ALL MY LOVE

To everyone who has ever felt the dark waters of depression creeping up their legs.

You deserve to feel the sun on your face.

And to Cooper, the best pup who ever lived.

ALL MY LOVE PLAYLIST

Music is a huge part of my life and a bigger part of Stella and Riggins' story. Each chapter has a song title from Noah Kahan's discography to help set the mood. Listen to the playlist on Spotify!

All My Love Playlist

A NOTE FROM MORGAN

Hi my friends!

First and foremost, thank you so much for choosing to pick up All My Love off your extremely long TBR. It means the world to me!

Back when I was in high school, I had this little silly idea of a second change rockstar romance inspired by one of my all-time favorite movies, *Sweet Home Alabama.* I never wrote it, of course, but it circled and circled my brain for literal years, shifting and morphing and always staying at the very edge of my mind.

When I started writing for real, I realized the story would be deeper than my silly goofy romcoms and it would require me to dig deeper into myself than I was comfortable. The characters needed vulnerability, they needed kindness and understanding and to be honest, that sounded absolutely terrifying. So I left it to simmer.

By the time the Revenge series was just about done, the idea had morphed into sometime bigger than I ever intended, twining with the music of Noah Kahn so perfectly, I knew it was time.

And god, their story is so beautiful. I think I love them the most out of all the characters I've ever written.

All My Love follows Riggins and Stella, childhood neighbors and songwriters who fell in love and drifted apart when Riggins became much too tangled in the lifestyle of his new rock stardom.

This story deals with issues of alcoholism and sobriety as well as depression (recurrent brief depression,) narcissistic parents and (off-page) death of parents. There is also a scene where the FMC is cornered by a man but no assault takes place. This is contemporary second chance rockstar romance.

I'm so excited to share these characters with you and I hope you love them as much as I do.

All my love,

Morgan Elizabeth

NOW

1

HALLOWEEN

STELLA

I'd know the bark anywhere.

I could be one hundred and six, and I'd still know that bark.

Tucking my notebook under the cushion of the porch swing, I stand, moving toward the steps and turning to face the road leading to my house, but I see nothing. Considering I live on the very outskirts of Ashford, the Pine Barrens butting up against the back of my property, people only come down this road unless they live here. I wasn't paying great attention to what cars drove past, though, so wrapped up in what I was working on.

Still, I hear and see nothing on the road. A winding driveway leads to the garage behind my house, but I didn't notice anyone driving up it.

Sighing to try and regulate my pulse, I push back on the railing of the porch that finally sold me on this house four years ago, moving back toward the swing to sit, convincing myself it was nothing.

I have to be hearing things. My mind is playing a cruel, cruel trick on me. It wouldn't be the first time it was an enemy of my own making.

Even after I sit back down, my blood pounds in my veins at the reminder of what I used to have and who I once was. I don't reach for the notebook I tucked away—even without trying, I know the muse is long gone.

Instead, I sit on the chair, my arms wrapped around my knees, my ears tuned to try and hear even the slightest whimper, to recapture the sweet memory once more, to hone it and sharpen what had started to become dull.

The funny thing about sounds is that your mind doesn't catalog the mundane as if it's the last time you'll hear it. It's easy for us to experience a moment and commit what it looks like and feels like to memory, but it's the sounds that fade the quickest.

When you want it most of all, when it's dark, and you're painfully lonely, and the heavy blanket of your emotions suffocates, you reach for it to remember what someone sounded like or the deafening roar of a crowd and... it's gone.

It's like that feeling when you have a song stuck in your head but can't fully remember what it sounds like, how the melody goes, or what the words are. If you could just listen to it, you'd get some peace, but instead, you can't even remember enough to think of the name.

I'd give anything to hear the bark once more when I'm aware it's the last time, so I know to catalog it better.

Closing my eyes, I lay back against the swing that's rocking gently on its own, and I try to recreate it in my mind, synch it up with one of the dozen memories that have haunted my dreams and waking moments for the past seven years.

And then it happens.

I hear it once more, the bark of a dog. My chest constricts when it's followed by the jingle of tags and a whimper. My eyes pop open and instantly begin to water as I scan the lush green of my yard, my heart dropping through the wood planks when I don't see her.

God, the memories that sound brings.

The pain.

I wonder briefly if the neighbors got a new dog. Maybe that's what I'm hearing, obscured through trees and space and too many emotions. I wonder what it will do to my ever-fragile mental state if that's the case.

Will I get used to hearing that sound, or will it always feel like a knife is rooted deep in my chest every time it makes its way on a breeze to me?

Before I can contemplate anything else, like, say, moving to Antarctica, where I'm pretty sure German Shepherds don't get much outside time to bark and tear open old wounds, I see it.

A black and brown blur bounding to me, her tongue out, ears back, tags on her collar clinking like music to my ears, a song I haven't heard in seven years.

My Gracie girl.

I almost trip down the three steps of my porch to the path before I kneel as she reaches me, letting her pounce on me and start licking my face, whimpering as she does.

It's her. Her snout is covered in greying fur, and she's bigger than I remember, but it's her. Either I've officially lost it, and I'm having the most wonderful hallucination known to man, or somehow, some-way, my dog is here, her paws on either side of my shoulders, nearly knocking me over with her excitement.

My mind doesn't have a chance to process the *hows* of why she's here, not before a pair of dark brown boots are in my line of vision, the toes worn and shiny, the rest matte and battered. My eyes travel up as my hand rubs into Gracie's coat, and the boots disappear beneath a pair of old, worn-in jeans, ending somewhere underneath a fitted black tee worn under a red and black flannel.

My eyes continue up even though I know what I will see before I even make it there.

He looks the same and wholly different, his jaw more cut than the last time I saw him, but his cheeks are less hollow than I remember, dusted with a fine layer of scruff that needs shaving. His eyes are the same bright green that haunted my dreams for years, but they aren't sunken in anymore, no longer set in deep under eye bags from lack of sleep and abusing his body. There's a single dimple on his cheek, his full lips quirked just a bit to one side. His hair is longer, light brown, with a light wave ending at his jaw. He runs a hand through it, pushing it away from his face before he opens his mouth and I realize this illusion is anything but.

"Hey, little star," he says, voice low and gravelly, bringing a million memories I buried deep back to the surface.

My hand pauses in the scruff at Gracie's neck before her nose pushes into my cheek impatiently until I start back up, scratching behind her ear.

"Riggins. What are you doing here?" I ask, staring at the man I haven't seen in nearly five years outside of magazines and television.

"Coming to see my wife," he says, and my world shifts on its axis.

THEN

There's a tiny clink on my window, and with it, I hop out of bed and slip on my shoes before opening it. It's dark, the moon nearly full, and its glow is lighting up Riggs' face more than normal. His hand moves in the dim light, a come on gesture I've seen a million times by now. Nodding, I grab the messenger bag I keep on the cushioned bench of what my mother calls a reading nook (it has instead become my writing nook, much to her dismay) before pushing the window open further and swinging my legs out.

With well-practiced moves, the toes of my battered white Converse touch the tree's rough bark next to my window before I step onto it. Then, I proceed to carefully climb down until my feet hit the ground.

We walk quickly in silence until we're two blocks down the road, where he parked his truck. Despite the late August weather, I'm shivering in the night air as we hop in. Before I even say a word, he leans in the back, grabbing an old sweatshirt and tossing it at me.

Smiling, I tug it over my head, trying to be discreet as I sniff the collar that smells like Riggs.

"I wasn't sure if you'd be up," he says as he starts the truck and puts it into drive. "You didn't text me back."

"Mom took my phone again," I say with a sigh. He looks over at me as he drives, his smile wide, and his dimple comes out. My heart pulses hard, looking at my best friend, the most handsome boy I've ever seen.

Riggins Greene was my neighbor for the first fourteen years of my life until my mother decided she didn't like my spending so much time with him and forced us to move to the other side of town. She would have moved out of Ashford altogether to punish me more, but that would also mean punishing my twin, Everest. Considering Evie is the perfect daughter, she'd do anything to keep her happy.

So now I live eight traffic lights away, a full three miles from him. Thankfully, there was only a year between my moving and Riggs getting his license, so there was only a year of riding bikes a mile and a half to meet each other halfway. Now, when we want to write songs, he picks me up, and we drive to our spot.

"What'd you do this time?"

I shrug but smile all the same. "I told her I don't want to do cheer this year. Sign-up forms came home."

"Oh, how dare you."

"I'm ruining my future career opportunities, you know," I tell him, quoting my mother. "Not having four years of cheer on my college applications is the end of the world."

He scoffs out a laugh, then reaches over and scrubs his hand over my hair, mussing it.

"As if you're smart enough to go to college," he says with a smile.

I slap my hand on his chest. "Hey, I'm plenty smart. That's why you had to have me, a sophomore, help you with your junior-year math homework last year."

"I know, little star. You're plenty smart."

I roll my eyes, but now that we're on the topic....

"What are you doing next year?" I ask, suddenly interested in my nails as he drives over familiar dirt roads.

"What?"

"Are you going to, uh, apply to colleges and whatnot this fall?"

He scoffs out a laugh.

"Hell no. We're taking the band on the road as soon as I finish school. Gonna try and get a label to sign us."

I know this, of course. It's what he's always talked about. But now that the future is looking much less distant, Riggins leaving Ashford with his band seems less like a daydream and more like a clear road he'll travel soon.

A road that will lead him far, far away from me.

"Mmm," I say noncommittally because I don't know how else to answer without sounding stupid or clingy. He has to leave me behind —my mom would never allow me to drop out of school and go with him—and he has to get out of here, out of this town where everyone looks at him with pity, where everyone knows about his mom and his dad and expects Riggs to end up just like him.

A washed-up daydreamer in a dead-end town.

But I don't have to come up with a better answer when the truck bumps a few more times before he puts it into park.

"Come on," he says. "Let's go write."

The only thing I love more than writing songs with Riggins late at night is lying under the stars with him. It's something we did long before we started writing before his mom died, and before his dad started drinking, back when our parents were still friends and would spend summer nights together, grilling and having a few drinks in one of our backyards.

Evie, Riggs, and I would wander just far enough so our parents couldn't hear us talking, lay in the grass, and watch the stars move.

It's because you got the cool name, Everest would say. *That's why you love the stars. All I got was a big mountain people die on.* I never argued because of the two of us, I always thought my name was the coolest. Riggs also never argued that fact, and after a lifetime of everyone comparing me to Evie and me coming up short, I kind of liked his quiet agreement.

We'd lay there all night, chatting about silly things like TV shows and movies and whatever was happening at school while our parents hung out. Even though he's just barely two years older, he never made me feel like it was a chore to hang out with us, even though I'm sure he was told to watch us rather than play with us.

"You're my best friend, you know," Riggs says under his breath as we lay on the big blanket we keep in his truck, staring at those same stars we watched back then. The same stars I hope we'll still watch together ten, twenty years from now.

"I know, Riggs. You're mine, too." Another beat of silence passes.

"You'll go with me, right?" I don't reply, not sure what he means. Or, to be clear, I didn't know if what I hoped he meant was what he *actually* meant. "On tour, once you're out of school," he clarifies.

My pulse races, but I don't answer.

"I need you with me. I can't do it without you, Stell."

"You can do anything you want, Riggs. You don't need anyone. You're... you're you."

"Fine," he says, correcting, reaching down to where my hand lays on the blanket, grabbing it and twining our fingers together. "I don't want to do it without you." A long beat passes as I concentrate on nothing but Riggins' hand in mine and pray my palms don't feel sweaty. "I don't want to do anything without you, little star," he says, using the name he started using back when we were little kids in the grass.

There's no question in my mind when I answer.

"Yeah, Riggs. I'll go with you," I whisper, and the words feel huge when I speak them out loud.

He doesn't respond, instead lifting our joined hands and pressing the back of mine to his lips.

Even though it probably doesn't count, I catalog it as the first time Riggins kissed me.

NOW

3

FALSE CONFIDENCE

STELLA

"What are you talking about?" I ask Riggins, the world spinning around me in a way that makes my stomach turn and my head feel light.

"You were always smarter than me, Stella. Don't pretend that's changed."

I stare for what feels like an eternity; the only thing grounding me is the dog I'm holding onto, my fingers buried deep into her fur.

"You never told me," he says, hurt flashing in his eyes.

I wonder if he can see the hurt reflected in mine or maybe the rage brewing even deeper.

"Most men don't have to be told they got married, and most brides don't have to remind their grooms." He stares at me instead of responding because, really, how do you respond to that?

You don't. *You can't.*

"You have to get out of here," I say, the words so low I'm surprised he can hear them.

"We have to talk, Stella. That's what I have to do. You had seven years to lick your wounds—" Suddenly, I stand, letting the indigence win but not letting the tightly leashed emotion out.

"Lick my wounds," I repeat, crossing my arms on my chest. "That's what you think I've been doing for seven years? Licking my wounds?" A hoarse laugh leaves my throat even though nothing right now is funny. "God, some things never change, do they? Still so fucking self-centered to think my life still revolves around you." He sighs and runs a hand through his hair.

"Stella, that's not what I meant. We need to talk about this. This is a big fucking deal. We've been *married* for seven years!"

"If you want, I'll get divorce papers written up," I say casually, feeling the knife twist.

I should have sent them years ago, snipped the invisible string keeping me tethered to him, but I never did.

"What?"

"You seem frustrated we're married. Simple fix. We'll get a divorce." His thick brows furrow, brows I used to run my thumb over when he was angry, smoothing out those harsh lines.

"What? No, that's not what I'm saying. We need to talk. You left with no warning, no note, nothing. I never saw your face again; you never talked to me—"

"Yeah, you tried real hard, out there on the road, fucking anything that would move, being a big rockstar, dating models and actresses. Must have been real hard on you, babe."

"What the fuck? You left *me*, Stella. What was I supposed to do? Now I find out all this time we were married, you never said a word, and it's *my* fault—" Something snaps in me.

"Leave," I say, the word low and bitter.

"What?"

"I said, leave. Get off my property." I look to Gracie who has laid down at my feet and swallow the rock of emotion there, knowing she'll be leaving with him. "Now."

At least this time, I knew to protect her bark, to capture it and cherish it so I'll have it later when the deep, dark waters start to pull me under.

"Stella, we—"

"Go, or I'm calling the cops, Riggins." The name slices through him, and I know somewhere deep down it hurts.

Good, I think. *I hope it fucking kills him, tears him apart, changes him the way he tore through me, changed* me *all these years ago.*

I never called him Riggins, not since I was little. I only ever called him Riggins when I was annoyed with him. He was always Riggs, or baby, or honey.

But now he's just... Riggins.

Except, really, he's not even that anymore. He hasn't been much more than a ghost of my past for years.

"We have to talk." I shake my head.

"No, we don't."

"We're married, Stella!" Finally, his calm mask slips, and somehow, somehow, I feel like I've won this round.

I won't give him the same outburst. I'm not that person anymore; I'm no longer wild, free, and loud.

"And we have been for seven years, Riggins. That hasn't changed. Nothing has changed just because, for whatever reason, you're standing here now. Nothing has changed, has it?" He knows I'm saying more than I let on, and I know it's a bitch move, and I know it's a blow that hurts him.

A lot has changed, and I know he had to have worked hard to make that change, but I can't find it in me to care.

He looks at me, those wide green eyes taking me in, trying to burrow in under my skin and read me the way he used to, but he hits a wall I carefully and precisely erected to keep everyone out, including him.

His mouth goes tight, and he gives me a slight nod.

"Gracie, come," he says with a wave before he heads toward his truck, and it almost causes my mask to slip and my armor to dent.

But I hold on tight, pressing my lips to her soft, furry head. "Go, Gracie," I whisper. She looks at me confused, and I fight tears, registering her look of betrayal before she turns and runs to the driver's side of Riggins' truck, where he is holding the door open and waiting for her to jump in. Before she does, though, she looks back at me as if checking on me. I nod like she would listen to me after all this time, but she moves, jumping into his truck when she sees it.

He climbs in behind her, slams the door, and drives off.

I watch his truck drive down my driveway and head back toward wherever he's staying. I walk into my kitchen and stare at the space I've tried to make for myself, noting the lack of color, the monotony, and the predictability that are perfect mirrors of my life these days.

And then I fall to the ground and sob until there's nothing left but numbness.

NOW

4

HOWLING

STELLA

Wednesday morning, I feel the bone-deep exhaustion that makes it harder than normal to leave my bed. I should've known it wouldn't be gone for long, the foggy blanket of depression, but it's been a good while since my last episode.

Recurrent brief depression, my psychiatrist calls it. I call it the waters.

My life is like the ocean.

Sometimes, I'm at the top, floating on my back, the sun on my face. Happy, warm. Whole.

Other times, I'm in the deepest, dark blue depths, so cold I can't remember what the sun feels like anymore. I'm numb.

So I spend my days on the edge of a knife, knowing that if I stay directly on the blade, I can swim in the happy blue sea, but the slightest breeze can send me plummeting into something dark. It becomes an emptiness in my soul, the wind blowing inside, howling within me.

It's a constant battle, but I don't want it to win today, so I force myself to roll out of bed and shuffle to the bathroom, squinting as I flick the light on. I use the toilet, diligently avoiding the mirror as I wash my face and brush my teeth and hair, clipping it back, all while avoiding the gaze of the stranger in the mirror. I don't want to see the blankness on her face, the bags under her eyes, the redness from my late-night crying jag.

Instead, I head downstairs to start the day, continuing my routine even though I'm off today. It helps, I've found, to continue the routine on days I feel the dark waters creeping up.

Shuffling to the kitchen, I flip on the coffee maker, grab a slice of bread, and slip it into the toaster before opening the cabinet above the coffee maker. Meticulously, I pull out three orange bottles, opening each and tapping until the pills fall into my hand. I then return them to their home and knock the pills back with water.

Getting medicated was the best decision I ever made for myself, but it requires routine, which has never been a strength of mine, especially on mornings when I feel that all-too-familiar weight in my legs. It's like treading through the shallow end of a pool. Every step takes just a bit more effort than normal.

While waiting for the coffee and toast to be made, I shuffle back to my bedroom, grab a white tee and a pair of jeans, and slide them on before combing my hair and putting it into a French braid.

I don't bother with makeup, a tiny rebellion against my mother, who believes leaving the house without a full face is a capital offense.

I may have shifted to fit my parents' mold, but no matter how deep I bury myself there, the little rebel still holds onto the small pieces of the old me I let her grasp.

Drinking my coffee and munching on toast, I note how quiet my house is for the first time in a long time. When I bought what had been my dream house since I was young, I slowly started to fix it up on my own. Even though there are four bedrooms, I stopped with just the kitchen, bathroom, living room, and main bedroom.

It's a majestic farmhouse, but I'm just one person. One day, I realized there was no point in fixing it beyond the needed rooms, so I stopped. It never bothered me before, though. But for some reason, the creaking of the wind against the outside, the emptiness... it feels heavy. Closing my eyes, I take a deep breath through my nose, praying it's not the start of another episode. It usually starts this way: taking note of how my life didn't amount to what I once was sure it would.

I shake my head, trying to dislodge those thoughts before they take hold, and at five-thirty, I grab my keys, hop in my car, and head down to the Ashford Diner to start another day of blissful monotony.

"Hey, Sandy," I mumble distractedly as I walk into work in a daze I can't seem to shake. To be fair, that's how every moment has felt since yesterday afternoon: a daze.

Because Riggins is in town.

Riggins is in town, and he came to my house.

He's in town with Gracie. That alone could make me cry for long, heartbreaking hours.

But even more, Riggins knows we're married.

How?

When?

It's been seven years since we got married and I left and five years since I last saw him. Now he's coming back into my life, shaking up everything in my predictable little world?

I've curated my life for the least amount of upset and confusion humanly possible, from living in my house on the outskirts of town to avoiding having to talk to people when I don't have my shield up, to being exactly what my mother wants me to be, to working at the family restaurant even though it was what I once swore up and down I'd never do.

The restaurant was started by my grandmother, and when she passed, was given to my mother who worked there her entire life. As soon as she had the keys in her hands, she tried to move it from a cozy family breakfast restaurant to a snazzy upscale brunch place.

If we lived in New York or Philly, it might have worked, but instead, we live in Ashford, population 992, and the people here have zero need for a mimosas brunch at ten on a Tuesday.

So now, Monday through Friday, it's pancakes and eggs and hearty breakfast foods in the morning, BLTs and patty melts at lunch, doors closing at three. On the weekend, we offer brunch options, but they're rarely ordered. It never stops angering my mother that instead of classy groups of girlfriends visiting for Bloody Marys, she gets rowdy groups of families and maple syrup smeared on everything.

When she realized the restaurant would never become what she envisioned, she gave up, hiring nearly everything out and making me manager when I returned back from tour so she would have to do the least amount of work possible.

In a way, even though it isn't what I'd ever have chosen for myself, I'm grateful. I have a steady job that keeps me busy and my mind from wandering too much. I don't need the money, but having a job in town also helps with nosy questions I don't want to answer.

I like the job, except for on Wednesdays when Mrs. Crawford rings the bells over the door, giving me a shitty look before I even have the chance to greet her.

Mrs. Francesca Crawford is my mother's sole remaining friend after treating everyone so terribly in Ashford, no one wants to spend time with her. Some people would see that as a wake-up call, but my mother, bless her heart, only sees it as proof that this *little hick town* is so much below her.

"What, no one works here anymore? You just sit around and dilly-dally?" I look down at the table in front of me, where silverware and napkins are sprawled as I roll them up for the upcoming day. "Is that what your mother's paying you for? No wonder you can't afford updates to that hole you bought, Stella." I bite my tongue and the urge to be just as rude back to her. I've done it in the past, and while the satisfaction simmers for a few moments, the utter and all-consuming chaos of dealing with my mother after the fact is so not worth it.

"Of course not, Mrs. Crawford. How can I help you?" I ask after giving our hostess, Amelia, wide, joking eyes and standing, ready to start my boring, predictable little life.

My safe life.

A life Riggins Greene no longer has the right to haunt

When I get home from work, that hope dissipates when I open my mailbox and see a single postcard with a familiar scrawl on the back.

Good to be home, little star.
All my love, Riggins.

THEN

5

YOUNG BLOOD

STELLA

The summer after Riggins graduated high school, Atlas Oaks picked up any and all gigs they could in the area, from countless shows at the Atlas, where they got their name, to dives up and down the Jersey shore and even a few in the city. It didn't take long for a label exec to catch wind and sign them. Throughout the winter of my senior year, they recorded their first in-studio album, and now they're traveling as an opening act for a larger Jersey band this summer.

The first tour for Atlas Oaks started in May of my senior year and spans to almost September. Of course, my parents said there was no universe where I could go with them. I suspected as much and even accepted it, knowing I would be finishing up my senior year and wanting to spend as much time as possible with Evie before she went to school in the fall, but now that they're gone for real, I wish I had fought more.

They've only been gone a week, and I'm *miserable*.

I'm quickly learning this town is nothing without Riggins, nothing without the band. It's strange realizing you have nothing and no one in your hometown other than your twin sister and a boy you've been in love with since you were a kid.

A week after Riggs leaves, I'm sitting at the kitchen table doing homework when my mother walks in, her designer bag hung over her shoulder, a pile of mail in one hand. She hangs the bag up as she walks into the kitchen, not acknowledging me, though I don't mind. The more invisible I am to her, the better my day goes.

She tosses her keys and phone on the island, eyes on her hands as she flips through the thick stack of mail. She eventually speaks to me, and the words make my stomach churn and send anxiety rolling through me.

"Lenore and I have decided you will be going on a date with her son next Friday." She says the words as if I'm not 18 but a child, and she's decided I'm going to the dentist for a cleaning rather than a date with a near stranger. Finally, my head moves up, and I stare at her, my brow furrowing as I fight my instinct of shouting, absolutely the fuck not.

Things with my mother have been tense for as long as I can remember, but in the past year, they've gotten even worse. I don't know if it's my decision not to go to college in the fall or the recent urge to step out of the perfect mold she built for me, but either way, it feels like I'm constantly on the verge of feeling her anger and disappointment.

"Thank you, but I'm not interested," I say diplomatically. I can't wait to tell Riggins how she wants me to go on a date with the douchey lacrosse captain when he calls me next. He's going to get a kick out of this one. Especially since Tripp constantly made fun of Riggins and me when Riggs was still attending Ashford High.

"It wasn't a choice, Stella. I phrased it very specifically," my mother says, her hands moving a bit slower as her fierce stare hits me. "You're already embarrassing me by not going to school, giving up on everything. I've convinced my friends it's because you want to help take over the diner, but I can't explain away you just staying in the house and doing nothing."

I wonder if she was always like this, cold as ice and only

concerned with public appearance, money, and status. And if she was, why the *fuck* did my dad ever marry her?

I take a deep breath, knowing that gaze doesn't bode well, but standing my ground. "I'm not dating right now, Mom."

"And why is that, Stella? Your sister is dating the mayor's son. I just don't know why you can't be more like her. She trusted me to set them up, and look how happy she is." If by *happy* you mean she does everything in her power to avoid him, then yeah, she's happy as can be.

"Well, I'm not Evie," I say. I don't add *unfortunately*, even though I know she's thinking it. She always thinks it. Why aren't you more like your sister? is a common refrain from her. Still, if I want to escape this conversation without a blowout, I need to do some damage control and explaining. "I'm just... I'm not interested in dating. I have my whole life to date and I'm in my senior year."

"It's not like you're going to be meeting any good boys at college," she says with an angry edge, and I should have known that would come next. When I told her my decision to forgo further schooling, it became a huge blow-up fight that boiled down to her cursing the Greene family for moving in next door to us, and Riggs was ruining her life, as if my life and hers were so closely intertwined and my not going to college would ruin *her* life.

What am I going to tell my friends, Stella?

It was always about appearances, after all, and your daughter's choice not to go to college was apparently social suicide in her circle.

"I'm just not interested in dating right now. I'm focusing on my..." I hesitate a bit because I want to say *songwriting*, but that would only make things worse. Instead, I say, "School work and enjoying senior year." When her jaw goes tight and her eyes go flinty, I know she's about to hit deep, about to say something with the intention of hurting me and causing pain.

"What are you waiting out for? Riggins Greene? Grow up, Stella Jane. He's a loser. To his credit, he left town to get away from his drunk of a dad as soon as possible, but do you really think he's out touring with his little band and thinking about you? You're here, wasting your senior year away, sad and depressed, missing some boy, and he's out living his life. *Without you.*" She looks at me and sees she hit her mark of my insecurities, and smiles.

"If he really wanted to be with you, Stella, he would have before he left. But he wants to go on tour, be single, forget about his silly little neighbor who's been prancing after him like a lost puppy her whole life."

"Mom, that's not—"

But what am I even going to say?

It's not true? I haven't been in love with Riggins since I was a kid? We both know that's bullshit, even if I stopped confiding in my mother when I was 10, and she started to use my secrets shared in confidence against me.

Somehow, still, she knows I've been worried about exactly that since he left, that he already forgot about me, that he'll move on with his exciting new life and leave me behind.

"Use your head, Stella. Before you waste your best years on him, use your head. Grab a good boy who's going to have a good job and who will uplift this family's standing. Stop walking around with your head in the clouds, delusions, and convincing yourself he cares about you."

I just stare at her, biting on my lip until it bleeds in an attempt not to say something I'd regret or show some kind of emotion she could weaponize against me. A minute passes before she shakes her head in disappointment and walks to lean against the kitchen counter, redirecting her energy and attention to the mail.

My body starts to relax, and I turn my face back to my math homework.

"What is this?" she asks a few moments later as she flips through the mail, her brow furrowing. She must be confused, seeing as she would never risk fine lines and wrinkles for nothing.

"I..." I start, but then my eyes focus long enough on what she's holding up. My chest fills, my day brightening for the first time since Riggs left.

She flips the paper, and I see his messy scrawl on the back. I can't stop myself from standing and snatching it from my mom's hands, excited and not even worried about her giving me a hard time for manners, instead hungrily reading his words.

The front clearly shows it came from Maine, one of the first stops as they tag onto the tour halfway through. The words, *Greetings from Portland* scrawled in pretty font above an image of trees and stars.

> *Little star—*
> *We're in Portland, Maine, our first show on the tour Blacknote set up for us. I miss you like crazy. It's so pretty here, you'd love it. When it's dark, the stars are the brightest things I've ever seen. We should come back some day, go star gazing.*
> *All my love,*
> *Riggs*

I sigh as I read it, letting my head drift to a world where Riggs isn't just my best friend who sees me as a sister he writes songs with, but a woman he loves, the one he writes his songs *about*.

He doesn't know all the songs we write together, I write with him in mind.

"What is that, Stella?" my mom asks, annoyed.

"Oh. A postcard from Riggins. Atlas Oaks made a stop in Maine first," I say, stuffing it into my agenda for school and trying to play it off.

"I still can't believe his father is letting him throw his life away like that," my mother says, moving around the kitchen, grabbing a glass and a bottle of too-expensive wine.

"Well, I mean, he has a record deal." I don't remind her that Mr. Greene has been falling apart more and more since Riggs' mom passed and doesn't care much about what he does.

"Anyone can get a record deal, Stella. It's not that hard. They're always looking for idiots who will work cheap and who aren't hard to look at. One in a million. He'll crash and burn just like that loser father of his, then come crawling back to this town, probably a drunk like his father, too."

"Mom, that's mean."

"It's the truth. I'm glad he got out before he could drag you into that world, too." Her look turns to an icy glare. "Even if you are still throwing your life away."

I got offers, scholarships, the whole nine from good schools, but I knew from the start it's not for me. *School* is not for me. I want to write music, I want to tour the world, I want to be with Riggins

And I'm good at it. All of the reviews for the debut EP of Atlas Oaks mention the beautiful songwriting. It's healing, some reviews say. Real and raw, another said.

I'm good at this, and for the first time in my life, I understand what I'm supposed to be. *Who I'm supposed to be.*

"Mom—" I start because this might not be the best time to talk to her about it, but there probably won't be a better one. But I'm put off when her face turns to one of horror.

"That's why, isn't it? Why you're refusing to do the right thing and go to college?"

"Mom," I try again, but she steamrolls me as she's wanted to do.

"Stella Jane, you are going to fail. You are going to fail and come crawling back. Don't be a fucking idiot."

"I like writing, Mom," I whisper.

"Then go to school and write papers."

"I like writing *songs.*"

"Stella, there are a million and seven foolish young girls just like you, falling in love with rockstars and convincing themselves they're different. You aren't special. You aren't different. But if you abandon your future for this, you are stupid." The burn at the back of my eyes starts. We've tiptoed around the topic of why I decided not to go college, but this is the first time we've talked outright about my dreams.

I think a part of me truly thought when I said it out loud, my mother would concede. She'd see and hear the music I've written and agree it's a worthwhile dream.

I should have known better.

"That's enough, Rhonda," my father says, walking into the room, his hand loosening his tie. Her face snaps to him, pure venom there.

"No, it isn't enough. We've been ignoring this disaster for years, and it's starting to ruin Stella's life. I will not have a loser of a daughter, and that's where you're headed, Stella," she snaps in my direction.

"Rhonda," my dad barks in a loud voice even I don't expect. My mom's eyes go wide slowly, and she turns her entire body to his. "Can I speak with you in the other room?"

For the first time in my life, I watch my mother obey someone else's command without arguing, her back straight as she leaves the kitchen stiffly. My father follows her close behind, his eyes meeting mine for a brief moment before he nods once and walks out of the room.

For the rest of the summer, I get the mail before my mother every day until Riggs comes home.

NOW

6

NO COMPLAINTS

STELLA

It's nearly ten when he comes in. I see him from the back, watch him walk in, pop his sunglasses to the top of his head, and start chatting with Amelia at the hostess stand, smiling wide as she flutters about, clearly frazzled that the local celebrity is in our restaurant.

He uses his thumb to point outside at the three tables out there, then tips his head in my direction without his eyes shifting here. From this angle, I can see her face screw up a bit in confusion, ask something, then he nods. Finally, she nods and walks outside to seat him.

When she returns and walks right up to me, I don't even have to wonder what she will say.

"Stella, you're never going to believe who is here," she says, excitement coating each word.

"Riggins Greene." Her smile drops, and if I weren't having an internal crisis, I would feel bad for ruining her fun. But I am, so I don't.

"Yes! He's sitting outside, asked you to be his server. Do you know him?" My eyes shift to the big window at the front of the restaurant, where we paid a local teenager with an amazing talent to paint a mural for the summer season. Even though an enormous sandcastle mars my view, I can see his broad shoulders and a grey teeshirt, his hair in a bun at the top of his head. He must have put his sunglasses back on, which I suppose will be a slight relief.

"He was my neighbor growing up," I say, not exactly lying.

"No way! Lucky!" Her eyes are dreamy and dazed, but as I open my mouth to ask if she wants the table instead, she speaks again. "He has a dog with him, asked for a bowl of water for her."

"A dog?" I ask, turning to look at her.

"Yeah, super cute one. She wasn't even on a leash. Seems a little strange but," she shrugs.

It's not strange to me because Gracie has always loved Riggs. He got her for me when she was a puppy, and I did everything to keep her alive and happy. When Riggs would come back to the bus or whatever hotel room we were staying in, she would run to him, never leaving his side. We could go on long walks in new places with new smells and new people to inspect, and if Riggs was with us, we wouldn't need a leash to keep her with us.

"*She's a free spirit, little star,*" I remember him saying. "*Just like you; she always comes back to me.*"

"Just like me," I had said with a wide smile, a smile he had liked a lot because he kissed me so hard, I thought it was going to bruise.

This is his plan, I guess. Gracie being with him is intentional, just like how he showed up at my place. He knows I can't resist seeing her again and, for whatever reason, he wants me to talk to him.

I do as he wants, grabbing a menu and walking out front to the three outdoor seating chairs. It's still a little chilly out, but it's the kind you know will warm up quickly as I walk to Riggins' table and hand him the menu. I do a close-legged squat to get on Gracie's level, brushing her fur back with my hand.

"How are you today?" I ask in a low, cooing voice.

"Now that you're here, I'm great," Riggs says, and when I look up at him, he doesn't have the cocky grin I expect but soft eyes and a sincere face. Instead of replying, giving in to my instinct to argue, I continue petting Gracie. A minute or so later, I begrudgingly stand, grab the pad out of my apron, and stare at Riggins without a word.

He stares right back, but this time, his eyes dance with laughter, his lips ticking up, his dimple coming out.

I glare some more before he gives into the apparent humor and lets out a laugh.

"God, you know, for a moment, I thought you really had changed into the robot your mom always wanted, but this?" His hand gestures at me, indicating all that is me. "Proves you haven't. Good to see, little star. I was worried there for a second."

Goddammit. Only Riggins Greene could find my glaring at him and refusing to talk to him a good thing.

"What do you want, Riggins?"

"I want to talk. We have to talk, Stella."

I roll my eyes and sigh. "I meant to eat. What do you want to eat?"

"You know my order," he says, and a part of me warms at the fact that he still gets the same breakfast order all these years later.

I stare at him, battling with myself to pretend if I should lie and say I don't know his order anymore, lie and tell him I blocked out everything that had to do with him, even if I still know he hates mornings but will get out of bed for breakfast every time. He drinks orange juice with his pancakes and wants the syrup on the side so he can dip them but the butter on top so they get all soft. "You're literally defeating the purpose," I once said. *"They're all soggy from the butter anyway, so why not just add the syrup? Then you don't have to dip every single bite."*

"Because then I couldn't watch you get all irrationally angry about it, little star."

Is this what I'm destined to do until he gets tired of this game? Constant reminders of a history I long buried? Forever having what I once had thrown in my face until he gets bored?

Instead of saying any of that, I nod, don't bother to write anything on the notepad, and turn on my heel for the kitchen.

When I bring out his food, I also bring the check, silently placing it on his table before turning, but I don't get far.

He grabs my wrist, and I see the scars there, tiny cuts on his fingers from guitars, from youth, from stupidity. I have matching ones on my fingers, and they used to be a comfort, knowing at the very least, we always had that in common.

The scars and the love of music.

"We need to talk, Stella. Come to lunch with me. Or dinner. Something." I shake my head.

"We don't, Riggins. We really don't have to talk. I'll get papers to you—I should have done it forever ago, but—"

"But you didn't want to. You liked having that tie to me, that hint of hope I'd get my head out of my ass. I know you, Stella. There was never a person on this earth who knew me like you know me, but it goes both ways." I shake my head, tugging my hand free, and lie again.

"No. I never did because I knew, like with every fucking moment in your life, you'd be stubborn and not just give me what I wanted, what I needed. You'd insist on seeing me and, Riggins, I closed that door years ago."

Lies, lies, lies.

Still, I continue to lie.

"You are not someone I feel the need to talk to. You are not someone I feel the need to have long chats with anymore. You showed me exactly who you were all those years ago, and I don't feel the need to get to know that person again. Let me be, please." I thought it would work, really. Telling him straight out, hitting below the belt.

But somehow, his eyes shift to be more determined instead of hurt, more focused instead of backing off.

"You're punishing me, pushing me away because of who I used to be, but I don't even know that man anymore, Stella. How is that fair, paying penance for a person I'm not?"

"And here I am, paying penance for the person you were then?" I ask. "That's life. It's not fair, Riggins. I learned that a long time ago." Then I finally leave, walking into the restaurant and ignoring Amelia's burning eyes on me.

I don't know when he leaves, but it's before I go out to check on him. There's cash tucked under his plate with the receipt, enough for his meal and a healthy tip I don't need or want.

What I do want is the printed-out photo of Gracie with, *Gracie, 1 year old in New Mexico,* scribbled in all too familiar scrawl on the back that he also left behind.

And below that,

You've still got all my love.

NOW

7

TIDAL

STELLA

"Hello, Mother," I say, walking into my parents' home for family dinner. Even though I try to put some emotion into it, I know I fail when her all-seeing look scans me. The weekly family dinner at my childhood home isn't nearly as optional as my mother makes it seem, though Evie gets a much larger pass, considering she's often on assignment.

Thankfully, my twin will be here tonight because the cruel, emotionless look my mother is giving me makes it clear she's in one of her moods.

"No makeup?" she asks in lieu of a greeting. I fight a sigh.

"I worked all day, and I'm not…" I pause. "I'm not feeling too well." She stares again for a moment, assessing me before rolling her eyes and stepping aside to let me in.

The house hasn't changed since I last lived here when I was 19, right before she kicked me out. Even when things with Riggins and Atlas Oaks came crumbling down, I didn't move back home; instead, I stayed with my sister until I found a place of my own.

Even now, this place still feels like a prison.

"This again," she says, exasperated. Like many in her generation, my mother thinks any claims of mental health degrading are just a weakness, a laziness my generation created.

"I'm fine, Mom."

"Oh, I know you are. This dramatic stint of yours... I would've thought you outgrew it by now." Now I really do sigh.

"You can't outgrow depression, mother." Her eye roll is almost audible as I toe off my shoes and hang my light jacket.

I should have just put on the fucking makeup; I already can feel the animosity between us growing.

"Depression. What do you have to be depressed about, Stella? If anyone should be depressed, it's me. Stuck in this town, my daughter constantly telling me how miserable I've made her life and refusing to make it any better." I take a deep breath, then move to the kitchen to get a drink: anything to distract myself.

This is not a new conversation.

I just need to endure it until she's done.

"I just don't understand," she says, her voice trailing behind me. "What could you be so depressed about?"

Thankfully, my father is in the kitchen. A tall, broad, quiet man with greying dark hair, my father was never one to argue with my mother. But as the years have gone on, he's more likely to tell her to stop, at the very least.

"Hi, Dad," I say, walking over to him and letting him pull me into a hug.

"Hi, sweetheart. How are you?"

"Depressed again," my mother says with another eye-roll, pouring herself a large glass of wine.

"Rhonda, drop it," he says, and my shoulders relax just a bit with relief. I can feel her eyes boring holes into my father and me, but I ignore her, grateful for the reprieve.

Now, I just have to make it through a few more hours.

An hour later, I'm sitting at my childhood dinner table, my eyes locked on the meal in front of me: meatloaf, mashed potatoes, gravy, and baby carrots. It's been in the five-meal rotation since I was a kid, even though I've hated both carrots and meatloaf with a vengeance since I was five and realized I could dislike foods rather than dutifully eating them just because my mother served them.

Everyone is at the assigned seats we've always had: my sister across from me, dad at the head of the too-long table, and mom at the other end.

Everest, or Evie as everyone but my mother calls her, is my fraternal twin. We look nothing alike, except for small, almost unexplainable similarities which make it clear we're sisters, but not necessarily that we're twins.

She sits, moving around the mashed potatoes. While I was served and expected to eat every bite on my plate out of spite, Evie was always expected to eat just enough to sustain a small toddler. Our mother had her different ways to pick at us, to keep us on our toes and in line. Mine was her disapproval of my friends, of my life choices, and, of course, of Riggins, but for Evie it was her undying disapproval of her body.

While she loves to fuck with me, to torment and remind me of all of the things I'll never be strong or smart or capable enough to do, sometimes I'm grateful I got this end of the stick. Evie stays in line and still gets torn down repeatedly.

Of course, she lets her because if there's one thing that is ingrained in my sister's DNA, it's striving for our mother's approval. I only come to these dinners because Evie will never be able to cut our mother out, and I think if she disowns me, there's a chance she'll push Evie to cut ties, too. And if I'm here, it's an extra person for my mother to focus her anger and sorrow on.

But it seems Evie is safe tonight since she seems intent on picking on me.

"Stella, next Friday, you're going on a date with Francesca's son, Parker." *This again.*

I blink at my plate a few times before looking up at my mother. Her hair is the same dark brown as mine but without the lowlights breaking up the color. She has it cut into a severe bob ending at her chin, and it barely moves as she looks up at me. There's a pair of pearls at her ears and a strand around her neck. Her black dress is perfectly tailored. She's dressed to the nines, despite the fact that I know today is her grocery shopping and clean-the-house day.

I also know she put this outfit on at 6 am before getting coffee and breakfast ready for my father before he left for work.

My father, who's nearly seventy, does not need to work. My parents could easily live off of retirement savings and the income from the diner, but I'm convinced that man refuses to retire because that would mean spending every waking hour with my mother, and what kind of torture would that be?

"What?" I ask.

"Next Friday, you're going on a date with Parker Johnson, Francesca's son," she repeats. I roll my lips into my mouth and fight back the version of me who argues with my mother. She's been missing for seven years, and I'm not letting her out now.

"I appreciate it, mother, but I'm not interested in dating." Her chin goes firm, her eyes going steely with her irritation at the fact that I'd deign to argue with something she's saying.

You don't do that in this household. I learned that lesson young, forgot it, and regretted it ever since.

"It wasn't an option, Stella. The date is made. He'll pick you up at your house and take you out for dinner and dancing."

Dinner and dancing. My god.

"Mom, that's really not my style; I'd much rather—"

"You're going," my mother repeats before taking a deep sip of her wine.

"Rhonda," my father starts, his voice low. "Maybe we let Stella decide who and when she wants to date." My father piping up means that this is going to be an issue, something he knows she's going to dig her heels in on.

I knew the moment I argued I should've said yes and gone on the date to avoid the drama, but something made me feel like I needed to argue, to not be the perfect daughter I've forced myself to become.

Riggins.

Of course, it's Riggins. I can't even pretend I don't know that, that him just being in town isn't impacting me, fucking with my new life, cracking the shell I had to craft after we broke up all those years ago.

Broke up, I think. *Such a funny choice of words, Stella.*

"If we do that, she's going to die alone," my mother insists.

Evie rolls her eyes and sighs loudly. "Stella is not going to die alone, mother."

"At this rate, she absolutely is. And before that, your father and I are going to be stuck with her—"

I see this spiraling quickly. Every once in a while, Evie gets brave and likes to stand up to our mother, but unlike me, Evie cannot handle the heat of her wrath. She can't handle the look of disappointment, and it tears her up each time.

"It's fine, Eve. I'll go." I turn to face my mother, pasting on my fakest, perfect daughter smile and nod. "I'd love to go. If you don't mind, send me over his information, and I can set up times and whatnot."

My mother gives Evie a, *see? Your sister listens to me,* look, then me a small, almost-approving smile. My mother never has a full-blown approving smile—just the hint of one, the promise that if you did everything perfectly, maybe somehow, some way, you might get that genuine approval. Something to always strive for.

Silence takes over the table, and the only sound is that of forks and knives on china, of Evie pushing food around and myself duti-fully eating, my father keeping his eyes downcast. I think we'll make it out of this okay, in one piece, before my fucking sister opens her damn mouth.

"Riggins is in town," she says, a smile in her words that I don't see because I keep my eyes staring at my plate, pushing things back and forth. But with her words, the already quiet room goes painfully silent, the ominous quiet before an atomic bomb explodes.

"What?" my mother asks, venom in the words. I clear my throat, tipping my chin up, and quickly glance at my twin, who is staring at me, not my mother.

Like she's trying to gauge my reaction.

"Riggins Greene is in town again," she repeats

"And how would you know he's in town?" she asks her jaw tight.

"It's a small town, Mom. Gossip travels quickly. Word on the street is that the band is on break for a bit while they write their next album." The knife in my chest twists, and I fight every instinct to let it show on my face. Is that why he's back in town? Does he need to write?

My mind keeps traveling.

Is that why he's finally reaching out to me? Is he out of inspiration, out of songs? Does he need my help?

"Did you know about this, Stella?" my mother asks, dragging me into the conversation where I don't want to be but leaving me with no option but to answer.

I roll my shoulders back, straighten myself, and do my mental check to make sure I fit her expectations. I started this when I came back, making the checklist of what she expected of me and how to be the dutiful daughter.

She told me if I skipped college and instead went on tour with Riggins and the boys, I would regret it. *He's going to chew you up and spit you out, Stella Jane, and then what will you have? Nothing. You're throwing your life away,* she said.

And she was right.

He chewed me up, spit me out, and destroyed me.

And then I had nothing left. I should have listened to her.

Becoming the daughter she wants me to be is my penance for not listening.

When I came back from tour, I was a shell of myself, so hollow on the inside you could hear air howling and twisting within me. So from then on, I listened to everything she told me, going to work at her restaurant, living under her thumb.

I came back with no idea of who I was, who I was without Riggins, without music, and without the band. I had built my entire life since I was five around the daydream of touring the world with him, and in one summer, it all fell apart.

I was a shell of myself, so when I built myself back up, I made sure my armor was bulletproof and that I became everything I needed to win my mother's approval. If I was nothing anymore, if I was a shell of myself, I might as well fit into the role she wanted for me.

"I did," I respond simply, removing the ability to read between the lines.

"You better not see him," she said.

I don't know why I don't tell her he's already stopped by my place and that he's come into the diner for lunch, but I omit it all the same. I'm contemplating the why of that when Evie speaks, exasperated by her words.

"Mom, she's an adult; she can see whoever she wants."

"Not if she wants to work at the diner. If she respects herself, if she respects this family, she won't see him. He's trash, just like his parents." Evie shakes her head.

"You used to spend every night in the summer out drinking on the patio with his parents."

"And then his mother passed away, god rest her soul, and his father became a drunk. And then Riggins followed right in his father's footsteps." She turns to me, telling Evie without words she's done speaking to her, and shifts her venom to me. "I don't want to see you out with him, Stella."

"Rhonda," my father, the world's worst mediator, says, but she doesn't even bother to move her head to slice her daggers at him.

"I'm not going to, Mom. Don't worry. That's... ancient history." She stares at me, inspecting my face for lies and untruths, but just like her learning to ignore my father, I've learned how to make my armor Rhonda-proof, to make a facade she'll approve of.

When she sees exactly what she wants, she nods, then changes the subject to gossip about someone in her group of backstabbing friends.

"Hey, Stell, wait," Evie says as I walk out the door toward my car. I close my eyes and take a deep breath, hoping she'll let me go easily but also knowing there's no chance in hell. My steps slow, and hers quicken until we're standing in a shadowy spot of the yard where, if our mother stood on the front steps, she wouldn't be able to see us.

It's the spot Riggs used to stand in, waiting for me to sneak out of my window back when he was mine.

I shake my head, knocking that thought out.

"Yeah?"

"How are you?"

"I'm fine, why?"

"Armor down, Stella. I'm not Mom, and I'm not going to narc to her, either."

"There was a day," I start, my words trailing off.

"There was. And then I came to my senses about the family we were born into." She gives me a look, but I just shrug. She sighs before asking what she really wants to, like I knew she would. Evie is the only person who actually knows what happened all those years: the good, the bad, and the very, very ugly.

"How are you doing with Riggs being home?" she asks, her voice low and cautious. I suck in a deep breath at her saying his name like that, calling him Riggs, but it's like I'm breathing underwater. But even though it wasn't the same, she loved him too. She knew him and grew up with him and saw him as a brother, and when he was gone, I know in her own way, she felt that, too.

"He came to see me," I announce for some reason I can't figure out. Her head moves forward, her mouth dropping open.

"What?"

"Three days ago, he came to my place. He," I scrunch up my nose, fighting emotions I don't want to address and tell her the worst of it. "Brought Gracie."

"Gracie," she whispers as if the dog was actually my child and she was the aunt we pretended she was as if she had ever met the dog ever, rather than just seeing pictures and hearing stories.

"What did he want?"

"To talk," I say, jiggling my keys in my hand.

I want to go home.

I want to go home and forget about tonight and the fact that the entire town is buzzing with conversations about Riggins and the fact that Riggins is back here in Ashford.

I want to grab my guitar and write a song and then ignore that song, cataloging the emotion so I don't have to feel it anymore.

That's my way, after all. Why talk about or process my feelings when I can turn them into something beautiful, get it out, and never have to think about it again?

"And did you?"

"Nothing to talk about," I say, tipping my head back, taking in the stars.

"Nothing to talk about? Are you insane? Stella," she starts, her eyes wide and worried. I take a step backward.

"I gotta get home, early shift tomorrow." Her face goes soft, concern laced within it.

"Stella—"

"Come for dinner soon. I want to hear about what you've got going on." I take another step back towards my car.

"Stell, we really need to talk—"

"Love you, sis," I say, then walk to my car and drive off.

I hold it together until I open my mailbox, pulling out the three pieces stuffed in there, including a postcard. My hands shake, holding it as I take in the green trees and happy type set across the photo, reading, *Welcome to Ashford!* When I flip it, there's no stamp and no address because it isn't needed, but there is a scribbled note.

> We really need to talk, Stella.
> All my love,
> Riggs.

I make it inside the house, the keys in my hand jingling as my hands shake as I turn the key in the lock.

It isn't until I lock the door behind me that I let myself cry until I can't breathe.

THEN

8

NEW PERSPECTIVE

RIGGINS

I get the text at three fifteen when she gets home from school. We've been on the road for three weeks, and I miss Stella more than I ever thought possible. I always knew she was my person since she moved in next door to me when she was five and I was seven, but being away from her has only proven that more.

And when I get the text telling me she's home and her mom isn't hovering around trying to make her life a misery, I always find a quiet place to talk to her.

"Oh, Riggs must be about to call his girl," my best friend Reed says with a playful tone. I roll my eyes, flip him the finger, and grab a drink and my phone.

"Tell her we say hi, yeah?" Beckett calls, always protective of my little star like a big brother.

I should think of her in the same big brother protective way, but lately, all I can think about is if she would ever want more. Her mother wants her to marry some rich douche that will help raise her social standing, and would probably commit quite a few felonies if she found out Stella chose me, but what if?

I don't let myself think too long on it, instead pulling the curtain separating the main area of the bus from the bunks and hitting her name on my cell.

"Riggs?" she says.

It's always Riggs for Stella. Hearing her say it is like coming home, both familiar and sweet, and like hearing all of the best things in the world at once.

"Hey, little star. How's home?" I sigh with the words, and everything seems to fall away as she fills me in on all of the Ashford drama going on that I've missed out on.

"Oh, and Mom is setting me up on a date," she says a few minutes in.

A wave of red anger rolls through me, the same variety that always comes when Stella talks to me about guys. She hasn't dated much, just a few here and there, and being her best friend other than her sister, I usually hear all about whatever asshole she's crushing on who definitely isn't good enough for her.

Except, I'm the biggest asshole who isn't good enough for her.

Not enough money, not enough prestige. The son of a dead mother and a drunk. I have nothing to offer her.

"God, she's still on that shit?" I ask.

"Yeah. I don't know why she won't just let it go. Evie and I are happy without her meddling. I wish she would just be happy for us. Let us live."

"Well, you know, she married an Ashford loser, and her life didn't magically turn her into some famous heiress, so she needs one of you to fulfill that dream for her." It's the truth, and everyone in town knows it. Rhonda Hart has always thought she was too good for Ashford.

According to my mom, everyone was shocked when she settled down with Hank, Stella's father because she was supposedly dating some fancy New York exec who would whisk her away from our little town. But when she started showing right after her shotgun wedding to Hank, it all became clear.

I don't tell Stella this, but I think the reason her mother is such a bitch to them is because she resents the life she's in, and she sees it as her daughters' fault she's there.

"Which is bullshit because let's be real, if the money and notoriety is what she wanted, she'd be trying to set me up with you, a literal rockstar on a trajectory to stardom and fame and riches. Instead, she thinks you're the dregs of society, and I'm doomed to misery for hitching myself to your star." Well, I guess that's a good sign, that Stella thinks I'm good enough for her.

"Because even when Atlas Oaks makes it big, I won't be an old money douche who likes going yachting and wears the collars of his polo popped and wears loafers."

She scoffs out a loud laugh, and I reach for my beer, cracking it open and taking a long sip. Her laugh dies down, and silence fills the line.

"What was that?" she asks.

"What?"

"That noise. Are you drinking?" she laughs, but it's devoid of laughter. "It's like noon where you are." She's not wrong: I probably shouldn't drink this early, but I'm still battling a bit of a hangover from the night before, and her talking about dating has me tense. I just need a little bit of mellow. A relaxer. It's not the same, not like my dad.

"No, it's just a soda," I say.

I don't know why I do it, lie like that to my best friend, or why it comes so easy. But when her easy, true laugh comes, I get it I guess. I didn't like the concern in her voice, especially when there was nothing to worry about.

"Oh," she says. "Sorry, I'm such a loser."

"Never, Stell. Now tell me how you're going to get out of this date," I say, sipping the beer again, but this time with a hint of guilt. It does help my never-ending anxiety that has plagued me since I was young, the anxiety that always lessened when I was with her.

Things will be better when she's on tour with us next year, though. When I can lay under the stars with her and write instead of missing her like crazy. We're churning some real interest, and if it continues, it could mean a big album and a headlining tour.

The dream. Our dream. All I need is Stella to be mine.

And when I hang up, I make my decision.

Whether I'm good enough for her, whether she deserves better or not, I'm going to make Stella mine when I get home.

NOW

9

STILL

STELLA

"You're back," I say, putting a plastic-coated menu he doesn't need in front of Riggs as he sits at the iron tables outside of the Ashford Diner. Even though I don't want to, I can't help how the corners of my lips tip up at seeing him here.

It's just because he brought Gracie with him.

Definitely.

"Best place for breakfast," he says with a shit-eating smile that makes my belly flutter in a way it's not allowed to.

"Do you need this?" I ask, waving the laminated menu. He shakes his head, and I move to turn and input his order without much of a word. He reaches out, though, grabbing my wrist and stopping all movement.

His thumb grazes the underside of my wrist, brushing against that tattoo we got together when we were too young to know about consequences and too optimistic that we'd always work, sending a shiver down my spine that I try to ignore, but I can't. I never could when it came to Riggins.

"Ignore me all you want, Stella, but I know you better than you think I do. I remember every single thing about you."

"Except that we got married," I whisper without meaning to, giving him more than I want to once again, and his lips tip up with my words.

"Yeah, except that, huh? Except now I do. Now I do, Stella. And I'm not letting you run again."

I don't respond.

I don't respond because I'll either say something mean and angry and impulsive or something worse... like telling him how fucking much missed him, how lonely I've been these past years.

Instead, I shake my hand until he lets go, his smile never fading, and I walk back into the diner, hiding in the back until Amelia reports that he's left, confusion and disappointment in her words.

When I walk to the table he sat at, there's another twenty under the plate and another photo of Gracie, a dog toy in her mouth as she trots towards the camera man.

Gracie, 2 years old.
All my love, Riggs.

On Sunday, he comes in after the morning rush, sitting outside with Gracie. I go out with water for her after Amelia seats him. I trip on the uneven sidewalk as I walk out with a dog bowl, spilling the water to the concrete.

"Still clumsy, I see," Riggins says with a smile, and I roll my eyes but don't respond. Instead, I grab the full glass of water Amelia brought him and pour it into Gracie's bowl, holding eye contact with him the whole time. He laughs and holds up his hands like he's waving a white flag. I pet Gracie a few times, then reach into my pocket, where her nose nudes a treat.

"Can I give her this?" I ask, feeling strange since this was once my dog. He nods, and I hand it to her, watching her munch on it.

"Remember that time on tour when you found that little dog bakery and bought a bunch of treats for Gracie?" The memory is one I haven't touched in a while, hidden amongst the other good memories I refuse to break out, covered in dust but precious all the same.

A small smile breaks on my lips despite my need to act indifferent, and I hug Gracie, burying my face into her fur. It's probably a health code violation, hugging a dog on the clock, but I'll worry about that later.

"Reed came in the bus, high as can be, and thought they were cookies. Picked one up and ate it." I can't hold back my small laugh now, moving back and looking at Riggins.

"He ate the whole thing and then told me I needed to work on the recipe," I say with a small snort of a laugh. "We didn't let him forget that one for weeks." I laugh some more, but Riggins isn't laughing. Instead, he's staring at me with a small, sad smile on his lips, taking me in.

"There she is," he says so low, the words filled with wonder. "There's my little star. Buried deep under that mask," I roll my eyes, but it doesn't dull his smile. "Gotta keep trying to break through," he says, as if to himself.

I stand, rolling my shoulder back and forcing myself to drop the smile.

"I'll put your order in," I say and his smile goes wider, but he lets me go all the same.

I serve him in silence, relieved when he doesn't try to pull more memories I've hidden away out of my archives, and when I come to clean up his dishes, it's the same as every other day.

A twenty and a photo of Gracie sitting in front of all the guys. In Riggs' messy scrawl it says,

Gracie and the band on her first world tour

All my love, Riggins.

Just like he's been every afternoon since he came to my house, Riggins sits outside the diner on Monday, Gracie settling beneath the table with him and turns his head to the windows, looking for me. Amelia doesn't see him yet, but I don't even bother to play the game of making him wait.

Instead, I walk past the hostess stand and snap a menu he doesn't need before pushing open the door, the bells jingling as I do.

"Morning, Stell," he says with a wide grin, not the shit-eating kind, not the kind that tells me he knows he's succeeding at getting under my skin, but a different one.

One I used to see a lot when we were kids, when he threw rocks at my window, the one he'd give me when he passed me in a hallway or would answer a video call. It always made me feel like he was undeniably happy to see me, so much so that he couldn't bother to play it cool, couldn't bother not to let a huge smile creep across his face, making his dimple pop out.

"It's not morning," I say, my jaw set. Last night I sat up late, sitting on my little front porch, annoyed that I've let him get under my skin. I don't hear from the man for five years, not a single peep, and suddenly I can't go a single day without him bugging me.

"It's morning for rockstars," he says with that cocky smile.

"Got it. Your normal?" I ask, not bothering to pull out my pad. His brows furrow, and he nods, but there's clear confusion there. He expects me to argue or give him shit, but I don't.

I'm tired.

I'm tired in so many ways, only one of them being I'm tired of arguing with him. I'm tired of pushing him away. I'm tired of falling behind on expectations and I'm tired of living alone and in my safe bubble with no friends. I'm just tired.

It's probably why I did what I did this morning. It's probably why I walk out just a minute or so later with a small plate.

I drop it on the table without saying anything about it, just putting it next to his water and starting to move away.

I don't know why I did it, why I went to the bakery down the corner after the morning rush and picked up the box of donuts I asked Patricia at the Ashford Baker to set aside for me. Why I put them all in the back room minus the French crueler, putting that on a plate and hiding it until Riggins showed.

And I definitely don't know why I didn't talk myself out of giving it to him this afternoon.

Mostly, though, I don't know what I expected when I gave it to him. Because when his hand reaches out, grabbing my wrist and tugging so I can't walk back into the diner and ignore him some more, it's not unexpected.

"Did I forget something?" I ask, avoiding his eyes.

"French crueler," he asks, words low and full of meaning. Much more meaning than those two words require or are worthy of.

I look at him, and his eyes are warm and a heartbreaking mix of sadness and hope and something I don't want to even touch on before I nod, a small smile I can't fight pulling at the edges of my lips.

"Your favorite," I say, remembering the mornings we'd ride our bikes and then later Riggins' car to the bakery and make sure we got one for him and a strawberry frosted sprinkle for me.

His eyes burn on me, and I want more than anything to break eye contact, but instead, I nod and smile fully.

"Yeah," I say, and with that, his smile spreads too, like melted butter on toast across his face, warm and inviting. He squeezes once on my wrist before letting go, right where that small heart tattoo is. When my hand drops, the spot where his fingers were is cold and uncomfortable, but I don't let myself think too much about it.

"Thanks, Stell," he says, with a tip of his chin.

I don't reply.

I just nod and walk back into the diner.

When I come back out, Riggins and Gracie are gone, but a twenty and a photo are tucked under the plate again.

This one shows a grown dog, not a puppy, but with no grey on her snout. When I turn it over, in Riggins' thick, masculine handwriting, it says,

Gracie, 4 years old.
All my love.

I tuck the photo carefully into my bag before going about my day, my head in the clouds and lost in beautiful, comfortable memories that until recently, were covered in a thick layer of dust.

NOW

10

PART OF ME

STELLA

Dinner with the man my mother thinks would suit me goes exactly as I had anticipated: unbearably and miserably boring.

He picks me up at exactly five pm, knocking on my door like a true gentleman, but before I even get a hello out, his eyes are glued to my tits in the scoop neck dress I'm wearing, and they don't leave the entire night. I'm not fully sure what that says about him either, considering calling my boobs B cups is being incredibly generous.

Parker takes me to the lone restaurant in Ashford my mother would approve of, where the waiters all wear ties, and there are candles on every table—the fake, battery-operated kind, which my mother deems plebeian, but in a town this size, you can only have your expectations so high.

The dinner goes about as well as one could expect, though fully devoid of any real conversation on my part or enjoyment, for that matter. He asks me about my job, to which I tell him what he already knew from my mother, and then he spends the next forty minutes telling me all about his job at an accounting firm, which sounds like the world's most boring career in the world.

When he pays for the meal, I'm starting to plan how to get out of a goodnight kiss at my door without him taking it as an insult to report back to my mother when he looks up at me with a smile.

"Okay, now that this is done, how about we get a drink at The Atlas?" I feel my jaw clenching, trying to think of an excuse, but unfortunately, tomorrow I don't have work in the morning. The last thing I need is my mom calling me on my fucking day off, giving me shit.

"Look, I know you got dragged into this same as me," he says, catching me off guard. "We both need to give our mothers a good story about this date, and I could use beer. Then I'll take you home, easy as that."

"You got dragged into this too?"

"You're gorgeous, Stella, but the whole town knows you're not looking for anything close to serious, and I'm too young to settle down, you know? A man's gotta sow his oats." He gives me a shit-eating grin, and I fight the eye roll and gag because, in truth, he's helping me out.

"Yeah..." I say instead.

"So let's grab a drink next door. I think there's music tonight. Then we have a full story for the pushy moms and can say we were having such a good time, that we extended things. That should buy us each a couple of weeks before they get on our case again."

For the first time all night, I give him a genuine smile. "Yeah. That would be cool."

We walk into the bar next door and he's right, music is in fact playing, a band on the small stage and instantly, it makes my chest tighten.

I avoid live music at all costs, and for a moment, faced with the opportunity to avoid my mother's wrath for a bit longer, I forgot why.

It's the way the crowd feels, the way the bass pounds in my belly.

The way a room of strangers can suddenly feel like they all have a common goal, a common love.

I used to run toward that feeling, live for the sound of a room of people all singing the same words, all feeling the beat the same way. Now, I never feel more alone than at a show. It's soul-crushing; the memories fly in and suffocate me, and the panic builds and brews. The recent reminder that is Riggins coming to see me doesn't make it any better.

But I can't let him continue to control me. It's unfair to me, unfair to my soul that used to love music so much, used to find it healing. When I used to sink in my ocean, through the pretty teal and to the blue and feeling the creeping tentacles of the dark blue sneaking in through my airways, I could listen to music and fight it back.

Now it's barely a balm, barely a relief at all to grab my guitar, to hum out songs and write down words.

It's fucked that I've let Riggins have that power over me.

So even though I hesitate as we step through the door, I force myself to straighten my shoulders, take a deep, fortifying breath, and move through the crowd, following Parker to the bar where we wait to get the attention of the bartender, then I see him.

Beckett James, drummer for Atlas Oaks. My entire body strings tight when I see him, even though he doesn't see me.

"You know, I'm kind of tired, maybe we should—" I start, but then the band playing crescendos into a deafening interlude and my words drown in the noise. Parker pays the bartender for our drinks, (a beer for each of us, even though I definitely did not give him an order for one) before we move away from Beckett, and my spine starts to ease.

There are four members of Atlas Oaks, and there's a good chance only Beckett is here. The oldest in the band, he was legal and able to drink long before the rest, so this might just be a hangout of his.

No one else is here, I tell myself, and it's a small comfort when I watch Beckett grab his drink and walk in the opposite direction of us.

Then I start to enjoy myself. I watch the band, who isn't great but isn't terrible, and take in the music, letting it fill my veins and cloud my head the way it used to, the way it hasn't in a long while.

My shoulders are finally starting to drop, the anxiety leaving my system when it happens.

"And now, we have the honor of welcoming a local celebrity to the stage!" My shoulders go up to my fucking ears, and my back goes ramrod straight. "If you're from around here, you definitely know of these guys, and even if you're not, you still definitely know of them."

"No, no, no, no, no," I murmur under my breath, but it's no use as I watch a familiar shape stand at the edge of the stage, more familiar shapes behind it.

"Welcome Atlas Oaks back to Ashford, you guys!" The crowd roars, the kind of noise that makes you know will leave permanent damage as Reed, Riggins, Beckett, and Wes walk on stage. Reed picks up his bass, Beckett sits behind the drums, and Wes and Riggins grab guitars, all three adjusting mics as they do.

"Hey, guys, it's great to be home," Riggins says, and something in me dies with the words. I can feel it.

Something I thought I had buried deep, something I thought I had cut out the addiction to Riggins from, it dies seeing this again.

I've spent seven years avoiding nearly every mention of them possible except for the few times my self-hatred won, and I'd spend a night in misery looking them up on the internet.

I do my best to avoid social media, where rumors and video clips run rampant. I rarely talk to old friends from high school because after I came back, all any of them wanted to ask was how tour went and how the guys were. I even avoid listening to the radio, where I might accidentally get ambushed by my past.

And then my mother sets me up on a date, and here I am, watching them live.

"Huge thanks to The Tailored Pigs for letting us steal a moment of your set. We haven't played live in like, four months, and it's killing us," Reed says, and through the lump in my throat, I smile because at least nothing about him has changed.

Reed was once my best friend in the world after Riggins, my confidant in all things. And then I left.

"I want to leave," I shout, trying to get Parker's attention, but he's as wrapped up in Atlas Oak as everyone else. I tug at his arm to try and get him to look at me, but his eyes stay on the stage while his arm wraps around my waist like we're an item like I'm his.

Just when I thought this couldn't get any worse...

"This is a song I wrote long, long ago with a girl from Ashford about being here and how it made us feel."

The first chord start of the first song that got some recognition. It's not a top 40 radio hit like some of their other songs, but it's definitely the song that got them off the ground.

I remember writing it, laying in the grass late at night, watching the stars as Riggins strummed the guitar, playing its different chords and progressions while I hummed out tunes and tried different words. It took less than an hour before we had a song that encompassed our emotions for this town, the way we loved it to our bones, but how it held so many complicated memories.

When I left the band and came back to town, I remember this song being stuck in my head on a loop for days and the way it caused me physical pain. I remember putting headphones in and blasting other music—any other music—to try and drown it out, but nothing worked.

Nothing at all.

And now it's everywhere around me, my words and Riggins' chords and our history swirling and swirling until I can't breathe, until my knees go weak.

Then, his eyes find mine in the room, and I realize Beckett must have snitched.

His hand moves on his guitar as the melody moves to deeper chords, as the anxiety of coming home creeps into his words, but his eyes stay on mine.

"I don't feel it when you're with me," I remember whispering, telling him that when we were together, the anxiety stayed away.

"You're the only thing keeping me here, little star," he had responded.

The vice on my chest loosens as our eyes stay locked.

Air comes back into my lungs, and I can feel my feet again.

It should be the opposite. It should get worse when he's staring into my soul like this, reading me like a book only he knows the language of, but instead, it's the same effect he's always had on me.

He finishes the song like that, then shifts into another older song, one much less anxiety-inducing about wanting to make it big and leave this town, a reminder that he did just that, maybe.

He always loved to stand on stage and watch me, to tell me stories through whatever songs were on the set list that night, and I wonder what he's trying to tell me tonight.

"Alright, guys, that's it. Thank you so much!" Reed says, and the band gets down, the old band coming back up, but when they start playing, it sounds worse, like the reminder of who Atlas Oaks is makes everyone else seem... less.

Or that could just be me.

But the sweet lull of live music has worn off, the anxiety of knowing Riggins is here taking its place and I turn to Parker.

"I want to leave," I say straightforwardly, tugging on his arm so I know I have his attention.

It's an understatement, of course. I need to leave if I want to make it out of here alive.

"What?" He cups his hand to his ear, and I move to my tiptoes, speaking louder so there's no chance he can't hear.

"I want to leave," I say, and then the band cuts out, allowing for a conversation.

"Come on, Stell, we just got here," he says like we're old friends instead of new acquaintances.

"I need to leave," I say, and there's no way he doesn't hear the panic in my voice. I need fresh air; I need space. The walls are closing in and I can't take in a good breath of air.

"I don't want to, Stella. A couple more songs," he says, then turns his head to look at the stage, essentially cutting me off.

Well.

It seems my gut instinct that he's a fucking twat was right.

I grab his arm and tug him toward the hall, which leads to an emergency exit and the kitchen. I stare at him, a look of irritation on his face.

"I need to leave, Parker. I'm not feeling well. Thank you for agreeing to tell our mothers a good lie, but I don't think we actually have to stay that long," I say, trying to keep things copasetic between us and, I think, failing miserably.

Just like my mom, he turns his personality in a moment, his body shifting so my back is to the wall, his body in front of mine.

I've never been a big person, and though Parker isn't tall, he's taller than me. If I thought I felt locked in before, that I needed air and space, I can multiply the feeling by a hundred now.

My eyes shift left and right, and I know no one will see us in this corner should things go from bad to worse.

"Parker, please. I don't feel well." The music has started again, deafening in the main room but slightly damped in this hallway.

"Come on, you know we can have some fun," he says, and my stomach aches, nausea creeping through me, acid burning at the back of my throat.

"Get the fuck back, Parker," I say, all semblance of friendliness gone from my voice.

"I looked you up, you know. You had a wild time with him. Now you're here with me, and what? Nothing?" *Fuck, fuck, fuck.* The good ol' boy is gone from his eyes, leaving what my brain interprets as a monster in its place.

"Get off me," I say, my voice growing louder, but it's like I didn't say anything at all. "Parker, get off me." My mind goes into how to get out of this mode. I could knee him in the balls, but his legs are closed, and if I fail, it might anger him more. I know there's no strength behind my fist, but don't they say something about adrenaline making you strong? Mothers can lift buses off of babies, and people can run through burning buildings.

Does that work when you're scared out of your mind, pinned in a hallway at a bar no one will find you in?

"Do you really want me to tell your mother what a shit time I had here?" He threatens, an evil grin on his lips.

How long had this been his plan?

"Parker—" I start, but I don't have to finish my sentence because he's gone, and I'm no longer being held to the wall by his body, by his presence.

I look around, trying to figure out where he went, only to see—

Riggins.

Riggins has him against the wall, held by the collar of his stupid fucking shirt, and his face is just inches from his.

"Who the fuck are you?" Parker asks, his ego still too big despite the fact that he is clearly at a disadvantage.

When we were kids, Riggins was lanky, all skin and bones, clothes hanging off him in a way I thought was cute, but as he got deeper into the scene, it was in a way I found concerning.

It seems getting sober changed a lot more than his ability to function as a human being. I have to assume he replaced some of his habits with working out. His shoulders have gotten toned and muscled, the sleeves of the tee he's wearing stretching around broad biceps and tapering to a trim waist.

I refuse to wonder what the rest of him, covered by clothes, looks like and if it's changed at all, too.

"Her fucking husband," Riggins says in a low growl, and my entire body tightens, both with the clear aggression in his words and with what he's saying.

"Fuck that, she's not married. She's been all over me all night, man. Not my fault the bitch doesn't want yo—" Parker doesn't have a chance to finish as he's lifted in the air and pressed to the wall.

He's kicking, but it doesn't phase Riggs, who shifts his hand, pressing him against the wall, pulls his arm back, and slams it into the side of his head. Instantly, Parker's body stops kicking. He's not passed out, but the fight has gone out of him.

Riggins doesn't care, his arm pulling back again and punching him in the nose, blood starting to drip.

"Riggins, stop!" I shout, "You're going to fucking kill him!" But he either can't hear me or doesn't care, his arm moving back again and landing in his stomach. I look around for someone, anyone, but there's no one near, no one paying attention.

"REED!" I shout, trying to find him. A few eyes shift in our direction, but no one steps to help. "BECKETT! WES!" I just need one of them to knock some fucking sense into Riggins or, at the very least, pull him off before he sends Parker to the ER.

God, what a fucking headline that would be.

But no one comes.

We're in a hallway out of the way, and no one is coming for us.

I have to do it myself.

"RIGGINS," I shout. "RIGGINS STOP."

He ignores me and Parkers eyes drift shut as he pulls his fist back once more about to slam it into his face for the third time and my gut tells me this will be the one that lands him in some kind of intensive care. I need to stop Riggins from ruining his career.

He saved me once. It's the least I could do.

I turn to him, putting a hand on his shoulder, away from his cocked elbow, and tug. His body freezes as soon as my hand touches the cotton of his tee.

"Riggs, stop. Stop. I'm fine. You saved me, Riggs."

Without him saying it, I know it's the use of *Riggs* that has his fist dropping, has him letting Parker slump to the ground, has him stepping back.

"Fuck," he says, and I bend, grabbing his wrist to look at his fingers, bruised and bloody.

"Goddammit, Riggs. You could have hurt your hand. We need ice." I look down at Parker, who is slowly standing, a slow trickle of blood leaking from his nose.

"I'm going to fucking sue you," he groans.

"No, you're not, Parker," I say calmly.

"The fuck I'm not, you—"

"There is a camera pointed here, right there," I say, pointing to a black dot. I'm 99% sure it's a sprinkler system, but I'm hoping...

Parker's eyes go wide or as wide as they can, considering one is swelling shut, and his hands go up in a placating move.

"Fuck, Stella, I didn't mean—"

The fuck you didn't, you creep, I want to say, but I don't.

"You tell my mother we had a good time, but we were not compatible. I'll tell everyone you fell and smashed your face." His jaw goes tight as he looks from me to Riggins, and when I let my gaze follow, I see Riggins' face is steel, ready to continue what he started.

Parker sees it, too, because he sighs, then nods.

"You're not my fuckin' type anyway," he mumbles, walking toward the exit. Riggins' body lurches for him, but I hold onto his arm tightly.

"Come on, big guy, let's get you some ice, yeah? I'm sure they have a first-aid kit somewhere. Who the fuck knows where he's been."

Riggins looks to me, the urge to run after Parker clear, but he chooses me instead for some reason, nodding while I go to Anderson, the familiar owner of the Atlas, and ask for ice and a first aid kit.

THEN

11

SINK

STELLA

It's been two weeks since my sister left for college and it's the night before my 19th birthday, and I feel so utterly alone, lost in the world. It's also been six months since I've seen Riggs in person, and Atlas Oaks is absolutely killing it on tour. I should be happy and excited for the future, but I'm not. Instead, I'm sad and lonely, and I feel like a part of me is wholly missing, with no way to get it back until he comes back.

This morning, my mother took my phone and all access to any kind of computer because she didn't like the way I responded when she told me she didn't like my outfit of jeans, shorts, and a tee. This means I can't text or call Riggs, can't check in with him on the road, and, most of all, can't find out exactly when he's coming home.

Tomorrow or the next day, his last text said, *then we'll write.*

God. That's what I want most of all. To sit under the stars with my best friend, to write songs, listen to him strum a guitar and loop melodies around the words I write. He's been gone on tour since May, and it feels like I've been missing a limb.

He's called me regularly since then, telling me about the wild parties they've gone to, the insane life of being a rockstar on the road, and the freedom he feels being away from Ashford. But, of course, he always closes with how much he misses me and can't wait to lay under the stars again soon.

Pick me up, I wanted to say. *Take me with you.*

But I won't say that. He's out there having a fucking blast, partying and hanging with stars we only dreamed about as kids, and he doesn't need his little sister-esque best friend paling around with him.

I may have been in love with Riggins Greene since I was five, but that doesn't mean I don't have common sense.

Clink.

The sound comes again and my heart pounds as I peer out of the window, looking for him.

And finally, he comes into view.

I think my heart might actually escape my body when I see him wave, when I see his smile go wide. I open my window and bend over the sill.

"What are you doing here?!" I ask in a whisper.

"Breaking you out, Stella girl. Come on."

I don't ask another question. I've never had to when Riggs is around. Instead, I grab my bag, sliding a pen and my notebook inside, then touch my toe to the rough bark of the tree next to my bedroom window, muscle memory clicking in as I move down it to the grass where he stands.

I don't play it cool like I told myself I would. All those weeks and months without him, talking only in texts and clandestine phone calls so my mother wouldn't find out, I spent them planning how to be cool and casual when I saw him again.

But now he's here, in ripped jeans and a tee shirt, his hair a bit longer than I remember, his smile wide, that dimple in his cheek, and I lunge at him.

Wrapping my arms around his neck I glue my body to his, and instantly his arms wrap my waist as well, holding me close, his head going into my neck and breathing deep like he missed me as much as I missed him.

Impossible, I know, since he was out there living life while I rotted away, but it's a lovely fantasy, I suppose. Riggins Greene missing me.

"God, I missed you," he says into my neck as if hearing my thoughts, and my chest hitches as I try not to cry, something I also told myself I wouldn't do.

He pulls away, just enough to see my face, his looking concerned before he pulls me back in, holding me closer, tighter than before.

"Stell, what's wrong?"

"I just," I start, sniffing into his neck. "I just really missed you."

"I know. Me too, Stell. Felt like half of me was gone." We stand like that for what feels like an eternity, a dangerous act considering we're in prime position for my parents to catch us, before he steps back, grabs my hand and we start the familiar walk to his truck.

Except his fingers stay twined with mine as we walk.

"STELLA BELLA!" I hear and before I can process it, the door to Riggins' truck is opening, Reed standing there and pulling me into his arms.

"Reed!"

"And it's your birthday!" he shouts.

"So I hear," I say

"And we're headlining a tour next year!" The shock from those words settles somewhere in my gut, the surprise tearing through me, both excited and proud and terrified and sad.

They're going to leave again.

Leave me in this town I hate when they're not here.

"No way!" I say, my eyes moving to Riggs, now behind Reed, arms crossed on his chest, face guarded. "That's amazing!"

"You're coming with us, right?"

"Well, I..." I start, looking back at Riggs, who is smiling now, his dimple out. "I wouldn't want to mess with your experience, be the annoying little sister type when you guys are being big rockstars."

This has been my refrain for some time, ever since he left and started telling me stories from the road, ending them with *I can't wait for you to come next time.* I always tell him I don't want to insert myself, to be a burden. Riggins looks to Reed with a, *can you believe her bullshit?* kind of way.

A deep, loud laugh comes from behind Reed, and I see Beckett with a wide, joking smile on his face,

"You're fucking with us, right? Sometimes, I think you're more of a part of this band than Wes is." He pulls me into him, and my arms barely reach around his wide chest as I do. I melt a bit when I feel his lips press to the top of my head, the closest thing I have to a big brother.

"Hey!" Wes says, coming out from behind Reed's house where I know further back a bonfire has already started.

"Tell me I'm wrong," Beck says, and Wes just glares at him.

"Happy birthday, Stella," Wes says, tugging me from Beck and into his arms.

"Thank you, Wes. I think you're a vital part of Atlas Oaks, by the way."

"See! Stella thinks I'm an important part of the band, you guys!"

"Alright, alright, let's get inside; we've got a lot to do to get ready," Beckett says.

"Get ready?" I ask as Riggins puts an arm around waist, tugging me in close. I look up at him and he looks down at me and suddenly it doesn't feel like it did before he left. It feels... different, the way he's looking at me.

"What, you think we could come home, and you could turn 19, and we wouldn't throw a party for you?"

Riggins

Stella's birthday party isn't anything to write home about, just a bonfire in the woods behind Beck's house, but it's everything I need. Being on the road was everything I hoped it would be and nothing I expected. Sleeping in new places, standing on a stage and singing to thousands of people, seeing new places.

The parties.

The further we got on the tour, the more the crowd started to sing our songs back to us, the songs Stella and I wrote here in Ashford, spreading through the country and becoming anthems for people I've never even met.

But most of all, I missed Stella. Not seeing her regularly felt like a piece of me was missing, my other half, my *better* half. Without her, I found myself reaching for beers to mask the boredom, to mend the gap in my soul. I'd smoke with the band and daydream about being under the stars, writing songs with her, and when I woke, a wave of sadness and loneliness would crash over me, so I'd grab a beer to forget that, too.

It was because I missed her, of course, just another reason she needs to come in March.

But mostly she has to come because nothing can stop her now, not her mother or school or anything like that.

And we can finally be together.

On the road, I realized that it wasn't just proximity or familiarity that had me constantly thinking about my best friend. I realized I fell when we were 12, when she refused to sit with her family at my mother's funeral, when she reached over and quietly held my hand when I fought back tears, never looking at me but giving me the same silent support she's always given me.

But now, sitting around a fire with my band, my best friends in the entire world, and some random people scattered about, a gaggle of girls who, now that I'm not the poor, sad kid who lives in the sad-looking house with the dead mom and the drunk dad, have a sudden interest in me, but the only person I can focus on is Stella.

"Okay, okay. Which one of us would survive in a scary movie?" Reed asks, taking a sip of his beer.

"What?" Stella asks.

"A scary movie," Reed says. "Like, *Texas Chainsaw Massacre*. Which one of us would live?"

"Not Stell," I say with a smile directed toward my best friend. "She'd somehow meet the serial killer and decide he was a nice guy. Bring him cookies or something."

"No, I wouldn't," she says, tossing a marshmallow at me; it bounces off my chest and into my hand. I eat it and wink at her, and she sticks her tongue out at me.

Fuck I missed her.

"You so would," Beckett agrees. "You trust everyone you meet."

"I'm so sorry I'm not a cynic like you guys." We all laugh before Stella speaks again. "Well, Riggs wouldn't make it either. Have you ever seen that kid run? It's like watching a toddler."

"No, she's so right, though," Reed says as he laughs, wiping tears from his eyes. "His hands go out at his sides, and he's all wonky and lanky."

"Fuck off, man," I say. "You'd die first. You'd trip on a twig or something and decide it wasn't worth it."

"True," Reed says with a smile. "Wes or Beckett would live. Probably Beckett because he'd just glare at the guy and scare him away. The serial killer would run away."

"As he should," Beckett says, stern face fighting a smile. It continues like that for a while before Stella leans into me, tipping her head to the sky. I'm two beers in and Stella's had one, and when I look at her goofy smile, I can't help but smile too.

"Stars are bright tonight,' she says, low. "But clouds are rolling in." I know what she's trying to ask.

"Wanna write?" I ask, hoping against all else, and she says yes. When her smile spreads wide as can be, I know the answer without her saying it.

I wonder if she's felt it, the ache to write, the way the words come out like molasses when she's not with me but flow like water when we're together.

Probably not. I can write, but not the way Stella can. She was born to write songs, to bottle precise emotions into words and chords.

In turn, I was born to make the music she crafts. The perfect duo.

"Be right back," I say, standing, then, on a whim, pressing my lips to her hair. We both freeze, and I stand straight awkwardly, turning toward the door of Beckett's house. "My guitar's in Beck's house. Be right back." She stands as well.

"I'll wander to the back," she says. "That way, maybe we can sneak out without anyone giving us shit."

As most of these parties end with everyone getting hammered and Stella and I wandering to the woods to write, we have experience with the crew giving us shit for leaving to be alone.

I don't see Stella sitting on the logs and chairs around the fire when I walk back out, my guitar slung behind my back and the bag I know holds her notebook over my shoulder. I head toward the woods, taking the long way around the fire so no one stops me, eyes peeled to look for her.

I don't see her, though. Instead, I hear her.

"No, thank you," I hear Stella say in her sweet but firm voice, the one she uses when she doesn't want to upset someone but also wants them to leave her alone.

"Aww, come on, your mom says we'd be good together," a voice says and a chill runs down my back as I look around the bonfire searching while walking towards the direction I heard her.

"My mother doesn't know much about me, but I'm sure you're very nice. I'm not interested, though," she says, and I shift my direction left a bit, still scanning for her, but she's so goddamn small, I can't find her.

"You're at a party to have fun; you should have fun with me," the man says.

"I came here with my friends, I—"

"We could be friends," he says and I finally get a view of her. Her back is to a tree, a man taller than me but shorter than Beck in front of her, fear and discomfort clear on her face. I start to jog her way, and the guys' hand lifts to touch her cheek. She moves, trying to get away, but he has her pinned.

"I really should—"

"She said no, man," I say, walking over, my hands in fists as I approach where the fuckwad had Stella pinned.

"Hey, bud, we were having a conversation. Our moms are setting us up; I just wanted to—" Realizing who exactly this is, my blood boils. Tripp Vanderveer was the lacrosse captain at Ashford High during my senior year. This is who Rhonda Hart was trying to set Stella up with, the guy who has enough rumors about how shitty he treats women, even I've heard it. My hand moves to his shoulder, ripping him away from my girl. He's been to parties here a few times, but I never know who invites him.

"You've got my girl pinned to a fucking tree; I think it's my place to be here." He turns to face me, and it's clear he's drunk and maybe impaired in some other way. But he wavers where he stands, so I know even though he's bigger than me, he's at a disadvantage.

"Maybe you should've kept a better eye on her," he says, "Finders keepers, man."

With his words, something in me snaps. I wish I could say I don't know what pushes me, but that would be a lie.

It's the look of fear on Stella's face.

It's the fact that she's not mine in the way I need her to be yet, the fact that there's so much unsaid between us.

The fact that I haven't seen her in too long, and now we're dealing with this bull shit.

I pull my fist back and slam it into his face, feeling his nose break beneath my knuckles. He stumbles back, holding his hand to his face and groaning as he does.

"What the fuck, man?"

I don't have time for him, though. Instead, I grab Stella's hand and start moving, walking toward the trees, toward escape.

Freedom.

"What was that, Rigs?" she asks as I tug her away from the bonfire, away from the chaos, away from the asshole who better be gone by the time I calm down and make it back to the house.

"He was scaring you," is all I can say.

"You can't just punch people because they scare me!" she shouts and I look over my shoulder at her as I continue to walk toward the woods, as I make my way toward our clearing where we can see the sky and maybe, *maybe* I can breathe again.

"I absolutely can, Stell. And I will anytime someone scares you."

"Well, you're scaring me right now, Riggins!" she shouts and I slow my steps.

"I'm scaring you?" I ask, slightly confused. She lets go of my hand and puts both of hers out to her sides.

"Yes! Who are you? Just out here punching people? I'm a big girl, Riggs. I can take care of myself! I have since you've been gone, and I'll keep doing it when you leave again!" Her eyes go wide like she can't believe she said that like it popped out and she didn't mean it, but I heard it.

She heard it.

The birds hiding away heard it.

"I'm not going to leave you again, Stella."

She sighs. "Yes, yes, you are. I heard Beckett talking. You guys are going to New York to record, and then they'll send you on tour again. Headlining. Congrats, by the way. That's amazing. I'm really fucking proud of you," she says, but the emotion isn't behind the words.

I step closer.

"I'm not going to leave you again, Stella." She gives me a soft look.

"You are, Riggins, and that's okay. It's more than okay." I shake my head because she doesn't *get it.*

"I'm not leaving you because you're coming with me," I say, my words low and quiet. Again, her eyes widen.

"I can't come with you, Riggs," she says, sweet and low. "I'd get in the way of everyone, of the band."

"You heard the guys. You are *part* of the band. You're... you're us." She shakes her head again, her face going sad as she does.

"I'd be a burden," she says. "The little sister wandering around, getting in the way." My brow furrows as I stare at her, confused how she can still think that.

"You are so far from a little sister to me, it's not even funny," I say, taking a step toward her, and she takes a step back.

"What?"

"You heard me. You are so far from being my little sister, it's actually comical you'd think you were." I take another step closer to her and she follows suit, moving backward.

"Riggins," she says, and her back bumps into a thick tree trunk. Rain starts to fall, soft and gentle.

"If you were my sister, it would be incredibly fucked to think about you the way I do every day."

"Riggins," she whispers, and soon, I'm pressed against her, her breaths pushing against my chest.

"Riggs," I whisper back.

"What?"

"I'm always Riggs to you. And you're my little star. Ironic when you're my goddamn sun, when my entire world revolves around you."

"Riggs." It's almost inaudible now, but I watch her lips form the word.

"I'm going to kiss you now, Stell," I say, then wait for her to argue.

I'm so fucking this up.

I planned so many things while I was on the road, so many things to tell her, so many ways to confess this to her, but now I'm fucking it all up, and she's going to say no, and our friendship will be fucked forever —

"Okay," she whispers, my heart beating out of my chest with the single word.

One word, two syllables, and both of our lives are changing forever.

I close the gap between us, gently pressing my lips to the lips of my best friend in the entire fucking world, and everything changes in a heartbeat.

The rain starts to come down hard, soaking us through instantly despite the tree cover, and the gentle press turns into a fevered sliding of lips against lips. Her hands move, one to my jaw, the other behind my back, mine going to her hips to hold her close. Her mouth opens, and I slide my tongue into her mouth, tasting her for the first time. She lets out a tiny moan, a sound so precious I know I'll keep it in my mind forever.

We stay like that for what feels like hours, kissing and tasting and learning each other, pressed against a tree as it rains, kissing my girl on her birthday and somehow, I know this will be forever.

But right now, there's nothing in this world except for Stella and me. Despite everything in this universe, I found her, and she found me, and it was always supposed to be this way.

By the time we stopped kissing, the rain had stopped, and the sky clearing to reveal the stars. I contemplate heading back to the house, but then I remember what we left there and decide to continue deeper into the woods. It takes a bit to reach our clearing, but when I do, I pull the blanket out of the bag in my guitar case, thankful the waterproof case kept both my guitar and the blanket with the water-proof lining dry, even though we're both soaking wet regardless. I spread it out in silence before grabbing Stella's hand and forcing her to lay down with me there, guitar and her bag long forgotten in the grass.

We lay on our sides facing each other and slowly, I take in her face, all the small subtle changes I missed over the past six months.

I find a new freckle on her cheek beneath her left eye, her cheeks have lost some more of the fullness from being a kid, or maybe because her mom feeds them the ridiculous healthy stuff, and Stell hates it.

"I missed you so fucking much, Stella," I whisper.

"I missed you too."

"I want you to come in March. The label is sending us out for real this time. And to New York to record the next album next month."

"Oh, my god, Rigg! It's happening!" She's so genuinely excited for us but still doesn't get it.

"I want you to come with me. With us."

"Riggins..."

"We leave for New York in a few weeks. We'll be there for a month or so, then home for the holidays. Then we're out to LA for a few months for press and whatnot. The album should come out in March. April, we go on tour." There's a pause before she smiles. "I want you to come. We'll write around here, then you'll come to New York with us. The guys and I already agreed; they're cool with it."

"You talked to them about it? About me coming?"

"I wouldn't be asking without the band knowing. You know that, Stella." She rolls her lips in on themselves, rubbing and rolling them together, deciding how to ask whatever it is she's about to ask, deciding if she's brave enough for it.

"What...." She clears her throat before speaking. "What would I be coming on tour as?"

As tends to be our way, I don't have to ask her to clarify, to ask what she means.

"Mine," I whisper, my hand moving to cup her cheek. "You'd come on tour as mine, Stella. The way you always have been since you were five years old, and you told me I was stupid because I was a boy and boys were inherently stupid."

"I still stand by that," she whispers, and I smile.

"Yeah, I know you do. But what about if that boy is so wildly in love with you that he can't breathe when you're not near? Can you make an exception for him?" Her eyes go wide, her mouth dropping open.

"You're in love with me?" I laugh because I thought it was obvious, thought I was *always* obvious. I grab her and roll to my back until she's above me, her body pressed to mine in a way I've dreamt of for some time.

"God, Stella. Have you gotten my letters? Or has your mom snatched them?

"I mean, I got most of them, I think. I've been following the tour dates, but I think a few were missing..." her words trail off.

"You've got all my love, little star. Always have, always will."

And then I kiss her again, letting my lips tell her everything my words apparently can't.

She was always better with words, anyway.

NOW

12

CRAZIER THINGS - CHELSEA CUTLER

STELLA

"Somethings never change, I guess," Josie, the owner, says with a smile, looking from Riggs to me.

I smile at her before grabbing what she hands me and walking out the rear exit until we're in the early summer cool night air.

"Sit," I say, pointing to a curb.

"Stell, it's not necessary—"

"You keep throwing the wife thing in my face, so let me return the favor. You're my husband. Let me take care of you."

Something flares in his eyes, something I don't want to notice, address, or even see, but he sits and holds his hand out to me, so let's call it a win. I kneel before him and turn his hand over, looking at the knuckles before shaking my head.

"God, did you have to do that?"

"Yes," he says simply.

"I was fine, I—" I start, and Riggins lets out a laugh.

The man laughs!

"Yeah, you had it totally under control," he says, and honestly, I can't argue much. Instead, I grab an alcohol swab and wipe it against a cut with not a hint of gentleness because he's an idiot who doesn't deserve it.

"Somethings never change," Riggins mumbles, and I know exactly what he means. That night at the bonfire, he had to save me in a similar manner, back before we were anything and then right after when we became everything.

I ignore that because I don't have the mental strength for those kinds of memories.

As I dab the cut on his pinky with an alcohol swab, he hisses, and I roll my eyes. "Such a baby." I use a butterfly bandage to pull a cut on his pointer finger shut. I hope it won't scar—we both have more than enough scars, inside and out.

"You've come far," I say, then pause and hope he'll pick up what I'm saying or fill in or let me off the hook, but I've never been a very lucky person. "From where you were last time I saw you." He sighs as I clean up the last of the cuts before he answers.

"Yeah, last time you saw me, I was a mess."

"Hmm," I hum, keeping my eyes away from him, not sure what I'll see there and not sure I want to know.

"You know, when my dad was alive, I thought he was weak. Stupid, to spiral like that when my mom died," he says, filling in the void with something I already knew, the words so low I almost don't hear them. I keep my eyes on his fingers, pretending to fiddle with the bandaids even though it's all done.

"As I got older, though... I got it," he whispers, and I can't help but look up at him. His eyes meet mine, and it feels like they burn down to my soul.

They say everything I can't say, everything he clearly wants to say but knows I won't take well.

I don't tell him that I understood it too. How, after I left the tour, I understood Mr. Greene a bit more, understood what sent him over the edge, what sent him spiraling. I didn't get it when we were kids: I thought it was selfish and irresponsible and ridiculous, but now I get how you could drown in that kind of sorrow.

I just learned to box it up, lock it tight, and bury that shit along with any other form of feelings and emotion.

"Yeah. I got it too, eventually." The silence hangs between us as I finish his bandage, close up the first aid kit, and press the bag of ice to his hand before sitting on the curb next to him. We sit there in silence, side by side, facing the back of the bar.

"It was a wake-up call," he says. "Him dying. I was going down that path, but worse. Faster. He was too young, but I was going to be younger." I can't bear to look at him while he confesses this. "I'd lost too much already. I thought... I don't know. After you left, I tried to get sober. I thought I had it, could do it myself. I don't think... I don't think I knew how deep I was in. I went to treatment after he died."

More silence and I realize that he's done speaking, lost in his thoughts or afraid to say more, it doesn't matter.

He's done letting me peek into his closet of rattling bones.

"I'm happy for you. I know it doesn't mean much—"

"It means everything, Stella," he says, cutting in, his hand reaching out and twining with my fingers.

I don't look at that either, my hand in his.

Like the feeling of the bass in my belly, it'll bring back too much. At least like this, holding his hand, it feels different. His hand is more calloused than I remember, more weathered, The bandages I placed making it feel even less familiar.

"I'm proud of you, Riggs. That's not easy," I whisper into the dark, and I mean it. He may have broken me, but he is still my first love and was once my best friend, my closest confidant.

"You keep calling me that," he says after a beat. "Riggs."

"Don't get used to it." I didn't realize I was doing it, not really.

"I missed it." I don't reply to that, instead keep staring at that rear door, my mind lost in a flurry of memories I thought I had chained up tight in the dungeons of my mind.

A reprieve comes when the back door opens, Reed popping his head out.

"There you are," he says. He looks the same as when I last saw him, but still wholly different. His longish hair that's short on the sides, his bright blue eyes, his wide, open smile. It warms something to see him again, and his eyes go wide when he sees me.

"Oh! Stella Bella!" he says, moving to me quickly and then reaching down, lifting me from my seat on the curb and pulling me into a tight, familiar hug. I swallow the lump in my throat. This night has been just... too much in so many ways. Too many ways. He loosens his grip, leaning back to look at me, his smile going softer. "Oh, Stell."

"Please don't make me cry," I whisper for his ears only, and he rolls his eyes the way he always used to.

"Such a girl," he says, and I step back finally, slapping him in the chest.

"I *am* a girl, thank you very much," I say with a smile, a common refrain when we were kids. The door to the bar opens again, letting in a loud burst of music before slamming shut, Beckett walking toward us.

"What the fuck happened?" he asks, staring at the ice on Riggins' hands.

"Stell got cornered by some ass who didn't know no means no."

Beckett's dark eyes burn as he turns to me, anger there. "You good?"

"God, nothing has changed, has it?" I ask. "I'm fine, and he's gone. All is well."

"Because Riggins beat his ass?" Reed asks. I don't respond, and neither does Riggins, but his smile says it all.

Beckett gives a disapproving head shake before speaking. "Good to see you, Stell."

He takes three steps closer to me, the tallest of all of the boys, and tugs me in, giving me a huge hug.

If Riggins was my soulmate and Reed was my best friend, Beckett was my big teddy bear of a brother.

A part of me both heals and breaks with the move, and I bite the inside of my cheek so hard it bleeds, trying to fight off the wave of emotion. He moves his hands to my shoulders, leaning me back to look at my face and read I don't know what there.

His brow furrows at whatever it is he sees, clearly not liking it, but doesn't say anything else.

"I'm gonna head out, I think," Riggins says, then stands, moving to where Beckett and I stand.

"How'd you get here?" he asks. I shake my head.

"I'm gonna call a cab," I say, not giving a real answer.

"He drove you?"

"It's fine; I'm going to take a cab home. Easy peasy." Riggins shakes his head, and behind him, I see Reed smile at Beckett.

"I'll drive you."

"No, I'm fine, really," I say, shaking my head. He gives me a stern look, irritation brewing in his eyes.

"Stop being stubborn; you've had a long night; let me drive you home."

"I'm in the most inconvenient part of town. I'm fine."

"Jesus, some things really *never change*," Reed says with a laugh. I glare at him, but that only makes him laugh more.

"Humor me, little star," he says under his breath. "I just saved you from a sketchy spot. Humor me so I know you get home safe. It's the least you could do, and then I can make sure he's not a bigger ass and at your house."

I don't think it *would* happen, but it would really fucking suck if it does. Begrudgingly, I nod.

"Fine," I grumble.

13

ORANGE JUICE

RIGGINS

The drive is quiet for the most part, with Stella lost in her head, and I'm lost in mine.

I wish I could say I don't know what came over me, what made me lose my fucking mind when I saw that fuckwad's hands on Stell, but that would be a lie.

I clocked her as soon as she walked in the doors of Atlas, my wife standing too close to that fucker for my liking but not close enough to signify any kind of real relationship.

Then my eyes saw her face, the utter pain there, the understanding and the memories that flooded her.

It might have been seven years since she confided in me, but I can still read Stella Hart like a book, even from across a crowded bar.

I wondered if she has seen live music since she left or if she avoids it altogether. At the first show we played when I knew she wasn't there, when I looked out to the wings and saw them empty, I thought I was going to vomit on the stage.

That was the first night of my true spiral, a spiral that lasted two years and ended only with the cold dump of water that was my father dying and a DUI. It's interesting seeing my father fall apart when my mother died, the pain and suffering he put himself through, the way he drowned it in beer and liquor, and then understanding I was doing the same fucking thing. Stella was gone, and I was filling that void with everything—anything–I could.

I watched her from the moment she arrived, watched her start to relax and enjoy herself, fall victim to the bug that is live music, and then, I don't know why, I turned to Reed and told him I wanted to play a song.

I wish I could say I don't know what came over me, but I knew. I wanted to remind her of who we are. Who we should be. Who we've always been.

So I played the first single the band ever released, something of a hardcore fan favorite, at this point, not something the top 40 radio fans would ever know. The first song Stell and I wrote together under the stars, the song that changed everything. When I look back, I think that was the day I decided my best friend would one day be mine in every sense of the word.

Only to fuck it up so badly just a few years later.

As I played, my eyes never left hers.

It was a dick move, and I knew it the second I saw the panic take over her, when I saw her breathing quicken even from the stage, when I saw her eyes go wide.

We climbed off the stage, shaking hands with the owner of the Atlas who once gave us a chance when no one else wanted to, then with the members of the Tailored Pigs, and by the time we were off, I had lost my view of her. The guys went to go get drinks and I went to pace the bar, find a place I could watch my girl from without making her uncomfortable, or at least make sure she was safe.

Then I heard her, and I lost my *fucking mind.*

It was a bad move. I know that for sure. I'm fully expecting a call in the morning from Lee, our publicist, ripping me a new one or maybe a blackmail call from the asshole trying to get some money from me.

I'd pay it.

It would be worth every fucking penny.

"I was surprised to see you there," Stella's low voice says. She always had this fucking intoxicating, gravelly, low voice, almost like she smoked her entire life. It surprised people a lot, that voice coming from the little thing she was, but it always felt like Stella. My old soul. My little star, living a million lives.

"Where?"

She hesitates, and when I glance over at her, she's biting her lip, second-guessing speaking.

"The bar."

"Cause I'm a drunk?" She coughs, choking on surprise, and I can't help but laugh. It feels rusty, a sound that hasn't been used in a while, but it feels good all the same. "They've got orange juice and soda at bars." She shakes her head.

"I'm sorry, I shouldn't–"

"I'm clean. Sober. All of the things," I say.

"I know," she whispers.

Something in me warms, the fact that she knows, that she probably searched me, that I wasn't some unknown, distant memory over the years. She clarified and confirms.

"I, uh... I look you up. Occasionally. Make sure you're okay; the band is okay. I spent..." There's a pause while she tries to figure out how to say what she's going to say or maybe if she even wants to, but she continues. "I spent a lot of my life with you guys. You were all a big part of my childhood and... later."

"Yeah," I whisper, afraid if I allow myself to say more, I'll scare her off, and this is the most conversation I've gotten out of her since I got home.

God, it seems even seven years later, I'm still fucking things up.

The road turns bumpy and unmaintained as we get closer to Stella's house, and I wonder how she gets back here when the weather is bad, if she has something other than that little VW beetle, or if she has a truck in that big garage.

As I pull up to her place, I realize there are no lights, not on the road, not leading up to her house, something she should change and quickly. It's not safe, her driving back here alone at night. Mentally, I decide where they should go along the driveway and what kind should go up her walkway.

Finally, I'm in her drive, parked next to the house instead of pulling all the way back, and she reaches for the handle.

"I'll get it."

"What?"

"I'll get it. I'll walk you to the door."

"Riggs, that's—"

"Almost watched you get attacked by some asshole tonight. Humor me, okay? I'm a little on edge." Another beat of her staring at me, trying to decide if she's going to argue with me before her shoulders relax, and she sighs.

"You always were very protective of me," she mumbles.

Until I forgot how fucking precious you were, I don't say out loud. Instead, I just get out, slam the door behind me, and walk around the front of the truck, tugging open her door and holding out my hand.

"Riggs—"

I don't miss how she's back to Riggs.

"Please, Stell. This truck is big and though a lot has changed in seven years, you haven't gotten any taller." She glares at me and I can't fight the smile. She takes my hand though, small and warm and twines her fingers with mine. I don't flinch when one of them touches a cut, a pain I'd feel over and over and over if it means I get to hold her hand.

She hops down, and I tighten my grip so she can't pull her hand out. When she glares at me, I ignore that, too, instead tipping my head up to the sky.

Something about this, holding her hand in my hometown late at night, looking up at the stars just like we did countless nights before, heals something in me.

"They're bright tonight," her voice says, dancing in the night air and tinkling in my awareness. When I look over at her, her eyes are on the sky, too, taking in the familiar lights.

"Clear night," I agree.

"I still go there, you know," she says in a whisper, still not making a move towards her house. "The clearing. Lay there, watch the stars."

It's a shock, but a good one.

If she were completely over me, over us, if it was a painful memory she never wanted to touch again, she wouldn't go there. She wouldn't go to a spot in the woods haunted by our love, by our dreams —the place we spent hours and hours daydreaming, writing, and falling in love.

I don't respond because I don't know how. I'm walking on eggshells right now, trying to find the balance between encouraging her and terrified to scare her off, anger her.

Finally, her face tips down, quickly meeting my eyes but not letting me hold the contact, before she takes a step towards her house, hand still in mine.

A win, I think.

My boot stomps up the steps and in addition to the loose floorboards, I take in the railing that needs some work, a new beam and some paint.

Finally, she drops my hand, digging in her bag to find a key and holding it up, but not unlocking her door. Just standing there in front of me.

"I don't... I don't really know what to say. Thank you feels...." She smiles, a small laugh bubbling through her words. "It feels like a reward for bad behavior." I return the smile. "But you know, thanks. For saving me and all."

"It's what friends do, Stella," I say without thinking, and her brow furrows in confusion that sends a strike of pain and misery through me.

"But..." her words drift off, and I shake my head, trying to get her to see."

"Please, Stella. Friends," I say, pleading in my voice.

"What?"

"If you won't give me anything else, please give me that. I miss my best friend. It's like... it's like I'm missing a part of me for seven years." I stare into her eyes, her chin tipped up to look at me like she did the stars, and I see it there. The sadness buried under her tough exterior, the way this is all weighing on her.

The way *I'm* weighing on her.

For a moment, I wonder if Stella will ever let me back in. If this is all a fruitless quest to find her again.

But god, I miss her. I miss her too fucking badly to throw this away, to throw her away. I've spent seven years trying to get her out from where she burrowed under my skin with no success.

"Friends," she whispers.

"I know I don't deserve it, but I'm selfish. I'm selfish, and I need something from you. A part of you. I've been missing the part you took all those years ago. Give me something, something small to fill the void," I whisper. I realize now how close we're standing, how I can feel her body heat in the chill of the early summer night. My head tipped down to look at her, hers tipped up to look at me, a decade of thoughts flashing across her face.

I almost step back, assuming she's not going to say anything, but I'm stopped when her warm hand settles on my chest, right over my heart, and the permanent reminder I have there like she somehow knows it's here.

"Riggs," she whispers, then closes the gap between us, sandwiching her hand between us.

I can't stop myself, every molecule of my body screaming to grab her, to touch her, to drag her into this house and remind her of who we are together. I grab her, wrapping one arm on her waist.

Time passes at a speed that makes my skin itch, that makes me want to scream, want to jump and speak before her, but I force myself to pause, to wait, to give her whatever time she needs.

I remember this about her. I was impulsive and would jump before I thought, but not my Stella. She always thought things out, breaking them down until she knew the exact pros and cons and potential outcomes before making a decision.

The only time she jumped without looking was when I asked her to marry me and look how that ended.

So I wait. I watch the thoughts and emotions cross her face, watch her deduce the ending of how things could go before finally, *finally*, she moves to her tiptoes.

I lean down and the world stops moving. The sun explodes and my body goes up in flames, a million memories and long buried emotions escaping as I press my lips to hers, soft and pliant, both so painfully familiar and eerily foreign.

And for the first time in seven years, I kiss my wife.

It starts chaste, just a pressing of lips on lips, but then she gasps, her lips opening a bit as she does, and I can't help but slide my tongue into her, tasting her as I do. Her body melts to mine, her hand moving to behind my neck and fingers twining into my hair. My arm moves, wrapping her waist, and we continue to kiss until I lose track of time, place, and reality. It heals something inside of me that's been broken for years, and when it ends, when she moves her head back just a bit, there is a flash of confusion, longing, and embarrassment. I feel hope rather than disappointment.

"Okay. Friends," she says in a whisper like the kiss didn't just happen.

A weight leaves my chest, but I don't actually speak, just nod and smile at her, a mirror of her as she steps away and moves to unlock her door, cracking it open and turning to me again.

"Good night, Riggs," she says. "Glad to have you back." It's a simple statement, but it sends a cascade of warmth through me all the same.

NOW

14

MEAN! - MADELINE THE PERSON

STELLA

Hammering wakes me up the next morning. After Riggins drove me home and walked me to my door after I had a huge lapse in judgment and kissed him, I took the world's quickest shower to scrub off the existence of Parker, then I took two melatonin and passed out. To her credit, my mother agreed I could have an extra day off this week since I was going on the date *she* insisted on, meaning I was able to turn my alarm off and sleep in.

Strangely enough, I had the best sleep I've had in months, passing right out even though I should've stayed up way too late overthinking that *kiss*, and not waking up once during the night like I normally do.

But now there is a low banging noise coming from outside my house, and I have no idea why.

I roll out of my bed and shuffle to the living room, seeing a familiar truck in the drive from the front window. Sliding my feet into a pair of sandals, I open the front door, not even bothering to check through the peephole.

"What are you doing?" I ask, staring at Riggins in a tight tee and a pair of jeans, holding a hammer in his hands.

"Oh, good, you're up," he says.

"What are you *doing* here?"

"Fixing your porch, obviously."

"I don't understand," I say, brows coming together.

"You've got a few loose boards, and that railing is a death trap," he says, tipping his head toward the railing of my wrap-around porch that is, in fact, a death trap. He puts the hammer down, straightens, and walks up the steps, moving until there's barely a foot between us. His hand moves out, touching the sleeve of the shirt I slept in, a giant oversized thing that's so worn and comfy, it's nearly see-through.

"Nice shirt," he says, his voice gravelly and low. I don't have to look down to know I'm wearing one of his old shirts from the very first tour they did, one I stole not long after becoming "us" and never gave back.

"It's old and comfy," I say in a whisper, looking up into his eyes.

"Hmm," Riggins says, then his hand moves, wrapping my waist the way he did last night and tugging me close to him until we're chest to chest. I have no bra under the shirt, not that I even really need it, but the warmth of him, the smell of him that's so familiar, sweat and musk and woods, it has my traitorous nipples stiffening under my shirt.

I shake my head at him, my hand moving to his chest but not pushing away.

I'm weak when it comes to Riggins Greene. I always have been.

"Friends. We agreed on friends, Riggins," I remind him in a whisper, even though I don't feel the warning as deeply as I should. His lips tip up in a smile, the dimple I used to spend my days making silly jokes just to see coming out.

"I lied," he says. I give him a glare, my hand starting to push on his chest, but his arm grips my waist tighter, his face going a bit serious. "Friends don't kiss like you kissed me last night, Stella."

"That was a mistake," I say. I expect him to be annoyed, to argue with me, but instead a full, boyish smile breaks over his face.

"Well, then, I guess my new goal is to make sure you keep making mistakes, isn't it?"

"This isn't who I am anymore, Riggins."

"Then I can't wait to get to know the new version of you, Stella. Make her my best friend, too." He tips his head down, passing his lips to my forehead before letting go and stepping back. "But the next kiss, it'll be you kissing me, too. I'm not fucking this up any more than I have already."

I don't ask what that means because I don't think I'll like the answer. Instead, I shake my head and step back, crossing my arms on my chest to hide any pesky nipples showing.

"You have to leave, Riggins," I say firmly, attempting a glare. He just keeps smiling at me and shakes his head.

"No."

"No?"

"No, I'm not leaving. I'm doing shit. I'm fixing this deck you're gonna break your neck on, then I'm working on this railing that's gonna fall in three minutes."

I glare at him. "I can handle it."

"You haven't. You've lived here how long?"

The answer is just under four years, so he has a fair point. I won't tell him that, though.

"Well, I'm suddenly very motivated to do it," I say, and even I can hear the urgency in my words. This is too much. He is too much. I feel like the entire foundation of my world is shifting, and I'm not able to keep my steady footing.

I *need* that steady footing.

Something in my words stops him, and he takes me in again, hands in his pockets, looking top to toe the way he used to, taking me in and categorizing, deciding if I was okay,

I'm not, of course.

In so many ways, I'm *not* okay.

And he knows. Somehow, he can see it the way he always could, seeing through my reassurances and lies and knowing what I need.

"I'll be done out here in forty or so. I can't, in good faith, leave this death trap. It's too dangerous at night and you live too far out for someone to come happen by you and help you. God forbid, if there was an emergency." I open my mouth to argue but he raises a hand and somehow I know there's no use in arguing.

I sigh.

"I'll leave if you agree to talk to me. Soon. My place, yours, don't care, but Stell, we need to fucking talk. I have a lot to say to you, whether you want to hear it or not, whether it changes anything or not. Twelve steps and all," he says, and in the same way he could always read me, I read him, knowing it's an excuse he's using.

In the same way, he let my lie go, I let his go. He's not wrong. At the end of the day, we do need to talk. Maybe closure will be good for me; the ability to slam that door behind me for good might be healing.

At the very least, it will probably have him stop coming to me, interrupting this new life I've created.

"Fine," I say. The single word makes his lips continue tipping until it's a full-blown grin that makes my stomach do somersaults.

"Really?"

God, he looks so fucking hopeful. He looks relieved, content, and at ease, something I hadn't seen since long before I left him. I should tell him it's just for closure, that I'm only agreeing to have some grand talk in order to finally end this, but I don't. I let it go and nod.

"Yeah. I have stuff to do inside," I lie. "Do you want coffee?"

He smiles wide before nodding. "Still black and one sugar," he says, and something about that, knowing it hasn't changed, his coffee order, the coffee order I used to make fun of him because he was 18 and ordering the most old man coffee on the planet.

Still, I back up into my house, start the coffee, take my meds, and start the toast like I do every day.

But this morning I pull down two cups.

"What the fuck is wrong with you, Stella Jane?"

It's not even an hour after I handed Riggins his coffee when I answer my phone, and I regret doing so without checking the screen or at least heading into another room rather than standing in the center of the living room with the front door wide open, where I've been pretending to putter around and clean. Secretly, I've been sneaking a peek at Riggins as he works on my steps and railing, watching muscles flex beneath his tight tee in a way I should absolutely not be interested in.

"Wha—" I say into the phone, brushing the hair from my face that fell out of my ponytail. Checking the clock across in the kitchen, it's barely eight am.

Why is my mother calling me just after seven on my day off?

She doesn't leave me wondering very long.

"Parker is at his mother's kitchen table with a *black eye,* saying you're fucking *married.*" There are a lot of things I could say in response to her exclamation, but I, of course, pick the stupidest of my options.

"Why is he at his mother's at eight in the morning?"

"What?"

"It's eight in the morning on a Friday. Why is he at his mother's already?" I ask.

"Jesus, Stella, what does it matter?"

"I just think it's weird, running to your mommy when you're thirty because you got your ass kicked." In my peripheral vision, Riggins' head pops up, looking in my direction and stopping whatever he was doing.

"He lives with his mother, Stella. What does it matter?"

"Oh, that explains a lot, I suppose." I walk over to the loveseat and sit on the arm, thinking about how I should've guessed the 30-year-old man still lived with his mother.

"How about you stop talking about poor Parker and start explaining yourself, Stella. I am *so* embarrassed. I set my friend's son up with my daughter, thinking they might be a good couple, thinking nothing of it. I should have fucking known you'd fuck this up."

There was a time that would hurt.

Before I went on tour, when I was just a literal child, unsure as to why my mother couldn't stand me to the degree she does, yes, it would have very much.

When I came home from tour, after the repeated, *I told you so's*, absolutely. Then it hurt even more when I tried to fit the mold she made for me, the one she wanted me to be, and she still wasn't happy with me.

And then I became numb.

The blue waters creeped up past my ankles and never fully receded. Instead, I just lived life trying to stay in the sun instead of sinking under. Her musings of disappointment, of, *why can't you be more like your sister,* or *if you had gone to college...* didn't hurt anymore because I stopped caring.

Most days, I'm simply surviving, and when you're simply surviving, people's poor opinions of you start to matter less and less.

"*Poor Parker* took me to a bar, got drunk, then pinned me in a dark hallway when I told him I wanted to leave, telling me I owed him *something*. A something he did not have the time to elaborate on when a kind Samaritan helped me out."

There's a pause, and for a split second, I think I'll get something from her. An apology or worry or concern or... something.

I should have known better.

"You went on a date with him, Stella. What did you expect?"

Okay, there it is.

That one. *That one* hurt. I put my head down, staring at my shoes and ignoring the presence that has filled the doorway, blocking the light.

"I expected a human to respect my wishes and my personal space, at the very least." I roll my lips together, fighting back my true responses, knowing they'll just make things worse. "I went on that date as a courtesy to you, not because we were a match made in heaven. It was a blind date, Mother."

"I set you up because you're nearing 30, still single, and throwing your life away." I take a deep, deep breath, trying to regulate my emotions the way my psychiatrist always tells me to, but any sense of calm is thrown out the window when she changes to a more treacherous subject.

"And why is that boy calling you his *wife*, Stella Jane?"

In the moment, Riggins yelling that in a crowded bar, protecting me and my honor felt *good*. Great, even.

But now I hate that he did it, hate that he outed us like that.

I've spent seven years holding on tight to that secret. Something I kept close to my chest, the last flimsy thread tying me to my past life, to Riggins. It always felt as if no one else knew, I didn't have to force a divorce, didn't need to finalize the ending of this part of my life. But with my secret out...

"Stella Jane..." she says in my silence, and I sigh, finally letting this secret out.

"Because technically, I *am* his wife."

The silence is scathing, burning up the line with her fury.

"What the fuck do you mean by that?"

I sigh. There's no point in continuing to lie. If she wanted to, she could get the information, I'm sure. I'm surprised no one had dug it up before then, that no one had dug into Riggins' life and found he had a wife, a marriage formed in the dead of night in a little chapel in Vegas, but done all the same.

"I mean, when I was 20, I married Riggins Greene in Vegas. It was never dissolved."

Again, the silence.

But as expected, it doesn't last long.

"Are you *fucking kidding me*?" she bellows, making me flinch.

"Mom—" I start, though I'm unsure of what I'd say.

"I said, are you *fucking kidding me*?"

"Mom, it's not—" I can't finish because, as she tends to do, she cuts me off.

"It's not what?! Not a big deal? Not important? God, Stella. I told you then, I *told you* getting wrapped up with him was going to ruin your fucking life. Now look at you. You can't even get a good boy to date you. And even if I could convince Parker to go on another date with you, you're *damaged goods!* No wonder you're sad all the time. You threw your life away!"

"I'm genuinely not sure what would make you think I'd go on another date with Parker, but okay, Mom. And I'm also unsure of how getting married, a marriage that, I'll remind you, you had no clue about until minutes ago, has *ruined my life.*" She scoffs, and although I opened the door, I wish I could slam it shut, knowing what's coming for me.

"What have you done with your life, Stella? You work at a fucking diner. You're a loser. You have no friends, no husband, no kids. No prospects. No fucking clue how you bought that shithole of a house, but it's just another decision in a mile-long list that you should have fucking listened to me about. But no. You don't; you throw it all away."

The waters rise, leaving me squeaking out a word.

"Mom—" She cuts me off again.

"Get a divorce, Stella."

It stings, even though it shouldn't.

I know I should.

I know that. It's no longer the secret it once was so there's no need to hold on to it. I could dissolve the marriage simply, move on with my life.

But...

"Mother—"

"I don't want to see your face unless you have those papers, Stella. Making a fool of me, tying yourself to that loser. Do you know how this looks to the town? To my friends?"

"That I'm married to an incredibly successful rockstar? No, Mom I have no idea. Probably pretty good." I snap.

"You're married to a fucking drunk, just like his father," she says. For some reason, that is what finally angers me. My mother making judgments and assumptions about people she doesn't know, never taking the chance to *get* to know them because she thinks she is better than them.

"He's not a drunk," I say, defending him, but she isn't listening anymore.

"I'm done with this. Get the papers, Stella. By Friday, I want you to get that divorce rolling, or we're done."

"We're *done*?" I ask, my stomach churning. But I know what she's about to say. It's the threat that always looms, hanging over my head.

"If you don't get a divorce moving, you'll be fired at the restaurant. You will no longer be invited to family dinners. Your father and I will be *done with you*. And if I get my way, Everest will be done with you."

Everest will be done with you.

I know she could easily turn my father, who never wants to rock the boat, despite how much he loves Evie and me, without much effort, but Everest? Could she convince my twin to stop talking to me?

It's not improbable; my sister, who has never been able to stand up to our mother, is even more eager than me to please her.

"You can't just cut me off—"

"If you don't do what I'm telling you, I will. I should have done it long ago when you started up this bullshit about being depressed as if you have a fucking thing in your privileged little life worthy of making you fucking *depressed*."

The ache in my chest builds.

"Get this sorted, Stella, get your fucking life together the way I've been telling you—"

Suddenly, the phone is gone, and a large body looms over me. Suddenly, Riggs' voice fills the room.

"I can tell whatever you're telling Stell is fucked because she looks like someone just punched her in the gut," he says, and my mother's voice rises an octave, arguing. "No, no. We're not doing this. Stella is an adult. She can do what she wants, talk to who she wants, and date who she wants. I know you see your daughters as nothing more than a chance to redo the life you're unhappy with, but it ends now. I'm back, Rhonda, I'm back, and I'm not some dumb fucking kid who's going to sit back and watch you tear her apart again."

Again, my mother's voice starts up, but all I can focus on is Riggins, who shakes his head like he's disappointed.

"She'll call you back if and when she's ready to, Rhonda. Until then, maybe worry about the shit the town says about you and how you treat your daughter rather than worrying about how her relationships will impact your social standing."

And then he pulls the phone from his ear and hits end.

"You can't do that!" I say finally, staring at him as he taps on my phone screen a few times, turning on Do Not Disturb, I think. He looks up at me with a small smirk, the dimple out.

"I just did. I'm tired of you living in fear of her. It's been too long."

"Who the fuck are you?" I snap, my sadness melting into irritation. I'm glad. Anger is much simpler to manage, easier to control, and morph into what I need it to be.

He tosses my phone on the couch before grabbing my hand, tugging me close, and wrapping me in his arms. I stand there stunned, my mind reeling, my body in a state of pure panic.

"I'm yours. I'm yours, and I'm back, and I'm here to protect you," he says to the top of my head.

The anger morphs again with the warmth of his body, turning back into that sadness and fear, but now also a bit of nostalgia and longing for something I once had.

"You did back then, you always protected me from her." I sniff, thinking of that, of those times when I knew no matter what, I would have someone in my corner and how much I didn't realize I missed not having that.

"You were always better than her, Stella. She knows it, too. That's why she is the way she is," he murmurs, words I feel more than hear as my face is buried in his chest. I fight the tears creeping up, pulling at my throat.

"She told me she'll cut me off from Evie," I whisper. "She still lives with them, you know. She still is.... Evie," I say, and to anyone else, that might not make sense, but to Riggins, who grew up with us and knows how deeply her sense of worth is entwined with our mother's approval, he knows that threat would scare me to my core.

"She's jealous of you, Stella. That's all," he whispers, his fingers tugging me until I look up at him. "You know that, right?"

I roll my eyes. "What does she have to be jealous of?"

"That you're beautiful. That people adore you. That you're so fucking talented, the entire world knows your work. That you're in this town not because you're stuck, but by choice. That you're *you*, Stell. Everyone should be jealous of you. Just look at you." I roll my eyes, but he keeps staring stoically at me.

He lifts a hand when he sees the single tear I've let fall. I hate it, that tear shows weakness, shows how much she impacts me. He wipes it with a thumb, but keeps staring at me.

"You were always worth more than whatever she thought of you, Stella. The only one who couldn't see it was you." He looks at me a moment longer. "Still hate people watching you cry?" My brow furrows.

"What?"

"Do you still hate letting people see you cry?" I sniffle, then nod. I wonder if he's thinking of the time I finally did let him see me cry, of the moment he broke through my walls.

Of the last time he saved me from her.

But he must see my hesitance more because he nods, a small look of sadness crossing his face like he realizes he doesn't have that privilege anymore, that he isn't my safe space anymore.

"Alright. I've got maybe five minutes until I can get out of here. Let you be alone."

A part of me wants to argue, to tell him to stay, to beg him to wrap me in his arms and let me sob there, but instead, the smart part of me nods, steps back, and wipes my eyes.

He stands there for a moment, then, true to his words, nods, turns, and goes back out the open front door. I hold it together for the five minutes he's outside, and the two additional minutes he spends cleaning up.

I don't cry until his truck is rumbling down the driveway.

And even though it's a great question, I never wonder why I don't just file those divorce papers to stay on my mother's good side.

But hours later, the world answers when I walk out my front door to get the mail, eyes swollen, long after the sun has gone down and nearly trip over a bouquet of sunflowers. The note inside just says,

All my love, R.

THEN

15

PAUL REVERE

STELLA

I only make it three blocks away from my parents' house before I breakdown crying and pull the phone out of my pocket.

A burner phone Riggins gave me because somehow, he saw it coming the way I purposely blinded myself to.

"Little star," his voice says, rumbling through the line. The relief I feel from his words fills the small gap left in my gut.

"I—I—she—I—" I start, but I can't get anything more out, can't speak through my body-wracking sobs. Through the pain lancing through me, both physical and emotional.

"Where are you?" he asks, his words firm and instant.

"Corner of Balch and Alderbridge," I somehow manage to say.

"Ten minutes. Do you have a jacket on?" I sniffle, once, twice, three times, taking a deep breath, I hear noise in the background—keys being grabbed, a door slamming, another opening then closing, his truck starting. It somehow calms me, despite my all consuming panic, the pain and anger flowing through me so I can speak slightly easier, air going into my lungs.

I don't miss how he doesn't rush me, doesn't question a thing, just waits for me to speak as he makes his way to me.

"A hoodie and a jacket."

"Okay, good, Stell. Good." His voice is low and soothing, almost the crooning singing voice he uses on stage. It's late September, and while most days are still pretty warm, at night, it starts to get cool like it is now.

"I love you," he says.

"I love you too," I whisper.

"It's going to be okay."

"I know," I say, and suddenly, I do know that. I do know that everything will be okay. I'll be okay, and we'll be okay. I made the right decision.

"I'm gonna stay on the line, okay? But I'm driving, so you're on speaker in the passenger seat."

"Okay," I say, my voice small and unlike me. Normally, I'd give him shit about talking to me while he's driving or about how he really needs a new truck that has Bluetooth, but I don't have it in me. Not at all.

It doesn't take long before he's here, and I hear his truck before I see it, but still, relief washes through me.

God, I feel sweet fucking relief at seeing him. I step up to the curb to get in, but before I can even open the door, he's parking on the side of the road, stepping out, and jogging around the front of the truck, pulling me into his arms.

I lose it finally, sobbing into his tee shirt (*he* did not grab a jacket or sweatshirt before leaving, it seems) as I remember everything that just happened, the cruel, angry words my mother spit out, the way my father just watched, the way I begged her to understand.

The ultimatum.

"It's okay, Stell. You're going to be okay." He sounds scared, and it's probably because he's never seen me like this, a mess, sobbing and miserable. I've made it my mission to be the happy one to Riggins, who has lived with grief and sadness enough as it is.

He's never seen me cry, not when my mother told me my entire life that crying makes you weak, that crying is for babies, not strong women who want to do something with their lives.

"She—she—she—" I start, trying to get air into my lungs to explain.

"I can put the pieces together," he coos into my hair. Feeling his warmth around me, his strength, smelling him, his voice rumbling against my crying face, I start to calm, the way I always do around Riggins.

I've always had an imbalance of some sort for as long as I can remember. I'd get sad for no reason, and it would last a bit before I'd feel good again. Once, my mother took me to the doctor, but when it wasn't an easy, *here, take this antibiotic, and she'll be good in two weeks*, my mother decided to ignore the diagnosis altogether.

But even when I feel the wave of my sadness creeping up, if I'm wrapped in him, I know I'll be okay.

It's always been that way. Just... more lately. More since he became *mine*.

That simple reminder has the last of my hiccups slowing.

"She kicked me out," I whisper into his chest. "I told her we were together and I was going on tour with you. She told me I wasn't welcome there anymore."

I don't know why my mother hates Riggs so much or why she hates his family so much, but the violence with how she spoke to me in the kitchen of our home was still a surprise.

"You'll move in with me," he whispers.

"You don't have to—" I start, but he pulls back, his hands on my shoulders, his eyes locked on mine.

"Are you mine?"

"What?"

"Are you mine? We haven't talked about what happened at the bonfire, but Stell, to me, you're mine now."

"Your.... Your girlfriend?" I ask, my pulse racing again but for a different reason now. It's been two weeks since the bonfire, and while we've had small kisses and held hands and been some new version of *us*, we haven't talked about what it meant, and we definitely haven't done more, despite how much my entire soul wants to.

"You're my everything, Stella. But yeah, for right now, we can call you my girlfriend."

I can't help it. Even though the rest of my life feels like it's crumbling, I smile. I smile *big*.

Because after a lifetime of being head over heels in love with my best friend, he's now my *boyfriend*.

When he sees my smile, Riggins returns it, pressing his lips to mine, kissing me, and making me *feel* like his as his hands bury into my hair.

It is as if everything in the world is going to be okay so long as we're *together*.

"You'll move in with me," Riggins says hours later as we lay on a blanket in the grass in our clearing, watching the stars. We went to his apartment before we came here, where I spent a good hour stress cleaning, throwing beer bottles in the recycling from Riggins having the guys over the night before, checking his fridge to see what we had to work with for dinner, before finally, he forced me to stop with kisses on my neck.

It didn't take long before we were making out on his couch for a good long while, learning each other with this new label but not going much further, even when I pushed for it.

It was *blissful*, his lips trailing down my neck, his lips making mine swell with the long, deep kisses.

I always wondered if making out would be awkward, bumbling, uncomfortable. But like everything with Riggs, it was anything but. It's natural, like it's what we were always supposed to be doing, like our bodies and our hands and our lips were made for this moment.

Unfortunately, when my hands started to creep around for more, he pulled away, pressed his forehead to mine, and smiled. "Let's go write under the stars," he whispered.

The one offer I'll never turn down, which brings us here.

"What?"

"Tomorrow, we'll go in when she's not home, grab your stuff."

"I don't—" I start. "You don't have to, Riggs. I'll figure something out. I have royalty checks coming in now, thanks to you guys." And I did, though I didn't think they would be enough to fully support an apartment and feed and care for myself. Something tells me my mother won't be allowing me to continue to work at the restaurant under these circumstances. I think she's hoping I'll find myself on the streets, homeless and desperate, then finally, after 19 years, break to her will.

"You're mine. That means I take care of you," he says, his head turning on the blanket to look at me, and the look there tells me not to argue at all, that I'll lose whatever argument I'm gearing up for.

Instead, I let out a small smile and nod. "Okay, Riggs." He smiles, too, and warmth fills me from my belly and out.

"There's my girl," he whispers, then presses his lips to mine.

It's all going to be okay.

I can't imagine it not when we're laying under the stars like this when Riggs is this new version of mine, when he's pressing soft, sweet kisses to my lips.

"I can't wait to leave here," I whisper into the night sky.

"Yeah? Where do you want to go?" I laugh.

"Anywhere but here, really. Far away from my mom."

"From me?"

"What?"

"Far away from me?" he asks, his voice low. I turn my head to look at him and realize he's already looking at me.

"Of course not. Where you are, I am, Riggs."

We lay like that, under the stars, him holding my hand, sometimes kissing, for what might be hours before he speaks again.

"When we make it big, when we can live anywhere in the whole world, where do you want to live?"

"What?" I ask with a laugh.

"We'll always have a house here, in Ashford, if only because this is our place. I want to take our kids here one day. Show them where we fell in love, where it all started. But we'll have another, wherever you want."

He's planning a future.

Our future.

And under the stars like this, the way we've always been, the opportunities feel absolutely endless, like we could do and we could be anything we want so long as we speak it into the universe like this.

"Anywhere?"

"Anywhere," he whispers, reaching down and twining his fingers with mine.

"I don't know. I just know I want a dog. My mom never let me have one." He turns his head and smiles at me.

"Okay, so we'll have a dog and a big yard for the dog. Where's this yard going to be?"

The fact that he never tells me I'm crazy or stupid or silly for my thoughts makes me feel warm and fuzzy all over. "Maine? You mentioned Maine in your postcard, the first one." I turn my head to look at him, his face directed at the bright stars over head and see his lips tip up in a smile.

"You would have loved it there. The stars, god. You think they're bright here? Out there it was like you could reach out and touch them."

"We should go one day."

"You say the word Stell, I'll take you to Maine." I don't say the word, even though I want to go. I want to go everywhere with him.

But right now, I'm happy here in my favorite place with my favorite person, forgetting the rest of the world.

I lose track of time, my mind blank from anything but the man beside me and the all-consuming peace I feel, but eventually, I look at my watch, taking in the time.

1:32.

Fuck, how have we been out here this long? It's then I realize Riggins hasn't talked in a while, simply humming in agreement at random things I say, at stars I point out, thoughts I have. We've done very little writing tonight, which is rare, but I think Riggins knew I just needed the stars and the open space, and writing was a way to get me there. He always knew best what I needed.

"You're quiet," I say.

"I'm busy," he says, concentrating on the stars.

"What are you doing?" I ask with a laugh. There's a pause before he turns his head to me, a smile on his lips.

"Finding the brightest star other than the North Star. That one's already taken."

"What?" I ask with a laugh, and his head turns back to the night sky.

"That one," he whispers, pointing to the sky. "That's the one I'm naming after you. My little star gets the brightest star." He moves, shifting so I'm now held by him, his arm wrapped around my shoulders, my head on his chest.

"You're crazy," I murmur.

"I'm okay with that." We go back to watching the sky before I speak in quiet wonder.

"Look, a shooting star," I whisper. "That one. That one could be me. Stella, the bright, shooting star," I smile into his chest but feel his head shaking above mine.

"Never. That would mean you're running from me. Getting further. I want you to stay put, so I can always find you when I need you."

"No need, Riggins. I'll always be right here, by your side."

"Promise?" he asks, but the word sounds strange, strained even, worry and panic laced in it. Looking over at him, his eyes are serious, worried, though stuck on the night sky. I move so my body lays on top of his, my eyes looking into his, my hands framing his face that needs a shave.

"Yes. I promise."

"When I fuck up, do you promise to stay by me?"

"Of course, Riggins. I love you."

"I love you more," he whispers against my lips.

NOW

16

HOLLOW

STELLA

My head pounds when I wake the next morning, the weight of disappointment and sadness heavy on my shoulders as I head downstairs.

Turn the coffee on.

Start my toast.

Grab my meds and down them with water.

It's the same every morning, a routine I've perfected, never changing out of superstition, I think. If I keep my days the same, if nothing changes, there's less possibility for something to throw me off and send me spiraling.

But I'm already headed there. I feel it in my bones, the creeping, exhausting dark blue lapping at my hips. Soon, it will be at my throat, and I'll be unable to move or accomplish much more than the essentials.

Seven years ago, I came home and conceded to my mother, becoming whatever she asked me to be to please her, but it was never enough. Now I'm starting to wonder if it will ever be enough if *I'll* ever be enough.

Even when she's ground me down to dust, will I ever fit into that impossible mold she made for me?

I shake my head, trying to dislodge the thought. Instead of stressing about it, I move to my room to dress in an Ashford Diner tee and a pair of shorts, pulling my hair into a ponytail and forcing myself to add some mascara and a swipe of blush. My mom might be threatening to fire me, but for today, at least, I still have work to do.

And hey, maybe if I look like a functioning member of society, I'll become one.

Wishful thinking.

The morning drags, my mind lost in memories and thoughts and worries, but when the bell above the door rings at nine am and my eyes move there, I can't do anything but smile.

Smile *wide.*

It's like how it was when I was young when I was 17 and working here on weekends when I didn't have some kind of practice or school, and the guys would all trudge in for breakfast, Riggins at the lead.

Before he's even fully through the door, his eyes scan the diner before they meet mine, his eyes going warm, the smile taking over his face.

He's happy to see me. Overjoyed, even.

God.

God.

A part of me knows the splash of elation I feel from him being *here* is dangerous. I should temper it with reality and past experiences, but I can't. I just *can't.*

Not when the entire band comes in for breakfast, just like they used to back when they were all exhausted from a long night, occasionally hungover and half awake.

Not when he walks up to me, slugs an arm around my shoulder, and says, "Gotta booth for us, little star?"

Not when they sit and start ribbing each other playfully in the same loving way they did years ago, including me, anytime I walk over to them as if nothing has changed at all.

And surely not when every time I look up, Riggins' eyes are locked on me, following me throughout the restaurant, winking every time he catches me staring back.

Each time, I can't fight the small smile on my lips. By the time they leave, the waters that were lapping at my ankles this morning recede, if only for a few hours.

This continues three days in a row, with the guys coming into the diner, led by Riggins, a few hours after the morning rush ends, hanging for an hour or two, just goofing around and laughing. Sometimes, they pull me into their conversations, and sometimes, I sit with them for a bit, but each time, it feels like a piece of me is healing, like a part of me is coming back.

A part I missed dearly, a part I thought was gone forever.

When I see him sitting outside, I know the routine has shifted. Walking out with a bowl, I'm excited to see Riggins outside by himself, Gracie at his feet, and bend to pet Gracie on the head.

"Happy Monday," he says.

"Happy Monday. No crew today?" I ask. His smile widens, and he shakes his head.

"Nah. It's nice out, I thought I'd bring Gracie. Plus, Reed takes up too much of your attention." I don't let my mind dig too deep into that one; instead, I stand and place my hands on my hips.

"What can I get you?" I ask, not even bothering to grab my pad. What's the point in pretending anymore?

He doesn't answer, simply asking a question of his own. "Is it busy in there?" he asks, tilting his head toward the diner but not looking away from me. I've realized that when I'm near, he never shifts his eyes from mine, almost like he's afraid if he does, I'll disappear. Something about it doesn't sit right with me, and guilt ravages me with the realization.

"No," I say with a shake of my head, both to answer his question and to shake away the emotions I don't want to be feeling. He pauses a beat like he's trying to steady his nerves, and nods.

"Sit with me," he says, his eyes soft and with just a hint of pleading.

"What?"

"Sit with me. Just…" There's nervous hesitation that I absolutely hate on him, on *Riggs,* the most confident man I ever knew. He doesn't *get* nervous asking a simple question. "Just sit with me. For a few minutes." He pauses, but I don't speak, continuing to stare at me for a few moments before biting his lip, the way he used to when we were kids when he was suddenly nervous or ashamed of something, like when someone would bring up his father after his mom passed or rib him for not having the coolest, hippest shoes. "Unless you can't, then that's cool. I get it if you have to do work."

My mind rakes over the things I have to do this afternoon, anything I haven't done yet, and realize all of my normal tasks are done, except for things I really can't do until the diner is closed. Thursdays tend to be pretty slow, and now that Riggins has been coming in, I try and keep my hands and mind busy while I wait to see if he'll actually show.

I find I'm not raking my mind for excuses, either, but for permission to do what I want.

When was the last time you did something for you, Stell?

The words my sister spoke ring in my mind. For the first time, I ask myself them. When *was* the last time I did something for me? For me alone, not for my mom or for work or for Evie or even years ago, for Riggs? When was the last time I did what *I* wanted without worrying about what others would say, how it would be interpreted, how people would react?

I'm not sure.

And with those words vibrating through me, I do something Riggs clearly doesn't expect.

I pull out a chair across from him, sit down, and tug my phone out of my pocket, sending Amelia a text telling her I'm taking a short break and to let me know if she needs me inside. She replies almost instantly with a chaotic line of letters and exclamation points that make me smile, followed by a *take as long as you need!* before I slip my phone into my pocket.

"Deal. How's it feel being home?" I ask, leaning back in the chair, my hand dipping down to brush the hair of Gracie, who has moved to be close to me.

Riggins' smile goes wide, and he begins to answer, telling me about how he's been finally clearing out his parents' house, visiting all his old spots, and hanging out with the guys.

I fill him in on what I've been up to, skirting around some of the subjects I'm not comfortable enough to mention yet, like my mental health and the songwriting I've been doing, before we start to move onto random topics. I marvel at how easy it feels, even after all these years.

Our conversations fall into a comfortable lull in ten minutes or so, Riggins halfway through his pancakes Amelia brought out as I pet Gracie's head that she's rested in my lap absentmindedly.

"I missed this most of all," he says, a soft look in his eyes.

"What?" I ask, confused.

"This. You and me, laughing about things, just talking. Being us. I miss my best friend, Stell." I can't help it; the words are spilling out without my mind's approval.

"Me too, Riggs," I say with a small smile. I have to fight not to be a sad one.

He stares at me for a moment, categorizing and dissecting the look, I'm sure before we move back to talking about little things, things with no real meaning or impact.

And for a short, blissful moment, I wonder if we could have this again, at the very least. This friendship and camaraderie I've missed.

I wonder if I could have my best friend back.

"I should go soon," he says eventually, breaking into my thoughts. " I have an AA meeting at four, and I have to bring Gracie back before I drive over to Stafford." It surprises me, both the mention of him going to Alcoholics Anonymous and how casually he says it.

"AA?" I ask stupidly. "I mean, I know what it is, I just didn't think..." My voice trails off, and I'm sure my cheeks burn with embarrassment, but his smile widens.

"Yeah. Been going for a while. Five years sober." He doesn't explain more, but I can do the math. Five years ago, at his father's funeral, where I came and held his hand, was the last time I saw him.

"Well, don't let me keep you," I say, leaning over to press a kiss on Gracie's soft head before standing.

"You're not keeping me at all, Stell. I'd do absolutely anything in this world to spend more time with you like this, just hanging out. It feels... it feels normal. It feels like how it used to be, the way it was always supposed to be."

He says exactly the way I've been thinking, but something about him saying it aloud makes it hurt more like he's confirming that we don't have that anymore.

It always tells me he might miss it just as much as I do.

But where does that leave us?

Where *could* it leave us?

My mind refuses to start to calculate the equations of possibility and what could be.

"See you tomorrow?" I ask, walking towards the door. He smiles wide.

"Tomorrow, little star."

When I come back to clean up Riggs' table, I find another photo, a more recent one.

Gracie, 5 years old.
All my love, Riggs.

NOW

17

COME OVER

RIGGINS

"Hey, Riggs," she smiles when I walk in the next day.

It sounds stupid, but seeing her, hearing her, makes my entire day better, makes my steps lighter, my smile wider. It's raining today and when I heard it on the roof of my childhood home, for a moment, I felt at peace. My hatred for the rain and the bad memories it usually brings wasn't there this time, instead just an excitement to see Stella again, to keep making headway in fixing our broken relationship.

For the first time in years, I feel hopeful. Hopeful we can make this work, hopeful that I'll get my star back.

I move to the corner booth that used to be the band and mine, everyone in town somehow knowing not to sit there and wait for her to come over. I get a weird joy each time I see the scuffed and stained table hasn't changed, my mind able to sync each scratch and spill to a memory. In the furthest corner, hidden beneath a napkin dispenser, SH+RG is still carved.

It's like our history still stands strong, a small comfort.

"How are you?" she asks as she moves over to my table with a glass of water and an orange juice, then puts her hands on her hips. I've been careful to come in later in the day, just like when we were younger, knowing the few times Rhonda Hart comes in is early in the morning to collect money. I'd like to avoid as much of the drama as I can before Stell and I are secure.

"Better than ever," I say, reaching to grab her hand. A small smile tips her lips, and again, my heart flips in my chest. It's just like those early days when she would blush at any flirting I'd do, and just like then, I have chords and melodies drifting through my mind. My hands itch to write them down, my soul yearning to lay under the stars with my girl and turn our story into art.

"You're so weird," she says with a roll of her eyes. "You're normal?" I nod. "Got it, I'll give the order to Frank."

"And then you'll sit with me for a bit?" I ask, sounding like a child wanting some attention, but that's fine. She looks around the restaurant; there are a few tables toward the end of their meal, but it's not too busy. Her lips are still tipped in an echo of a smile when she turns back to me.

"Yeah. I can do that," she says.

There's a lull in our conversation nearly an hour later, an empty plate pushed away from me as Stella still sits across the table. We've laughed and talked about everything under the sun, from stupid stories from tours to updates on Evie's job as a music journalist. It's just like it used to be, where time would barely exist for us.

It's easy. It's familiar. It's perfect.

I should have known it wouldn't last long, though.

"Why did you come home?" Stella asks out of the blue.

"What?"

"Why did you come home? Why did you come back to Ashford? I know you have a real house somewhere nice. Why come back to this town with so many memories?"

"Why do you think?" I ask instead of answering, trying to balance my answer accordingly.

"Honestly?"

"Always." A beat passes as she picks at her nails before she looks me dead in the eye and answers.

"I think you came home because you need to write, and this is where you do it. I'm who you do it with. I think a part of you wanted to see if you could make it work, what we used to have, the writing relationship." She shrugs, then looks at her nails again. "It sounds self-centered to say you came home for me, but it makes sense. You're about to record a new album; it's the only thing I can think of."

There's a long moment before I answer, trying to think of the best way to explain. She's not completely right: I came back to clean out my parents' house, to put it on the market and close that chapter. But I'd be lying if I didn't say that I've been stuck since the last album, no true idea on what to write.

The first album we released after Stella left was angry, so many songs about heartbreak, but also a lot about getting drunk and having a blast and the band. The second album after I got clean was full of self-realizations, songs about getting sober and not being as bullet proof as I once thought. It was about self hatred and self acceptance and loss.

But now the label is looking for our next album, and nothing has come when I put pen to paper. I'll admit, a part of me thought being here again might give me some kind of inspiration, that being where it all started might help.

"I'm tired of being angry," I say, my voice low. "I'm so tired of being angry and being sad, Stell. I spent years being so angry. At you, at my dad, at the world. I came back because I needed to remember why I started this and what I loved. I want to write about love and friends and being happy again. I haven't been able to do that since I wrote with you."

"Oh," is all she says, and suddenly, I wonder if she wishes I had lied, telling her I came just for her. But where have little lies gotten us? A bunch of small lies always make the biggest mess.

"Stella, that's not to say I didn't come here wishing deep in my soul that I'd see you, that I'd cross paths and get to try and make things good with you. That's what I want, Stell. That's what I want most of all, to make things good with you." I reach across the table to grab her hand and hold it, mostly reassurance for myself, but she slides it out of reach, continuing to stare at her nails. I sigh.

"We need to talk, Stella," I say, my voice low and soft like she's a scared cat.

"Riggins..." Back to Riggins. Fuck. Somehow, I made this worse. Somehow, I've convinced her to crawl back into her shell.

Well, I guess there's no point in playing it safe anymore. I sit up straighter, reaching and grabbing the hand she's staring at before she can pull away. When she looks up at me, I see the mix of emotions, the confusion and the panic and the fear there.

"We need to talk. We're married, Stella. So much has happened between then and now. Fuck, so much happened then, and I have a feeling we both only remember or know half of it. We need to talk. We need to... Fuck, little star, I still love you." Her head jerks back like she's confused, like that shocks her, which is wild to me.

How the fuck does she not know I love her?

"I love you, Stella. I always have. And I miss you so fucking much. I have for five years. Longer, if we're being honest, because I lost you long before then. I miss you in my bones. You are my person. A part of me is missing when you're not near." Her eyes start to wander, but her shoulders straighten, resolve in her face as she pulls her hand away.

"Riggins. It's not that easy. It's not that simple."

"Why not?" I ask.

"What?"

"Who says it's not that easy? Who is to say it isn't as easy as deciding we both were young and stupid and stubborn—" she tries to cut in, but I steam roll over her, knowing I chose my words wrong but unable to change it now. "And we just need to talk. Who says it can't be as easy as that?"

"I do," she whispers. "I say it's not that easy. You destroyed me once—" Frustration bubbles under my skin, and I speak without filtering.

"Then let me help fix you, Stella." Her entire body goes stiff.

"What?" She says the single word stilted, something I don't realize until after I fuck up. I should tread carefully, but I don't.

"I destroyed you; let me help fix you." There's silence before she speaks, a surprise, in a way, because I think she believes she's not broken, or at the very least, has convinced herself of it.

"There's nothing to fix, Riggins. I'm fine." Her jaw is set tight, but I don't stop.

"You're not you, at the very least, Stella."

"You don't know me anymore." She stands, and my gut drops, but my anger wins, the stubbornness canceling out common sense.

"You keep telling yourself that, but it's bullshit, and we both know it. You put on your armor, protect your heart because I broke it years ago, but this armor? It isn't you. It's exactly that: protection. From me, from the world, from yourself, from your mother. You became what she wanted because it was the safe option, but you lost yourself doing it." I pause, looking her dead in the eye to make sure she hears my next words and understands how serious I am. "And I'm making it my job to bring you back."

"You have to leave," she whispers, her voice pained.

I went too far.

I needed to go too far, to knock some sense into her, to tell her I see through her bullshit, but I went too far all the same, and that wall is back up.

"I'll head out, Stella, but I'll be here. I'll be here in this shit town we both always hated until you're ready to talk to me. I'll be here under the stars, waiting for you. And when you're ready to talk to me, *really* talk, I'll be here."

And then I leave to give her the space she needs.

I give Stella time to collect her thoughts.

She told me over and over again she needs time, needs to think, to come to terms with things, and I bulldozed in, first by forcing her to be my friend again, then forging some kind of in-between because I miss her more than anything.

But she needs time.

When we argued at the diner, I knew she needed time. So I gave it to her. I left, told her to let me know when she was ready to talk, and I headed back to my dad's house.

And waited.

And now it's been nearly a week without any word from her. Instead of spending time with Stella like I want, I'm sitting with Reed, watching some old movie on the couch of my dad's house, the same couch we had my entire childhood, stewing.

"Alright, it's been long enough," he says, finally pausing the movie.

"What the fuck man?" I ask, turning to him, ready to knock him out. My emotions are too close to the edge, my temper fire engine red, and this dumb fucking show is the only thing keeping me from absolutely losing my mind.

The sole distraction I have.

"What's going on?"

"What's going on is you just turned off my show." He rolls his eyes like I'm a moron.

"Where's Stella?" he asks, and now it's my turn to roll my eyes.

"At her place, I assume. Or at the diner."

"Yeah, and you're here moping around like a dipshit. Why aren't we there instead of watching this stupid fucking movie?"

I don't answer, instead averting my eyes until I find a loose thread on the seam of the couch, tugging until it snaps then rolling it between my fingers into a little ball. "Riggins," he says, his voice firm.

He might be the goofiest of us all, but he's got this dad vibe that always means business.

"We got into a fight," I say, my words low.

"You got into a fight? When?"

"Thursday."

"It's Monday."

"Yeah, and she hasn't reached out."

"She hasn't reached out?" he asks like he doesn't understand.

"Yeah. She needs space, and I'm giving it to her. When she's ready, she'll talk to me." Reed opens and closes his mouth once, twice, three times before cocking his head to the side, like he's trying to understand what he's seeing or what I'm saying, maybe.

"Okay, okay. Back it up really quick. What did you fight about?"

I sigh but know he won't let it go until I explain, so I do, telling him about going to the diner, about her thinking I'm only in town because I'm out of inspiration and my pushing her to talk. I tell him about calling her broken and how I fucked up once again. "So yeah," I say. "She told me to leave, so I did. Now I'm just giving her time." Reed has remained quiet this entire time, silent despite the subtle change to his face, but finally, he speaks.

"You're giving her time?" He asks it like I'm an idiot.

"That's what she needs."

"She's had seven years of time, Riggins. Seven years that you didn't chase her."

"Can't chase someone who doesn't want to be chased, Reed. She wanted nothing to do with me that whole time." It's then that Reed laughs, a sad noise that twists something in my gut. Something I very much do not like. It's like he knows something I don't, and he can't believe I don't know it.

"You're so fucking stupid, Riggins. Really." My jaw goes tight.

"What the fuck is that supposed to mean? She ran and never looked back."

"Never looked back? God, man, all she's done is look back. She's been writing all that time, hasn't she?" Cold creeps into my gut.

"What?"

"What do you mean, what?"

"I mean, what the fuck are you talking about?" His face loses a shade of color, and panic starts to brew in my veins. He shifts on the couch so he's better facing me.

"She didn't tell you?" he asks, but it's less of a question and more of a shocked statement.

"Tell me what?"

"I don't... I don't think it's mine to share, Riggins."

"Reed, I swear to fucking god—"

"She's been writing. Songs. *Hits*, Riggins. She ghostwrites hits." I feel it then, the tingling feeling of shock as it washes over me, a mix of panic and excitement and... "They're all about you, of course."

He says it like it's a foregone conclusion, but it takes the air from my lungs and fills me with hope and dismay.

"No," I whisper, shaking my head, but somehow, I know it's the truth. It explains so much, like how she afforded that money pit of a house, how she wasn't worried when she lost her job, and how she knew so much about the industry she's had nothing to do with for seven years.

Or so I thought.

"I mean, I can't confirm they're about you, but...."

"Name," I say, my voice not even sounding like my own.

"What?"

"What's her name?" Reed looks to the side, his Adam's apple bobbing as he swallows, avoiding looking at me, and I know, somehow, it's going to cut me deep, whatever her name is. "What's her fucking name, Reed?.

"Marie Stevens."

Marie Stevens.

Marie was my mom's middle name, Stevens her maiden name.

How had I never realized that? Sure, both are pretty nondescript names, but how did I not put them together?

"She couldn't have forgotten you if she tried," Reed says low, his face filled with compassion and a hint of pity.

Suddenly, the path is clearer. My plan completely shifted and altered. Reed is right; I can't play this safe, and I can't let her stew. I've been letting her stew for too long. She thinks I let her stew because I didn't care, and right now, I'm just proving that point.

I need to do something big.

I need to scream from the rooftops about what she means to me, who we are. Who *she* is to me.

"Call Lee," I say, grabbing my phone and opening a search tab, typing in Marie Stevens in the search bar. A long discography of songs shows up, songs she's written, and speculation of who she is; none of them are correct. Some of the songs are familiar, songs that when I heard them on the radio or at awards shows, they hit me with a sense of longing and sadness I didn't understand.

I should have known.

"What?" Reed asks.

"Call Lee. I need to get on a show," I say, pulling up a music app and typing her fake name in there, my pulse racing.

I'm terrified to get to know the version of Stella I've never met, but it's time. If she won't tell me herself what happened over the years, I'll let her music do it.

18

YOU'RE GONNA GO FAR

STELLA

"Over easy, right Mrs. Marcuso?"

"You've got it, sweetie! You've got a great memory." I don't tell her my memory had very little to do with it since she's been coming in every morning since I was 20 and ordering the same thing.

Turning toward the kitchen to give Frank my order, I stop short, watching Amelia get increasingly flustered at the man standing in front of her despite this not being his first time in the diner. He points at me and smiles wide. I roll my eyes, walking over to him.

"Stella Bella!" he says, using the old nickname, and then pulls me into a big bear hug. Reed always gave the best hugs, and with every-thing going on, I really need one. Badly.

It's been four days since Riggins last came to the diner, four days since I asked him to leave in a fit of anger.

It has been four days since I spoke to him.

Funny how you can go years without seeing someone, they come back into your life for a few weeks, and suddenly you feel that loss all over, like it's fresh and painful.

"What are you doing here?" I ask when I pull back from the hug.

"Why do you think I'm here?" he asks reasonably. I make a face without my brain's permission, and he laughs before his face goes serious. I know he's here because of Riggins, but I also have to wonder in what respect? Is it because Riggins sent him here, or maybe because he's worried about him? Is he spiraling?

"Come on. Eat lunch with me," Reed says, genuine hope on his face. "It'll be like old times."

"I'm working," I say, even though a part of me wants to say yes so, so badly.

I miss him. I miss my old life, a version of me that I've packed away tightly, but I've slowly been picking at the tape and keeping it shut this past week. It's been nice having them back in my life, but it also feels like opening a door that needs to stay shut to keep what's left of me safe.

"You have your break coming up, Stell. It's slow now. You totally can slink off for an hour or two, and we'll be fine," Amelia says. I turn to my employee and glare, but she's so starstruck, it bounces right off of her.

"See! You'll be fine! Come get lunch with me, tell me all about your life since I last saw you."

That sounds about as enjoyable as having my eyelashes plucked out one by one. Can't wait to tell the guys who have been touring the world and going to awards shows and living their dream that I'm stuck in the hometown we all swore we'd leave, working in the diner my mother owns and as lonely as humanly possible.

I shake my head.

"Actually, you have to leave. If my mom finds out you're here, she's going to freak." She hasn't been in since that call despite her threats of needing to get my divorce rolling by Friday, but I know round two of that argument is lying in wait.

Reed looks momentarily confused.

"The Stella I knew didn't care about what your shit of a mother thought," Reed accuses, and if it were anyone else, I'd be mad, but he says it with his signature smirk and goofy boy face; I can't be mad.

"Yeah, well, now she pays my bills," I say, lying just a bit, but what does it even matter anymore? "And considering Riggins is back in town, I'm already walking on eggshells, waiting for her to find out he's been coming in here after he punched Parker."

"Let me guess, she has no idea?" Reed asks, that same cocky smile tugging at his lips. I shake my head. "Would be a shame if everyone in this place finds out you're ma—" I slap my hand over his mouth, and he laughs the deep, loud laugh that used to wake me up in the middle of the night under my hand. He was never able to hide his laugh, make it quieter even when he tried his hardest.

"I'll go," I whisper, then say louder, my hand still on his face, to Amelia. "I'll be back, an hour tops."

"Two!" Reed says with a wide smile.

I roll my eyes and ignore Amelia's, *take as long as you need!* before I let Reed lead me out the front door.

Lunch is on the outskirts of town at a burger joint we all used to go to way too late at night. I haven't been here since I came home; the memories are too sharp, but when I walk in, the smell alone brings them in on a wave.

Good memories.

Sweet ones.

We stand at the counter and order, Reed insisting he pay for my meal despite my arguing. "I'm a famous rockstar, Stella Bella. I can handle the cost of a burger and fries."

I know better than to argue, so I let it go.

"So, what have you been up to? Anything exciting?" Reed asks, his smile genuine as he sips his soda from an old translucent red plastic cup, the same ones the place had when we were all kids. I shake my head.

"Nope. Just the normal. I'm working at the diner. Living in

Ashford. I'm boring. But you—you've got an exciting life," I say with a smile. "How's life been?"

He shrugs. "Same old, same old," he says, his face going a bit sad as he does. "You know how it is. New city every week, shows and fans and... all that. Just bigger now. Wilder."

I can't even fathom *wilder*. His lips tip up with the words like he can see my mind working.

"A different kind of wild, though. Fans screaming our names, trying to get backstage. We have full-time security now, which is wild." I laugh at the idea, the mental image of a 6'5", built as fuck grumpy Beckett needing a bodyguard. Reed laughs. "Beck hates it." I smile at the way he still can sense what I'm thinking. "But it's not the same partying wild. We drink, me and the guys, but not blackout drunk every night anymore."

"Riggins?" I ask. It's a multi-part question: Did you stop because of Riggins? Does Riggins drink on tour? Reed shakes his head.

"Riggs doesn't drink anymore, obviously. But he'll hang with us when we do. It wasn't always like that. It took a bit for us to believe it would be okay if we drank around him, but eventually, he convinced us. We all met with his AA sponsor about a year after he was sober and asked him questions until we felt comfortable." There's a heavy silence that comes with the reality of acknowledging Riggins' addiction.

"He's changed," Reed says after a few beats of silence, and it twists a knife.

"I know that," I say in a whisper. Just a week or two of being around Riggins, and I can see it. I see the version of him I fell in love with is back, no longer a cloud of alcohol and addiction hanging around him.

But it still doesn't ease my worries, doesn't cure my anger or the pain he caused.

"I was pissed for a while, too," he says, and my head moves back in surprise.

"What?"

"I was pissed. How he was, how he threw his life away, threw our life away. He threw you away. It pissed me off. It took him a while to prove he was sober, that he really meant it. There was a year there, before his dad died, where he would try to get sober and then relapse. It was a cycle that felt like it would only end in tragedy, but we were young and scared that if we talked to him about it too much, it would backfire." He looks beyond me like he's lost in memories. "I wish we'd talked to him sooner. There was that one time, but after that, we never said anything, not outright. And it only made him want to hide how bad it had gotten. It made him hide his drinking."

I remember that part all too well, the final nail in the coffin of Riggins and my relationship.

The confusing concoction of emotions that continues to swirl in my gut twists again, and I'm back to being annoyed with Riggins for putting all of us through it.

"It's not fair, you know," Reed says, his tone turning once more gentle and concerned. His hand reaches out, and he grabs mine. "Holding his mistakes against him this long, holding this grudge." I open my mouth to argue, but he shakes his head. "No, I'm not saying you can't be mad. Be mad forever, Stella. But let him tell his side first. You two... there's too much there for you to just throw it out. That's what I had to come to terms with. Our friendship was too old, too valuable to throw it out. I heard him out, and we talked. It was good. And he's better now. My best friend is back."

I give him a sad smile that wavers with my effort not to let a teardrop. "I'm happy for you, Reed. Really, I am. You were as worried as I was about him back then. I'm glad you got your best friend back, glad you guys got the career you always dreamed of, and glad you get to tour the world. But me? I'm also better," I lie. "I'm better because I got space, I got to breathe." I shake my head, trying to fight the tears. "I lived for him for so long; it took me a long time to learn to live for myself." That hangs in the air between us before, finally, he tips his head to the side, furrowing his brow, and asks me something that shakes me to my fucking core.

"Are you, Stella? Are you living for yourself?"

I can't breathe, much less answer.

"Or are you living for everyone else? Because this?" His hand moves up and down my body, indicating who I am now. "Is not my Stella Bella. This is not the girl who daydreamed about the stars and would make stories about pretend worlds just to make us laugh. This isn't the girl who wrote songs that could tear me in two before she even lived life before she got out of the small town that was holding her down." He shakes his head.

I don't speak because I don't know how to answer.

He's not wrong.

I'm not the version of myself he knew, not the free, comfortable version. I'm my mother's version. The safe version.

"Knowing you were writing, it was a bit of a comfort." My gut jumps at the knowledge that Reed knows I still write songs. "Knowing that even when you were far from us, doing your own thing, you were still following your dreams the way you could." I don't respond, ripping apart the paper wrapper of the straw instead.

"But seeing you like this?" My gut drops. "I don't feel as good about it."

"Well, we all have to grow up sometimes, you know? The real world isn't as forgiving as daydreams," I say through a tight throat. He smiles at me sad before nodding. There's another beat of silence like he's waiting for me to say more, but I won't.

I'm relieved when two large burgers and a mountain of fries are placed in front of us, giving me a much-needed distraction.

Unlike his friend, Reed knows when to stop pushing, knows if he doesn't stop I'll shut down and cut him out, so he changes the subject to my relief and we spend the next twenty minutes chatting about nothing of importance.

Finally, when we're all finished, I stand, knowing I have to get back to the diner.

"This... this was great, Reed. Really. I missed you."

"It's good to have you back in my life, Stell. Our life." I know he means the band, and he means Riggins, but I shake my head.

"This is the last thing I'll say on it, Stell," he says, and I take a deep breath, trying to brace myself. "Friendship. Give him your friendship. Even if you can't ever give him what you both really want ever again, if you're too afraid to get hurt again, we'll all understand. But you both need each other, even if it's just as friends. You're in the same room together, and for the first time in seven years, he's whole again, Stella. His light is gone when you aren't around. And I haven't seen you over the past few years, but I think the same goes for you, too. Did you shine the past five years, Stella?"

I think about it, but I already know the answer.

I built my armor up so high, so thick, there was no chance for any light to get through.

But Riggins and the band being back has cracked it wide open, making me question everything again.

"I have to get back to work," I say instead. He stares at me for a bit before nodding and leading me out of the burger joint and to his car. But as I try to leave, he grabs my wrist, his fingers touching the heart tattoo with the small letter 'R' on my wrist.

Riggins' heart on my sleeve.

"Give him a chance, Stell."

I can't respond, through the lump in my throat, so instead, I give a noncommittal nod and open the door.

I think about Reed's words through the rest of the day.

19

THE VIEW BETWEEN VILLAGES

STELLA

Later that night, while I'm sitting on the swing on my front porch, my phone rings, blaring the ringtone I set for my sister, and I smile as I answer.

"Hey, Eve," I say. "What's up?"

"You need to turn on High Fever," Evie says, fully ignoring me. My brows furrow at her panicked voice, at my even-keeled sister not even pausing for me to finish saying hello.

"What?"

"You need to turn on High Fever right fucking now," she says louder, panic and urgency in her words.

"What are you talking about?" I ask, standing and moving back into my house.

"Stella. Are you near your computer? Or you can use your phone."

"You're scaring me," I say, but I open my laptop on the kitchen island, typing in the password quickly as I balance the phone between my shoulder and ear.

"I need you to turn on the live stream. I'm serious, Stella."

"Okay, okay, I'm on it," I say, trying to ignore the way my heart is pulsing. There's only one reason Evie would tell me to turn on High Fever, the music channel that often has artists on for acoustic sessions.

"Faster, Stell. Faster."

"I don't understand what—" I start as I wait for the page to load, a live stream clearing and cutting my words out.

It's Riggins on a chair, camera trained on his face, sitting with a guitar in his lap, those fingers I know all too well strumming gently and playing a song I recognize too fucking well.

Not because we wrote it together or because I've heard it on the radio.

No, because it's a song I wrote after we broke up.

A song I wrote in a spiral, the first time I saw a photo of Riggins walking around Central Park, a blonde on his arm. She was a pop star, and the tabloids spent weeks speculating about their relationship when they were seen slipping into restaurants, and she was seen stepping into his building a few times.

I got drunk that night, replaying the clip over and over of her moving to her tiptoes, of his arm wrapping on her waist as her head tipped back.

All I could think about was how fucking badly I wanted to be her because she had him, and I never would, not again.

It was the first song I sold, a large country band buying the rights and when it hit #1, I was able to buy this house.

It felt good, writing for the first time, reclaiming that small part of me I tucked away, so I kept doing it, writing dozens of hit songs, but this one... this one will always be my favorite and least favorite wrapped in one. The memories hurt, but in the good way that felt like stretching a limb that's gone numb.

So I wrote the song he's playing now, a song about having a crush on a woman I've never met because she gets him when I never will again.

He sings it with such pain in his voice, the same pain I felt when I was writing it, his eyes closed and his face reflecting the same pain in his voice. Wes is in the back behind him, strumming an acoustic guitar, and I wonder if the rest of the guys are there, too.

The song winds down, and I watch it in shocked silence, my phone still held precariously between my ear and my shoulder as the camera pans to the host.

"Wow, what a change for you!" The host of the live streaming show says, his face filled with shock and confusion. Clearly, Riggins didn't tell him what he was going to do and I wonder if he knows, of he know who wrote that song, what it means to Riggs. To me.

Because I know, somehow, he found out. The only other person who outright knew is Evie, who is mysteriously quiet in my ear, where my phone is still held.

Riggin's eyes don't look at the host when he speaks, staring straight into the camera, straight at me, whether he knows it or not.

"Yeah, it's a song that means a lot to me," he says, and I'm surprised I can hear the words over the rushing of blood in my ear. I continue to stare at the screen of my laptop, my jaw going tight with irritation when the camera pans back to the host, forcing me to lose sight of Riggins.

The host laughs, confused and amused in a way that grates on my nerves, though logic tells me it's simply because I'm dying for the camera to pan pack to Riggs, to see him again, to hear his voice, to let his eyes bore into me again despite the distance.

"Does it? I don't think many would have pegged you as a country fan," the host says with a chuckle, and I want to strangle him. Who gave him this job, anyway?

"I'm a Marie Stevens fan," Riggins says when the camera is back on him, and suddenly, I can't breathe. The phone in my hand slips out, crashing to the couch and then the floor, but I can't even worry about that; I can't even focus on the words coming from my phone, Evie's voice panicking, I'm sure.

"Marie Stevens?" the host asks, but I'm grateful when the camera doesn't show the idiot again, somehow knowing this moment is important and instead zooming in on Riggins so he fills the entire screen.

"She's a songwriter. She's written dozens of number-one hits." There's a beat, and suddenly, I feel nauseous, cold, and clammy like I might get sick, but still, I can't look away from the screen, knowing that as he tends to do, Riggins Greene is going to ruin my fucking life once again.

"She's also my wife."

I don't watch the rest of the stream. Instead, I run to the bathroom and get sick.

NOW

20

NORTHERN ATTITUDE

RIGGINS

The banging on my door isn't exactly unexpected.

It's a bit sooner than I expected, to be fair—she must have caught the stream as it was broadcasted. Wes and I went to the city this morning and recorded it, and I've been waiting for Stella to figure it out. I wonder who told her. I don't think it was Reed, but maybe it was.

Or it was probably Evie, with her music journalist ear to the ground at all times.

Shuffling to the front door, I open it, Stella's fist still pounding on the air as it opens.

"What the fuck are you doing?" she asks instantly, her face red with irritation.

God, she's beautiful. She's even more gorgeous than she was five years ago when I thought she was the most beautiful girl on this earth. Even with the underlying sadness and exhaustion that seems to be ever-present, she's stunning. And right now, angry, red-faced, and ready to tear me to pieces, I've never been more turned on by her.

"What?" I say, knowing damn well what's going on.

"That unplugged session on High Fever! What are you doing!?" I step back in the house, leaving the door open in invitation for her to step in, but she stays planted on the front step.

"What do you think I'm doing?"

"I don't fucking know! Losing your goddamn mind?!"

"Why would my singing a song you wrote mean I'm losing my mind?"

"Don't play coy with me, Riggins Greene. I'm not talking about you singing my song. I'm talking about you calling me your fuck-ing *wife!*"

"But you are," I say with a smile. "You are my wife." Her face goes redder, and she takes a step forward. For a moment, I think she might hit me.

"What are you doing, Riggins? Why would you do that? I'm going to have reporters hounding me now!"

"Telling the world you're mine."

She throws her arms up, walking into the house as she scoffs.

"We went seven fucking years, no one knew anything. You didn't know anything! Now, when this ends, I'm going to have all your little fans coming at me. I had privacy. I had anonymity. No one cared about me."

"That's bullshit, and you know it. *I* care about you."

"I'm not even going to touch that, Riggins. You threw me into the spotlight without even thinking about how that will impact me." That's a lie because I thought long and hard about how it would impact her. But Stella was always meant to shine, not hide behind a pen name. "And my mother is going to—"

I cut her off with a groan. "Jesus, Stella, why is that always your biggest concern? How your bitch of a mother is going to react."

"She's my mother, Riggins, she—"

"Is fucking horrible to you! She treats you like shit and always has." She hasn't told me much about her relationship with her mother since I've been back in town, but I know she set her up with that fuck wad and wasn't even a little concerned when she found out he tried to assault her daughter. But even if things were amicable, Rhonda

Hart would always be no better than the dirt under my shoes for the way she treated Stella.

"She's my mother."

"That doesn't mean she deserves your time, your energy, or your grace, Stella." She stares at me, and for a moment, I wonder if I broke through. But then she shakes her head.

"We're not here to talk about me or my mother. I'm here to talk about you and what you did."

"I'm not going to apologize for telling people who you are. The world deserves to know how amazing you are." She shakes her hair, and I move to close the door, reducing any way for a quick exit because it's time we finally talked.

"I can't believe this. Why can't you just leave me alone? We talk one time in seven years, and then you come back to town and try to change *everything*. You've been fucking stalking me for a week—"

"Getting lunch at the only diner in town is not stalking."

"Then go to another town! Another state! You're a fucking celebrity; you have millions of dollars! You can go anywhere, and instead, you choose Ashford, New Jersey, the town you fucking hated your whole life! You were itching to leave here the second you turned sixteen. You get out, and seven years later, you're back. Why, Riggins? Did the words dry up? No more angry songs to write about your bitchy girlfriend who left you?"

She's referencing the first album we released after she left, which was full of angry breakup songs about her since that was all I had in me at the time.

Anger and confusion and addiction.

"Wife," I say instead, the word rolling through the room low and angry.

"What?"

"You weren't my girlfriend when you left. You were my wife."

Stella rolls her eyes, throwing her hands up in the air.

"So what, you go on live television to sing a song I wrote about you as payback? The song I wrote about the all-consuming jealousy I felt seeing her on your arm? Great job, Riggins, great job reminding me how I spent the seven years you were gone trying to keep my head above water, not even looking at another man because it made me sick to my stomach, and here you were, going on dates with a pop star. Having a grand, sweeping, on-again, off-again relationship with her. God, her little fucking fans are giant and will crucify me!"

"Willa?"

"Yes, Willa Stone! Your long-term, on-again, off-again girlfriend?"

"Jesus, Stell, you thought that was real? It was all bullshit!" I say in irritation, but she just rolls her eyes at me.

"I've seen the photos and the clips, Riggins! As hard as I tried, that was my favorite kind of torture—late at night, when I started to miss you, I'd open my computer and search for you. Find the pictures and the articles about you. I'd spend hours learning all about how your life was without me. Looked pretty fucking great. So why don't you go back to it, Riggins? Stop trying to dig up the past."

I step forward, reaching for her, but she steps away, pain in her eyes.

"Stella, I—" I start, apologies at the tip of my tongue, but she shakes her head.

"No. No, Riggins." She steps back, moving away until there is a good five feet between us. "You know, I didn't write that first year after I left. I couldn't. I tried so many times; I wanted to get the feeling out, put them in their little box, and walk away, but every time I touched them or tried to write, it hurt too bad; my mind was blank. I thought... I thought I was broken. I thought I was nothing without you." Finally, a tear drops, and it breaks my heart knowing I did that. That I hurt her.

"The first song I wrote was a year after we got married. Two days after you didn't show up at coffee five years ago." My brows furrow in confusion, but she shakes her head when I open my mouth, continuing on. "Some tabloid reported that you were out with her, and I don't know. It was like the confirmation that I needed to know we were really done once and for all–"

"We were never done, Stella," I say, taking a step closer. "Never." She shakes her head sadly.

"That night, I wrote the song you played today. Funny timing, you know? Since the reason I realized we can't ever work was because of her?"

THEN

21

GIRL CRUSH - LITTLE BIG TOWN

STELLA

"And next," the pretty blonde host of the entertainment news show says as I move through my room, cleaning up. "A hot new couple on the rise?"

I've taken to watching the shows like this while doing mindless tasks. It serves multiple purposes. It's not music, which is important since most of my playlists end up shifting toward Atlas Oaks, and radio stations now have them in their top 40 lineups, making it hard to avoid.

But I also watch the show because ever since I left the band and Riggins last year, I've found myself searching their names regularly, trying to keep up on anything that might happen. I think part of me is always waiting for news that something happened, that Riggins' drinking won him over once and for all and I'll have to face the devastating prospect of living life without him, forever.

But at this moment, I wish I hadn't started the habit at all.

"Riggins Greene and Willa Stone were seen walking through Central Park together, hand in hand," My mind freezes, but unfortunately, my body doesn't as I turn to look at the television behind me, the screen my worst nightmare.

Music Power Couple is scribbled in bold pink letters above the photo, one of Riggins' hand holding Willa's, the powerhouse singer-songwriter whom I've admired for years.

"The couple, both rising singer-songwriters, have been seen around the city a few times, though we can't quite get a pinpoint on when these photos sent in anonymously were taken. We're just happy to see Riggins looking happy after the tragic death of his father last week." My stomach churns, and I feel like vomiting.

We had made plans to meet up after his father's funeral, and for the first time in a long time, his eyes looked clear, his face filled with grief and sorrow, but not loose from liquor, and I thought maybe... finally, he'd found the light. Maybe my leaving had snapped him into looking deeper at himself; maybe he had changed, and we could make an honest try at this once again.

Because god, I miss Riggins. I miss him to my bones, to the pit of my stomach. I miss my best friend, my cowriter, my first and only love.

But he didn't show. I sat at the cafe for hours waiting for him, like an idiot, believing this was it: our chance at a fresh start. Our shot to once and for all make things right. And when he didn't show, I went home and cried until I couldn't breathe, finally coming to terms with my new reality: Riggins and I were done.

I spent the night searching for discreet divorce attorneys, someone, anyone, who could write up the papers I needed without making a scene of it, narrowing my choices down to three.

When I woke this morning, I stared at that list, deciding it was something... tomorrow Stella could deal with. Or next week Stella. Or maybe next month, Stella.

Hell, we've already been married two years; what would it matter if it's longer?

But now, now I'm staring at a screen grab of Riggins standing next to a gorgeous tall blonde, her looking up at him like he personally made the sun rise, his hand holding hers, dark sunglasses on his face as he looks ahead at wherever they're headed, but in that protective way I've seen so many times before.

My blood freezes in my veins and the reporter shifts to some other hot topic, an actress getting caught saying something into a hot mic accidentally, but that photo is burned into my brain.

When was that taken?

Where was it taken?

I'm going to be sick, I think to myself as I move to my computer, typing in a few keywords in a search bar and waiting for the results.

Riggins with a pop star, my brain screams, and even though I try to fight it, my gut knows.

My gut knows that when I click on the first result, I'll see that, even though they can't confirm the exact day or time, the photo submitted was allegedly taken on Thursday. This means while I was waiting in the coffee shop where we agreed to finally talk about what happened two years ago, where I had planned to confess about Las Vegas and the wedding, he was out gallivanting with a famous pop star, living his best life.

Forgetting about me.

I start to spiral.

For the first time, at the very least, I can feel the spiral happening. I can feel the dark blue waters creeping up on my ankles, lapping at my shins, but this time, I let it.

The numbness is better than this churning, this envy.

Envy.

How fucked is that?

My fingers start to move on the keyboard without my mind's permission, searching for more photos of Willa, seeing a gorgeous woman, everything I will never and could never be. Gorgeous lush curves where I have none. Long blonde hair, the same shade my mother always told me I should get at a hair salon, while Riggins told me he loved my dark locks. A voice that wins awards, lyrics she writes about love and loss and life, more eloquent than anything I ever have been able to put on paper.

Can I even blame Riggins for choosing her over me? For choosing to spend a sunny day with this beautiful woman rather than dissecting the issues of our failed relationship in his hometown?

Fuck, I would choose her too. I think I have a crush on her, too.

Not just because she's beautiful and talented and everything I'll never be, but because she has him.

Instead of getting sick, completely dissociating, and curling up in my bed to cry when this all-encompassing pain crashes over me, I do something I haven't done since I left the tour.

I reach for a pen, paper, and my guitar, and I write.

And write.

And write.

And when I'm done, I pass out on the couch, sleeping until noon, those dark blue waters keeping me sound asleep.

When I finally wake up, I finally do what I've been putting off for too long.

I call the lawyer.

NOW

22

CAVES

STELLA

"We never dated, Stella," Riggins says, pushing me out of my trip down memory lane. I sigh, closing my eyes as I do. When I open them again, somehow, the anger is gone. I'm just tired. Tired of this back and forth, of this digging up of the past. Of the disappointment.

"Riggins, you don't have to lie to me anymore. Really. We were kids with big dreams, and in a way, we both got ours. You're allowed to live your own life. Just... sign these papers for me, so I can live mine too," I say, then reach into my large bag slung over my shoulder, gripping the envelope in my hand.

"It was all fake, Stella." He runs a hand through his hair like he's frustrated I'm not understanding. "After my dad died, the label threatened to drop us unless I went to rehab, but they didn't want everyone to know I was going because what's the fun of a sober rockstar?" His laugh is incredulous and angry. "It's part of the reason that when our contract was up, we left Blacknote and went to Catalyst Records. The album after was all about my sobriety. About loss and... well, you. Blacknote didn't like that; they liked the wild rockstar vision." He shakes his head like this is just part of it, but I'm aghast. How did I not know this?

"Stella, I'm breaking about a thousand NDAs telling you this shit, so if you want to ruin my heart and my career, this would be a good place to start. But Willa doesn't date, or at least not really. She has fake relationships for PR; the more interesting and controversial, the better. She doesn't believe in falling in love, but the public won't believe love songs if they don't believe she wrote them about someone. So we were a perfect match. I needed to clean up my image a bit and hide out while I was in rehab, and she needed someone the public wanted to see her with. That was it. We're just friends. Good friends who both used each other to get what we needed from the industry."

I stare at him, noting the honesty in his eyes but trying to be strong and hold myself to the plan I made.

Come here, give him the papers, and end things forever.

The papers that have sat in a desk drawer for years. Papers I've never been able to send because a part of me never wanted to break that final thread that held us together.

But it's time.

It's just hurting the both of us.

I pull out the envelope and hand it to him with no words. He accepts, opening the silver fasteners, pulling out the stack of papers, and staring at them for long, long minutes.

I should leave.

I should turn and leave before he can argue, but instead, I stay, dissecting the look on his face as it moves from confused to sad to angry.

"What the fuck are these?" he asks, waving the yellow envelope the papers came in.

"Divorce papers," I reply, doing my best to keep my voice neutral, no emotion there.

When he looks at me next, I see it all there. The hurt, the confusion, the frustration, the regret.

But no anger.

He's not mad. It makes my stomach churn because I can handle anger. I can handle him being mad that I'm severing this tie, but sad? Disappointed? That's a harder pill to swallow.

"Got that. I'm asking why the fuck you're giving them to me."

"So we can cut the bullshit, Riggins. We—"

"Riggs," he says through gritted teeth.

"What?"

"You call me Riggs. Not Riggins."

"Are you really nitpicking this bullshit?"

He steps closer, and I take a step back, my back hitting the wall, leaving four feet between us.

"You always call me Riggs. My Stella always calls me Riggs."

My jaw goes tight.

"Well, newsflash, *babe*, I'm not your Stella anymore. You don't know me anymore."

"No, I don't know this weird robot version, but I know *you*. I know you to your core, Stella. And I don't know what happened—"

"What happened? Are you insane?" That takes him back, his head moving with my fierce reaction, but all of my bottled-up feelings are bubbling to the surface, pushing back the well-composed neutral version of me.

"Stella—"

"I said, are you insane? You don't know exactly what happened?"

He shakes his head. "No, because you refuse to talk to me about anything!"

I laugh, but there's no humor in the words. "Fine. You want to know what happened? I asked you—no, I begged you to slow down with the drinking, and you agreed. Promised me the world and told me things would get easier. But you didn't, did you? You just got sneaky with it. Do you know that I can't even smell mint mouthwash without wondering if that person has a drinking problem they're covering up?" I can see that hits the mark, guilt suffusing his face.

"We woke up that morning, and you didn't remember marrying me, Riggins. We got married, and I woke up happy as could be, and you didn't even fucking remember."

"You didn't say anything! You—"

"Don't with this bullshit, Riggins. Because what bride wants to remind her husband the next morning they got fucking married!" I shake my head and take a deep breath to try and regulate myself. "I had to get away. So I did."

"Stella..."

"And then you never came after me." His brow furrows, confused, and he opens his mouth to argue, but I'm on a roll, speaking over him. "And now here you are, back in my life, raking up shit."

"I'm not raking shit up, Stella. I'm trying to fix things. We were always meant to be together, and I fucked that up. So I'm here, better and clean and healthy, trying to fix it!"

I shake my head again. I can't believe that's what he's here for. I won't believe it. Doing so means I'm risking everything. The safety and sanity that I've crafted for myself over the last seven years, the walls I've built to protect my heart. He absolutely destroyed me once, and I barely survived. A second time might kill me.

"Let me go, Riggins," I say in a near whisper, the tears clawing at my throat. "Let me go. Go live your life and do it without me. Stop dragging me down. I live in the same old town we grew up in, but you got out. You're a new person. Take it. Run with it. Be Riggins Greene, rock star. Be everything you were always supposed to be." He takes a step closer, and I close my eyes, not wanting to see him.

"And you'll be what?" His voice asks, low and concerned. The same way he'd talk to me in the middle of the night when I'd confess my fears in the safety of the dark.

"I'll just be Stella," I whisper.

"You were never just Stella. You were never meant to be *just* Stella."

"Well, that's what I am now."

"No, it's what you've convinced yourself you need to be to fit in this town. Small and meek and unassuming." He takes another step closer until there's just a foot between us, and my breathing stops with the determined look in his eyes.

I know if I wanted to, I could tell him to back up, I could leave, and he wouldn't follow, but I can't make my feet move. I can't force myself to do that.

"But you were always extraordinary, Stella. The brightest star in the sky." His eyes take in my face, reading my deepest secrets and uncovering all of my truths. It feels like it lasts a lifetime before he sees what he needs to.

A whisper of hope.

The confusion battling within me, the bright pull I'll always feel to him that sometimes seems to fight back the darkness of my fear.

And I'm so tired of fighting. I'm so tired of lying to myself, of telling myself that I don't miss him, that I don't crave him. Would it really be so bad to give in just this once? To scratch the itch, to ease the burn? Then we could go right back to before; I could finally move on...

Closure. It could bring me closure.

"Fuck this," he says, pinning me against a wall and kissing me as if the world is about to implode.

The kiss detonates something inside of me in a way that our kisses in the past never have. That wall I've erected between us caves in, leaving me open to accept whatever he's willing to give me.

Whatever he's dying to *take*.

As soon as I do, any and all rational thoughts leave my mind. No thoughts on how this might destroy me later, nothing about how I'll regret it in a bit. Just the all-consuming joy of being back in Riggins' arms.

His lips move on mine, and my lips part like they've been trained to do so, his tongue sliding in and tasting mine. My hands move to his neck, tangling in the hair at the base of his neck, and I moan, trying to get closer to him.

"Jesus fuck, it feels good to hear that sound again," he says when he breaks from my mouth, lips trailing down my neck, nipping and sucking as he goes.

My neck has always been wildly sensitive; kisses and nips there always made my entire body erupt in flames, and it seems he remembers that. His lips move, shifting so his thigh is between my legs, the firm span of it pressing where I already need him.

I moan again, the sound deep and feral. The pleasure and need rocketing through me catches me off guard, but I should have known.

I always knew I was born to be Riggins'. My body was built to respond to him.

"Riggins," I whisper as he sucks on my neck. His hands move to my hips as his lips move back to mine, kissing me wild. He uses the new grip to move me, shift me, and encourage me to grind on his thigh. I'm rocketing toward pleasure and release at record speeds, but I don't have enough of my mind in place to feel self-conscious. Instead, my hands grip tighter on his hair, pulling his face closer to mine like if there's any space between us, I'll cease to exist.

"Please," I whisper, the words meaning so much more than a plea to convince him to take me over the edge.

I'm begging for *him*.

For Riggins.

The versions of him I refused to let myself even contemplate.

The one who loved me wild.

The one who always made me see stars.

The one that could make my body sing.

Instead, he shifts, hands going to my ass and lifting until I'm wrapping my legs around his waist, pressed to the wall. It's then I feel how hard he is, my hips rocking to find something, anything to take the ache away.

"Tell me to stop," he says, standing in front of me, pressing me to the wall, my legs wrapped around his hips.

I shake my head, his lips trailing down my neck, sucking and nipping and causing me to moan.

"I can't," I whisper.

"Need to hear you say yes, Stella. I won't wake up knowing you regret this." I close my eyes and take in a deep breath, trying to channel my common sense and come up with a real answer, but all I can focus on is how much I miss him. Miss this.

How much I miss being Riggins' entire world.

I don't say yes the way he asks, but I say what I *need* to say.

"Destroy me. You've done it once before. What's a little pain with my pleasure?" He lets out a deep groan, but it seems to be what he needs to hear because he steps back, his hands gripping my ass tighter, my hands gripping at his neck, my hips tipping forward to grind against him as he moves away from the wall. His teeth nip at my neck, harder than before, harder than he ever would have dared all those years ago.

A feral noise leaves my throat, loving it.

He walks through a doorway I instantly recognize as his childhood bedroom, and I giggle a bit at the idea of us finally fucking in this bed after years of not. I barely have time to take in the room before he's throwing me on the bed.

"Shirt, off," he says, reaching behind his head to grab his tee shirt and I watch as his creeps up his front.

Normally, I'd argue. It's all I know how to do with Riggins these days, but, for the first time, winning is outweighed by need. Absolutely, all-consuming *need.* The kind that burns in my veins soothed only when his fingers touch mine. They the waistband of my shorts, tugging them to my ankles, grazing as he goes, taking my underwear.

I pull my shirt off with my bra as well, tossing it in the corner. My chest rises and falls as he stands straight again. So much has changed —his shoulders are broader, and his skin is healthy. Muscles twine down his arms, carved but still lean, his stomach flat, taut muscles disappearing under his jeans. His hand, long fingers, and tiny scars and calluses move up, brushing through his hair before moving to the button on his jeans with ease.

I lean back on my hands, my legs stretched and crossed as the ankle, watching. His lips tip up, his dimple showing as he looks at me before shaking his head like he's entertained by me. I would laugh or smile or say something, but then he's pushing his jeans and boxer briefs down, and I'm at a loss. His hard, thick cock juts out, bobbing as he stands tall again.

He crosses his strong arms on his chest and lets his eyes survey me as I have been him. His gaze goes from my face, taking it in, weighing how I feel as he always seems to do now, down to my breasts, not large but one he always loved; nipples peaked before moving down to my belly. When I shift, I uncross my legs and widen them a bit. Letting him see me.

"Jesus fuck, Stella," he whispers like he's in awe before moving onto the bed on his knees, crawling up to between my legs; I shift back, pulling my head to the pillows, but I prop myself up again when he stops before he's laying atop me.

"Riggins, what—" I start, but I swallow my words when a hand goes to both thighs, widening me further as he lays between my legs.

His eyes look up, and his face is suddenly feral, serious, and crazed with desire.

"I've been waiting to taste you for seven years. Now, be patient, and let me enjoy this."

"Let you enjoy this?" I ask with a laugh, looking from my body to him. But the laugh stops when he runs his tongue over me, from the entrance to clit, and quickly sucks there. A deep, low moan leaves me as I tip my head back, but I look at him again when he stops.

His eyes are on me, serious and full of fire. "And you're going to watch, little star."

Something in me knows that's a demand, and I take it seriously.

I watch as his head lowers, lips wrapping around my clit and sucking hard. I scream out a moan, hips bucking up, but one of his wide, rough hands moves to my belly, holding me in place, his eyes still boring into mine. I pant, and then I scream as his free hand moves between my legs, two fingers sliding inside me easily and crooking.

"Oh, my fucking god, Riggins!" I shout, the fire in my belly pooling, heat taking over my body. I'm so close. It's been just a minute or so, and I'm already at the edge of the cliff. I can't even get *myself* off this quickly, but here he is, gathering up years and years of pent-up sexual frustration and channeling it into something I know is going to be huge.

My hand moves up, inching and rolling my nipple, making my pussy clamp around his fingers, and he must like it, the look or the feel, I'm not sure, but either way, he moans around my clit where his tongue is expertly flicking me. I scream, my free hand moving to tangle in his long hair, holding him in place as I start to help, to ride his face, to help him finger fuck me.

It creeps up, starting at my toes and traveling up and up and up. Right when it's about to crest, his eyes lock on mine, his teeth scrape my overly sensitive clit right as he crooks his fingers and pushes them in deep, and I explode.

I come, and I come, and I *come*, my body quaking, his tongue lapping as I moan his name, dragging out this orgasm until I feel wrung out from it, at which point he moves finally, looking at my panting body, pleased.

Finally, I let my eyes drift closed.

I'm still catching my breath when Riggins crawls up my body, caging me there before kissing me wild. I taste myself on him, feel it on his chin, and it makes me gasp in pleasure.

The satiation that was lingering in my bones just a moment ago is gone, leaving nothing but a burning need in its place. His body lays along mine, and I can feel every inch of his skin against me. "I really, really wanted to make this last long," he says, pressing kisses down my neck, sucking where my neck meets my shoulder when he gets there. "But there's no fucking way. Seeing you, so fucking beautiful, so fucking sexy, hearing you come with my name on your lips? I need you, Stell."

"I have an IUD, and I was tested recently; everything came back negative," I say, breathing heavily. I think I would give anything to get him in me, to feel that connection and closeness right now.

"Me too," he breaths, "Are you saying—"

"I'm saying I need you inside me now, or I'm going to lose it," I whisper. "Please, Riggins. I miss you so fucking much. It consumes me. I wake up, and I miss you; I go to sleep, missing you. I just *need* you. Pleas—" I barely get the last word out before he's sliding into me, both of us moaning loudly as he does.

It's as I feared. Or hoped, maybe. Riggins fits me perfectly as if he was made to be mine and mine alone. Full to the point I can feel a stretch, his pelvis pressing on my clit as his hips press into me, a riot of pleasure filling my veins.

"Oh, fuck,"

"Stella," he groans. "Stella."

My hands move to his neck, fingers looping around his neck, his face coming to mine to kiss me again as he slides out. I moan again, the sound consumed by his lips as he breathes heavily and bites my lip. His hair falls in a curtain around me, and it feels like right now, all that exists in this world is Riggins and me.

There is no history, no past. No addiction, no depression. No music industry, no disappointed mother and no forgotten wedding. It's just Riggins and I, clean slates. Two stars in the universe, lighting each other's worlds.

He slides in and out of me, and one of my hands brushes up and down his back, scratching and grasping, trying to pull him closer, get more. My legs hook around his hips, both opening me so he can thrust in deeper, so he can hit right where I need him.

"I missed this so fucking much," he says, moving and kissing my neck before removing to look into my eyes again. It's like he is afraid if he looks away, this will all disappear, and I get it. It feels like I'm in a dream. My heart's greatest desires and hopes balled up into one thing that has to be too good to be true.

For a minute, I have Riggins back.

My Riggs.

The realization cracks something up in me and the pleasure gowns and builds, starting in my belly and moving to my lower back, pressure and excitement as I reach for my orgasm.

"That's it, Stella. That's it, baby, Fuck you're beautiful. *So* tight, so wet, so hot," He groans in my neck as my head tips back before he moves again, pressing our chests closer, his weight in one forearm as his other hand moves behind my head, pushing so I'm forced to look at him again. He keeps sliding into me but doesn't increase the pace or the pressure, keeping me idling on the edge.

"Look at me, Stell," he says. I do, I am, I have been, but this time, I look at him through the haze of pleasure. Then I see him.

Cracked wide open, I see Riggins staring at me. He's open and honest, and I see it all. The guilt, the fear, the anxiety, the sadness.

But I also see the love.

It's like he's trying to show me why he really came home. It wasn't the marriage or the town or the music.

It was me. It was us. It was because just like me, he has only been half alive for nearly a decade and he's tired of living without me.

"You're back," I whisper like it finally makes sense to me.

"I am," he says, his voice a heated, strained whisper. He continues to fuck me. "I am, Stella, and I'm not going anywhere. You were made to be mine. You were made for me. And I'm back. Now fall. Fall, and do it saying my name," he says, then slams into me, grinding as he does.

"Riggins!" I shout, my eyes slamming shut, my head tipping back.

And I come.

I come hard, stars shooting behind my eyelids as my eyes slam shut. The room goes quiet; the only thing I can hear is the pounding of my heart. Pleasure cascades through me, my back arching, my hips tipping to try and get him in deeper still. And then I hear his deep groan of my name that reverberates through me, launching a smaller second orgasm through me as I feel him fill me, pulsing.

We stay like that for long, long minutes before he rolls off me, and we lay next to each other.

"God, I missed you," I say. A moment passes and I continue to stare at the ceiling, drained in the best possible way, pleasure still lightly simmering beneath my veins.

And then, the next beat, I'm being pulled into Riggins' chest, his booming laugh filling the room.

And it, too, feels right.

NOW

23

YOUR NEEDS, MY NEEDS

STELLA

Tangled in the sheets of his bed, both of us naked and sated, his thumb brushes the letter 'R' tattooed in a heart on the inside of my left wrist, the one we got together on our wedding night. I got his heart on my sleeve, and he got a shooting star.

Memories crash over me when my eyes finally catch on to the flower on Riggins' pec, a flower in shades of black and greys on his chest, over his heart.

My fingers trace the lines, my heartbeat picking up as I remember doodling a sunflower in the margins of my notebook, remember telling him I wanted to get a tattoo and him saying we would after tour.

I don't speak as my fingers trace the dark outlines, a wilted sunflower, its large head tipping down, the stalk straight and upright, drawn down his sternum.

He must know what I'm thinking about when he says, "I got it after I got sober."

I open my mouth to argue, but he shakes him, leaning in to press his lips to my forehead, shutting me up and forcing me to listen. My hand flattens on his chest, feeling his heart beneath my hand as I do, its steady rhythm against my palm.

Somehow, I know this tattoo is about me.

"Why... why this?" I ask, not really asking a million questions I want to ask. Why a sunflower? Why here? Why no color, why is it wilted, tipping down?

But he knows the way he always does.

"You were always my sun, Stella. The center of my universe." Again, I try to open my mouth, to argue, I think, to tell him that wasn't true, but he keeps talking. "Without you, I couldn't find the light. But I also knew I let you wilt. I watched you wilt all those months on tour, watching me spiral with no way to pull me out. I kept you in the dark until you couldn't stand straight anymore. I needed this reminder that I did that to you, that I once had the sun, and I lost it."

"Riggins," I whisper, but I don't know what else to say, if I should lie and make him feel better or if I should just let it go. I don't have to decide because he twines my fingers on his chest with his, pressing his lips to our joined hands, and looks at me, letting me see everything behind the veil that hides his emotions, his guilt and sadness and shame laying out in front of me,

"Sunflowers are amazing, you know," he says, almost conversationally. "Even when they wilt, their stalk is so strong, they stand straight, like they don't want anyone to know they're suffering." He shrugs like he's not about to blow my world apart. "Reminds me of you."

I take in a shaky breath, unsure of how to respond, how to proceed, or how to fucking breathe when he keeps blowing my world apart. I came here to serve him divorce papers once and for all, and instead, I ended up fucking him and laying in his bed late at night, my fingers running over the bold lines of a tattoo he got to remind himself of how much he hurt me.

What am I supposed to do with that?

"Give me a chance, Stell, I'll make sure you get all the sunshine you need to flourish. You'll never wilt again, not because of me."

"Riggins," I say, my voice low, not sure how to respond, how to move forward, but he shakes his head, presses his lips to my naked ring finger, then to my lips once more.

"We've got time, Stella. Don't tell me no now."`

His words are so earnest, so pure and kind, that I can't do anything other than put my head down on his chest.

I can ignore the outside world for another day. I've done it this long; what's one more night?

THEN

24

SOMEONE LIKE YOU

STELLA

"Hey, little star," a voice says, shifting my headphones to the side and lips pressing to my neck.

My body jolts in panic and eases in the same millisecond, the nerves receding as soon as I know it's Riggs' lips on my skin.

"You scared me," I say with a giggle, leaning and turning so I can press a kiss to his lips before he sits in the chair next to me.

"You were lost in your own little world. Writing?" I nod, my pen continuing to draw outlines on a flower I was drawing in the margins.

"Yeah, and doodling."

"Doodling?" I smile and nod.

"I want a tattoo," I say in a whisper.

"A tattoo?" he asks, his lips quirking up from a smile. "But you're afraid of needles." I shrug even though he's not wrong. I've been terrified of needles since I was a little kid.

"I think if I'm gonna be a rockstar's wife, I should have at least one." His smile goes wide, his dimple coming out before he buries his head in my neck, kissing me there and making me giggle, my fingers moving through his long hair.

We're on the first headlining tour and it's been a life changing and life affirming experience. Being out here, seeing the world, watching the guys live their dreams.. it's been amazing.

"We're not even engaged yet, though; pretty bold calling yourself a rockstar's wife," he says with a smile on my neck, and I roll my eyes, pushing him away.

"You're the worst," I say. "You know, don't say that too loud, or the tabloids are going to hear. The next big article in *US Stars* will be all about how you broke up with me."

The one downside of watching Riggins and Atlas Oaks blowing up quicker than anyone could expect, and people are invested in America's new favorite rock band, meaning we've all become quite acquainted with the tabloids and the lies and twisted truths.

"Ugh, don't remind me," he says. "You know I'm just making fun of you, though, right? Once life settles, when the time is right, we're gonna get married, Stell. This tour is just..." There's a pause and he sighs, exhausted to the bone. "A lot." I move closer to him, brushing my hand through his hair and looking at him.

"I know. After the tour, we can talk about it and plan and all of that fun stuff. But does that mean I can't talk to you about being yours, for real? I just..." I tip my head down, slightly embarrassed. "I'm just excited to be yours." Riggins' body moves with a deep sigh, and his hand moves, too, tipping my face up.

He looks tired, so damn tired, like he hasn't gotten a good night's sleep in months, which is strange because most nights, he doesn't wake up until noon, even the nights we go to bed at a semi-reasonable hour.

I love tour, being on the road with the band, seeing the fans and the country, but I'd be lying if I said I wasn't excited to go home, back to Ashford, to live a bit of normal for a bit.

"You've always been mine, Stella. Always."

"I know," I say in a soft whisper. "I just can't wait for it to be official."

I don't tell him that I'm hoping once we are legally official, that it will ease the feeling in my belly that aches like something is so off, like I'm just moments from waking from a dream. Like I'm waiting for the other foot to drop and ruin everything.

"Once tour is over, we'll set a date. If you want a big thing, we'll do it. You want something small, it's yours. I just can't give it my full attention until tour is over." He stands, walks toward the small fridge on the bus grabbing a beer, cracking it open, and taking a long drink from it.

I let out a short laugh, masking the worry because this has become a more and more common occurrence.

"Are you drinking at—" I look at my watch, squinting at the early time. "One thirty?" I ask with a laugh. His face goes blank, losing all of the sweetness from before.

"Yeah, why?"

"I just... it's early, is all." His smile goes boyish, but it doesn't paint me with warmth the way it normally does. It turns into concern instead. I picture afternoons after school sitting at Riggins' kitchen table, doing homework together and watching Mr. Greene come in, grabbing a beer from the fridge and drinking it in one long swallow.

"That's the rockstar life, baby," he says, and the way he says it makes me feel hot panic.

"It's just... I worry about you, you know? You drink more beer than water some days," I try to tiptoe over the issue. It's probably me being silly, probably just the knowledge of his father that has me uptight.

His brow furrows. "Okay, and?" he asks, something dark twisting in his words. "You're too young to drink legally, so you don't get it. It's not actually that big of a deal, Stella."

I bite my lip but nod all the same.

"Oh, yeah, of course. I just... I worry about you, you know?" This doesn't land the way I want it to, his face going frustrated, so I explain to the best of my ability. "You're on stage every night, jumping around, sweating. You need water and electrolytes and stuff." I smile my fake smile I used to give my mom's friend when I felt uncomfortable but couldn't show it for fear of feeling my mother's wrath. A smile I never thought I'd need around Riggins. "We gotta make sure you're taking care of yourself. So you can marry me, you know?" His face transforms again, and he smiles wide, then tips the can back and empties it before leaving the empty on the counter.

Then he's walking back to me, sitting and moving both of us so I'm sitting in his lap and we're both facing the small table in the tour bus and the scrap of paper with words, single lines of lyrics and little pictures doodled in the margins.

"So a tattoo?" he asks with a press of his lips to the skin beneath my ear.

I welcome the change in subject.

"Yeah. I want one. Beckett says they won't even hurt, and I can close my eyes the whole time."

"Beckett's full of shit."

"What do you know?" I ask, my thumb brushing his cheek. "You don't have a tattoo either." His smile widens and it fills me with warmth and joy.

"When tour is over, we'll get one. Together. What do you want?"

"Really?" I ask, excited.

"Whatever you want, little star." I turn in his lap, grab the notebook I'd been doodling in, and point to one of the flowers in the margins.

"I want this," I say, pointing to the letter R in a heart. "Your heart on my sleeve." I look over my shoulder and see he's smiling wide. He likes that idea.

"I'll get a star and an S. My little star with me all the time." I like that a ton.

"And a sunflower," I say, getting overconfident.

"A sunflower?"

"Yeah. They're my favorite."

"Alright, Stell. I'll find an artist back home; we'll get it together." Another kiss is pressed to my neck, and his hands start to travel over my belly and dipping down. "Now, the guys are out for at least another hour or two. What do you say we take advantage of the small amount of alone time we have?"

Now, that is an offer I can't deny.

And when I'm sweaty, smiling, and satisfied on the bed we share in the back of the bus, I completely forget about how he drank that beer in two swallows.

NOW

25

GROWING SIDEWAYS

STELLA

I wake up to banging.

A steady knock outside my house has my pulse pounding until I hear intermittent dog tags jingling.

Gracie.

Gracie is outside, which means Riggins is probably outside, too.

Sitting up, I take note of my body, the achy exhaustion in my limbs, and the quiet, foggy blanket covering my mind.

I left early in the morning before Riggins woke, driving home in silence, overthinking every moment that happened the previous night. Him singing my song, going to his place in a rage, the papers. The kiss. Everything that happened after the kiss.

The contentment I felt falling asleep in his arms.

I was surprised when I was able to fall back asleep when I got home, but I told myself the day prior had taken an emotional toll, draining me. But now I know to my bones that's probably not it. I feel the rising tide of another episode coming on, the waters lapping up to my knees now, holding me down.

With a sigh, I roll out of bed and use the bathroom before sliding on a pair of sandals and moving toward the front door, where the banging is the loudest. I'm still in Riggins' tee and a pair of my own shorts as I tiredly lean on the door frame, watching as he bangs a hammer into loose nails on the porch.

"What's going on?" I ask.

His head lifts, followed by his body, and Gracie runs to me, dancing in front of where I stand until I pet her. "Funny, that's what I said this morning when I woke up to an empty bed. No note, no text, nothing. Just an empty bed, your car out of my drive."

I squint at him, still tired and confused, trying to understand. "Are you... are you *mad* at me?" I ask, bewildered.

"Considering everything that happened yesterday, I'm trying my fuckin' hardest not to be, Stella, but I'm having a hard time doing so." My head snaps back, and I stare at him.

"You're not allowed to be mad at me," I say, and Riggins stands to his full height, staring at me with false shock.

"I'm not? My wife spends the night in my bed, I don't have nightmares for the first time in seven years, and then I wake up, and she's gone?" For a moment, I stand there, stunned because *I don't have nightmares for the first time in seven years* is running through my mind but then I snap out of it.

I can't have him helping me slide into the easy we used to be before everything imploded. I mean, fuck, he's only been in my life for a couple of weeks, and my life is already going back to the mess it was when he was in it.

"I'm not your wife, Riggins. Stop saying that." I step out onto the porch.

"You're not?" he asks, stepping closer and crossing his arms on his chest, the hammer still in his hands. "The papers we signed in Vegas state differently." I groan and sigh, looking at the railing of my porch as if it will give me the energy and strength to deal with him.

It does not, in fact, give me anything.

"Then we'll get a divorce! Sign the papers, and we can end this shit. It was a dumb decision we made as kids! This is *crazy*, Riggins." The words twist something I refuse to acknowledge in my gut, while the practical, rational side knows it's what makes the most sense. It's been the same battle for seven years: cut the last tie holding us together or hold on tight to the last fraying thread of hope.

A loud clatter occurs, heavy metal on wood, as the hammer falls to the steps before he takes a few steps toward me, pinning me against the side of my house.

"You bring up those stupid papers again; I'll do what I always used to do when you would say something that pissed me off."

I feel my brow come together in confusion. "What—"

"Fuck you until you see things my way." My mouth drops open, his just inches from my face, and even though there are a million things I *should* be worrying about at this moment, all I can think about is the fact that I probably have morning breath.

"Excuse me?" I ask, my voice a stuttered whisper.

"You let your walls down for me last night. Let me in. You came barging in, ready to rip me apart. But instead, what happened was out of your careful little calculations." My breath stops.

"What?" I ask again, my words barely audible now, but he hears it all the same.

"You think I don't realize your new life is entirely weighing pros and cons and deciding a million outcomes before you even try anything? No impulse. No excitement. Nothing." He looks.... *disappointed* as he speaks like he can't believe this is the life I'm leading.

"I don't—" I try to explain because he might not be wrong, but that doesn't mean he has to be *right*.

"At my place, though, you didn't take a moment to calculate. You went with your gut, and fuck, baby, I'm glad you did." His head dips down then, shocking my system as his lips touch the skin beneath my ear.

"Riggins," his breath is spreading warmth through me, his beard that needs a shave grazing against my skin. "Riggins, we can't."

"We can," is all he says, his lips grazing skin.

"We aren't that anymore."

"We could be."

I shake my head, but even I know it's half-hearted. I'm barely even fighting anymore.

"We can't. We don't work; we proved that years ago," I whisper, but I don't push him away, and I don't give any other indication I'd want him to back away from me.

"You're punishing me, pushing me away because of who I used to be, but I don't even know that man anymore, Stella. How is that fair, paying penance for a person I'm not?" he whispers, hitting a sore spot, a place I've contemplated more than a few times since he's been back.

"I just need time, Riggins."

"Time," he whispers against my skin.

"Yes. I need time." He nods, something I feel rather than see.

"If you can promise you're not using it as an excuse, a chance to rebuild that wall I broke down yesterday, then yeah, I can give you time. I can give you all the time you need."

Relief washes through me and I answer before I can second guess it, answering with my heart rather than my head.

"I promise." His face goes liquid with pleasure, and the waters lower a bit, his sun warming my bones.

"Okay, Stell. Then I'll give you time," he whispers, then his head dips once more, pressing his lips to mine before backing away. "Gracie girl, come on," he says, and I watch as Gracie follows him, trotting to his truck. Then, I watch him drive away.

On Thursday, Reed is leaning on his elbows against the table in the diner, loudly and exuberantly telling me a story of a time when they locked Wes outside of the bus with no clothes on.

"God, you should have seen it, Stella. He was frantic," he says. I look over at Riggins, who is watching me. A small smile is on his lips, as he does. This is what it's always like when he comes here; his eyes are always on me like he's afraid to miss something.

It's two days after my failed attempt at serving Riggins with divorce papers, and I'm learning his definition of *space* is a bit different from mine. He is still coming in at noon every day I'm at the diner, sitting in his booth and watching me until I'm done for the day. Then he follows me home and presses a kiss to my lips before he leaves and goes on with his day, doing I don't know what.

It's... easy.

It's everything we used to be.

But it's unnerving. I've come to learn that good things, sweet things, don't last for me.

And it seems like today is the day the other shoe is going to drop.

"No." I hear the words ring out in the diner, my mother's firm, angry voice entering my psyche.

My head swivels in the direction of the door to see my mother standing at Amelia's station, her jaw tight, her eyes filled with venom.

And the venom is directed right at Riggins.

Without my permission, my body moves toward the front of the entrance, ready to diffuse this situation.

"You are not welcome here," she says, not paying me any mind.

"Mother," I say, my voice low and trying to avoid a bigger drama than I already see rolling out. We have a handful of customers scattered at tables throughout the diner, but in a small town like this, juicy drama travels fast.

Her head turns to me quickly, and I don't see the mother I know, the one who is cordial, if a bit cold. Instead, it is ice and brutal anger. A glance of someone who doesn't like you in the least and barely tolerates your presence. "I'll get to you next," she says, stunning me.

"I told you I didn't want him to be here. Riggins Greene, leave, or I'm calling the cops. I have the right to refuse service." Her lips tip up in an ugly smile I've never seen before. "You were pretty well acquainted with the back of a cop car last time you were in town, weren't you? And if I recall, Stella wasn't too impressed by that either." My brows furrow in confusion with her words and the way a hint of pain scrapes along Riggs' face with the words, but Reed steps in before I can let it register.

"Hey, Mrs. Hart, maybe—" Reed tries to say.

"I don't want to hear from you, Reed. You're no better than that one. You leave my establishment before I call the authorities."

It's getting too out of hand, her words getting angry for no reason, and I wonder if she's fully sober, remembering the days when she would come home from luncheons with her friends just a bit too tipsy —that's always when she would be her most cruel. And with all the eyes in the diner on us now, I need to shut it down before it gets much, much worse.

"Mom, come on, let's—" I don't know what I'm going to say. Maybe *let's talk about this out of the eager eyes of the entire town* or *let's not do this here*, but I don't get the chance to determine which version I'm going to argue because she looks at me, and snaps.

"I told you to get that divorce, or I was done with you, Stella. Did you? He's bad news, just like that father of his. Even Jeanette enabled their shitty behavior."

Now, I can put up with a lot of shit. I can put up with my mom talking shit to me, with my never being enough for her. I can even put up with her talking shit about Riggins because, at some point, I reinforced those thoughts she had about him. I cried in her house when he broke me, and she listened.

But Jeanette?

Absolutely not.

Jeanette Greene was the woman who took me in for six hours when I tried to run away from home after failing another one of my mother's invisible, unwinnable tests when I was ten. The one who dried my tears and told me my mom was just confused. That I was beautiful and smart and *enough*, and when I was 12, and she died, a part of me died with her.

She was a good person, unlike the woman who actually raised me.

"Absolutely not," I say, speaking the words out loud, my back straightening, my jaw tightening. The armor I've built around me to be her perfect child despite everything shatters, and I revert back to a version of me I hid long, long ago.

"Excuse me?" My mother says, seething.

"I said, absolutely not. You do not talk about Jeanette like that. One, she isn't here to defend herself. You yourself taught me not to talk ill of the dead, but your obsession with talking shit about Mr. And Mrs. Greene is absolutely criminal. And two, that woman was more of a mother to me than you ever were. She was kind and comforting and never—"

I don't get to finish my sentence because searing pain strikes my cheek, my face turning as my mother slaps me across my face.

"How fucking dare you," my mother says with pure fucking venom, with a voice I've never heard before. "How dare you? I am your mother. I raised you."

"I..." I start stuttering. My cheek is throbbing, and I think, at this point, I'm in pure shock, unsure of what to do.

I'm twenty-seven, and my mother just slapped me in the entryway of my workplace.

"Get out. Get your shit, and get out of here. You're fired. And this time, when he breaks you again, I hope he does it well and good, makes sure you don't come back from that shit. I'm done with you, Stella. So is your father, and so is Everest."

The words rocket around my brain, and I think people talk in the restaurant, but they could be whispering or screaming, and I wouldn't know the difference. I can't focus on anything, absolutely nothing.

"Come on, Stella," a low voice says, a comforting one, a voice my body melts for, firm hands wrapping around my bicep, another tucking around my waist, pulling me until my face is pulled from looking at the pure rage that is my mother. "Come on, sweetheart.

Amelia, right?" Another voice I can't place says. My ears are ringing now.

"Can you grab Stella's stuff? Bring it out?" I think someone agrees but I can't function, my feet moving without my knowledge as I'm guided toward the exit, the bells tinkling overhead.

Suddenly, my mind registers somehow, somewhere, that might be the last time I hear that noise, those bells.

Fresh air hits my face and my lungs, the smell of impending rain hitting my nose, and suddenly, it's like the world fast forwards, and I'm rushed back into my body.

Riggins is holding me, my body pressed to his as we stand on the sidewalk outside of the Ashford Diner.

"She hit me," I whisper.

"Yeah, baby. She did," he whispers into my hair.

"My mother slapped me."

"Yeah, Stell."

"She hit me in public. She hit me." I'm starting to lose it. I can feel it. The emotion is leaking into my pores, the panic and disappointment and anger and sadness all mixing like chemicals in a nuclear reactor that is my chest, needing an outlet.

"She hit me, Riggs." And then I break.

The tears come, and somehow, the way he always did, he knows it's coming before I do. Somehow, he remembers how much I hate having people see me cry and is giving me that bit of decency, that bit of humanity. He turns me into his body, using one arm to wrap my waist and hold me up, the other to hold my head down and I break, as I cry into his shirt.

"Here, Riggins," Amelia's voice says. Riggins moves, jostling me a bit but not too much before grabbing what must be my bag. "I'm sorry, but she said if you guys don't leave, she's going to, uh," she hesitates as I take a deep breath to force my tears to slow, my sobs turn into gasping breaths into Riggins' shirt. "Call the police."

That snaps me out of it, and I step back, looking at Amelia, then

Riggins, then at the open door, my mother standing in it, her arms crossed on her chest.

And despite the fact that I know my face is swollen both from her hitting me and my tears, I move to stand in the doorway.

"You're going to call the cops? I dare you. I dare you." A maniacal laugh leaves my lips. "You do, I'm happy to tell them how you assaulted me, then fired me. Bet that would look great at your Sunday morning brunch, explaining the assault charges to your little friends." Her face goes red.

"How fucking dare—" she starts, but I cut her off, feeling free for the first time in my life. Free of her expectations, of my unexplainable need to earn her approval.

I'm done.

"No, how dare *you*. How dare you treat me, your own daughter, like I'm shit on your shoes?

"That's enough, little star," Riggins says in my ear, his chest somehow plastered against my back, rumbling the low words right into my body.

"Enough? Enough? A lifetime of taking her shit, nothing will ever be enough, Riggins."

"I know, baby. I know. Come on. Don't let her win, yeah?"

Somewhere in the far reaches of my mind, I remember that. I remember him whispering that to me as I cried on a street corner, not unlike how I am now when I cried because she kicked me out at nineteen.

He was right then, too.

Riggins Greene might not be perfect, and he might be fucked in a million and seven ways, but he was right about that.

My standing here, arguing with her, is what she wants. It somehow confirms I am what she thinks I am, and not in a good way.

"You're right, she's not worth it," I whisper, then turn away from my mother.

NOW

26

STICK SEASON

STELLA

Though my hands shake and my stomach feels like it might lose the little I've eaten today, I walk to the parking lot behind the diner with my back straight, my chin up. I had a lapse in front of the store, but I refuse to let anyone else see me like that, to see her break me.

Not until I'm home alone and can lose it by myself, where I can process everything that's somehow happened. My eyes scan the lot, finding my car easily, and I move toward it, but Riggs' hand on my elbow tugs me, pulling me away from my car.

"Come on, Stell, this way,"

"What? My car's right there."

"I know, but I'm driving you home." I sigh and stop walking, turning to face him.

"I'm fine, Riggins, really. This was a long time coming, but not a surprise." I pause, then tip my head. "The slap was a surprise, but maybe it shouldn't have been. I'm fine."

"You're shaking like a leaf, Stella."

"I'm fine." I insist.

"Humor me," he says, crossing his arms on his chest, mimicking me.

"Why do you care so much? Why are you doing this, Riggins? Really. You keep swooping in and saving me, but for what? Why?"

"Because you're mine. You're my wife."

I sigh, the sound deep in my chest. "Honey, I appreciate it, really, I do, but I'm fine. Seriously." He stops moving altogether, and I look at him. "What?"

"Honey," he says, staring at me with awe and wonder. "You called me honey." I stare at him, taking in his face, the new lines and creases in his face and trying to match them with the mental image my brain conjures when I think of him, the sixteen, eighteen, twenty-one year old version my mind has committed to memory.

I remember all of the times I called him honey.

I also remember all the times he held me while I cried, all the times he hid me from prying eyes when I did, always embarrassed to do it in front of people. I remember all the times he protected me and saved me and decided arguing wasn't worth the effort.

I'll cave.

I always do when it comes to Riggins.

"Fine," I whisper. "You can drive me home."

Riggins opens the passenger side door, and he watches me climb in before he reaches across me, pulling the seatbelt and buckling me like a small child.

"I can buckle myself, you know."

"Humor me," he says again, then slams the door.

As he walks around the front, a few fat raindrops fall onto his windshield.

"It's starting to rain," he grumbles as he gets into the car, pushing his damp hair back, starting the car, and backing out. "Fucking hate the rain," he says a minute later to himself.

When we turn off on Main Street, I finally speak. "What's wrong with rain?" I watch him make a left at the red light on Main and Alderbridge, driving out of downtown toward my house. The scenery quickly turns from businesses to green fields bordered by trees.

"I hate the rain," he repeats.

"What? Why? Since when?"

I shouldn't ask.

I know that.

But there's still a part of me that feels like I know him, and this is strange. So off from the version I used to know, the version that could sit in the rain for hours if it wasn't cold, letting it wash the day and shit mood from him.

"Reminds me of something I lost." My chest feels tight, the panic brewing and changing from curiosity to pain, growing painful spikes.

"Something you lost?" I ask stupidly, the words barely rasping out through an aching throat.

"I lost everything, Stella. You became my whole world on a rainy day in Ashford, and on a rainy day in Vegas, I lost everything. That night in Vegas hasn't come back, at least not all of it, but some parts did. It kills me every time, knowing I had you, that you gave me everything, and I threw it away. I threw you away."

His head turns to me, and I see it there.

The pain.

The loss.

It's not just some line, it's real.

"I tried everything to try and move on. I figured you made it clear you were done with me, so it wasn't fair to keep reminding you of how I hurt you. But god, rainy days.... It's like a darkness comes over me. That half of me that used to be filled with your sun is cold and dark, and I'm reminded again of how much I lost. I lost you, Stell. I lost you, and it's all my fault, and I can't go back and change it, and that fucking kills me," he says, his eyes on the road as we continue to drive.

I can't handle it.

I can't handle it.

I can't breathe in this car with him confessing everything I once wanted to hear.

I thought we could be friends, but I was wrong. I can't be just friends with Riggins, and I'm too scared to give him more, which means I can't be anything to him. That realization tears through me, ripping at the places I thought had healed.

I can deal with the cocky version of him, showing up at my place with a smile and wanting to talk like nothing happened.

I can deal with the version who shows up at my work every day, stubborn as ever, waiting for me to give in.

I can deal with the version that wants to rescue me, that wants to take care of me.

I *can't* deal with this version full of sorrow and regret and loss. It hurts too much. There were days and weeks and months and years when that's all I wanted. I wanted him to show up at my house with that look and beg me to listen to him, to apologize or just be there, to care.

He never did.

And now, all these years later, he's looking at me like that.

"Pull over," I say through a croak.

"What?"

"Pull over." My voice is slightly less croaky and more firm, and even I can hear the panic in it as I reach for the door handle. I don't know if I'd jump out of the car but the way I'm feeling, the way I feel like the walls are closing in on me, I wouldn't doubt it.

"Stella, what?"

"Pull the fuck over!" I shout. Riggins does as I ask, pulling over abruptly. Before the tires even stop fully, I'm flinging the door open, ignoring his yells as I run.

I run into the empty field, hoping the exertion and the movement of my muscles will get this feeling out of my chest, but it doesn't. It just keeps building and building and building until I slowly realize it's not just rain running down my face but hot, warm tears.

When I collapse on the grass, the sobs start.

That day in Las Vegas, a rainy day with nothing to do and filling that time by saying vows at a little chapel.

I gasp for air as memories hit.

My mother slapping me, the look of hatred on her face.

I can't get a full chest of air into my lungs.

The first time Riggins kissed me in the clearing, rain falling around us.

They all slam into me, painful and burned, not stopping even when I fight to keep them back. I sob and sob, heartbreaking, gut-wracking sobs that you might be able to hear for miles, but all I hear is the rain.

The rain and Riggs.

Riggs pulls me into him as he sits in the grass next to me, rain soaking him to the bone as well. His hair clumps in stringy, wet strands around his face, but he looks so fucking handsome all the same. Water drips off him, off his long eyelashes I used to stare at while he was sleeping, and I wonder if we had a baby boy, would he have long eyelashes like his, too? It twists in me, the painful reminder, and I need space; I can't fucking breathe when he holds me.

Or maybe it's the opposite; maybe I can only breathe when he holds me. Maybe it's that I got so used to not breathing when he's not holding me that when I finally got the oxygen, it feels unbearable like blood flowing back to a body part that lost circulation, pins and needles in its wake.

"Let me go," I beg

"No."

"Please, Riggins. I'm begging you. Let me go." I fight his hold, but he holds tight, containing me.

"I won't, little star, I can't let you go."

"Please, I need you to just leave me. Go back to your life, go live your life, live your dream." I pound on his chest, not caring that I might hurt him, just desperate for him to let me go.

Life was so much easier a few weeks ago when I was numb. He came back and stirred it all up, wracking the pain up.

"I can't," he says, low and pained and I pull back to look at him and it could be the rain, but his eyes are glossy as well.

"What? What are you talking about?"

His head shakes, a sad, slow movement. "Don't you get it? I can't live my dream, Stella. I haven't dreamed in seven years. My dreams are nothing without you little star." I smack his chest, angry at him in so many ways."

"Don't say that."

"It's the truth, and you know it. And you can't live yours, either, not without me. I see it in your face. You're a fucking shell of who you used to be. Where is she, Stell? Where is my star?"

"Long gone. Burnt out."

"No. She's hiding. I know she's under there because every once in a while, she comes out. She smiles at me, and my life feels like it has fucking light for the first time in a decade. Like my sun is back." I open my mouth to argue, but to say what exactly, I don't know. "I love you, Stella. I never stopped—Did you?" he asks.

"No," I whisper in the field for no one else to hear but me and Riggs.

Except then Riggins opens his mouth to say something, to say more that will shift my understanding of our relationship and of my world, and I decide I can't take it. I can't. I think if he says more, I'll lose it, and I might never find it again.

Instead, I do the only thing I can think of to prevent that from happening. I put my hands on either side of his face and pull him to me.

Then I press my lips to his.

NOW

27
PLEASE

RIGGINS

"Where are you bringing me?" she whispers into the quiet of the cab of my truck, shivering despite the heat cranked high. We're both absolutely drenched, and the rain continues to fall.

Normally, it would just be yet another reminder of her, of what we once had, but right now, my jaw burns from where her cold hand pressed on my skin, my lips on fire from where hers touched mine.

It wasn't the first time we've kissed since I've been back, but I know, down to my core, it was different. Something new, something changed. Like she came to a realization, whether she wanted to or not.

A part of us had healed.

And finally finally, she admitted she still loves me.

As I carried her limp, exhausted body back to the truck, I had to fight the full-face grin eating at me. It's not exactly appropriate to smile while you're carrying your wife, who just had a full-out mental breakdown in the middle of an empty field.

"My dad's place."

"Riggins, no—" she starts, hesitation that sends disappointment ripping through me even if it's deserved, even if it's valid.

"Not for anything, just need to make sure you're okay. After everything that just happened..." I let my words trail off and I know she's looking at me, but I don't look to her as I turn away from the way to her house, where we were headed, and toward my childhood home.

"That's really not necessary—" she starts again, but I move one hand off the wheel toward her, reaching for her hands and grabbing it without even looking and squeezing once. I lace her small fingers with mine without looking at her, tug her hand closer, and press my lips to her fingers.

"Please. After everything that happened with your mother, with us out there in the rain, I don't want you to be alone." I let a beat pass, making room for her to argue, but she doesn't, so I add, "Plus if your mom tries to come to talk to you, we both know she won't come to my house." Her hand squeezes mine a bit, a half-hearted effort like the move was too hard for her, fully drained of energy and the will to be her.

"Yeah," she says, and I take that as acceptance, and we drive in silence.

When we get there, she follows me in, taking in the house we spent so much of our childhood in, watching movies and playing games, me, Stella, and her sister Evie, on the days that Mrs. Hart wouldn't let us play at their house.

"Not much has changed," I say, peeling off the shirt that's still near soaking, keeping my back to her as I grab a new shirt and slide it on before grabbing a pair of old sweats and a tee from the bottom drawer. "But it works in our favor. These are yours." I toss the sweats to her. She lifts up the old, baggy grey sweat pants, Ashford High emblazoned down one leg, and for the first time all day, maybe longer, a smile cracks her lips.

"God, you still have these? I always wondered where they went."

"I think you left them in my truck once, and, well, they're yours again." She puts them against her body, hips that have filled out in the best fucking way, but it's clear they'll still fit. I toss the tee her way.

"Bathroom is... well, you know where it is. Bring me your clothes, and I can pop them in the dryer." She doesn't speak; she just looks at me, nods, and then walks away.

I change my pants to a pair of loose sweats, tossing my wet clothes into a pile and frantically trying to neaten up the bedroom.

It doesn't take long for her to walk back toward me, a lump of wet clothes in her hands. Her hair is out of the ponytail she always wears, just barely passing her shoulders in wet strands that were clearly finger-brushed. My tee is way too big on her small frame, but I can still see the swells of her breasts and force my eyes not to linger on the way her nipples peak beneath the dark fabric, clearly not wearing her wet bra.

Then I take in the full image, Stell, my Stella, wet hair, wearing sweats and barefoot in my home. It's familiar and new all the same, and it makes my heart ache.

I clear my throat, run my hand through my own wet hair, and smile.

"Pizza for dinner and a movie marathon?"

And then I get the second smile from her, letting my mind categorize and capture it before she nods.

Stella

It's hours after pizza and too much time watching TV in his bedroom, long after he convinced me to sit in the bed next to him instead of sitting on the floor, long after I let myself pretend this was normal, that we were sixteen and eighteen and there wasn't an ocean of trauma between us if only for a night.

Long after, my eyes started to blink longer, long after he insisted I lay down, resting my head on his chest, his arm wrapped around me protectively.

Long after, I quietly admitted, if only to myself, that I missed this, the steady rhythm of his heart under my ear, the way we could spend hours doing absolutely nothing so long as we were together.

I always had the feeling of home when I was with him.

It was always like this: even if my own family was a disaster, even when I never felt like I belonged there, I always belonged here. There were days when things felt so dark, when I felt those waters lapping at my ankles, ready to pull me down, but his arm could save me, keep my head above water.

In fact, I only fell under when I left him for good.

"What did she mean, saying you're fucked in the head?" he asks, his voice low as if he could hear my thoughts. My gut churns with nerves. I was hoping he missed that jab, but even now, even after all these years, he never misses a thing.

I contemplate for a long time how to answer, if I should answer at all, but what does it even matter? What's the worst that's going to happen? He's going to run away, think I'm crazy, and decide I'm more work than I'm worth?

"I have these bouts of depression every once in a while. The first time it happened, I couldn't leave my bed for two weeks before my mother forced me to go to the doctor. Probably the one kindness she's done to me. They helped me. Figure out what was going on, how to handle it, and what kind of meds would work best for me. It doesn't happen too often now that we've got me on the right meds, but it still happens sometimes. She thinks it's just... me being dramatic mostly. But when she wants to, she uses it as a weapon, another reason I'm fucked up in her mind, not worthy of her or her attention." His hand never stops grazing up and down my back, caressing me, and I focus on it in order to stay out of my head, stay out of the thoughts that are swirling and sending me spiraling.

Time passes, and his hand keeps brushing up and down, a silent metronome as my mind starts to spiral into thoughts of Riggins thinking I'm insane or a lost cause or too much work, his silence clearly confirmation of that and I should just leave, but I don't think Reed has brought my car yet and I—

"Is it because of me?" he asks, breaking into my spiral of thoughts and letting me into his, where his mind is.

He thinks it's his fault, and for some reason, I want to ease that worry. I'm a mess, but it's not his fault.

"I don't think so," I say, and his body I didn't realize had tensed eases, like four words took a weight off of him. "I think... I think it was always there, that darkness. You just... for a time, your light made it hide in the shadows." He stays silent, letting that sink in and I'm mostly asleep when he finally speaks again, so asleep, I'm still not sure if it was a dream or not.

"I'm sorry I took your sun away, little star. I'll never make that mistake again."

I wake up in the middle of the night and feel rested despite the room being dark. It's the kind of rest that goes bone deep into your soul, the kind you want to write down because you're not sure you've ever slept that well and know you'll definitely not do it again anytime soon.

And before I'm even fully awake, I know it's because of the warm chest against my back, the heavy arm on my waist.

Riggins always liked to hold me. Even when he was asleep, his body craved touching mine, like a touchstone. I loved it because it always felt like he was holding me together, keeping all of my broken pieces together while I slept, keeping me safe.

Sometimes I wonder if that's why the episodes come now, I wonder if part of it is because I don't have someone at night, holding me together, making sure I don't shatter.

That thought has my eyes opening. Gently, I extricate myself from under him, rolling a bit and putting a pillow under his arm the way he used to sleep when I wasn't around.

When he tugs it in close, shifts a few times like his body knows something is different, I pause, but when he relaxes with a sigh, I do too.

I note Gracie is asleep on the dog bed in the living room when I walk out that way, and I rub my hand over her head. Her head and eyes are alert, but her body is unmoving.

"Go to bed, girl," I whisper, and I shouldn't be surprised when she licks my palm and then puts her head down, curling in on herself. She was always a smart dog, even as a puppy.

My shoes are by the door and I quickly and silently slide them on, grimacing at the fact they still feel wet. I grab my bag and as quietly as I can, head out the door where Reed brought my car at some point last night.

The exhaustion hits when I'm two traffic lights from my house, creeping into my veins like my well-rested state is tethered to Riggins.

One traffic light from home, I let out a loud yawn, masking the sob that tried to break from my chest.

I refuse to cry.

I can't—I've done it too much this week as it is.

NOW

There's no warmth next to me when I wake up, and the irritation brews in my veins, despite the fact that I know I need to give her time. As I pad out to the kitchen, there's a scrap of paper, half ripped like it was pulled from a notebook in a rush, words scribbled not on the lines, but wherever they fit.

Stella.

I stare at it, at the words, realizing her handwriting has barely changed in all these years; it's still the same loops and curves and lines as all those years ago when I used to watch her pen make on any scrap of paper she could find.

It's a comfort, in a way, to find the small things that haven't changed.

R—

Back at my place, woke up early and need my meds.

She signed it with a star, the way she always used to. The star tattoo on my wrist, the one I woke up with in a Vegas hotel, burns with the knowledge it's her star on my wrist. That my heart is on her.

Well, at least she left a note, I tell myself, despite the disappointment from waking without her only slightly eased.

I also have to keep reminding myself that this is absolutely not a sprint. It's a marathon, and I have to pace myself if I want to make it to the end with her.

Putting the paper back on the counter, I head to the bathroom to brush my teeth and get ready for the day.

The bumpy road of her winding drive reminds me we should figure out a better solution before the winter because even with a plow, a dirt road is a bitch with freezing and melting snow.

When I come into view and see her on her porch, I can feel more than see her eyes tracking me as I pull up. She's sitting on that front porch swing, a notepad in her lap that she swiftly shoves under the cushion like she doesn't want me to know what she's been doing. She doesn't walk my way as I get closer, nor as I put the truck into park and step out or when I walk up the three steps I repaired for her. Instead, she stares, preparing, taking a sip from a big lavender-colored mug and gently placing it on the railing of the porch as I move until I'm right in front of her.

"What are you doing here, Riggins?" she asks and it doesn't really bug me anymore, her calling me Riggins instead of Riggs. Partially because I still get *Riggs* when it matters, but also because it reveals her mood, her confusion and a hint of irritation, so different from the version I remember of her.

Old Stella would walk on eggshells, always afraid to show me too much of her burning star, worried it wouldn't be received well.

This version doesn't care at all, letting any thoughts she has fly, turning whatever eggshell between her and me into dust.

I smile and then extend a hand to her, marveling when she takes it without arguing.

We're finally getting somewhere.

I tug, pulling her up to me until her chest is against mine, one of my hands moving behind her neck and sliding up into her hair, the other wrapping around her waist. Without prodding, her head tips up, one arm moving to loop around my neck, the other resting on my chest, over my tattoo.

I press my lips to hers, our lips melting together the way they always did long ago, sliding and opening, an invitation on her part, an instance on mine as I slide my tongue into her mouth, tangling and tasting her sweet coffee.

I stop there, knowing I could kiss her forever, spend the next thirty years making up for lost time and then some. Nipping her lip, I break the kiss and rest my forehead against hers.

She's panting from that small press of lips, and I can't help but smile.

"If you're not going to stay the night and kiss me in the morning, I have to come and get one," I whisper and watch her brows furrow in confusion.

"You're not mad?" I can feel my lips move, smiling wide.

Her being worried I'd be mad if she left is a good sign for my cause of winning her back, once and for all. A great sign, even. I can't help it but move again, resting my lips to hers once more before answering.

"You left a note."

"I know, but—"

"You need time, Stella, I'll give it to you," I say. "I'll even give you space, but don't you mistake it for me stepping back or giving up. I'll let you steer this ship, steer the pace, but I'm here, Stella. We're here. I'm not letting you leave again. I'll follow you around the world, but I'm not letting you go." Her face goes soft, and I realize this is the time; this is when I need to tell her everything.

Because I'm starting to remember bits and pieces of that day, and I never forgot the way I felt about her.

"I love you, Stella. A lot has changed, but that hasn't," I say, my pulse pounding, but I can feel hers doing the same, synching with my heart inside my chest. I smile and show my hand. "Until I'm compost, food for the worms, little star."

I repeat the words I whispered in a Vegas hotel room before we got married seven years ago. Her eyes go wide, realizing what I just said. A moment passes before she closes her eyes, taking a deep breath.

"I need space. I need space, and I need time. A lot just happened. I need to... I need to mourn the shit with my mom. I need space. I promise this isn't some ploy to get away from you. It's not saying no, just that I need space." She swallows, taking a deep, steadying breath. "When I've processed everything, we can talk. We'll talk about... us. What to do next."

I lean back, taking her in, reading her face. Something is off, something I can't quite decode, and I can't tell if it's because she's not telling the truth, her mask in place, or if it's because there's something more, a new tell I haven't learned yet. But I also know pushing her won't help at all. I take in a deep breath and let it out. "How long?" I ask finally.

"What?" Her brows furrow in surprise.

"I'll give you space, but how long?"

"Riggins—"

"If you don't give me a date, I'm coming to your house every day and checking on you." I don't mind giving her space, but I also know Stella better than I know myself. I need a date, or she'll keep pushing me away.

"A week," she says finally, an exhausted sigh leaving her lips.

"A week?"

"Yes. Give me a week to process." I stand there, considering her offer and taking her in. Suddenly, I see it. She's exhausted. All of this:

me and her, dredging up the past, her mother—it's a lot. Too much, I think.

"You're tired," I whisper, a hand reaching out, cupping her soft cheek, my thumb scraping over the skin there.

"I am," she whispers.

"Okay, little star. Sleep. Take care of yourself for me. One week, I'm coming back. We're going to our spot. Showing Gracie where we fell in love." She rolls her lips between her teeth, and her eyes water. I'm pushing too hard. I know it. But I can't seem to stop myself when I feel so fucking close.

"Riggins," she says, and it sounds like a pained plea.

"A week, little star. I love you," I whisper against her lips, leaning in and pressing hers to mine in a barely there touch. "Go inside, go back to sleep."

Then I move down the stairs, to my truck and head back to my place, once more trying to force myself to try and remember that rainy day in Las Vegas.

It's been two days of Stella brushing off my texts and calls. I'm over it. I gave her seven days before I reached out, and she asked me for more time.

I agreed. I thought she needed it after everything that happened with her mother, after the kiss in the field, after she slept in my bed. This is a lot of shit I'm throwing at her, a lot of confusing thoughts and feelings, and we're raking up so much history that, for her, apparently, had settled beneath the silt of her new life.

She needed time to come to terms with the fact that I'm here, that I'm here *for her*, and I'm here to be hers again.

But the next time I text her, she tells me some new bullshit excuse for why I can't see her, and I'm over it.

"I'm going over there," I tell Wes, grabbing my keys.

"You really think that's a good idea, man?"

"No fucking clue, but it's what my gut is telling me to do, so I am."

"Riggins..." he says, his eyes looking concerned, but I know the look in mine is determined.

"Once, long ago, I ignored that feeling in my gut, ignored how it would tell me something wasn't right, that Stella needed me, needed something. It told me something wasn't right, but I was so stubborn and so fucked up I ignored it. I've lived in misery for seven years because of it." My friend looks at me, sighs, and shakes his head.

"Alright, man. Just don't make us lose her again, yeah? She's your wife, but she's all of ours. You know that."

I do, and I fucking love that she has that, even if she doesn't realize it. Stella might have lost her mother, but she has a whole family waiting to welcome her back home as soon as she's ready.

"Got it, man.

I walk up her steps, testing the floorboard I nailed down last time I was here, and find myself pleased that it doesn't move nor make any noise. But I also noticed a spot where the siding is loose and needs to be replaced, and the gutters probably need to be cleaned and inspected.

The place is a shithole, if I'm being honest, but it's so totally Stella.

She always loved this house. When we were kids, we'd drive around Ashford on one of the few days she could get away during the day, just wandering and looking at houses, planning our future together. I may have hated this town and the way everyone in it knew my life history, the way they'd look at me with clear pity in their eyes, but she loved it here regardless and always wanted to settle down in our hometown.

She always made me drive down this dead-end road on the outskirts of town, passing it at least three times before we were allowed to move on.

That's the one, she would whisper, eyes wide and filled with hope and desire. "That's the one I want."

"It looks like a heap, Stell," I'd say, smiling because I knew what her response would be.

"We'll fix it together. It'll be a little project for us."

And it seems like at the end of it all, she did just that. She got her house, I'm assuming, with royalties from Atlas Oaks or maybe from her ghostwriting since her mother definitely doesn't pay enough for her to buy this, and she fixed it up.

Mostly.

Kind of.

Shaking my head to knock myself out of the past and the regrets I feel like I swim through every day, I reach for the doorbell and press it before pushing my hands into my pockets, waiting for her.

Nothing.

I wait a full minute before trying again, then another few moments before I realize there's a chance the bell doesn't work, considering the house is ancient and that would require wiring. While Stella's handy, I don't think she's mastered that in the years since I've seen her.

Pulling my phone from my pocket, I scroll and tap her name and lift it to my ear. I can hear it ringing in the house, so at the very least, the phone is in there, but after a handful of rings, I get her voicemail.

She's ignoring me.

Or maybe... maybe there's something wrong. That knot in my stomach tightens, remembering the dark bags under her eyes the last time I saw her, the exhaustion that I could almost touch in the air. Maybe she's sick. Maybe she needs me.

I make my decision, the only one that makes sense. I reach for the doorknob, half praying it's unlocked to make my life easier, half praying it's locked because the thought of her being unprotected makes me sick. It's a mix of panic and relief when I realize it's not locked.

Turning the knob, my heart races with the worst-case scenarios. She lives alone in this big house; what if something bad happened? Maybe a carbon monoxide leak or a slip, and she hit her head. Maybe she was kidnapped, or— my anxiety that I've never been able to conquer jumps to a new level when I look around her house, stopping dead in my tracks.

The living room seems like a tomb, untouched but clean, but even from here, I can see the kitchen is a disaster. As I step into the house, closing the door quietly behind me and moving deeper, I get a better view of the large kitchen.

Cups and plates piled high in the sink, the cabinet underneath open, revealing the garbage piled high. The entire place clearly needs a vacuum or better yet, a deep clean. Maybe she's sick?

I try calling her name.

"Stella? It's Riggins. Came in to check on you." I wait for a moment before I hear something in the hall to my right, a fumbling, a low curse, and then her voice.

"All good, Riggs," she says.

God, I fucking love hearing her say my name like that, but even now, it's barely a balm on my nerves. At least she's alive, I guess.

"You should head out, though. I'm, uh. I'm sick," she says. "Wouldn't want you to catch it."

She's lying. My gut churns with nerves and worry as I step toward where she is. There's laundry on the floor, a few men's shirts scattered, and for a moment, I wonder if maybe she wants me to leave because a man is here, but when I pick it up, it's an old tee of mine. She used to steal them to sleep in, fitting her small frame more like a nightgown than a tee.

I'd smile if I wasn't nervous. Instead, I drop it and keep walking toward her.

"Coming in to check on you, Stell," I say.

"Seriously, Riggs, there's no need to; I—" Her words stop as I push open her bedroom door.

It's a disaster, clothes sprawled around, more cups and mugs and plates on surfaces, Stella in the middle on a huge four poster bed that looks like something out of an old time movie rather than in the 21st century.

But it's Stella who has my gut churning. Bags under her eyes, clothes askew. Her hair is a mess in a bun on top of her head, but even from here I can tell she hasn't brushed it potentially since I last saw her.

What's most concerning, though, is her eyes, where the light has turned off.

Something is wrong. Very wrong. I walk over to her slowly, like she's a stray cat I might spook, who might go into hiding again if I move too quickly, and her shoulders fall, her head tipping down to look at her sheets.

"Stella..." I start

"I'm okay. Just.. having one of those weeks."

"One of those weeks?" I repeat, then finally make it to her and reach out, grabbing her hand as I move to a squat, looking up at her. Her eyes are watering now, filled with emotions I don't want to see there.

Sadness. Fear.

She's afraid of what I'll say about what I walked into.

"Stell," I whisper.

"I'm fine, really. I'll be good in a day or so, and we can have our talk."

"Our talk?"

"That's why you're here. I've been ignoring your calls and texts, you want to get this chat over with. And we will, Riggs, promise. Just not.... Not now."

"You think.... You think I'm here because I'm mad and want to have a talk."

"Well, yeah, Riggins. But I'm not up for it, I'm sorry. I'm really tired, Riggins. You see I'm alive. You can go,"

"Stella, I—" I start, but she cuts me off again, leaving her back to me as she pulls back the covers and slides under, curling into a ball.

"Don't worry about locking the door. No one comes this way, and I have an alarm system." Yeah, that worked at keeping me out real fucking well, I think but don't say.

I stare at her back for long minutes before I make my decision. I turn, close her bedroom door, and walk down the hall past the mess and the clutter. I look in her kitchen, checking the fridge, then the cabinets, before I get in my truck and drive off.

NOW

29

COME DOWN

STELLA

I listen intently, curled into myself, as I hear his boots leave my house, his truck backing down my driveway. I listen as Riggins does exactly what I requested of him, leaving me be. With everything happening, all of the raked-up emotions and memories, this episode has been rougher than usual, and I'm not even sure if I have any tears left to cry. It's not fair to be disappointed and hurt that he actually left when I told him to, but a small childish part of me hoped he wouldn't have.

What might be minutes or hours later, though, I think I'm hallucinating when I hear the low rumble of a truck driving down my drive again. I don't move, convincing myself it's just the mail truck driving a package to my front door or someone getting turned around and using my driveway as a U-turn.

But the sound of the engine cuts out, and a door slams. When the front door creaks open, the jingle of dog tags and Riggins' voice travels through the living room into where I lay.

"Come on, girl. Let's go find her."

My bedroom door opens again, and something wet brushes my cheek.

It isn't tears, not this time.

It's Gracie's nose on my cheek, nudging and whining.

"Take care of her, girl. I'll be back," he says, not speaking to me but the dog who settles in the spot my curved body makes, her head propped on my hip.

"Riggs?" I ask, not looking at the door where, somehow, I know he's standing.

"She's gonna keep you company, little star. Rest. I'll be back," he says, his voice low and sweet.

"Riggins—" I start, but then my bedroom door is closed. Gracie's face turns to me, her knowing eyes reading my soul before she moves, cozying up closer to me. Looping my arm around her, I snuggle my dog and fall back asleep.

"Stell," the voice whispers, pulling me from sleep. "Stell, sweetheart." It's Riggins' voice swimming in my dreams and waking me, and the soothing touch on my forehead is him as well.

"Riggins?" I ask, my voice croaky.

"I'm here, baby. Come on, let's get you cleaned up. I'll make your bed, then you can come back."

"What?"

"Tub," is all he says. Gracie moves as he does, jumping to the floor. I sit up, squinting around the room, noticing it's at least dusk now, the room darker, and Riggs' hand is out, offering for me to grab it. When I look up at him, his face is kind and understanding, devoid of judgment.

So, for some reason, I take it.

I let him help me out of my bed, let him hold my hand as he walks me out of my room, like he's afraid I'll fall or run if he lets go.

"I'm okay, Riggins. Really. I'm... I'm coming out of it. You don't have to stay here," I tell him. I'm not lying—I do feel myself slowly digging out from it, swimming to the surface. There's sun glittering beneath, and in a few days, I'll be back to my fucked sense of 'normal.'

In the hall, the clothes are cleaned up, and I can hear the dryer running in the mudroom behind the kitchen.

"I know I don't have to," is all he replies as we move toward my bathroom.

When we reach it, I notice it's clean—not immaculate, not like a professional had some hand in it, but it looks like Riggins has wiped down the surfaces and gathered all the dirty laundry.

For a moment, I wait for the shame to hit me, for the embarrassment as it starts to fully click what has been happening here, what Riggs has been doing while I slept with Gracie, but that tired ache still living in my bones doesn't allow for me to expel the extra energy.

"Do you want me to leave?" he asks."While you get in?" My brow furrows as I try to understand what he means, what he's saying. That's when I notice the warm, steaming bathtub, small bubbles dotted along the surface of the water.

He ran me a tub, the smell of the lavender bubble bath I've used since I was a kid, even though it's probably horrible for my skin and the world, filling the room.

For a moment, I almost argue, telling him I don't need a bath, but unfortunately, I know that isn't the truth. With not having to get myself up and out of the house for work each day, I've kept my daily activity to the absolute minimum, taking my pills and feeding myself just enough to survive another day, but not much more than that.

At my worst, that's the most I can do to survive day the day until it starts to ease.

I look from the water to him and shrug.

"Nothing you haven't seen before," I say, my words low as I tug the shirt I've been wearing for at least two days over my head and push down the shorts with a similar fate before stepping into the tub. He makes me hold his hand as I do like he's afraid I'll fall if he doesn't.

Sighing, I settle into the tub, leaning my head back on the edge of the tub and closing my eyes.

"You didn't have to do this," I say. "Or clean up. I hope you didn't do too much."

"Nothing I didn't want to do, Stell."

We don't speak as I sit in the tub, Riggins sitting on the toilet seat, watching. Not in a way like he thinks me naked in a tub is hot, but in a way like... god, I don't know.

Like he can't believe he has the privilege of sitting here, watching over me.

A few minutes later, I can feel him moving behind me until he's behind the big tub. "Sit up," he whispers.

"What?'

"Sit up. Let me do your hair," he says.

"Riggins."

"Humor me."

For some reason, I do as he asks, sitting up, then tipping my head back when he asks. He starts gently working on the hair tie which I know from experience of coming out of one of these episodes is tangled with my hair.

When it's free, a thumb presses into my shoulder, and he whispers, "Tip your head back." I do what he asks, not questioning it, and he takes a cup, slowly pouring warm water from the tap over my head, avoiding my eyes diligently. His fingers work slowly once it's all wet, scrubbing in shampoo, using the tips of his fingers to rub at my scalp, and slowly loosening knots before rinsing out the suds. Next is conditioner, which he slathers in my hair, then takes a comb he must have found somewhere and slowly, meticulously begins to brush out the week of neglect.

As he does, silent tears roll down my cheeks, the quiet, kind gesture ripping through me, both healing and painful somehow.

He never questions it, never asks if or why I'm crying, never even mentions it. Instead, he just keeps brushing my hair until it's smooth.

He rinses it out once more, and then he leaves, coming back with a fluffy white towel.

"Stand, Stella. The towels are fresh from the dryer, and I have new pajamas on the counter."

I look to see a folded stack of grey sweats and a tee shirt. I'm unsure of when he grabbed those, but I'm thankful all the same. The water sloshes as I stand and step out, and I don't have any modesty left in me as he wraps the towel around my body and then a second around my hair. When I dry off, I forgo lotion, instead sliding right into my pajamas before Riggs grabs my hand, leading me past the bedroom and to the kitchen.

It's clean now, a mix of relief and embarrassment passing through me, and he sits me at the table, putting a grilled cheese and a soda in front of me.

"Do you need to have food in your stomach for these?" he asks, lifting the orange bottles I know so well. I keep my eyes down, avoiding his, but shake my head no. I know he stands there reading the labels as I lift the sandwich and take a bite, suddenly hungry.

A good sign in the grand scheme. My appetite is the first thing to return as I'm stepping out of a depressive episode.

"You didn't have to do this," I whisper to the sandwich as he puts pills onto the table next to me.

"I know," he says. "I didn't do it because I felt like I had to." Gracie comes into the kitchen, her dog tags clinking, and she rests her head on my lap. I scratch behind her ear before responding.

"Then why did you?"

"Because even if you aren't ready for that again, you're mine. That means you're also mine to take care of."

I could cry then, but I choke it down and start back on my sandwich.

It's after my dinner, after Riggs unraveled my hair from the towel and gently brushed it out, and long after I got back into my bed with clean sheets and bedding, Riggs climbing in with me wearing a pair of sweats he didn't come here in.

"When did this start?" he asks, his body wrapped around mine.

"It's always been there, but I think something broke in me when I left," I confess. "You called me your sun, but when I left, it was so dark. I couldn't... I couldn't see a way out."

"That's why you changed," he muses, not an accusation but an explanation like it makes a bit more sense to him now.

I don't know why I do it.

It must be the meds or him taking care of me, or maybe I'm just in some kind of delusional state that has me telling him everything that happened after I came home, but I do all the same.

"I came home, and my mother... well, you know what she said before we left. It was a lot of I told you so's, and I wasted my life. She wasn't wrong—she told me I'd get hurt." I feel more than see the look he gives me, it fills the room with regret, but I ignore it. "I didn't know who I was without you and the band and writing, so I became whatever she thought I should be because it didn't matter to me anymore. Might as well make someone happy. You know?"

He doesn't respond, but really, how do you respond to that?

"So I started working at the diner and lived the way she wanted me to. But I didn't get better. It didn't help me find... me." There's a long beat while he runs his fingers through my now dry hair, the feeling soothing and calming. We might lay like that for hours or just minutes, I'm not sure. I'm coming out of my episode, but I'm still lost to time, especially when I'm in Riggs' arms like this. It's in this daze that I confess to him.

"I'm sick," I whisper, the words my mother has told me a million times before. *I'm not depressed, I'm just sick.* As I got older and got help from professionals, I realized it wasn't a lie, not really. Just an illness of the mind rather than the body.

His hand around my back continues its circuit, up and down and back again, before he finally responds.

"What does that mean to you?" he asks. I shrug but don't answer. "Is that you speaking or your mother?"

He was always able to read my words like a manuscript he would pick apart to see what I was really trying to say.

"I have recurrent brief depression." Silence sits between us, but not uncomfortably, no judgment in the air, so I continue explaining.

"It comes every so often. I can usually feel it on it's way, and it usually lasts less then a week before I can pull myself to remember who I am without the clouds. I guess I'm one of the lucky ones because it doesn't last indefinitely." More silence, his hand swiping up and down, up and down. A metronome to my confessions.

"I'm on meds, which helps. They come less now. But sometimes things happen, trigger things. It's..." I sigh, the words catching in my throat before I push them out. It's part of the menagerie of reasons I'm scared to try again with Riggins, the fear that this will be too much for him. "It's who I am now. You want me to give you a chance, but for what? This is who you'll get now." He shakes his head almost instantly, the hand on my back moving to my jaw and tipping up from where my face was buried in his chest and forcing me to look at him.

"I'll take you any way you'll give you to me, Stell. That's what you're not getting. Sad, happy, scared, I'll take it so long as you're also mine."

I roll my lips into my mouth, tears welling.

"Some days, I can't get out of bed," I whisper. "I can't make myself do it. My house turns into a disaster, and I don't shower or brush my teeth." I'm telling him both as a warning and a challenge because who the fuck wants that? Who wants to live with that, to spend their days knowing one day, I'll wake up like this.

"Is it okay if I lay there with you?" he asks. My brow furrows, and I shake my head gently, not in a no, but because it makes no sense.

"What?"

"The days you can't leave bed. Can I lay in it with you?"

I think that's the moment I let a small part of myself go back to Riggins, knowing this time, I'll never truly get it back. The moment I give into the need in my bones to be his again, to let him take care of me, to battle the fear and the uncertainty, even if I'm not ready to say it out loud.

When I wake up the next morning, I'm transported to being 19 and going on tour with Atlas Oaks.

It was just a few days in, and my phone had been ringing off the hook, calls and texts from my mother flooding in, all of them spewing hatred and anger, telling me I was throwing my life away, each one somehow getting worse and worse, meaner and meaner. Eventually, Riggins had to confiscate my phone, only handing it to me if Evie called or texted, giving me his when they were on stage in case something happened and we got separated.

I remember it then. Feeling the dark waters creep up on me, feeling like I might shatter at any moment, but I also remember feeling like it was endurable, doable, *survivable* so long as Riggins was holding me.

It was always like that, like his strong arms, even when they were gangly and unmuscled, were holding me in place, keeping me together.

The first time I felt the waters creep up and he wasn't there to hold me when I realized I might drown without that life preserver holding me just barely afloat was the first time I made an appointment with a psychiatrist.

But now, with his vice grip around me, I feel like he's holding the pieces together. Not saving me, not curing me, but holding it together while I heal, keeping me above water while I rest and catch my breath so I can do the final work to pull myself to the surface.

"Morning, little star," he whispers into my hair, always able to know when I was awake and when I was asleep.

I mumble an incoherent sound, and he laughs against my back, the sound rumbling through me.

"Still not a morning person?"

I mumble another response but don't answer, not really. I was never a morning person as a kid, and that didn't change into adulthood, though I usually have a better routine in place, so waking up before the sun isn't a total drain.

He turns me then, moving my body until I'm facing him and I let him, both because I don't have the energy or mind space to argue, but also because I don't want to. I want to face him, to see his sleepy morning face, interested if he'll have the boyish tired look he used to have, the one he had when I left his bed while he was sleeping last week.

When I see his face, the light playing on the lines that are sharper than my memory has cataloged them, I see he does still have that sleepy, boyish look.

I can't help but smile at him, his own smile widening as I do, that dimple I always loved deepening and begging for me to brush my lips to it like I did when we were young and in love.

His hand moves, brushing my hair back, then stopping on my cheek and resting there. "How do you feel?" he asks, low.

I take a moment to take stock of myself, too exhausted and drained to lie, but I don't take note of my physical being, of how my body feels, but my mind. The exhaustion is still there, but the feeling of heaviness, like a weighted blanket covering my body, is lighter.

We're at the tail end of this episode, it seems.

"Alright," I whisper.

"Don't lie to me," he says.

I can't help it—for what feels like the first time in forever, as it always feels after an episode, a smile tilts the edges of my lips. My hand reaches up, pushing the chunk of hair breaking up his handsome face to behind his ear. A mirror of the move he did just a moment before.

"I'm not. I'm feeling alright, not one hundred percent, but I'm feeling... better. I'm sure that has a bit to do with you." I don't know why I confess that, but it hangs in the air between us, a bright shining confession I both want to take back and want to repeat so he knows the truth of the statement. I do neither and I'm relieved when he doesn't ask for clarification, instead asking me a question.

"This happens often?" I sigh and fight the urge to turn away, to hide. He's seen me at my darkest, and I know, in a way, I've seen him at his. We're even now, I guess, in a weird, twisted way.

"Often is... I don't think it's the right word. It's not regular, not every day, but not *irregular*."

I do the math, knowing this was a longer episode than normal like the stress of the world kept it around a bit longer. "This one lasted ten days, which, for me, is longer than my normal."

He doesn't say anything, which makes me both anxious and relieved, simply watching me, his thumb brushing over the curve of my cheek as his eyes take my face in, categorizing and memorizing everything.

I do the same, taking note of changes that I haven't noticed on his face yet. Small changes over the last seven years, small lines beside his eyes, the way the boyish softness has left his cheeks.

"What helps?" he asks after long moments.

"What?"

"Is there anything I could do to help?." I stare, blinking and trying to understand his question before answering.

"It's not necessarily predictable, but stress... doesn't help."

His face shows pain, clear as day, guilt, and pain, and I instantly want to remove it.

"No. Not like that. It was... just a lot. The last couple of weeks have just been a lot. My mom was... my mom was the trigger. I also had work to motivate me to get up and get moving, which probably didn't help when she fired me. I didn't have to leave the house, so... I didn't."

I didn't want to leave my house for fear of seeing anyone in our small town and having to endure their inevitable questions, either about my mother or Riggins or whatever other stories have been spun in the days since Atlas Oaks returned to Ashford.

"Leaving the house helps?"

"What?"

"Leaving the house. Does it help?"

"Sometimes. Exercise and fresh air and sunlight help, but it could also be a placebo."

Eventually, he nods and moves, letting go of me and rolling away. My body instantly misses his touch, his warmth. Suddenly, I feel alone and small again.

But then his hand is held out to me, his tee and sweats rumpled from sleep as he hovers above me.

"Come. Get dressed," he says.

"What?" I don't move; I just stare at his hand and then at him, confused.

"I said get dressed, Stella." I sit up, holding the blanket to myself.

"Riggins, I—"

"Get dressed, Stella. Leaving the house helps. Sunlight and fresh air help, so we're getting it." I don't say anything, but his hand stays out, waiting for me to grab it. "Come on. We're taking Gracie for a hike."

NOW

30

BAD LUCK

RIGGINS

In less than half an hour, we're in the car, driving to the easiest entrance of the woods. And then we start.

"Do you ever come here?" I ask after a few minutes of silence where we both watched Gracie sniff about nineteen thousand new scents, excited as can be. She might be a bit of an old girl these days, but on a walk, she's still a puppy.

"Sometimes," she says, voice low and defeated like she hates to admit it. "When I'm... lost."

Some people might not know what she means, but I'm not most people. I'm Stella's. I always have been.

The only person in our life who saw it, even then, was my mother. She'd watch us play together, shaking her head and smiling.

"Those two," she would say more times than I can remember. "Meant to be."

Stella's mom would give a tight smile, unimpressed, and my dad would smile and nod, knowing whatever my mother predicted was almost always true. Stella's dad would take us in curiously.

Stella would gag and tell me I was the grossest boy in the world, of course.

But as we got older, I saw it. The way I could anticipate her needs, her wants, sometimes before she even could. The way she always knew when I needed her, sending me a little how are you text or asking if I wanted to go to the woods. The way we one day started writing together and never stopped, an outlet we both desperately need.

So yeah, when she says she comes here when she's lost, I get it.

"I hiked a bunch once I got sober," I say, suddenly eager to fill her in on the past seven years, or at least the good parts of it. "All over. Every stop. Guys would go out and party, and, at first, I couldn't be there. Orange juice or soda at a party felt... depressing." Her eyes are on me, watching me talk as we pad along the trail, but I don't look at her. I can't.

"So I'd put on some boots and head out. It reminded me of you, of us. Of the last time I was at peace. It helped, I think. Even though you weren't there, you were, you know?" A long beat passes before finally, she speaks, a slow, low rumbling of my name.

"Riggins..." she doesn't know what else to say, though, so my name just hangs in the air between us.

"I was mad at you for months. Years, even." The words are low and slow, a confession of sorts.

I feel bad throwing this at her now, with everything she's been through, but at some point, we need to talk about it all, and I know she doesn't want me to use kid gloves with her.

"I couldn't understand... I didn't understand it," I say, referencing the night of the DUI when she answered and told me she was done. We walk a bit further, and finally, she speaks.

"Do you now?"

"Yeah. Most of the time."

I think there will always be some times when I don't understand.

Riggins, move on. I'm done.

Those five words haunt me.

On my worst days, I don't understand how she didn't come when I needed her the most. The look on the officer's face when he asked if there was anyone else I could call when she didn't pick up after call-ing, once, twice. The way I begged for them to call her again, knowing she'd pick up because she *had* to pick up.

And when she did, when I was in my deepest, darkest moment, she didn't fucking come.

Riggins, move on. I'm done.

They plagued me when I was detoxing, when I was getting sober. Those first few days at rehab, that's all I heard, those words swirling around me, reminding me of what I lost.

I get it now. Or at least, most days, I do.

Most days, I get it.

But some days, the quiet of the line, the way the lights played off the wet street as I sat on the curb, those five words... they ricochet through me, haunting me.

"But you weren't there when I needed you," I whisper. "Some-times, that wins. I know I wasn't there for you, that I fucked up first, but sometimes... I needed you, Stella."

It's selfish, I know, to bring this up, all things considered. I lied. I was a drunk. A user. I hid it, and I broke her even after she begged me. She told me what she needed from me, and I promised I could be that for her.

But I wasn't.

"I couldn't be what you needed," she whispers. "Not then. I was too hurt, too angry. I couldn't do it, Riggins."

"I know. I know that Stell." Silence hovers over us again as we watch Gracie run further ahead, chasing a squirrel, oblivious and content in a way I wish I could be. I once was, but then the world and reality came in, and it all came crashing down.

We reach the clearing, a place that used to be ours and still is in its own way, but also, part of me fears nothing will be ours again.

I can spend every waking moment trying to convince Stella to talk to me, to give me a chance, but there's always the real chance she'll never let me in again. A small chance, but it's still there.

I look around the space, memories flooding in before I turn to her and finally speak.

"Why'd you leave?" I ask, whispering quietly. I don't know what I expect, but it probably wasn't a response and definitely wasn't the response I get.

"I couldn't come in last anymore," she whispers, sitting with her back against a tree. I stay standing a few feet away, but her eyes don't come to me, don't look at me at all.

"You always came in first, Stella," I argue, slightly confused.

My entire world revolved around Stella. There was never a time when I doubted that we'd be endgame, that she was mine.

"No, I didn't, Riggs. And that's okay."

"Stella, no. I was... you were always first. No one came before you." She shakes her head in a sad move before finally looking up at me and I see it there. The resignation, the sadness and sorrow. The hurt.

"Not someone. Something. Music always came first for both of us. I was okay with that—I got it. It... it's in your bones, in your blood. The music, the band, it's what made you *you*. I was willing to be second to your music. I got what it meant to you, and considering you let me in on that, considering we did it together, I was more than okay with it. But I couldn't come after the lifestyle you chose back then."

"You didn't—" I start, but my words trail off because that's not fair. Lying to Stella now, when it doesn't even matter that much, when the lies won't save anything if there's even anything to save.

It definitely won't repair what's broken.

And that's what I need to focus on now: repairing and rebuilding rather than saving.

"I didn't know," I whisper. "I didn't know how bad I was."

"I know, Riggs," she says in a consoling tone. I sit too now, my back to a different tree, three or four feet separating us that feels like an ocean, but somehow I know getting any closer will ruin this tentative peace, this fragile willingness to talk to me about all of this.

"I thought I had it under control." I look down at my hands in my lap, taking in the small scars on my fingers from playing for years and years, a scab on my thumb from the time I tried to climb a tree in these very woods and found a jagged edge but didn't want to tell my parents since we weren't supposed to be there at all. Stella snuck out a first aid kit, patching me like she always did.

"I thought... I thought I was invincible. Saw my dad fall into that deep hole and knew there was the possibility of that addiction running in my veins, but I thought I would be stronger. " I sigh, letting my head fall back on the tree and stare up at the fast-moving clouds. "I thought I was better than it than him. That I could... No, I thought I *had* to take part in all the road had to offer to prove he was just weak, that my mom died and he spiraled because he was weak."

Shaking my head, a heavy sigh leaves my chest.

"I was a victim of my own ego. But history has a funny way of repeating itself, you know? You left, and in my gut, I think I knew why. I think I knew you knew I was using in secret, and it made me... righteous. Then I became angry and dug myself so deep when you left. I was fueled by heartbreak and loss and everything my father probably felt but worse because in my heart of hearts, I knew I could have avoided it." I pick a piece of grass and start tearing at it, feeling Stella's eyes burning on me, but for once, I'd do anything to avoid her all-knowing gaze.

"My dad... he wasn't in control of my mom dying. Her cancer, we saw it happen, slowly and painfully, and we watched her leave, but nothing he did could've changed that outcome." Finally, I look at her, meeting her eyes as I tell her my deepest truth, hoping she understands. "I watched you crumble on tour, watched you watch me fall deep, watched you beg me to stop. I watched you lose yourself while trying to quietly save me without scaring me off, and I let it happen. I could have stopped it all, but I chose not to. And that?" I throw the crumbled bit of leaf to the ground. "That kills me every day."

There are so many responses she could give me, so many things I thought she might say when I confessed this. I've had the conversation with her a hundred times over and over in my head, then a hundred times more since I came back to Ashford and saw her.

You were stupid.

I hate you.

You should've tried harder.

And then on days when I'm feeling more hopeful, I've contemplated options like *it wasn't your fault* or *we were so young* or *it's okay.*

But I never accounted for this.

"What was the wake-up call?"

"What?"

"Your wake-up call. It wasn't when I left."

"When my dad died," I whisper into the quiet. A bird chirps overhead, and Gracie's tags jingle as she looks to the sky to find the source.

"I know," she whispers. I know she knows, of course. She sat beside me and held my hand even though we hadn't talked in two years.

"Then I hit rock bottom," I say, another fact we both know too well. "The guys threatened to end everything if I didn't get better. They would be done with me. I think they knew if I kept going, there'd be no band anyway, so they helped me, encouraged me." I smile, remembering. "The first tour, a year after rehab, everyone was fully sober. It was the most boring tour of all time."

The reviews from that tour were also atrocious. *Riggins' sobriety took the joy from his performance,* one magazine said. "They were scared if I saw them partying, having a good time, I'd spiral too. Before the second leg, I had to talk to them, tell them I'd be fine, that being in the same room while they drank or smoked wouldn't send me down that path again." I shrug, remembering their disbelief

"It took a bit for them to believe me and longer for them to stop worrying I'd fall back in, but we got there."

"Wow," she whispers, her eyes wide because she knows how the tours were, how the after parties were, or at least how they were getting. Drugs and drinking and women and chaos everywhere. Every day, I thank whoever kept me from going even deeper, whoever up there stopped me from touching anything more than weed and liquor.

My mom, probably. I always liked the idea of that one, of my mother, watching over me, probably hurt and disappointed, but trying to save me all the same.

"I'm proud of you," she says, breaking into my thoughts, the words quiet and unsure. "For doing it. Getting out. For living your dream but also for valuing your life. That was what I always wanted for you."

More silence passes before I make my confession. I'm not sure if she'll like it, but I will make it all the same.

"I did it for you, I think." Her head snaps up, and this time, I don't avoid her eyes. "The hope of it, of this. Of being able to talk with you again one day, for you not to look at me with pity and shame in your eyes, to sit in this spot once more."

"Riggins..." she says, the word trailing off.

"I know things will never be the same. I don't... I don't want them to be. But I want you, Stella. In my life. I want you." A bird sings overhead, but I keep staring at Stella and putting it all on the table. "And not as friends." Silence spans again, but I don't break it, leaving her to process my words and her feelings. Eventually, she speaks.

"I don't know if I can give you me," she says in a low, scared whisper.

"That's okay," I tell her. "We can take it day by day. It's less scary that way. I learned that in AA. You take it day by day, figure out what you can handle, and don't worry about the day after, the next week, the next month, or the next year. A year of sobriety sounds fucking impossible when you're deep in there, but a day? An hour? That's doable. That's what we have to do. Take it day by day," I tell her, hoping she understands, that she'd be willing to do that with me. She stares at me, deep and assessing for long minutes before she nods. My chest lifts, warmth taking over with the hope.

"When I'm having an episode, that's what I tell myself. An hour. A day. I can handle being sad or numb for a day. An hour. If I tell myself it might last seven days, a week, a month at my worst, that's impossible. Unimaginable. But I can handle an hour."

I don't say anything, waiting to see if she wants to expand or if that's enough sharing for now, and when she looks to the sky, bright blue and filled with puffy white clouds, my body relaxes, thinking that's it for now.

"I'm scared," she whispers.

"I know," I say. "I am, too. But what's the point of swimming to the surface if you're not going to fight to see the sun?" She sits perfectly still, and I wonder for a moment if I pushed too hard. But still, I wait, and my patience is rewarded.

"I'll fight, Riggs," she whispers finally.

It's then I know we'll be okay. Because if Stella is willing to fight, I'm never giving up. Never.

"Beckett's birthday is Friday," I say when the silence stretches long and winding. It may have been minutes or even hours, but time always passed that way when we were together. Easy and slow as we let ourselves get lost in thoughts and inspiration and words and melodies.

I wait until my heart has calmed a bit from asking about the past. It beats rapidly again but in a different way.

"Yeah?"

"Yeah." I look at her, and her eyes are on me, questioning. "Come to the party," I say.

"Come to the party?" She echoes, and I stand, taking a few steps in her direction and offering her my hand. I'm not sure how she's going to react, but when he reaches out, grabbing mine and allowing me to tug her to standing, it surprises me. Then she's just inches from me, her face not far from mine.

"Yeah. As my date."

A million thoughts fly over her face, only few I'm able to capture and interpret before the next comes.

Confusion.

Concern.

Excitement.

They're all there, all at the same time, but I force myself to latch on to the good ones, telling myself only time can help with the others.

"Date," she whispers, but it isn't a question, more like she's weighing the simple word and deciding how it feels on her lips. "Okay," she finally says.

And just like she used to, just like when she would smile at me on my dark days, she lights up my world with a shy, quiet smile. A super-nova in my dark sky.

THEN

Usually, talking to my sister helps to ease my worries, but for the first time since I can remember, it's not working. The guys are out at press events, and I stayed behind. We're at the tail end of the tour before it starts back up in March. Two nights ago, we celebrated the tour almost being done and my 20th birthday, and for the first time since I joined, I resented this tour.

And what it's doing to Riggins.

"You should talk to him, Stell. No one has ever been able to get through to him like you," my sister says.

I just finished finally confessing everything I've been feeling. I love everything about being on tour with Riggins and the guys. It's everything I daydreamed about for what feels like my entire life, but I've never once gone so long without seeing my twin.

When she went to college just two hours from home, she came home once a month, at the very least, and we'd snuggle in bed together, giggling like we were ten in our childhood room, then later in Riggins and my apartment.

But now, when she comes home, I'm somewhere else, across the country

It hurts not having her. Riggins might be my other half, but Evie is my soul.

So every few days, I sneak off to peace and quiet while the boys go out wreaking havoc or practicing or doing some kind of press stop and call Evie, filling her in on everything that's been happening.

Unfortunately, being on tour has shown me some of the darker sides of our dreams, including Riggins' growing obsession with drinking at all hours of the day. We wake, and before I even get ready for the day, he's holding a beer. By the time their shows end, he's stumbling off stage, and he isn't stopping there.

It was fun at first, drinking and partying with the band, and random celebrities and musicians came to hang out and get wild, but now I'm concerned. Alcoholism runs in his family, even if he refuses to acknowledge his father, and it looks like he's following the same path.

"It's just, I've seen his dad. You know how he completely spiraled after Jeanette died. He's drinking himself into an early grave, and I'm worried Riggs is right behind him."

Before Evie can respond, I hear it.

"Are you talking to your sister about me?" Riggins' voice booms. I didn't even hear him coming onto the bus, but now he's standing over me, anger clear on his face.

"Hey, Evie, I gotta go," I say, not even waiting for a response before I end the call and toss the phone on the sofa. It vibrates with a text almost instantly, but I leave it where it lies, standing and reaching for Riggins.

When he steps back, just out of my reach, dread curls in the pit of my stomach, dark and ominous.

"What the fuck, Stella?"

"Riggins, I—"

"So what, you think I'm out of control?" he asks, a taunt in his words. "I'm going to, what did you say? Drink myself into an early grave just like my father?"

"That's not fair—"

"You must be so disappointed," he says, continuing to talk over me. "Getting hooked to the loser kid, an out-of-control drunk just like his dad. You could have had any of those rich bastards your mom begged you to date, but you chose me, and it's not what you expected. Heads up, Stella, you're on a fucking rock tour. What did you expect, tea parties and dollies?"

Something changes on his face, moving to something mean and cruel, and I brace for impact. He's never been mean to me, and I've never seen this angry, defensive side of him, but I have seen it in his father. "Or maybe you just imagined some silly little whirlwind romance, you and me writing across the country, sitting under the stars while everyone else fucking enjoys themselves."

It hurts.

It hurts badly. It must show on my face because, for a split second, his face goes soft, like he regrets the cruel words, but then it's gone as he straightens his face and his body and crosses his arms on his chest.

"Look, Stella. We're all of legal drinking age. I'm sorry you aren't. Maybe you were right all along; you shouldn't have come. Maybe this is just too much for you."

Another knife to my gut.

"This is what a tour is like. Drinking and parties and music. It's not that I'm a fucking alcoholic; it's that this is how the real world looks once you're out of your little bubble of Ashford. If it's too much for you, you know how to leave."

I open my mouth to say something, though I don't think a single word would come out of my throat if I tried, the lump there so large, so painful, but there's no time as he stomps down the center of the bus, slamming the door behind him as he leaves, an eerie quiet in his wake.

That's when the dam breaks, and I fall to the ground and cry as I've never cried before in my life. I cry about the life I thought I'd be living and the way this tour has not been what I thought. I cry about how maybe Riggins is right; it's my own fault.

I've watched movies and TV shows and read books, I should have known. I cry because I don't know what that means for Riggins and me, the only boy I've ever loved, ever wanted to love me my entire life.

I cry because it just might mean my mother was right all this time, and this was the absolute worst decision I could have ever made.

"Stell?" a familiar voice says what could be seconds, minutes, or hours later, but I don't move. I can't. I continue to sit in my heap as two sets of feet come my way.

"What the fuck?" a deeper voice says. *Beckett.*

"Stella," the other voice whispers. *Reed.* Strong arms are grabbing me, lifting me, moving me to the couch at the front of the bus, Beck's cologne filling my nose.

"Stella, what happened?"

"I fuckin' told you we needed to talk to him sooner," Wes says under his breath, but still audible. "His shit is getting out of control, drinking the second he wakes up, not stopping until he passes out. He's irrational, and now he's taking it out on Stella." He says my name like it's a crime to be unkind to me.

"I didn't think..." Reed starts.

"You all walk on fucking eggshells around him, but someone needs to talk some fucking sense into him before shit gets bad." A new bolt of fear and nerves strikes through me as I realize it wasn't all in my head, that it isn't just me being immature and inexperienced. Riggins has a problem, and Beck sees it, too. He moves, sitting on the couch with me.

"Stella, what happened?" Reed asks, ignoring his bandmate.

"I... I... I," This is getting nowhere, so I force myself to take one, two, three deep breaths in, filling the very bottom of my lungs as I do before I sniff and proceed. "I was on the phone with my sister. I... I'm worried about him. He drinks all the time. He wakes up and grabs a beer. I was just... I was venting to her because I've never had to address anything bad with him. Ever. We've..." My mind drifts off as

I try to confirm, try to sift through a lifetime of memories. "We've never actually had a real disagreement before. I've never had to talk to him about anything, much less... this."

Beck's hand moves, brushing my hair back, and I keep talking. In the corner of my eye, I see Reed and Wes look at each other, exchanging silent words.

"He walked in when I was talking to her. I was venting, you guys, I swear. I..." I pause, trying to justify. "I swear I don't think he's like his dad or that he's bad or—"

"We know Stella," Reed says low. "We know. We get it."

"I was just venting to my sister the way I always do. She's... she's my sister!"

"We know, Stell," Beck says, the most comforting I've ever heard him be. I look at Reed, Riggins' closest friend.

"He was so mad, Reed. He yelled at me." Beck's arm tightens around my middle, and his voice rumbles against me.

"He yelled at you?"

"Well, not like..." I almost say he didn't scare me, that it wasn't mean, but that's not the truth, is it? It was mean. It did scare me.

"He was just frustrated," I try to justify.

"No, he was fucking mad someone finally called him out for his bullshit," Beckett says.

"What did he say, Stella?" I roll my lips into my mouth, unsure if I should say anything, if I should share this, but this is his band. His best friends. And despite everything, even if he really truly does want me gone and thinks I'm not fit for this life. I want him to be happy and healthy.

I do think he needs help.

"It really doesn't matter, you guys. It's no big. I think.. maybe I should just let him enjoy the road, head home, and see you guys when it's over." Beck's arms get tight, and honestly, I'm a little reticent to look up at Reed with the sudden violence cracking in the room. Those two weeks would be the most miserable ones of my life, after living this life I fucking love, despite the partying, after being with Riggins like this, after being out of Ashford and away from my mother... "And he might be right, I'm technically underage, and you all—"

"None of us wake up first thing in the morning and crack open a beer, Stell, and just a reminder, Riggins is the youngest in this fucking band," Beckett says.

I did know that. I did. I just...

"What did he say, Stella?" Wes asks, his voice firm, and I know there's no avoiding this.

"He said if this was too much for me, I should go home and that he's just enjoying himself. And again, he's not technically wrong, I—"

But there's no one here to reason with anymore.

With those words, Beck sets me aside, and then he is out the door of the bus, Reed and Wes following, calling his name.

I just sit there, unsure of what to do, but a sinking sadness seeps into my chest that makes it nearly impossible to leave this spot.

Instead, I lay down where I am, cry a bit more, and fall asleep without making any real decisions.

"Little star, wake up," a low voice says. It's a familiar voice, a comforting one, a voice I love. Even though there's heavy waters lapping at me, telling me to stay asleep where it's warm and safe and easy, I crack an eye open.

I'm still lying on the couch on my side, but there's a blanket pulled over me now, up to my shoulders. It's dark in the bus, but my eyes are locked on Riggins, his face illuminated by a low light coming in through the window behind us.

"Riggins?"

"Hey, baby," he whispers, then moves his hand, pushing my hair back. It feels good, like he's pushing off the drowsiness and the sadness that was swallowing me whole. I turn my face into his hand, and he cups my cheek there.

"I'm so sorry," he whispers. My eyes open a bit more, then my brows furrow in confusion, trying to remember, to understand...

We had a fight. Our first fight ever.

The memory wakes me up fully, the warmth of his hand unable to fight back the chill as I sit up. It all comes back. Talking to Evie, Riggs hearing, him yelling at me, telling me to go home. Beck and Reed coming, Beck storming out and Reed following...

It's then I see it.

The giant shiner on Riggs' eye.

"Oh, my god, Riggins—"

"Looks worse than it feels, I promise," he says with a smile. "Come on." He holds his hand out for me to take.

"Riggins, we need to talk," I say because we do. So badly. I shouldn't have buried my concerns, but I should have talked to him about it sooner so he wouldn't feel like I was ambushing him.

"I know, and we will. Just... come with me, Stell. Please."

I've never been able to say no to him, not since we were five and he dared me to touch a frog in his backyard and I did it just because he gave me that look. Even then, I thought it was worth doing what he asked for that look, even if Evie totally tattled on me and got me in wild amounts of trouble for not being *ladylike*.

So I grab his hand, slide on a pair of shoes, and walk out of the bus with him. We're in Colorado, parked outside a large hotel chain in the middle of nowhere. According to Don, the bus driver, we're staying outside city limits both because it's the cheapest option for the label and because even though they're relatively new, the boys are getting popular. There's less of a chance of being ambushed by fans here, which I'm super grateful for, all things considered.

"Where are we going?" I ask as the warm summer night air wraps around my arms.

"Just be patient, little star," he says, the familiar words wrapping around me the way they always do, chasing out the last of the cold, watery chill that my bones had been soaking in all day. We walk around the building to a grass field, a tall man standing near some dim lights.

"Who's that?" I ask.

"Reed." We slowly approach him, my belly churning and not even bothering to ask where Beck is, knowing somewhere in my belly that he gave Riggins that painful-looking black eye. Wes is probably off hiding somewhere as is his way.

As we approach, it's pushed from my mind as I watch Reed start to struggle more with something in his arms.

A...

A wiggling ball of fur.

"What is that?" I whisper.

"Yours," Riggins says as we get slower and the ball of fur turns into a dog before my eyes. A puppy.

"Mine?"

"Yeah," he says, and I reach out to touch the puppy, but before I even can, she's jumping into my arms. I catch her, but just barely.

"Oh my god!" I squeal as she starts licking my face excitedly. "Oh my god!"

Riggins knows I've wanted a puppy since I was a kid, putting it on my Christmas list every single year even though my mother adamantly refused because dogs are disgusting.

"She's a German Shepherd. She'll be pretty big, eventually," Riggins says from behind me, his hand on my waist.

"She's precious," I murmur, burying my face in her fur for a moment before moving to look at Riggins and smiling. I also note Reed has at some point disappeared.

It's then I notice the rest of the area, a big blanket on the ground with candles lit all around, a guitar, a bag.

"What is this?" I ask, giggling as the dog nips at my ear.

"You can let her down," Riggs says. "There's a leash and a post in the ground."

"What?" Nothing makes sense right now, and for a moment, I wonder if I'm still asleep.

"Put her down, Stell," Riggins says, voice serious.

Suddenly, I'm anxious.

Suddenly, I'm remembering everything that happened this afternoon, remembering the look in Riggins' eyes, the anger on Wes and Reeds' faces.

"Put her down," he repeats in a lower whisper.

"Riggins," I say, but do as he asks, bending a bit, hooking the leash to the stake in the ground as I put down the dog.

"Stella," he whispers, hooking an arm around my waist and pulling me into him. My arms go around his neck on instinct, my body trained to move to him like a sunflower, tipping my head up as I do. "I fucked up," he says.

My instinct is to tell him it's fine, that it wasn't a big deal. He's under a lot of pressure, and he's right; I am underage, and maybe it's my fault, but I fight that urge.

"I've been overwhelmed. It's a lot, being on tour. The pressure to be this...." He sighs and then looks up at the stars as if the answers will be written there. "Great musician, and I'm just... I'm just me. I don't know what I'm doing. You're right—the guys are right. I'm going too far. I'm drinking too much, I'm having too much fun—"

I open my mouth to argue, but he shakes his head and corrects himself. "No, that's not fair. I can have fun without drinking as soon as I wake up. I can have fun without getting blackout drunk every night."

Relief washes through me. I move a hand, brushing his hair back. "That's all I was trying to say, Riggins. And in my defense, not that I think I need it,—"

"You don't, Stell, you don't need to defend yourself. You did nothing wrong."

"I was just saying, I vent to Evie about everything. You know that. Something enters my brain, and if it feels uncomfortable. I call her up and talk it out with her."

"I know. And I love that you have that. I also want to be that for you, though. I want you to feel safe coming to me, talking to me about anything. Everything. Even if you think it will be something I don't want to hear. "

"I just..." He shifts, so I have no choice but to look at him, his features filling my entire line of vision, and his face is so serious.

"Stella Hart, you're my person. Evie can be yours, and I'll share that honor with her until the day I die, but you're mine. You're it for me. You've always been it for me. I was already thinking about the things I heard you say to Evie. They were already rattling around in my mind, and that's why it threw me off. It was a confirmation of my biggest fears."

"Your biggest fears?" I ask, confused and worried at the dread in his eyes.

"I'm terrified I'm going to fuck up so big, so badly, you're going to run one day. You're going to realize your mom was right, that you can do so much better than me, that you deserve more."

"Riggins..." I start, ready to tell him all the reasons I love him and need him.

"I can't lose you, Stella. I..." His head tips up again, and in the low light of the stars, I can see the glistening of his eyes. "I can't lose you. I've seen what happens when you lose your person, your reason for living."

"Riggins—" I start, the panic filling me because I can't be his reason for living. I'd absolutely fold under the pressure of that. But then his hand moves, fumbling into his pocket and pulling out a ring that he holds between us. My heartbeat skyrockets.

"Riggins..." I say again, but it sounds different this time.

"I love you, Stella," he whispers. "I love you more than all the stars in the sky, Stella. You are my star, my sun. I wouldn't survive this world without you, and I never want to find out what life is like without you." The ring in his fingers glints gently in the starlight, but my eyes are locked on Riggins.

"I want you to be mine forever, Stella. I want to lay under the stars with you, write songs, and explore the world with you. I want to go to Maine and look at the stars there, and I want to make all of your crazy dreams come true. I want to raise our kids in Ashford and let Mrs. Montgomery tell them she always had to yell at their parents because they talked in the halls too much, that she always knew we'd be together." I choke out a laugh, and that's when I realize I'm crying.

"This isn't an engagement ring. You deserve more from a proposal than an apology after our first real fight. You deserve the moon, Stella. It's just a promise ring. It's me begging you to give me another chance, to forgive me, to give me time to plan your real proposal." His lips turn up in a smile, and I can't help but return it. "This is me begging you to forgive me."

I let myself think about it for just a moment, but it's useless.

I know what I'm going to say.

I've been irrevocably in love with Riggins Greene since I was five and I realized I had a crush on him. Fell further when I was ten and he punched Timmy Stewart for saying my pigtails were dumb looking, and I kept falling when I held his hand at his mother's funeral.

I knew he was it for me when we snuck out to sit under the stars, the first song we wrote together. I've known since he left to chase his dreams, and mostly, when he came back and told me his dreams were nothing without me.

I've always wanted Riggins to be mine, and I've always wanted to be his.

So there's no choice but to smile dreamily and nod. And when he stands, slides the thin promise ring band on my finger that I don't bother to look at—it could be the ugliest, least me thing on the whole planet, and I'd have accepted it—then kisses me, dipping low as I giggle, the band cheering in the background.

I didn't even realize he never made promises about changing his lifestyle until it was much, much too late.

NOW

32

FEAR OF WATER

STELLA

He knocks.

When Riggins comes to pick me up for Beckett's party, he knocks on the front door like this is a real date. Butterflies erupt in my belly and I wipe my hands down the front of my rose colored dress that I'm halfway regretting wearing. It's much too fancy for a house party at Beck's, but I'm unsure of what this is—a date, or just a party.

I chose an all-lace maxi dress with a plunging neckline showing the sides of my barely there breasts, a slip dress underneath the lace stopping right beneath my ass. It's a mix of sexy and boho, so it feels like me still but pretty. Special.

I take a deep break, running my fingers through my waves before opening the door.

He stands there, his hands in his pockets, his longish hair pulled back into a mini bun at the back of his head, a black tee and dark jeans on, and he looks so fucking handsome.

I open my mouth to say... something, anything, but I don't get the chance when he takes a wide step inside my place, hands going to my waist and guiding me until I'm against the wall of my entryway, his lips moving to mine instantly.

It's not a sweet hello kiss, not kind and pleasant. It's hot and needy, and when his body presses against mine fully, I moan into the kiss. The slit in my dress comes in handy when his hands move to my ass, and I'm able to spread my legs around his waist as he continues to hold me against the wall, grinding into me where I need him most.

We haven't done anything since that one night and definitely haven't done anything more than kiss since I agreed to give him a fresh shot, and right now, that need is building in me.

I moan as his tongue tangles with mine and again as his lips start to trail, leaving wet, sucking kisses along the sensitive skin of my neck.

"Riggins, please," I whisper in his ear. "Please." I'm asking for more. I'm asking for everything. I don't know if I'm ready to give him that or if I'm ready to take it from him, but right now, it's all I can think about. He puts his forehead against mine, shaking his head. "I don't want to rush this, Stella. I don't want to hurt you."

"What *is* this?" I whisper, dazed by the kiss and letting my worries run free. "What are we? One day, I'm just me, I'm floating along, surviving—"

"Surviving," he says, his brows coming together, the word sounding foreign on his lips, like he doesn't quite understand the meaning of it. Even from the close angle I can see he doesn't like the word. I roll my eyes and smile.

"Yes, surviving, Humans do it all the time. Living from one day to the next."

"No, no, little star. You should never be just surviving. You should be thriving. And I'm so fucking sorry it took me so long to come back, to find what has always been mine, and to take care of you." My heart skips a beat with his words.

"This is what I mean, Riggins. What is this?" The panic starts to rise with my already heightened emotions. "You slide back into my life, no warning, then start following me to work every day, saving me from creeps, taking care of me when I'm having an episode, helping me stand up to my mom, and I'm just supposed to be like, yeah, totally, this is normal?" He smiles wider and moves so I'm standing again, but he's still caging me in, keeping me in a place like he's afraid I'll run.

"I mean, that would make my life a bit easier, but you've never been one for that."

I roll my eyes. "I'm serious, Riggins. I'm so confused. What is this? Is this a date? Are we just friends?"

Suddenly, his face goes dark, a million emotions cascading over it. His breath ghosts against my lips, smelling of cinnamon mints and coffee.

"My biggest regret in life—and Stella, I have a lot of them. So fucking many, from not letting my mom know how much she meant to me, to not making sure my dad got help, to making the guys suffer because I was a fuckwad, to so many more I probably can't even remember because I'd drink until I blacked out and do and say dumb, hurtful things and not remember them in the morning. But of all the shit I've done, the one I regret most is letting you walk away from me. Not fighting for you, for us. And selfishly, part of that is because it means I spent too many years without seeing you smile, without smelling your perfume, or without feeling your fingers twine with mine. Seven years since I sat under the stars with you, since we wrote a song together. Seven years since, I felt at peace, even when I was tearing myself apart. My biggest fucking regret is watching you walk away and not chasing after you, not doing everything in my power to make sure you knew how fucking much I love you."

"Riggins," I whisper, but I don't know what I'm trying to say. Am I asking him to kiss me? Am I asking him to stop, to back off, to leave forever? "What is this?" I ask for a third time instead of either of those options, my lips brushing his with the movement of my lips.

"This is us, our second shot, Stella. That's what this is. Please. Take it with me."

Something in me shifts with his words, my world careening a bit, and for some reason beyond my understanding, I nod.

"Stella!" a voice yells when Riggins, Evie, and I walk into Beckett's house, the same one he had all those years ago, not upgrading to something more grand despite his increased budget and stardom.

Evie waited in her car until Riggs and I showed up, refusing to walk in without us, and as I see her give a forced uncomfortable smile, I'm half wondering why she came here, even if I'm glad she's here. "And Everest!" Reed comes into view, moving around bodies until he's pulling both Evie and I into his arms.

"You call me Everest again, I'm pulling out my blackmail from when we were kids," my twin deadpans when he steps back, bumping into some girl I don't recognize. She glares at him until she realizes who he is, and her lips tip up, coy and intrigued.

Reed ignores her, as he always does. That was always his way, ignoring all of the super fans who wanted a roll in the hay with the bassist of Atlas Oaks.

There's not too many people here, maybe fifteen plus a handful I saw milling about outside, smoking and sitting around a bonfire, but Beckett's house is small, so it feels bigger than it is.

"You wouldn't," Reed says, a look of fake hurt on his face.

"Try me," my sister says, and I can't help but laugh.

"Stop it you two, or I'll pull out my blackmail and we all know I know way more on both of you than you could possibly know on me," I say and both of them laugh.

"God, Stell, still as vicious as ever," a voice says, and then Wes and Beck come into view.

"Shut it, Wesley," I say with a smile, moving to give him a hug and then step back. "You guys remember my sister, right?"

Beck's eyes go warm and knowing, and for a split second, I wonder if I imagined it as his grumpy guard drops back down into place. "Evie," he says, low and without any emotion in his voice, before pulling me into a hug and wordlessly walking off.

I meet Reed's eyes and give him a, *what the fuck* look. His face is a hint of confusion, a hint of humor as he shrugs at me.

Evie elbows me in the side, and I lean to hear her,

"I think I just saw someone I know. I'll be right back," she says. I move to look around, then back at my sister to ask who, but before I can, she's gone, disappearing into the small crowd.

When I turn back it's just Reed and Wes in front of me.

"What the hell was that?" I ask, confused, still looking around to find her.

Reed shrugs, smiles, and opens his mouth like he has something to share with me, but then a strong arm is wrapping around my waist, tugging me back into a chest. I let out an *oof* and would normally panic, but I know that arm.

I know that chest.

I know the smell and feel, and I *definitely* know the rumble of Riggins' laugh on my back.

It feels safe.

It feels like I'm *home*.

Hours later, I'm sitting outside on a log around a fire, listening to the crackling of the wood and the occasional loud laugh from the house. I left the house to escape the chaos when all four of the guys huddled in a corner, and Reed started screaming at someone to take a picture for them.

Seeing him in this new frame has been a challenge, so close to how things used to be that it almost triggers a panic inside of me, something I don't want to feel, doubts I don't want to give air to. I don't think he's going to start drinking after just one party, especially not after talking to him in the woods and seeing him prove to me, again and again, he's turned a new leaf, but I can't help but wonder how parties like this impact him, how they make him feel.

A few minutes of my staring into the crackling fire, my eyes dry from my intense stare. Someone sits down across from me at one of the six logs lining the area around the fire. When I look up, I see Beckett staring into the same fire as I am, quiet, not saying a word or looking at me.

Silence takes over, suddenly louder than when it was just me. It's not uncomfortable, but it's... different. It never was when it was me and Beckett. He was always the quiet, brooding type, but I liked that about him. Liked how I could sit in my own thoughts when I was with Beckett.

Riggins was always my heart, the one I could share everything with, for better or worse.

Reed was the funny one, the one who would do absolutely anything to make someone smile, the one who I could talk about dumb shit with.

Wes was the ladies man, the one who would pick up a new girl on tour every single night, and I always knew I could go to him for anything and he'd always tell me how it was.

But Beckett? Beckett was the one I could always sit in comfortable silence with. The one who punched Riggins in the face when he found out he'd made me cry, the one who I know probably gave Riggs the most shit when I was gone for good. He was also the one who, when I had a line but not a melody, I could come to him and wait for him to find the right staccato or beat for the words I wrote.

I missed them all, but I missed Beckett most, I think.

"He's better, you know," his deep, rumbling voice says, shocking me since he's never been the one to speak up first. It's not his style.

"What?"

"Riggins. He's better. In control."

My stomach flips, but I nod in agreement. I can see that; it's obvious. And It's been confirmed by the others.

"Yeah, I know. Reed told me."

Beckett stares at me for a long beat before shaking his head. "Reed sees the best in everyone. He would tell you Riggs was better even if he slipped up a bunch just because he misses you and misses seeing you two happy together."

He's not wrong; Reed would do that, and I'd be lying if that voice in my head hadn't been whispering that to me in the dark as well.

"But me, I'll tell you like it is." This is also true. He would. "You left; he got worse. Real bad, Stell, but I think you know that." I nod in confirmation, but no words will leave my lips as I hold his deep brown eyes. "Got better, on and off, then his dad died, and he fucking lost it. You know that, too." I nod again, remembering the way Riggins described it all to me.

I remember going to Riggins' father's funeral. Remember holding his hand even though I didn't feel like I had the right, and I remember him disappointing me again, and I remember feeling like such a fucking idiot for believing in him, believing we could be anything.

"The label ordered him to go to rehab." Now that, that's news to me.

"What?" I ask, trying to place this new piece of information into the timeline I already have in my head, trying to understand where it fits.

It doesn't, but Beckett nods. His head turns looking out to the woods behind his house, woods I once ran off into with Riggins, woods where I had my first kiss with him, woods where I've written more songs that I can count.

"It was kept quiet, but yeah. He went to rehab." There's a pause while I try and think of what to say, but he fills in the silence. I knew he went, of course, but I never really thought of the logistics or what got him to go. "It wasn't easy; he thought he could do outpatient and get sober that way, but he needed professional help, full-time. He'd gotten too good at hiding it by then." My gut twists. "I told him I was done with the band if he didn't go. The music, the fame, the fans... none of it was worth it if he drank himself into a grave. The others followed eventually, and he agreed, especially after the DUI."

"A DUI?" I ask, confused. Beckett looks at me with a similar confusion across his face.

"Well... yeah." He says it a bit confused but keeps speaking. "I mean, it wasn't made public, though. All of this wasn't important for anyone else to know, but I think now... it's important for you to know." I stare at his profile, thinking how it would have been so much easier if it was Beckett, whom I had a crush on all those years ago.

"Why?" I ask in a low whisper.

"Because you're not all in yet. You're scared. I can see that. But Stell, I'll say he's been clean, he's been alive, but he hasn't been living since you left. Tonight? Tonight, he's *living*. He's back, Stella. And it's selfish as fuck, me asking you to give him a chance because I missed my friend, but I'm going to ask anyway. I'm going to ask you to give him a chance. If you want him as much as he wants you or even close to it, give him a chance."

This time, he lets the silence stretch, lets me think and ruminate on the words he just spilled,

"I'm scared," I whisper into the dark, a confession I'm embarrassed to say out loud. "I'm so scared, Beckett."

"I know," he says.

He doesn't try to tell me the reasons I shouldn't be scared, doesn't try to counter my fears. Instead, he challenges them. "But are you too scared to reach for something beautiful? Because you two? You two are beautiful, Stell. You two are something that doesn't come around often, a once-in-a-lifetime kind of love. Are you too scared to try and have that?"

"I thought Riggins was the songwriter, Beckett?" I say with a laugh, trying to break the tension and failing miserably.

He shakes his head seriously. "No, that was always you, Stell. But you know that. You know you were always part of this band from the start, and when you left, we were never the same. Not just Riggins—all of us."

I sit there gaping like a fish, trying to figure out how to respond when his name is called from behind me. Beckett raises a hand and stands, but not before he bends down and presses a kiss to the top of my head.

"Glad you're back, Stella," he whispers there, loud enough for no one but me to hear, then walks off.

I sit quietly for a while before I leave for the bathroom to take a few deep breaths with no one around.

And I look at myself in the mirror.

Are you too scared to reach for something beautiful?

Am I?

Am I too scared to try this again? Because if I am, I should stop this all together. The right thing, the kind thing to do would be to tell Riggins I can't do it, cut my losses before one of us gets really hurt.

More hurt than we already got.

But if I'm not...

I stand there, staring at myself for long moments before finally, I make my decision. If it was even really a decision at all.

When I leave the bathroom and step back into the party, I look around for Riggs but can't find him. Without my permission, my stomach starts to churn, nerves and old fears kicking in.

Finally I meet Reed's eyes and before I can ask, he tips his head toward the back sliding door and he's there, sitting at the edge of the deck, staring out at the stars, a cigarette balanced in his fingers.

I walk out and sit next to him, shifting my eyes to the same stars he's watching.

"Want one?" Riggs asks, offering his pack of cigarettes. I remember sitting outside gigs, smoking with him because it felt cool and grown up, even though I hated the taste. Eventually, I got used to it, started to crave the quiet peace of a smoke break.

It was the first habit I dropped after I left.

I shake my head with a smile.

"No, I don't smoke anymore."

He returns the smile and stuffs the pack back in his pocket, crushing the butt beneath his shoe and popping a piece of gum in his mouth. "Oh, me neither," he says finally.

I give him a small smile and a confused look. "You literally just lit a cigarette."

His smile goes wider, his dimple breaking out on his cheek. "Yeah, well. If you don't smoke, I don't smoke."

I think that small statement answered whatever questions I might still have.

I'm scared, but not too scared.

Riggs can show me and everyone can tell me over and over he has changed, but at some point it becomes my job to believe in him. To trust it will all be okay.

"What are you doing out here by yourself?" I ask, leaning back on my hands and staring off into the stars the same way he is.

"It gets hard sometimes, being at a party. The band, they all look at me like I'm about to break like they're constantly worried I'm going to grab a drink and spiral again."

"Are you?" I ask, and I think it surprises him, my asking. I wonder if people ever ask or if they tip-toe around the question like I have been.

But where is that getting us? Between not trusting him and holding old hurts against him, where is that getting us besides wildly confused?

"Am I going to start drinking again?"

I nod.

Without a moment of hesitation, he shakes his head. "Fuck no."

"That sure?"

His hand moves, reaching out and twining his fingers around mine.

"Drinking made me lose the most important thing in my life once before, and I've been living with those mistakes ever since. It also made my father lose his life, made me almost lose my career, and almost lost my friends. No, Stell. There's no going back there for me. Never."

"What if I say no?" I ask, and without even explaining myself, I know he knows what I mean.

What if I say no to this? To us. What if I decide it's too much, that there's too much between us, behind us, that I can't get over it.

"Then life will go on. I'll live life without my other half, but I'm not picking up a drink, Stell. I'm done with that."

He says it without wavering and when I look at him, I know it's true. I think to a point, that's what I needed. To know his sobriety wasn't hinging on whatever delicate thread of a relationship we have right now.

"Ready?" he asks. "To go, I mean." I realize I've spent long minutes staring at the stars, contemplating... life, I suppose.

I look at him and see the hope in his eyes. Not hope that I'll be ready to go, but hope that I'll be ready for more.

Ready for us.

And even though I'm terrified of getting hurt and how that would ruin me, I finally have the clarity I need to take the jump once more.

"Yeah, honey. I'm ready," I whisper.

"When you came back, I was scared," I whisper as he drives toward my place. I remember there being a time when I'd count the street lights from his place to mine, knowing when I counted to eight it meant we'd be parting soon, and I'd have to go back to my mom.

"I know," he whispers back, eyes on the road.

"My depression... the waters," I say, trying to explain in a way I hope he'll understand. "They got the highest they ever were that first time I left. I thought I was going to drown."

His hand reaches out for mine, grabbing it and squeezing hard.

We're silent for the rest of the drive, silent as he parks in my driveway and as he opens my door and twines his fingers with mine. We stopped at the top of the steps of the porch he fixed for me.

Finally, I stop and stare at him, remembering Beckett's words again.

Are you too scared to reach for something beautiful?

No. No, I'm not. I've let fear win for too long. Where has that gotten me?

"I'm not scared of the water anymore, Riggins," I say, looking at him. His hand lifts, brushing his hair back. "I'm not scared of drowning." I whisper the words into the night sky and feel the strength the stars have always given me, the courage to speak truths that are too scary to say in the bright light of day.

"Why?" he asks, the simple, small word carrying so much in just a single syllable, a single beat.

"Because I know you'll keep my head above water. You'll build me a boat if I need it." He steps closer until there's no space between us, pressing his forehead to mine and nodding, his skin moving against mine.

"Always, Stella. I'll always be there, waiting for you on the other side. If the waters start to rise, I'll be your lifeboat. And if you need to float in them for a little while, I'll be there holding your hand."

"I'm still scared of you," I whisper.

"I know," he says. "I know." It's a simple admittance, but it means a lot all the same. It means even more when he doesn't try to refute or diminish my fear, just accepts it.

"But I'm not too scared to try again," I whisper.

His eyes close slowly as he takes in a low, deep breath, filling his lungs. "I think that's the most beautiful thing I've ever heard."

NOW

33

BURY ME

STELLA

Standing with Riggins at the top of my steps, the butterflies flutter in my belly like this is our true first date, and I'm nervous for what comes next as if he hasn't kissed me breathless before or seen me naked a million times over.

"So tonight was..." I start, biting my lip with nerves, which is *crazy*.

This is *Riggins*.

The one person on this earth I could always be myself around.

"It was great. Thank you for inviting—" There's no time to continue my ramblings because his hand is on my waist, tugging me close. I let out an *oomph!* as he tugs me in, but I have no time to think when his other hand moves over to my jaw, tipping it up right before his lips are on mine.

With the touch, my body melts, and my arms lift, my fingers twining behind his neck as I move to tiptoes. He kisses me deep and full like he's trying to consume me, but slow as if he's trying to catalog the moment, remember it forever, just in case.

"If you need me to stop, that's okay," he says when he breaks the kiss, his voice low and gravelly. "Last time, we were both lost in emotion. I don't want any regrets this time."

He's right. Last time we were wrapped in too many emotions and while I don't regret it, not in the least, I know that this time would be different. If I invite Riggins inside, if we sleep together, it's because I'm finally agreeing this is something more. Or maybe that we were never anything less. Either way, I can't go back to being just friends, to pushing him away.

If I invite him inside, I'll be accepting I am Riggins' and he is mine, and we're ready to try this again, regardless of my fears.

"But I need you to tell me now. If you need time, I'll give it all to you. But if I follow you into this house, we're making this real again in all the best ways. You'll be mine again." I stare at him for long, long heartbeats, and I can see the nerves and fear in his eyes, but I just smile. I smile, move to my tip toes, and press my lips to his.

I'm not scared.

"Do you want to come in?" I ask in a whisper. His lips tip up in a familiar smile, and he moves. I'm squealing as he lifts me up bridal style and opens my front door. He steps inside, closing the door behind us. Gracie comes running to the door as he does. "Sit, girl. Be good, I've gotta go make mommy feel really fucking good."

I try to fight a laugh, but I can't when I watch her turn and go to the dog bed he brought over for her, like she fully understands and is over our bullshit.

Riggins just keeps walking until we're in my bedroom, letting my body slide down his as he lowers me to the ground, pressing his lips to mine gently, then moving to my neck. His hands move to my back, finding the zipper of my dress and pulling it down.

The loose material falls off my shoulder with a shift of my arms, and then I stand in front of him in just my bra and underwear. His fingers move to the back of my bra, expertly undoing the clasp and letting that fall too, my clothes a puddle at my feet. Once more, he pulls me in tight until I'm flush with his body.

His hands explore, one sliding up into my hair and holding me still as I stare at him as he looks down at me, the other dipping down into the back of my underwear, grabbing a handful of my ass.

My lips tip up because if there's one thing I know about Riggins, it's that he loves my ass. He returns it, then lets his hand shift to the waistband of my underwear, using a thumb to tug it down.

His lips hit mine, kissing me gently and slowly with no real urgency; he works my panties down with one hand until they're low enough that I can help out and step out of them.

Then I'm naked in front of him, my body pressed against his clothes. I try to speak, to tell him I need him, that I want him naked and in me. I want his skin on mine, but the words dry up as his hand moves to my belly and slides down, a rough finger brushing over my clit and then circling it. My knees go a bit weak, and I loop my hands over his shoulders to hold myself up.

"Already so wet," he whispers. "Is this for me?"

I nod, unable to speak as his finger slides further down, gathering my wetness and dragging it up to my clit. I let out a little *ah!* And his head dips down to press kisses against my neck.

The incessant circling continues, my hips bucking to try and get more, and he gives in, sliding down and pushing two fingers inside me. We both groan with the move, and he starts to pump them in and out, slowly fucking me, the heel of his palm grinding against my clit as he does.

"Riggins," I moan breathily, somehow already so close to the edge.

His mouth on my neck nips before his hand leaves me, his lips moving to mine to press once before stepping back. Then I watch as he lifts his fingers, eyes locked on mine, and licks them clean.

"You're evil." He just smiles. I take a step closer. "My turn," I whisper, dying to undress him, to touch and tease him the way he did me. Last time was so rushed, so emotion-filled, I almost feel like I was robbed of the chance to explore this version of him I don't know.

His hands go out, offering me full access, and I nearly shiver at the opportunity. I start with his tee, tugging it up and over his head, tossing it in the corner, and moving to the button of his jeans. Before I unbutton them, I press kisses to the skin across his chest.

His fingers move to rub at my scalp, push my hair back. He can't keep his hands off me and I don't mind.

I keep moving, pressing kisses down his stomach as I do, marveling at how his muscles tense and tighten as I move lower.

"Stella," he says.

I ignore him, my thumbs hooking into his underwear and jeans before pulling them down. Finally, I'm on my knees and he's watching, looking down at me. My pussy clenches at the look of it, of him towering over me, me on my knees before him. Lifting my hand, I grip and tug his cock the way I remember he liked before tapping my tongue on the head.

Riggs watches each and every move, every movement of my tongue, as I circle the swollen head of his cock.

Finally, I close my lips around it, tasting the precum there and letting out a low moan as I suck lightly. My eyes stay on him the entire time, so I know he likes it, watching his eyes drift close with pleasure, which is why I'm confused when he stops me.

"No," he says, shaking his head and using a hand to collect my hair. Pushing it over my shoulder. "No, not this time, beautiful girl." I fight the urge to feel like I'm being rejected. He sees that and bends, grabbing me under my armpits before pulling me up and sitting me on the edge of my tall bed.

"Any other time, little star, I'd be fucking feral, looking at you on your knees for me, pink lips wrapped around my cock." He pushes me back, then pulls on my legs, tugging my ass to the foot of the bed. His thumbs move to either side of my pussy, spreading and looking at me before running a finger up my center, stopping to circle my clit before repeating the circuit.

"Right now, I really want to make my wife come."

"Oh, god," I moan as his fingers slide into me.

"Jesus fuck, you're wet. Is that what having my cock in your mouth did to you?" he asks, and I can't do much more than a nod as he crooks his finger inside of me.

"Play with your tits, Stell. I remember you used to like that, to play with yourself while I play with you."

Gone is goofy Riggs.

Gone is the sweet one, the one desperate to prove himself to me.

Gone is Riggins, my friend.

In his place is this new version I've barely met, this one who commands my body, who I can't do anything but obey.

So I do.

He smiles when he sees it.

"Even all these years later, you're still my good girl, aren't you?"

And now, this new version is also *talkative*. My pussy clenches, and his lips tip up.

"Huh. Seems my girl likes me talking to her. What else does she like now?" His thumb moves to my clit, rubbing once, twice, and my hips buck.

"Mmm, she definitely likes that. Well, you've been pretty good; why don't I let you choose?" I groan, and somehow, his smile gets even wider. He's getting some kind of sick joy from this, from watching me suffer. "I make you come on my fingers, or I make you come on my cock. Which do you choose, Stella?"

I don't take a moment to consider, spitting the words out. "Your cock, Riggins. Please."

He barks out a laugh, and it's funny, in a way, to be this turned on and still find things funny. I'm reminded of the days when things were easy when *we* were easy.

All thoughts of easy are gone when he takes the head of his thick cock and runs it through my dripping pussy, pulling a deep, pained groan from him. My hands on my breasts tighten.

Finally, he notches the head and slides into me, slow and careful, stretching me wonderfully. His eyes are locked to mine like he's reading me, looking for any shift or change in my demeanor. He slides halfway out gently before sliding back in.

He's being careful.

He's being gentle.

I hate it. I need the passion and the excitement and the lack of restraint that is Riggins and I now.

"Let go," I groan, my fingers digging into his head. "Please, god. I'm not fragile. Fuck me, Riggins," I moan. He stops completely, buried deep, before his eyes go dark.

"You don't want gentle," he says, and I shake my head, hand moving to dig my nails in his back to get him closer, to get more.

"I want you, Riggins. I want whatever you can give me." His lips tip up but not in the playful way from before. In a wild way, that has me clenching on him as he slides out once more.

Finally, he gives me him.

He slams back into me with no restraint, and I moan loudly, my head snapping back as I do. The fire instantly ignites in my belly, and my nails dig in as he slides out and in again. His eyes survey my body as he moves, as one hand moves to my breast, tugging roughly on my nipple.

He watches with rapt fascination as he pounds into me, as I not only take his thrusts but arch into them, begging for more.

"Fuck, Stell. Look at you. Loved you then, loved fucking you then, but love you even more now." I moan at his words, writhing, feeling it crest and crest, the pressure building in my belly. He continues to speak through gritted teeth. "Love that I know you can take me, that you love when I'm fucking you hard and take what I need."

"Yes, yes, Riggs. God, yes. Whatever you need." I'm floating, lightheaded with pleasure and desire, and Riggins and all things bright and shiny and happy.

"You're mine, Stella."

"Riggins—" I moan,

"No." A deep groan leaves his lips, but he keeps slamming into me, harder now, a hand on each side of my hips using me as leverage to slam deeper, harder with each thrust. Each move pulls a deep groan from his chest, and I can't do much more than look up at him, take what he's willing to give me and feel every sensation.

"Now take your hand and rub your clit until you moan my name as you come. You moan, and I'll fill you up with my cum. Then you're gonna know that even as it drips out of you, you're mine. Forever, Stella."

That's all it takes. My hand is barely even on my clit when my back arches, when I scream his name, clamping down on him and coming harder than I ever have in my life. My body feels on fire as he continues to slam into me, groaning out bits of words and phrases like *beautiful* and *fuck* and *so good* before he finally shouts *Fuck, Stella!* As he buries himself as deep as he can.

The feel of him spilling into me triggers another small orgasm, my body shaking before I go limp beneath him, totally spent and completely changed.

THEN

Things have been good. So good, I'm scared to jinx it. Every night, Riggins is by my side, no longer partying every night. On nights there's a show, we all go out together and drink and have fun, but it's controlled, easy. Fun.

No more beers when he wakes up, no more kissing him with vodka on his lips, no more feeling like I have to keep up with him. Even the guys seem more relaxed. I hadn't realized how on edge they were until the big blow up, but now that everything is out in the open, it feels like a weight has been lifted.

My body feels euphoric, my mind open again so words and lines and lyrics are coming back to me. I've written more in the last month than I had the entire tour.

And now we're in Las Vegas. The city of sin and lights and excitement. I'd been excited about this stop since I saw it on the schedule. I thought we could explore the city with the extra day here before the first show tomorrow since it's a bucket list city for me, but it seems I've brought the rain with me, dragging it from the East Coast to the place where it rarely ever rains.

"I brought the rain," I say to Riggins as we look out the window of the bus. He laughs, pushing my hair behind my shoulder.

"I love the rain," he whispers in my ear, sending a chill down my spine. "Always reminds me of you. Of the rain and the stars. Of the first time I kissed you."

"Can't see the stars if it's raining, you know."

"If I'm with you, there's always stars, Stell. My own personal sun." I laugh loudly, turning to look at him, and he shifts me so I'm in his lap, hand on my jaw.

He's so fucking handsome. His hair has some lighter highlights in it from the sun, from my forcing him to sit on beaches and explore anytime we have a free day in a new place. He'd drag me around, showing me the places he bought me postcards from if it was a stop they had made with the last tour or showing me the location on the postcard.

This tour still has two months to go, but it's been utterly life-changing. Everything I hoped for and so much more. Everything we pondered on as kids under the stars, making wishes on shooting stars.

"What should we do today?" I ask, my lips pressing to his neck. "We've got a whole day in Vegas, just me and you." The guys ran off the second the bus stopped, excited for what I'm sure was a night of debauchery, but we stayed behind for some much-needed alone time.

"What are you thinking?" he asks, his arm wrapped around my waist tightening.

"Not sure. I'm too young for gambling," I say, biting my lip, the same nerves and guilt I always feel creeping in.

"Gambling is overrated," he whispers, lips on my neck, scruff scratching at my skin.

"There's uh, we can explore the casinos," I suggest. "Go shopping?" He laughs, knowing I hate shopping, that my mother's sole version of spending quality time with her daughters was spending too much money together, making it an unpleasant pastime for me.

"Or..." I say, trying to think as he turns me in his arms so we're face to face. I look up at him, his lips tipped and his eyes dreamy as he looks at me, his thumb brushing my cheek.

"Let's get married," he says low, his finger running through my hair, but it's dislodged when I jerk my head to look at him.

"What?"

"Let's do it. Let's get married."

"Riggs, we can't, we—" I stutter, trying to calm my heart.

"Why not?"

"Uh, because we're barely even engaged, and we have no papers or anything." I stare at him, my head spinning. I keep making jokes about getting married now that we're engaged, but he usually rolls his eyes and laughs at me, telling me we need to wait until the tour is over and...

"Papers?" he asks, confused.

"To protect you," I say, my brows furrowed. "Prenups and agreements. We need a lawyer and—"

"We don't need a prenup."

I tip my head and give him a look. He loves me; I know that. But even I, a hopeless romantic, standing in front of the only boy I've ever loved in my life, know he needs a prenuptial agreement. Even though I have absolutely zero interest in whatever money he has or might one day have, I want him to have that protection.

"Riggs, you're.. you're growing. Quickly. You're going to be huge by this time next year. We should make sure you're protected or something, we should—"

He shakes his head, pressing his lips to mine, his face shifting to that childlike excitement I've seen before. The kind that always makes me giddy and excited to be beside him, to be his.

"You're not going to leave me, right? Run and try to take all of my money?"

I give him a look that says you're insane because he is. "No, of course not, I'd never—"

"And you love me, right?"

"Of course, honey, I just—"

"Then let's do it." He steps back, and he's smiling wide, and it's hard not to feel that excitement, to get wrapped up in it just as well as his hand reaches for mine.

"Riggins."

"I love you, Stella. I'll love you until I die. I'll love you until I'm compost. Until I'm nothing more than food for the worms," he says, his voice a low rumble, something I feel more than see as he's pulled me up against him again.

"That's pretty fucked up, Riggs."

"It's true, is what it is." He stares at me for long beats and I let him, taking in his face all the same. The face I've loved for so long, I could draw it in my sleep if I had any real drawing skill. I scan it for mistruths and concerns but find nothing. Nothing but love for me.

"I love you, Riggins." It feels like a confession and agreement all the same, and somehow he knows. He knows this is my way of him winning, of agreeing.

"Then let's do it," he whispers, his lips ghosting mine. "Let's get married, make you mine for real."

"You're sure?" I ask in a whisper.

"Never been more sure of anything in my entire life."

NOW

35

A TROUBLED MIND

STELLA

Tires crunch on my drive and when I look out the window, a thrill runs through me when I see Evie's car rolling up. Gracie scratches at the door and when her car stops, I let her out, following close behind and watching my twin kneel down and scratch behind my dog's ears.

"What a good girl, Gracie! You love your aunt Evie, don't you?"

Something about that hits me deep in my gut. When Riggs and I broke up, I thought any chance for a family of my own and, in turn, Evie being an aunt to my kids was gone. But suddenly, the warm glow of the future isn't so far anymore.

"Hey, sissy," she says, standing up and walking toward the porch. "Got time for a coffee with your favorite human on the planet?"

"Is Reed here?" I ask jokingly, looking behind her. She rolls her big eyes and slaps my arm before walking past me and into my house. Gracie and I follow her, and I find her at my coffee pot, the cabinet where I keep my syrups open.

"What kick are you on today?" she asks. "Peppermint mocha? Caramel?"

I move to follow her, sitting on the stool at my kitchen island. "Neither."

She stops moving altogether and stares at me, eyes wide. I fight a laugh.

I'm so glad she came over today. This is exactly what I needed, my sister picking at me instead of my mind continuing to wander and replay the events of the last few weeks over, dissecting them until I start to find faults in the beauty of it all.

"Sugar cookie," I say, letting her off the hook with a laugh. "It's hidden behind the rest because I'm obsessed and don't want it gone.".

"Well, now I know, what if I use it."

"Please, do. I'd love you to see how much better it is than your zero calorie sweeteners and skim milk," I say, giving her a look. "And mom won't come ragging in, somehow sensing it."

"Stella—" she says, her voice tense.

After my argument with my mother, after everything went down, she called me to tell me no matter what our mother says, she's not going to cut me off. It would be like cutting off a limb. While I'm pretty much at the breaking point with our mother, it's harder for Evie to cut free from her. Every molecule of her self worth is tied with approval from her.

It worries me, but I won't tell her that.

"A latte, please," I say, skipping past that conversation.

She stares at me for a moment then nods and makes our drinks in silence.

In the summers after college and after school in high school, we both worked at the diner so she knows how to make a solid latte. Still, back then, I always held a grudge over my sister, who was often told she would get paid if she missed work for any of the mother-approved activities she was signed up for.

I never got a free pass because all I ever wanted to do was sit in the woods with Riggins and write music, and that was absolutely not on the approved list.

Ironic, really, considering that after all those years of competitive cheer and dance and taking etiquette classes between pointe classes and tumbling days, she went to college out of state and fell in love with journalism. Music journalism, to be exact.

"What brings you to my humble abode today?" I ask her as she sits at the island, sliding a mug to me.

"I'm in between assignments, so I have some extra time on my hands. I wanted to see what the uglier twin was doing." I glare at her, and she smiles wide, the dimple I once was so jealous about popping up. I ball up my napkin and toss it at her, hitting her between the eyes.

"Why are you like this?" I ask.

"Because we didn't fight nearly enough as kids. Feels like a right of passage we missed."

"What childhood were you living?" I ask, with a laugh. "I feel like all we did was fight."

"No, we argued about whatever bullshit mom was making us battle over. We were children forced into a gladiator arena, begging to survive."

I tip my head to the side and don't argue because she's not wrong.

"Anyway, obviously, I came here to ask about last night." I avert my eyes, suddenly very interested in my drink. "Well, how was it?"

"How was what?" I lift my drink and take a sip at the worst moment.

"Fucking Riggins. Your husband. How was it?" I choke on my drink as she laughs, standing to grab a paper towel and handing it to me.

"How did you—" I ask once I catch my breath.

She rolls her eyes. "I'm your twin sister, Stella."

"Does that mean you have a direct line to my vagina?"

She screws her face up in disgust. "God, no, you weirdo. I just can see you've got that freshly fucked happy face on."

I stare at her, trying to decide how to answer. It only takes a moment to realize there's no getting around it, so I just spill. "It was good, Evie. Like, oh my fucking god, toe-curling, better than I ever remembered, meant to be kind of good."

"Meant to be kind of good?"

I shrug. Lying to Evie is like lying to myself: there's no point in it. "I don't know. It's all very messy still. *We're* very messy, but... it feels natural, being with him again; it feels right. Like a part of me has returned back to my soul. Like I'm whole again."

"You seemed it," she says. "At Beckett's party. Happy. I haven't seen you that happy since..." her words trail off but I know the answer. Since the last time I was with Riggins and the guys.

"Yeah," I say. "By the way, where did you go? You ran off, and then I never saw you again. I only knew you were alive because I checked your location."

"You checked my location?" she asks with a squeak.

Weird.

"Well, yeah. I saw you were home this morning." Her shoulders ease and I file that away for later, something to try and pick apart and understand. She clearly doesn't want to be on that subject, so I change it away from all things Riggs and Atlas Oaks.

"So, what's going on with work?" A few months ago, Evie got hired at one of the biggest music magazines in the country, writing articles about the industry. "What did you just wrap up?"

She rolls her lips into her mouth to hide a proud smile and looks at the table, before putting her mask on again and looking at me.

That? That I recognize. I perfected it long, long ago, hiding the pride of something I felt I accomplished because our mother would see it as a weak spot, something for her to pick at and tear apart.

Got a 96 on a test? *What are you an idiot? You could have gotten a 100.*

Soccer team won? *Fine, I guess, but did you make any goals personally?*

"Evie! What is it?"

"Headlining article," she says, no longer able to hide her excitement. "A cover deal. 1o-page spread. About Rainy Daze." My jaw drops.

"Everest! I cannot believe you didn't tell me! Shut up! Congrats! That's huge! Is that where you were last month?" Her smile widens, and she nods.

"I didn't know if they were going to go with my angle because it's something new, I thought up, but it was a blast. I also didn't want to tell you because.. well... you know."

I do, unfortunately. For years, Evie has tiptoed around all things music industry around me, especially if it's someone I ever once knew in a personal way in another lifetime.

"I know, but who cares? I'm so mad at you for not telling me," I say.

"I'm doing more," she says, her words low and nervous. My eyes widen.

"More?" Her smile widens and her mask shatters and I know... I know she's been dying to tell me all about this, but was too nervous it would send me spiraling.

"It's something I pitched, inspired by... well you. And the guys. And the diner. How they'd come there after local shows and eat breakfast hungover to decompress. You said they did it on the road, too." I nod, because we did. We'd go to some local diner hungover and eat breakfast together no matter what. It was a ritual I missed when I left. "I'm going on tour with a band for a month, and every Sunday, we'll go to a diner, and I'll get to interview them."

"What about the rest of the month? Or is it just Sundays?"

"I'll see how they spend their free time, how they get ready for a show, how they interact with fans. A full, in-depth article about life on the road with whoever the magazine sends me to talk to." My mouth drops open with shock.

"Why... Why didn't you tell me?" I ask, and the betrayal is clear in my voice. I wish it wasn't, but I can't help it.

"Oh, Stell," she says, reaching over and grabbing my hand. "I didn't..." There's a pause before she squeezes my hand, and her smile turns sad.

God, I hate that look.

"I'm fine, Evie," I say, trying to reassure her. "You're my sister. My twin. I want to know when something exciting like this happens!"

"I know. I know. It was shitty of me. I meant well, I was just... nervous." I nod, understanding. She's seen what my episodes can look like and how memories can trigger them. "But now it feels... it feels like everything is falling into place."

I can't fight the smile that pulls at my lips again when I nod.

"It does. It feels like everything is where it should be. Like the universe is righting itself. I'm..." I hesitate to explain, to confess, scared that saying it out loud will jinx it. "I'm happy, Evie. I feel like a part of me is back." She gives me a small smile and squeezes the hand she's still holding.

"Are you scared?"

I almost answer instantly, almost reply with a no, and then almost jump in with a yes, but then I stop and think. I let it bubble in my belly, let the question really penetrate.

"Of Riggins?" I ask, clarifying so I can give some modicum of a real answer. The one person I've never in my life lied to is my sister, and I don't want to start now.

She nods. "Of Riggins. Of starting things with him. Or continuing them. Are you scared of being... together again?"

Saying yes feels like a betrayal to Riggs, a betrayal to everything he's done and all the progress he's made.

But saying no feels like a betrayal to my soul, a lie of the worst degree.

Am I scared?

I use my sister as a sounding board, bouncing ideas and thoughts off of her.

"I.... Yes. And no? I'm not scared of his sobriety. I'm not scared that he's going to hurt me again with that." Her face softens like she's happy with that answer, and I am, too, because it's not a lie.

Not a single part of me doubts Riggins' sobriety or his commitment to it. He's clean, and he seems completely content with that. It's clear the band is heavily supporting that effort.

But while that was a big part of why things went to hell, it wasn't the only thing.

"But I don't know where I fit," I whisper, suddenly anxious and uneasy. I feel weird saying that out loud and telling my sister that. Admitting it. It feels childish and selfish. "He's Riggins. He's a rock star. The band is monumental, and I just feel... I'm just Stella. I don't know where I fit in there. I think I struggled with it then, too, but now that I'm older, I can't just ignore it."

"You fit with him, Stell. You fit with Riggins, and you fit with the band. It was clear to everyone then, and it was even clearer at Beck's party."

"You think so?" I ask, hope blossoming in my chest.

"You know it's true. You just have to take the jump and believe it, too."

NOW

36

MESS

RIGGINS

Her car in the drive signals her coming home, but so does Gracie's head popping up, ears perking.

Staring at her, I decide Gracie needs a sister. Stella missed most of her puppy years, and I know that has to hurt. My mind runs through options, such as what kind we should get if she should come with me to get it, or if it should be a surprise again. The last time was me being a manipulative shit, me trying to make up for mistakes without doing a damn thing to actually change.

Would it be a red flag to her if I bought another and surprised her with it? Would it bring up bad memories, remind her once again of what a fuck up I was? I am?

I shake my head at the thoughts, instead picking up the glass of orange juice I poured and taking a sip.

She hates orange juice, always has, but she's been stocking it for me. Whether she's doing it consciously or not, it's another sign she's slowly accepting that we are on our way to being something now.

"What are you doing here?" she asks as she walks into the kitchen, where I'm leaning against the countertops that need replacing. The entire kitchen is a country style that doesn't fit my girl one bit, but we'll get to it once we make the upstairs livable.

I set down the glass I'm pretty sure she bought at the thrift store in town. None of her plates, cups, or utensils are the same, yet they all match in a strange way, a skill she had even when we were living together, when we were living off the dregs of my minimal advance and then royalties that took forever to start trickling in.

She'd go into the thrift store in town and leave with an entire set of dishware. None matched, but they were all in the same color family or with the same decoration, so somehow, they worked together.

I reach an arm out as she moves to walk past me and stop her, tugging her close so her front is against mine, my body at ease now that the steady rhythm of her pulse is under my hand.

"Kiss," I whisper, and her eyes go soft even though she fights it.

I used to do that every time she walked in the door, refusing to say a single word to her unless she gave me a kiss. Sometimes just to be a brat, she'd avoid me and give me the silent treatment back, not saying a word, the only clue that she wasn't actually pissed at me being the way the corners of her lips would tip up.

Sometimes, it would go so far that I'd grab her, toss her onto our bed, and plant kisses everywhere but her lips until she was squirming and whining beneath me, finally reaching for my jaw and pressing a kiss to my lips.

Then, of course, I'd finish the job, but I'd do it whispering all of the sweet nothings and dirty promises I'd held at bay until then.

But it doesn't have to go there this time, her chin tipping up, her arm moving behind my neck, pulling my face to hers and pressing a sweet, soft kiss to my lips.

It's shit like this, the simpleness of a hello kiss and having her in my arms, of being here when she came back from running errands that I tend to miss most of all.

The casual, warm love of being with Stella.

"Hey," she whispers against my lips with a dreamy look in her eye when the kiss breaks, and I know she feels it, too. The comfort of us, how easily we've already shifted back into it, into the way we always were and always were supposed to be.

There's a fuck ton for us to work through before we can move forward, but for the first time since I found out what really happened in Las Vegas, I feel like there's hope. A cloud has parted, letting the stars shine through in the dark night sky.

"Hey," I whisper back, my lips brushing hers with the words. "How were your errands?" I asked as her head moves back a bit, so she can look at me.

"Fine. What are you doing here?" Her small hand reaches up and brushes my hair back. I have it in a small bun at the top of my head, but I've never mastered the ability to tie it up and get it all in the bun. Right now, I think I never want to learn. I want to always keep it this length just so she has to repeat that move over and over again.

"I was working on the floors upstairs, then I ran out to get stuff for dinner. I was gonna go back to working on the floors, but then I heard you pulling in."

Her brows furrow. "You're working on my floors?"

"Yeah, well, a bit. I ripped up the carpet. Got a guy coming early tomorrow to drop off a dumpster for all the shit. Some of the old floors underneath are salvageable, but most need removing and replacing." She's staring at me, her mouth open a bit, but I keep going, explaining my thought process. "Baseboards are shot, so I ripped those out, fixed anything that needed patching. Luckily, most of everything is in okay condition, just ugly. Eventually, we'll need to replace the windows since they're drafty and old, but they work for now. Next summer, most likely."

I don't add how I was thinking of having someone come next summer while we're on tour to build an extension or maybe an additional house out on her land, a small recording studio for when the muse hits. If we're going to be staying in Ashford forever, I need a way to record without having to go to the city regularly.

But even I, in my optimistic delusion, can see that would scare

Stella off.

A long beat passes as she lets my words digest, and then finally, she asks, "Why?"

"What?"

"Why are you doing this?" A moment passes as I try to think of the honest way to answer, how to tell her what I'm thinking and feeling.

But I decide this is safe to admit.

"This was always your dream house, Stell. I told you when we were kids I'd fix it up for you. I haven't always kept my word, but I'm trying to change that." Her eyes glaze over, unshed tears shining, but she nods all the same like that's the reasonable, acceptable answer, as if it's not impacting her at all.

"Okay," she says, continuing to nod, then putting her stuff down on the counter, moving her hands to her hair and pulling her hair into a ponytail at the top of head. For a moment I think about how funny we must look together, my bun and her ponytail, but it's gone when she speaks again. "How can I help?"

"What?"

"We always said we'd do it together. What can I do? It was your dream, too, Riggs."

And a part of me thinks this might be it, the small bit of acceptance and acknowledgment of the fact that we have a potential future together.

It's fucking beautiful.

But it makes me want to do other things than work on fixing floorboards.

"You can help by getting your ass into your bed right now," I say, dipping my mouth to her neck as I press my hips to hers. She giggles in a way that heals something in me.

"What?"

"And as much as I like you in my hoodie, take it off. The rest of it, too."

"Riggins!" she says in a squeal as my hand snakes up her shirt, my lips sucking on the spot beneath her ear.

"Got a lot of dreams to make happen, but we've got even more time to make up for."

"It's.... boring," she says, looking around the room we just finished to her exact specifications.

I laugh, the sound deep and echoing around the empty room. God, it feels good, laughing from my soul, the way I always did with her.

"Well, little star, it's exactly how you wanted it." And it is. Dark, thick hardwood planks for the floors, basic, clean baseboards, white walls, and gold hardware on the doors. Nothing special, nothing like Stella or what I would have picked for my bright, colorful girl, but it is what she picked out for herself. After a lifetime of someone else choosing things for her, deciding what she could and should wear or decorate or listen to, she needed the ability to choose for herself even if I knew it wasn't *her*.

"It's just so..." She walks out of arms reach to the center of the room, and I watch her as she walks in circles, looking around with a confused look. I lean in the doorway, crossing my ankles and my arms on my chest, watching her mull it over, trying to find the right words. "Boring. Plain."

"Well, still, it is white walls," I say with a smirk, and I have to fight it so as not to spread into a grin when she sends a glare in my direction.

God, I missed this so much. Missed Stella being herself around me and so unafraid to give me shit. I missed having her as a friend, but when she suggested being friends, I think I knew that would never be enough for me.

"I know, you ass. I just... I don't know. It's not me."

"No, it's not." She keeps looking around, screwing up her face like she's trying to decide what's wrong, what's missing. "What are you thinking, little star?"

"Color," she says instantly, a distracted tone in her words. "Lots of it."

"Then let's go get some color," I say, stepping out of the door frame and moving until she's in front of me. I pull her into my arms. "Let's go get some color, baby."

Her body softens in my hands, her arms moving and draping around my shoulders, a small smile playing on her lips. I kiss her, pressing my lips to hers in a way that once felt expected, natural, normal.

I used to take her kisses for granted, take the way she felt in my arms for granted, because it was all I ever knew. She was all I ever knew, and I had never even thought about a life without her.

Then I lost her.

So, as I kiss her, I make sure to file this and every other kiss she gives me away.

I'm watching her race up and down the aisles of the home improvement store we're in, a pep in her step I haven't seen since she was a kid, long before the tour. It makes me wonder just how long it's been like this, how I missed how much she's been suffering even when she was mine, even before I fell into the depths of alcoholism.

"Look at this one!" she says with a smile, holding up a pink swatch. "It would be so cute with this one." She lifts a bright yellow and then a deeper, darker green. "Flowers!"

"Flowers?"

"Along the baseboards. A little field of flowers. Like the ones that grow in the clearing in the spring and summer." Stella smiles at me, adding moments of our life, our secrets and the bones of who we are into a room in her house.

"Whatever you want, Stell," I say, crossing my arms over the handle of the orange cart filled with painting supplies as she grabs more swatches, excitement, and happiness on her face.

A few minutes pass, and I stay there, watching her, a peace I haven't felt in too long running through me as she grabs colors and puts them together, occasionally shaking or nodding her head.

I missed Stella being Stella, not anxious to plan the future, not lost in the past. It's something I know I'll need to fight to keep, but for now, I'm happy to just live here, bask in the warmth of her happiness.

We're waiting for the paint to be mixed and looking at brushes when familiar notes come through the speakers. I reach forward, grabbing her wrist, her head moving to look at me, a small curious smile on her lips.

"Do you hear it?" I ask, my chin tipping to the open ceiling of the home improvement store.

"Hear wh—" she starts but stops when the noise coming from the speakers hits her ears. One of those top 40 hits stations is on, and right now, our first big hit is playing. My hand moves, and I wrap an arm around her waist, tugging her close, slowly swaying our bodies to the love song we wrote together.

A song about laying under the stars, deciding we were it for each other even though we were young and stupid. A song about finding your person and knowing you'll spend eternity with them.

We sway like that in the paint aisle for a few moments before she speaks.

"I missed you, Riggins," she says, so low I almost don't hear it.

"I promise I missed you more," I tell her, moving to spin her out, watching a smile break over her face, a small giggle leave her lips. She spins back into my arms, and we start swaying again.

"Come on. Let's go paint our house," she says when the song ends, her palms framing my face before she presses a kiss to my lips.

I don't correct her when she calls it *our* house.

I fully plan on making everything ours.

NOW

37

STRAWBERRY WINE

RIGGINS

Hours later, I walk up the stairs to where she's playing loud music in the first finished room. I lean against the doorframe as I watch her draw another green line, adding a few leaves before cleaning off the brush and adding pink to it, painting a flower to the top. She's good at this, decorating and designing. When we were young, she loved making our small space more fun, making it ours.

Whimsical, she called it.

She wanted to live somewhere whimsical and fun, a clear contrast to her childhood home, I think.

Finally, she notices I'm in the doorway, her head picking up to look at me and smile.

She's so fucking beautiful like this, her hair in a ponytail, a swipe of paint on her nose.

"You've got a little..." I say, placing the extra cans of paint I brought upstairs down on the floor and walking toward her. "Right here." My finger taps on her nose where a streak of light blue paint is. "You're a mess," I say, laughing at her. "Maybe we should just rescue your clothes."

She laughs, free and clear, filling the empty room with much-needed life. "What?"

I don't explain with words instead I get to my knees on the cloth tarp beneath her and pinch the old Atlas Oaks tee between my thumb and forefinger. "It's Vintage, OG Atlas merch. You can get good money for this," I say with a smile. "Wouldn't want to get paint on it."

She sets the brushes down and lifts her arms, surprising me. But I don't look a gift horse in the mouth as she lets me take off her shirt, revealing her small breasts and flat stomach. I toss it in the corner.

"Not enough money in the world to get me to sell that," she says. "You see, years and years ago, my husband made it for me."

I ignore the way my heart skips a beat with her words because it's the first time she's acknowledged me as her *husband* outside of an argument or trying to patch up my torn knuckles. Instead, I remember the time when she was 15 and the band and I decided we wanted to give a real go at this. We were playing small venues and kids' basements and a few shows at the Atlas, but we really only had one true fan.

Stella.

So, for her 16th birthday, we made her a stack of Atlas Oaks Shirts.

"Besides, how is taking *off* my shirt supposed to make less of a mess?" She's in just a pair of boy short underwear because she didn't want to get paint on another pair of pants.

I follow suit, taking off my tee so I'm just wearing my jeans. I try to fight a smile when her eyes trail over my body as I toss my shirt in the pile with hers. Then I bend, grabbing a paintbrush with green paint on it, stepping closer to her.

"Don't you *dare.*" I move forward. "Riggins," she says in warning, but I get closer still. She tries to scramble back, but I get her with a swipe of color across her stomach. "Riggins!" The shock doesn't last long, though.

Quickly, she grabs a brush, dipping it in blue, and comes back at me, hitting me in the shoulder. I laugh, taking off my pants so they don't get destroyed, and then I go after her, swiping more paint across her nipple.

"Ahh! You're going to get it," she shouts.

We move like this for a while, chasing each other with paint brushes and swiping color across our skin before I decide I want more, putting mine down and grabbing her. We faux wrestle for a bit until finally, I have her exactly where I want her.

"I win, which means I get to do whatever I want to you," I murmur against her lips. Even now, though, she's stubborn.

"What makes you think you win?"

"You're pinned beneath me, Stella. I think that means I win." She glares and I can't stop laughing. "Now, I'm going to move, but my prize is I get to paint a picture on your stomach." Her eyes go wide with heat and excitement and I have to force back yet another a laugh.

God, when was the last time I laughed this much? The last time I was this free? Probably well over seven years ago.

"Not with my cum, Stell. Maybe next time. Now close your eyes so it will be a surprise." She scrunches her nose in irritation, and again, my laugh echoes around the empty room.

"Now be still, Stella." She giggles, but it turns to a low moan as the cool paintbrush moves across her belly and closer to her pussy, then way. She tries to look down, but I push her face up again.

"What are you *doing?*" she asks.

"I'm making art, Stella. Be patient." I continue, grabbing more paint and liking the heated sigh that leaves her lips as the cold paint touches her skin again. Enough that I decide she deserves a prize for being so good, moving my fingers between her legs, gently rubbing her clit. When her hips buck, I tut at her, moving away from her with a smile.

"Riggins!" Her eyes start to open.

"Closed, Stella. Keep your eyes closed and stay still while I make you my masterpiece, or you're never going to come." She groans but closes her eyes again. I brush a few more swipes of the paint against her belly, watching her muscles tense and flex as I do until I'm done.

"You can look," I say and instantly she opens her eyes, moving to her elbows and looking down.

"Riggins loves Stella," she says quietly with a small smile at the messy letters I wrote on her skin. "You're kind of a softie, you know."

"Mmm, would a softie do this?" I ask, moving my fingers to her pussy and sliding them in. A quiet *ahh!* leaves her lips.

I finger her, watching her body accept me, listening and feeling how wet she already is, and my free hand moves to my cock, starting to stroke as I watch myself work her.

"Oh, fuck, Riggins," she says, eyes stuck on where my hand is pumping my cock. "God, that's so hot."

"You like that? You like seeing how fucking hard you make me?" Her eyes move to me, then back to my cock, and she nods. I crook my fingers inside her, and she moans again.

Perfect.

She's absolutely perfect for me. My balls tighten just watching her, knowing I'm the one bringing her pleasure, but I refuse to come anywhere but inside her.

"Stella"

She starts coming, her back arching, her body shaking as I press into her spot, but I don't stop despite her coming. Her moans turn frantic like she can't handle what's happening to her, and one of her hands slams frantically into the pallet of paints.

I can't even laugh.

Especially not when that hand, coated in pinks and purples, moves to her breast, grabbing and tugging at her nipple.

And not when she screams my name, a second hard climax ripping through her. I realize the first was just an intro, but this one now controls her. I keep jacking my cock, edging myself as I watch her body convulse as she frantically moans my name, stopping only after I move my hand away.

Her body goes limp. "I'm not done with you, Stella," I say, and she lifts her head, quirking a brow at me. I smile as I use my soaking hand to coat my cock, sliding it up and down, twisting at the head, and groaning as I do. Her mouth drops just a bit, watching, and I watch the fire in her reignite.

"God, a fucking dream you are. Ready?" I ask as I line myself up with her dripping wet pussy. She nods, and I slide in slowly, inch by inch.

When I'm planted inside, I look in her eyes.

"You're mine, Stella. This place, it's ours. This life? We're going to share it." She opens her mouth to say something, but I pull out and then slam back in, her eyes drifting shut with pleasure. My hand moves to her clit, rubbing quickly because I know I won't last long, and she needs to get there again. "I'm going to fuck you every day, listen to you moan my name every time I make you come. We're going to live a good life from here on out, Stella."

Her hand moves to my forearm, planted on the ground beside her hips, smearing paint and squeezing, a silent confirmation when words won't work.

I move one of her legs up, letting it drape along my shoulder, and we moan in unison at the new angle, the new depth. It makes her pussy squeeze me even tighter.

"Fuck, Stella. You feel so fucking good. I love this pussy. Is it mine?" She nods, but that's not enough. "Use your words, Stell. Tell me you're mine."

"I'm yours, Riggs," she moans. "All of me is yours."

Her words take me over the edge, the way she quivers around me, the way her small tits bounce each time I pound into her.

"Come for me, little star," I say through gritted teeth, my eyes locked on where my cock is disappearing in her cunt as I fuck her. "Now."

It's all it takes. It's all it ever seems to take these days, a rough demand and getting my cock deep. Stella screams my name, the empty room making it echo in the most erotic symphony I've ever heard, and with it, I bury deep, groaning her name as I spill inside of her.

"I love this room," she whispers, breaking the silence. We're still on the floor of the room, the old sheet all bunched beneath us. There's paint in her hair, splotches and splatters, and a few smears from my hands, but somehow, it looks good, great even. She looks free and easy.

She looks like mine.

Especially when I see the paint dried on my one hand, the hand that matches the handprint on her hip where I held her. Our bodies are a map of what happened in this room not too long ago, where my fingers traveled and where hers moved; her breasts are covered in a happy sunshine yellow, and her belly is filled with shades of pink and red.

I'd take a photo, but I know I'll never forget the way she looks right now.

"Yeah?" I ask, my fingers starting to trace some of the swirls and dots, committing them to memory.

She nods. "The light is great, but it's the quietest room in the house. It is far enough from the kitchen and living room that if some-one's down there, you can't hear anything really. I used to hide up here when they were doing work in the kitchen, could barely hear when they left for the day." I hum but don't speak, hating that she did even a part of this house alone, that my touch isn't on every update she made to it.

The place we once thought would be ours.

But I'm shaken from that with her next words, words she clearly doesn't overthink much because her body stills when she says them, like she wishes she could take them back or is hoping I didn't hear them.

"I always thought it would make a good nursery."

But I do hear the words.

Her body doesn't move a centimeter as she waits to see if I heard her or understood what she was saying, what she didn't mean to reveal.

It's like she's worried it will anger me or that she's crossed some line, which is fucking insane because she's Stella, and I'm Riggins, and we were always meant to be here, to be us. To be in this house talking about nurseries and which rooms would be best for one.

It just took us a fuck of a lot longer to get here than I anticipated.

"How many?" I say, the words low as I try to leave my pain out of them, the pain of knowing we lost seven years before we could have this conversation.

"How many?" she asks, confused, like now that she accidentally spoke out loud, she's careful with her words to make sure it doesn't happen again.

"How many kids do you want?"

"I—"

"Twins are in your blood, which would be cool. I always loved seeing you and Evie, your bond. I hated not having siblings, so I definitely don't want less than two. I think three would be good, but I wouldn't be the one carrying them." My hand splays over her belly, suddenly incredibly intrigued by the idea of her swelling with our child.

God, where did this all come from?

"Three?"

"Well, yeah. If we had twins, though, maybe four. The third would always be on the outs, not having that bond. But what do I know? Maybe that's not how it works." She lets my words work through her mind, confused still, and I fight a smile, knowing it would just annoy her.

"You're... you're talking about babies."

"I mean, I'm not talking about dogs. Though, I do want another of those, too. Gracie's getting old." Her face somehow gets softer, as if she can't believe this is happening. "You were talking about nurseries, and I don't think you meant plants." My mind starts working, and suddenly I'm nervous.

"Unless you were, with all the light talk. I just—"

"No, no. I was..." There's a pause before she finally touches me, her hand covering mine over her stomach.

God.

That feels so good. So goddamned right.

"You had it right. I just... I'm surprised."

"Why would you be surprised?"

"We never..." There's a pause, and she licks her lips before moving forward, where she clearly doesn't feel comfortable. "We never talked about this kind of stuff back then."

"Yeah, but we are now," I say, a million different things in those few words. I wonder if she knows what they mean to me, if she understands fully.

Because suddenly, it feels like there is a future for us.

And it's going to be beautiful.

Two days later, when she finishes painting her flowers, and I've finished getting some of the paint off the hardwood, I notice a new frame in her bedroom with a piece of the cloth we fucked on.

God, I love this woman.

NOW

38

CYNIC

STELLA

We get a week.

One week of blissful togetherness, of normalcy, and living in the now before reality comes crashing in.

Break

Riggins is at his AA meeting while I make dinner for both of us when I decide to shuffle out to the mailbox and grab the mail. Walking back to the house, I tuck a package I ordered under my arm as I sort through the envelopes. I move past a royalty check, a magazine, spam, spam, spam, catalogue, spam, then—weird.

My hand pauses and my feet stop moving toward the door, a white envelope in hand. An unlabeled envelope. I flip it over and see both sides are blank.

Weird.

I move up the stairs, staring at that envelope while I push open my front door and close it behind me. Gracie bumps against my legs as if I've been gone for a year instead of two minutes, but I barely realize she's there.

Instead, I walk to the kitchen island, dump the rest of the mail on the counter, the package I'd been waiting for long forgotten, and flip the envelope over. There's something inside, a stack of papers, I think, but nothing on the outside. How did it even get to me? I'd like to believe I would have noticed a car driving up or someone putting something in my mailbox, but I know that's not true.

Anyone could have delivered an envelope without me noticing.

A fan, maybe? My name is officially splashed across the internet, so tabloids won't take long to figure out who I really am, to find the marriage documents from Vegas. As soon as I saw the first headline of *Riggins Greene's Secret Wife Revealed!* I stopped checking, living in the bliss of not knowing.

Something tells me that it's all about to end.

Slowly, like it's a Pandora's box and I'm about to release something terrible into my world, I slide my finger under the flap.

Am I? Am I about to ruin everything? I asked myself.

Still, I break the seal, the paper ripping and revealing colorful papers beneath. Slowly, I pull them out.

The acid in my stomach churns as it comes to understanding what they are, what I'm looking at.

Articles from the last week about our marriage. About Riggins' history, relaying all the gory details of our breakup. Another with details about the DUI the record label concealed and his rehab trip, speculation about how it happened when he came home.

There's even a photo of me holding his hand at his father's funeral. Then there's an article about *me*—Everything you need to know about Stella Hart, Atlas Oaks' front man's secret wife. Quotes from artists I've worked with, people in town who know me or think they do.

It all feels horribly invasive as if I no longer have control or privacy.

The room starts to shrink around me, dark blue waters lapping at my ankles as I lay all of them out on the counter. Some are painting me as a home-wrecker, sympathetic articles about Willa Stone, the *heartbroken pop star*.

The public doesn't know about the fake relationship they sold too well.

I should have known this would happen. Even when we were together, when the press was just barely starting to get interested in Riggins and the band, the shit they'd publish was ridiculous, so far from reality that sometimes, we'd laugh about it.

But right now, as I carefully spread the photos and articles on my kitchen island, I can't find any humor in it. Not when front and center is an article showing Riggins out partying, clearly wasted beyond recognition, the photo allegedly taken the night I left. While I was on a plane back to New Jersey, sobbing the whole way, he was out partying.

It looks strange right next to a photo of me in a white dress we bought on the strip, Riggins in his usual dark jeans and a tee, standing in front of an officiant at a little chapel in Vegas. How the press got that photo, I don't know. *I* don't even have a copy of it.

All I can remember is how fucking hopeful I was at that moment and how it all came tumbling the next day. For the first time in a week, I wonder if I can do this. If I can handle the scrutiny of the media, the constant reminder of the hurdles we've jumped.

For the first time, reality hits me. I told him I was ready to try, but I didn't think about the outside world when I made that jump. I didn't think about the scrutiny I would face, that we would face, and if I was strong enough to withstand it.

Can I do this?

Can I handle this? My mental state is fragile as it is, so can I endure the constant reminders of the most painful days of my life?

For the first time since that day, I let my brain go back to that morning, dissecting where we went wrong, the moment Riggins broke my heart, and I let myself wonder if this fairytale we've been living in for a week can ever overcome that.

THEN

39

CATASTROPHIZE

STELLA

When I wake the next morning, I'm the happiest I've ever been. I'm a bit hungover, and for a moment, I think that splitting a bottle of champagne was probably not the best idea we've had, especially since I've been the one asking him to drink a bit less, but it was a special occasion.

We got *married!*

I shift a bit, doing a total body scan to see how I feel, and I'm pleased when the only real discomfort is a slight headache and an ache in my wrist. Last night, right after we got married, we went down to a tattoo shop, where I got my first tattoo. A small heart is on the wrist of my left hand, and the letter R is inside of the heart. Riggs got a star for Stella in the same place, a star I can just barely see from where he's curled up on the bed.

He looks so fucking handsome, peacefully sleeping, his hair a mess, his face soft and boyish, and I start to tear up for a moment like the sap I am, thinking about how I get to wake up to him for the rest of my life.

All of my dreams are coming true.

We can now travel the world together, write songs, and be

together. I can sit at the wings of the stage and watch him play and live out his dreams. I'll write music for Atlas Oaks and other bands who have already started to reach out to me about ghostwriting. Eventually, we'll start a family, and we'll bring our kids on the road with us and have our home base in Ashford. We'll take them to our spot in the woods and show them where we fell in love.

Love songs start twining through my mind, and I wonder how long we have until soundcheck if it's enough time to get Riggs' guitar and start playing around with a new song.

My giddiness must be contagious because slowly, I watch Riggs start to stir, and I reach up, brushing his hair back from his face. When his eyes open, his greens out of focus, I whisper, "Good morning, husband," with what I know is a goofy smile.

He blinks again, one, twice, three times, then smiles a bit wonky.

"Husband, huh?" He asks, slowly sitting up and leaning against the headboard, pulling me in close.

"Well, yeah," I say with a small laugh.

Riggs presses his lips to my hair. "One day, soon. Once tour is over," he says.

And suddenly, my bright, golden morning has a rain cloud.

"What?" I asked, hoping I heard him wrong.

He speaks into my hair, oblivious to the panic coursing through me. "You know I can't wait to marry you, but we're going to do it right when it finally happens." The world spins as he pulls back and sits up. I watch him stretch, but the confusion and nausea that hits me has nothing to do with the champagne. "What happened last night?" he asks, looking around the room. With the words, my gut drops to my feet.

"What?"

"What happened? How'd we get here?" He looks around the bridal suite of the hotel he insisted we stay in last night to celebrate, and I think I'm going to vomit.

"I don't... we... You don't remember last night?" I ask, and he stares at me, slowly blinking as the pieces come together. I close my eyes and breathe deeply before asking my question. "Were you... were you drunk last night?" Suddenly, he looks nervous. Anxious, even. He tips his head, giving me a boyish smile that usually works at easing my concerns.

"Just a little," he says.

"Just a little? You don't forget an entire night after just a little bit of drinking. When did you start drinking, Riggins? Where was I? I would remember you drinking enough to black out."

"Come on, Stell. Don't be like that."

Don't be like that.

Don't be like that.

He doesn't remember last night.

He doesn't remember getting married. Doesn't know it happened. The ring he slid onto my finger feels heavy and hot, just like the tears burning behind my eyes.

He was drunk.

Was it my fault? I ordered the champagne. It was my idea. I shouldn't have done that. I'm the one who's been asking him to slow it down, and there I was, asking him to do the exact opposite.

But I didn't black out, and my tolerance is obviously lower than his.

He leans over to the bedside table and grabs his phone, completely immune to the panic I'm feeling. "Fuck, the guys texted. I'm late for sound check." He stands, looking around and pulling on his jeans. "You good here?" I stare, feeling my heart breaking with an understanding of what happened and uncertainty about what to do next. I nod weakly, and he looks around his brow furrowing.

"Hey, hey," he says, moving to where I'm now sitting in the bed and pulling me into his arms. "I'm sorry, okay? I just had a few drinks. We had a good night, I just got carried away, yeah?" I roll my lips into my mouth and bite down, nodding. "We'll talk tonight, okay? We'll go straight to the room after the show and talk." I nod again, and he pulls back. The look in his eyes is conflicted like he knows he has to go but is scared to leave me like this. I shake my head and sniff.

"It's fine, Riggs. Go. We'll talk later." Another moment passes before I hear his phone buzz again. Probably Reed calling to tell him to get his shit together, and he sighs, pressing his lips to my forehead.

"Love you, little star."

"I love you, Riggs," I whisper, and then he's gone, leaving me to stew in my panic.

"Hey, babe, what's up?" my sister asks, picking up on the third ring. There's laughter in the background, and I'm pretty sure she's with her friends or in her dorm with her roommate. Normally, I'd let her go, let her live her life, but right now....

I don't know who to talk to. I'm lost and I'm scared and I just need my sister.

"Evie," I whisper, and I know with that one word, she knows. It's that twin bond, or maybe it's just that she knows me so well. Or maybe the word comes out as broken as I feel.

"Stella," she says, then the sound of a door clicking and silence fills the line. "Stella, what's wrong?"

"I did something so, so stupid," I say, my throat closing, panic filling me with admitting that.

Why didn't I tell him?

Why didn't I tell him what happened last night, that we got married, and he clearly was too fucked up to remember?

I know the answer, of course—I was too embarrassed, I was too hurt. But also, I think, in a way, I was protecting him, knowing that it would kill him if he knew he'd forgotten something so important if he knew he hurt me.

Every moment between now and then is making it harder to tell him, knowing I waited.

"What's wrong, Stella, what happened?"

Her concern is what breaks me, what pushes the painful lump in my throat to start to breakdown into tears, then uncontrollable sobs as I curl up on the bed I woke up in this morning.

The bridal suite.

God, how fucking stupid was I?

"Stell, you're scaring me," my sister says as I continue to sob, as it all comes out, the pain and the anguish of what happened, of the truth.

I take a few deep breaths, trying to calm myself, to make it so words can actually leave my lips, before I speak.

"I... we're in Vegas," I say, something she already knows. "The guys all went gambling and drinking, but I couldn't, obviously, so we just..." I pause and look at the ring on my finger, the one he slid on last night, something we picked out in a random jeweler store on the strip.

A wedding band with tiny diamond stars dotted across.

"*Stars for my little star,*" he'd said before kissing my hair and asking if there was a thicker version for him. There was, but it didn't fit so we kept the box with the too big ring he took off almost immediately after the little chapel ceremony, so he wouldn't lose it in my purse.

God, god, *god*, I'm so stupid.

"We wandered around. We had fun, it was like... normal. Jesus, Evie." I take a deep breath before confessing. "We got married." Silence fills the line.

"I'm sorry; what did you just say?" Her words are stilted and nervous.

Wait until she finds out it only gets worse.

"We got married. We got tattoos," I say, croaking out the words, staring at my wrist, directly under my ring finger, a heart with the letter R in it. His heart on my sleeve. Riggins got a star in the same spot. "We had champagne to celebrate." I take a fortifying breath before the next words. "It's all my fault."

"What's your fault?" she asks gently. With the pain in her words, the lump in my throat returns, and I reach for a water bottle, trying to wash it down. I play with the bottle in my hands, watching the water sway with the motion of my hands before I speak.

"I don't know what to do. He doesn't remember anything from yesterday."

"What?" she asks, stunned.

"That's why I called. Shit, Eve, I don't care about marrying him. I'd do it a million times. But he *doesn't remember it.* He woke up and acted like nothing happened. He just left for a sound check." She's quiet again, my logical twin thinking through options and words.

"What did you say?"

"Nothing. He has a show tonight, and I didn't... I don't know. I froze."

"You need to talk to him," my sister says, her words firm. "If he's drinking still and hiding it... that's not good," she says.

"He's not..." I start, panic racing through me at something I hadn't even considered. "He's not hiding anything. We just split two bottles of champagne and..."

"Stella, that wouldn't make him black out," she says gently. I ignore it. My mind isn't ready to process something like that.

"I just... I feel lost. I don't know what to do. I love him—" Her sharp words interrupt.

"Is that enough, Stella? I love him, and I love him for you, but in a situation like this, is love enough?" I don't ask her to clarify, instead pausing and thinking about her words.

Is love enough? Is the love I feel for Riggins enough to survive this?

Yes, I tell myself instantly, knowing it's the truth. Yes.

"Yes," I say, feeling the word deeply and into my soul. "It's everything else... he's worth it. I crack the cap of the water bottle and bring it to my lips as if I need to wash down the words, but I sputter and cough as I take a sip, moving it back to look at the label.

It's the same water brand that we keep on the bus in the tiny kitchenette.

Except that is *not* water.

It's vodka.

"Oh my god," I whisper.

"Stella?" my sister asks, but I'm barely listening as I put the bottle down and then start digging through his bags.

Three more water bottles.

I open each, smelling the same Vodka smell. I feel sick to my stomach, then move to the trash, finding more water bottles. Two smell like nothing, but one.... One empty bottle smells like vodka.

Evie was right.

"I'm coming home," I say, my voice cracking as I fight tears once more. I start moving things, tucking my clothes into my bag and Riggings' things into his. I'll have to stop by the bus to get the rest of my stuff anyway, so I'll drop his off when I do. I hope no one is there to stop me or ask me to stay.

Because I need to get away.

He can call me later and talk, but I need space.

And my sister.

NOW

40

BUSYHEAD

STELLA

His truck steers down my drive as the sun starts to dip, headlights on and bumping in the dark. I'm on my porch swing, and I tuck the notebook under the seat just like I did all those weeks ago.

I feel just as conflicted about him being here as I did then, too.

I've been sitting here for over two hours, but I haven't written a line. Instead, I've been stuck in my head, trying to come to terms with the tabloid articles that were delivered to me, the knowledge that he was out partying the night I left, conflicting with the bliss that it has been being back with him for the past two weeks.

I won't deny I love Riggins Greene. I can't deny that he will always have a part of my soul, a part that I'll never get back. I'll always have a part of my soul that aches to be with him, but sitting out here, I can't decide if I can be with him. If I can deal with the constant pressure and speculation that he's seeing someone else, the rumor mill that tries to sell papers at the expense of real people. I know he would never do that to me, but the pressure of the constant rumors could easily grind me down to dust.

I loved being a songwriter with a pen name because it gave me a layer of disconnect from the destructive world of the music industry. But now that barrier is gone, and if I keep things up with Riggs, things will only get worse.

Do I want that? Can I endure that?

Even with just the two hours that I've felt the invisible pressure of the press since I opened those articles, I felt the waters rising at my feet. Am I strong enough for this? Does he not deserve better?

And finally, with the news that he was out partying the day I left, I'm finding myself back to my original concern: I left and Riggins never looked back. Not a call or a text or a knock at my door.

When his dad died, we made plans to get coffee and finally talk, but he never showed up.

So why now? Why is he finally now choosing to come back into my life? The scared, fragile part I've been trying to quiet for weeks whispers, *what's stopping him from disappearing again?*

He steps out of the truck, Gracie jumping out after him, and I wonder just how many bruises a heart can take before it becomes permanently damaged.

"Hey, little star," he says casually as he walks up the stairs, stepping close, a wide, happy smile on his lips.

It kills me.

It kills me because I want this—it's all I've ever wanted, really, but I don't know if I can. I have enough issues with balancing reality and the mixed-up version my brain makes of it. Will adding another layer of concern and confusion make it that much worse? Will I be able to function with the threat of tabloids hanging over me?

Without my permission, my mind moves to all those times when we were young, and Riggins would come back to me drunk, a carefree smile on his face. I'd hide away my frustration and concern, nervous to let him know how I was feeling.

I'm not that girl anymore, though.

His brown furrows when I don't respond, when my face stays tight, when I don't stand and kiss him like I have every other night he's come home to me and I've been on the swing.

"What..." he says, pausing. "What's wrong?"

"What did you do the night I left?"

"What?"

"The night I left. I cried for three weeks in my sister's apartment. What did you do?"

His face goes blank, confirmation I wish I didn't have.

"Stella, that's not fair." He's right, of course. It's not. He had an addiction, something he's worked hard to overcome and something that he feels immense guilt over.

I take a deep breath before saying my next words.

"This is our future, Riggins. People bringing up every fuck up, every rough spot in our relationship forever." His brow furrows, and to his credit, he looks genuinely confused, as if he can't fit the piece into the puzzle of what could be wrong with me.

"What?" he asks, stepping closer.

"Don't," I say, shaking my head. "Please, please stay there. I need... I need to keep my head clear." Something shifts in his face, and his arms crossing his chest.

I know in my gut I'm being a bit irrational, that this is all just picking at old wounds, but wouldn't it be easier to know now this isn't going to work? That I can't handle it before we get in too deep.

But I also know in the depths of my soul I can't endure losing him the way I did before. Maybe if I take the power, if I make the decision myself, it will be easier...

"What's going on, Stella?"

"Someone slipped these into my mailbox. It's tabloids from this week."

Again, to Riggins' credit, when he pulls out the news article, he stares at it for a quick moment before rolling his eyes and shaking his head. He sighs and looks relieved.

"This is all bullshit rag magazines. This is just my life, Stella. Tabloids and magazines speculating about every aspect of my life. When I don't give them shit, they start to piece together old photos, make it look like something new and exciting, and put questions and thoughts into people's heads. You're gonna have to get over it. This is who I am. Who we are gonna be."

My mind tries to put together the idea of me just being okay with people repeatedly speculating that my....husband is cheating on me, the way that could fuck with me, the way I could start to believe it. If I have the backbone to handle this, this life.

"This is the reality of us being together," he says, like that is an inevitability, us being together. He's so sure in this, in us, but suddenly, I'm not.

I can't imagine a world where I'm fine with people speculating about him, about us. A world where it doesn't phase me, a world where it doesn't eventually grate on my already wavering mental health. Maybe all of my concerns back then, the drinking, the partying, the lifestyle, maybe it was an excuse for me to leave before it became too much for me.

I love Riggins, but what if all those years ago, we didn't work because we never would work. If it was all meant to be? Hell, I didn't see him for years, and he wasn't hurting for it; I never even fucking tried to reach out that first year after I left.

"What if I can't handle it?" I ask, my inner fears breaking through.

"What?"

"What if I can't handle this, this life? The speculation, the tabloids." I admit the thoughts I've been stewing in for the past few hours, my deepest fears. Because even if it's all fake, even if it's just some PR fantasy like he said, it's still going to eat at me. The lies are eventually going to dig under my skin until I start to believe them. "I'm already so fragile. You've seen what happens when I break when I start to drown."

"And I told you I'll be your lifeboat."

"But what if you're the anchor pulling me down." His face goes blank, and I feel like I'm letting him down, but maybe this is for the best.

It's better to cut this before we're too deep, before it hurts too much before I get to the point once again where I can't breathe without him.

I barely survived it last time.

I don't know if I can survive that kind of hit a second time.

"What if I can't do it? What happens then?"

"We figure it out then, Stella." Somehow, I think he knows where I'm going with this.

"I don't know if I can take that kind of risk." The words tumble out low and pained, and I stare at my hands as I speak them aloud. They're somehow still dotted with paint from the other day, from painting the room upstairs with him and what happened later.

How have I come so far in just a few days, from that high of being with him, being us, about talking about a fucking family and a future to here?

To ending things with the love of my life?

"Why the fuck not, Stella? That's how relationships work. You try to make it work, and if something isn't working, you fix it. You don't go into expecting to have problems."

"Except I'm not going into this blind this time, Riggins. Neither of us are. You broke me, Riggins. You broke me in a way that I try and convince myself every single day that I'm better. That I'll be okay again, knowing full well it's full of bullshit. But us? You and me? We won't work long term. We can't. This should have never happened."

I look up at him again, feeling the tears well and feeling silly and childish for my next words. "I was drowning once before, Riggins, and you got to go live out your dreams while I suffocated. You forgot that I even existed. I was no one to you the day I left."

His face goes dark and confused.

"You're not allowed to be mad at me for living my life, Stella! You left me! You left me, and I fell apart."

"I left you, yes, but you never came after me. I spent years doing everything for you, giving up everything because I loved you more than anything, and I left, and you just... accepted it. You never even tried, Riggins. That's what hurt the most. Not once. Not a call, not a text. You never tried to come to me." Silence fills the porch, and it's almost tangible.

"What are you talking about, Stella?"

NOW

41

GLUE MYSELF SHUT

RIGGINS

The world stops spinning, and I repeat my question while she looks at me blankly.

"What are you talking about?" I ask, my voice calm and cool, calculated even.

The world shifts with that sentence, something she's hinted at multiple times before, but I never understood. Suddenly, I start to wonder if there's more to it.

"It wasn't your job to chase me, of course," she says, continuing. "I realize that was partly on me, too, but I tried. I tried to let you back in, and I sat there like an idiot for hours, so I wasn't going to come for you after that. But that first day on tour, you realized I was gone; you didn't come for me. You never bothered to even try! You didn't even try to fight for me! You went out partying!" she says, pain in the words.

"I was giving you space, Stella—"

"Space! I didn't need space, Riggins. I needed *you*. I needed to know I mattered, that I was more than the booze and the liquor and the music. Just one—one time, I wanted to come first. For *anyone*. I never came first for my mom or my dad, but I thought I came first for you. When I left, I realized that I didn't even make the top ten after I didn't hear from you for a whole fucking year."

The words spin, and I'm so fucking lost, so confused. She didn't hear from me? What the fuck is she talking about?

"I wrote to you! I wrote to you the entire rest of the tour, a post-card for every stop just like I did in the beginning, and you sent them back! Each and every one, you sent back, return to sender."

"What?" She says, confusion and shock in her face but I'm lost now, irritation in my bones.

This is it.

Somehow, I know this is it.

This is the make or break moment, where I lay it all out on the line, give her everything and see if we're going to work.

Whether she's going to understand or we're going to be done, at least we won't leave with any questions between us.

"You sent them all back. I knew I fucked up, darkened the brightest star I'd ever known, and I figured you sending them back was your way of telling me to leave you alone. I wanted to respect that. Then you come to my dad's funeral a year later, hold my fucking hand, finally, *finally agree to* talk to me, and I find out you're seeing some fucker, and I'll admit, I lost it."

"Riggs—"

"I hit rock bottom that night, and I spiraled so deep I couldn't find the surface. I called you, and you said you were done with me. *I'm done, move on, Riggins.*" My throat is aching with unshed tears, and my chest is ringing and falling with heavy breaths, but what does it matter anymore. Might as well put it all on the line now.

"What are you talking about?" she asks, and suddenly, cold starts to creep over me, which has nothing to do with the night air.

"What am I talking about?. God, Stell, even now, you can't fucking admit it. I can admit—I *have* admitted what a fuck up I was, I *am*. But you weren't fucking innocent either."

"Riggins, I don't... I really don't know what you're talking about.

I look down at my feet, ashamed to meet her eyes. "I was young, drunk, and I was *alone*, Stella. My dad had just died, my mom was gone, I had no one left. I called you, and you picked up, and you told me you couldn't do it anymore. Then, you hung up."

42

SHE CALLS ME BACK

RIGGINS

The entire world feels bleak and empty, the longing for a drink creeping through my veins. And then I feel it, her small hand sliding into mine, the familiar smell of brown sugar and vanilla lifting on the breeze.

It's a ghost haunting me, but then the hand squeezes, another hand resting on my bicep, and I give into the urge to look down.

And there she is. Still short as fuck, but her hair is a bit longer, with a bit of a wave to it as it brushes past her shoulders with pretty highlights woven through it. Her blue eyes are looking at me, wide and calming, the way I always felt when she was near, her full pink lips pressed together.

She looks older, but she doesn't. She looks changed but wholly the same.

"Stell," I whisper quietly, worried she might be a mirage, something my sick mind manufactured to further torture me, and worried if anyone in the area sees me talking to the air, it will be the breaking point. Everyone is already always on edge around me, walking on eggshells.

"Riggs," she whispers, her hand tightening in mine, shifting until our fingers are twined the way we always used to hold hands.

I decide to say fuck it, to give into the delusion. It hurts too much not to, and there's enough fucked up bullshit in my life right now not to take this moment of peace my mind is offering and succumb to it.

"You came."

"I loved him, too," she says simply.

And she did.

She loved my dad more than I did sometimes, much more understanding when his drinking overtook him after my mom died. When I would be angry he was the way he was, she'd always tell me to give him grace, to find understanding.

And when we were finally together, she'd always tell me, *imagine if you lost me, Riggins. How would you deal?*

The irony of that never ceases to amuse me in a sick and twisted way. The way I lost her and spiraled, became my father.

My father, who I'm burying today.

Nearly ten years after my mother left, after ten years of drinking to forget his soulmate was gone from this world, he drank himself to death.

I can only hope that now he's at peace and by my mother's side. I hope she forgives him for leaving me to fend for myself.

I forgive him.

I get it.

But now... now my person is here. She's here after over two years of not talking to me, of sending back my letters and ignoring my calls and never coming back for me. Two years after she disappeared randomly in Vegas, not a trace or a note.

She's here, holding my hand.

"Please stay with me," I beg without thinking, without altering my response to sound better or less desperate or more casual. She must see something in my face, the pain there or the watering of my eyes as I once again fight tears, or maybe the way my hand tightens on hers because instantly she nods.

"Of course, Riggs. Of course."

And she does.

She never lets go of my hand, not as I greet fellow mourners and accept condolences I don't feel I deserve from people who wrote my father off years ago. Not as I toss a handful of dirt onto his coffin as it's lowered.

She never does. Even when I loosen my grip, she's there, holding firm.

And when everyone is gone, when it's just us in a graveyard, watching an industrial machine scoop dirt onto the last remaining physical vestiges of my father, she turns to me, staring and waiting for me to say something. Anything, I think.

I break contact with the quickly disappearing coffin and look at her.

Stella.

My little star, my sun.

It's been so fucking dark without her.

I'm still not sure what happened, not really, but I can make an educated guess. I told her I stopped drinking and didn't. Then I blacked out, completely forgetting the night before as I stealthily drank the entire night until I couldn't remember a thing.

It took nearly six months and a turn for the worse before the guys sat me down and told me I needed to slow down. I've been better, I think, since I last saw Stella, managing the drinking and the urges on my own.

But all that did was make it easier for me to remember how much I missed her, how much I lost.

I ache every fucking time it rains, remembering our first kiss or the last time I held her as mine.

"Thank you," I whisper, unsure of what to say to her. Her small hand reaches up, brushing my hair that's much too long and disheveled behind my ear, her skin touching mine and sending heat and comfort through me.

"Whenever you need me, Riggins, I'm there."

My mind races through responses, ranging from shithead versions of a rage-filled me about her leaving when I needed her to asking her to never leave my side again, but I know this doesn't change a thing. This is just Stella being Stella, coming when I need her most.

"Can we talk?" I ask without thinking. She opens her mouth, doubt written on her face, but I keep speaking, verbal vomit that won't stop.

This feels like a chance I shouldn't have been given, and I'm grasping it as hard as I can. Maybe this was a gift from my dad, one last moment to try and make things right. He always loved Stella.

"Please. Coffee. Lunch. Anything. I just..." I take a deep breath, letting my eyes close for a moment to find my footing even though all I want to do is look at her, to commit her face to memory in case this is it for us, for me.

I wouldn't blame her if it was. I don't hold her, leaving against her, even though I've spent every day for a year trying to put the pieces together to figure out the tipping point.

It always ends in my not putting her first, with my lies, my deceit, and my addiction.

I just hope I didn't push her all the way away. That I—

"Yeah," she says, cutting off my thoughts, her eyes going soft. "Yeah. We should talk." It feels fucked to smile this big in front of the spot where my father was just lowered into the ground, but here I am all the same. Her lips tip up, too, like she finds my smile funny. "Cafe Pine at noon," she whispers.

"I'll be there," I tell her. Then, I lift her hand and press my lips to it the way I did years and years ago in the clearing where we fell in love. Moments later, I'm pulled away by a grieving family, and she waves at me, stepping away and mouthing tomorrow at me.

For the first time in what feels like forever, the sun shines on me, its rays actually warming me to my bones.

My sun is back.

The grocery store in Ashford isn't huge, but it always had a pretty decent flower section. I remember the months when Stella moved in with me, stopping here on my way home from a day practicing with the guys or out at a studio any time she didn't come, and bringing her flowers home. Usually sunflowers, her favorite, but sometimes I'd grab her fluffy pink peonies or a mix of wildflowers if they had them.

It's the day after the funeral and I'm checking out with a bouquet of sunflowers before I meet Stella at the coffee shop.

It's time.

It's time to finally talk, clear things up, and win my girl back. I've spent the last two years battling on and off to get sober, succeeding, and failing, but I'm going on three months now, and the world seems... clearer. I get it now, why she left. I was a drunk, and I'd gotten so bad that I was willing to push her to the side in order to keep up the habit. I was willing to throw it all away for just one more drink.

But eventually, I got past the anger of her leaving, with Reed talking to me and letting me see things from his perspective. He tried to get me to go rehab or join AA, but I don't need that shit. I'm fine, especially with the wake-up call that's been my dad's passing.

And now I'm about to get my girl back.

My bright, shining little star. Fuck, just five minutes in her presence warmed me to my bones, a heat I hadn't felt in years.

It's as I'm checking out, a pack of gum, a soda, and the flowers the only things in my basket, that I feel an unwelcome cold presence behind me, a foreboding of sorts.

"If it isn't Riggins Greene," a familiar, sickly sweet voice I would be more than happy to never hear again in my life coos. That's the only way you can call the way Rhonda Hart speaks—a coo filled with hatred and anger and pure venom.

"Hey, Mrs. Hart," I mumble, grabbing my things and turning to leave.

"What, no time to chat?"

"Unfortunately, no, I have places to be," I say. *Like making up with your daughter, getting everything back to where it was always supposed to be,* I want to say but don't since she never liked my dating her daughter. She didn't even like me being in her daughter's stratosphere, but I think that's more because she spent her entire time making those girls everything she never was, everything she wanted to be.

Rhonda Hart was born and raised in Ashford, but she always wished she was somewhere glamorous, like New York City. I always wondered how Hank, the girls' dad, convinced her to stay here and how she never got to live the big life she aspired to. Either way, I think once that dream became unattainable, she looked to her daughters to live that life for her.

Her daughters who happily haven't let Ashford, except for the few months Stella left with us. But that wasn't the way she wanted Stella to live, so it was null and void, really.

"Are those for Stella?" she asks, irritation and anger in her words as her chin tips toward the flowers. While she was never pleasant with me, the anger and hatred in her eyes is new. Different.

"I'll talk to you later, Mrs. Hart," I say, trying to move around her. Where the fuck is Stacy, who normally works the self-checkout, eager to talk to anyone and everyone?

"I just thought you should know she's moved on," she says casually.

I should ignore her.

I should keep walking, leave the store and sit in my car outside the coffee shop until it's time to meet with Stella. Or call Reed, dump all of my thoughts and feelings on him so I don't explode with the nerves of talking to Stella.

Instead, I turn and look at the woman who would be gorgeous if it wasn't for the envy that stains her face.

"What?" I ask, my words much less stable than I would have hoped.

"She's moved on, Riggins. What did you expect her to wait here for you while you were off gallivanting with your little band?"

I force myself to take in a deep breath, to not jump to whatever conclusions she is trying to push me toward. That's what she wants, after all. She's always wanted the most distance between me and her daughter. I might not be the poor, white trash kid of a blue-collar contractor anymore, but I'll never be the type of man she wants her daughter to be with. I'll never have the "right" kind of money or influence for Rhonda Hart.

"It's great to see you, Mrs. Hart, but I do have things to do." I move to leave, but she moves to block me from leaving.

"Don't believe me?" she asks snidely. "I have proof, of course." She reaches for her phone and taps the screen a few times before looking back up at me, gauging my interest.

I should leave.

God, I know it. I should leave.

"She's dating Tripp," she says, and I take a moment for my mind to place the name but once I do, my jaw grinds.

The asshole who pinned her to a tree when she was 19, expecting more from her than she was willing to give. The son of one of Rhonda's bitchy friends,

Rhonda takes a step closer, a catlike smile on her lips, and turns the phone to me. "See?"

I do.

Stella's head is tipped back, her mouth open in a laugh, her hair trailing down her back as she does. Her arms are around his neck, dancing I assume, based on the bodies and couples around them, and he's looking at her with... awe on his face.

I know the look well—I used to have the same anytime I saw Stella, anytime I looked her way. Awe that she was with me, that she chose *me*. Awe that she was so incredibly talented, at her ability to string together words and melodies in a way that could evoke emotions you didn't want to share with the world. Awe in her kindness and her beauty and her grace.

And he's looking at her, holding her, with that look on his face.

The phone is gone and Rhonda swipes a few times, then shows me the screen again. Stella in a knee-length blue dress, her hair hanging in long wavy sheets, his arm on her waist.

It's clear to anyone looking that they're together.

My words croak when I speak.

"When were these taken?" I ask, begging some god I don't know I believe in that it was six months, or eight months ago. Fuck, even if it was right after she left, I'd be okay with it. Just not—

"Two weeks ago at his mother's wedding." I feel nauseous. My fingers hold onto the bouquet of flowers loosely, barely grasping them.

"I set them up, of course. Finally, she let me choose a nice, suitable man for her." She takes her phone again and looks at it, exaggerated joy and peace on her face. "Doesn't she just look so happy? A mother does always know best."

I can't speak.

My mind is stuck on Stella moving on, on Stella looking at someone that way, a way that I used to think was just for me, special.

"Well, you look like you have somewhere to go," Rhonda says, and I look to her, lightheaded and confused, but her smile…

Even years from now, I know that smile will haunt me.

"Have a great day, Riggins."

Then she turns, the cashier I was begging to come just minutes ago now standing there confused. Rhonda walks over to her excitedly, like she's an old friend she hasn't seen in ages, even though she hates the working class of Ashford more almost as much as she hates me.

I force my feet to move, to take me out of the grocery store. Fresh air. I need fresh air.

But when I get out there, it's not enough.

I can't get enough in my lungs. It's not air I need.

It's oblivion.

And without the hope of winning back Stella, I let myself fall into it.

THEN

43

DIAL DRUNK

RIGGINS

The red and blue lights flash as I sit on the curb, an officer standing over me as I hit send on the phone.

I only have one number memorized, but it's fine. It's the only one I need.

When I picked up the first beer I bought at the small liquor store next to the grocery store, I knew I did something wrong. Deep in my gut, I knew I made the wrong choice, those bright, sunny sunflowers in my passenger seat staring at me as I sat in the driveway of my childhood home and drank it down in one gulp.

I fucked up.

What were the chances that Rhonda Hart, who has hated me for as long as I can remember, was telling the whole truth?

Probably low.

But there I sat, digging myself deep in the same way my father did, drinking to mask the heartbreak and grief.

And now I'm on the curb waiting for my car to get towed for driving intoxicated.,

It rings and rings and rings before the answering machine picks up. I fumble the phone, hitting end and quickly redialing, hoping the officer who let me make a call from his phone won't mind.

It rings and rings again, and the dread curls in my gut before the ringing stops.

"Hello?" she asks. Her voice sounds distorted and strange down the line, but I don't care.

I can't care: she answered. She answered and everything is going to be okay now. I hear my voice crack as I speak.

"Stella. Stella. I need help." I mean it more than just in this moment. I need help with getting my life together. I needed help when I was convinced I could get sober and healthy alone. I need help before I become my father. "I fucked up," I say into the phone, and then spill it all.

"I need help. I'm a drunk, and I need to go to rehab, and Stella, I'm so fucking scared of losing you for good. You are my other half, and I want to get better for you. I don't care if you're with that asshole; you were always meant to be mine. It was always you for me, Stell. I want to be everything you need me to be, but I need to get sober first. I don't know if I can do it without you. I don't know if I want to do it without you. You're my person. My best friend, the love of my life. I fucked up today, and I shouldn't have been drinking, but I know I need to do something to get better. I'm begging you to give me the chance to prove I'm what you need. I just…" I swallow back a sob. I should be embarrassed, my words slurring and in cohesive, but I don't know if there's room for embarrassment at rock bottom. "I just need you, Stella. I love you."

Silence fills the line before there's a sigh.

"Riggins?"

"Stella, I—"

A cold creeps over me as she speaks, her words firm and irritated, with no room for arguing. "Riggins, move on. I'm done." The words ring in the silence, my mind silencing all of the background noise as they swirl in my mind.

Move on, I'm done.

Move on, *I'm done.*

Move on, I'm done.

We're supposed to meet to talk about us and she's done? I'm calling her at my darkest moment, and she's done.

With me? With this? With us?

I don't know.

The phone is silent at my ear and I have a feeling when I look at the screen, I'll see it's blank, no one on the other line.

She hung up.

Because she's done.

A hand touches my shoulder, and I waver, the liquor in my system making me off balance, and the world comes slamming back in, the noise filling my ears and overwhelming me, the blue and red flashing of the lights nearly blinding me, the rain I don't remember starting soaking through my shirt, and I barely maintain my grasp on the phone.

"Son, everything okay?"

Nothing is okay.

Nothing at all.

Because Stella is dating some asshole, and now she's telling me to move on as if I'll ever be able to move on from her, and I'm being moved into the back of a cop car, and I need another drink, and Stella is *done* with me.

"She hung up on me," I murmur as the police officer steps back once I'm settled in the back seat, hesitating as he prepares to shut the door.

"What?"

"She hung up on me. I told her I needed her, and she hung up on me." The older man's face gets soft for the first time all night, and he moves to squat, bringing him face to face with me. I see the sincerity on his face despite the swirling of the world.

"Sorry, kid. That's fucked." He looks over his shoulder, probably at his partner or someone else, before looking back at me. "Let this be a wake-up call, though. You're at rock bottom, already lost your girl, it seems. Don't let this shit," He lifts a glass bottle I didn't realize I had been carrying up, shaking the small amount of its contents. "Take anything else."

And when he closes the door, my mind can't stop reeling on that.

Don't let it take anything else.

And I don't.

NOW

44

PASSENGER

RIGGINS

"I called," I say to her, noting the panic on her face. "Those words haunt me. Those nightmares I mentioned? That's what I hear in them, over and over. I see the night my heart stopped beating. The night I stood in the rain, cops looking at me like I was a loser." She shakes her head like she's trying to refute the statement. "I called you, told you everything, how I hit rock bottom, and I loved you more than anything, and that I needed help. That I was struggling, Stella. I was lost and scared, and I told you I was sorry, and I would go to rehab, and that I needed you, and you said you were done. That I needed to move on, and you hung up on me. I got drunk after your mom showed me pictures of you and that guy—"

"My mom?" she says, confused, then shakes her head. "What guy? When?" The confusion is amplified now, turning into panic.

"When?" I ask, confused.

"When did you call? When did you talk to her? When did you call me, Riggins? Letters? What letters?" She's starting to hyperventilate, and suddenly, pieces that I've been given over the last month or so are moving together in my mind.

A heartbreaking understanding starts to take over and I wonder how I didn't see it sooner. How she didn't.

I step closer to Stella, slowly so as not to spook her, my hands moving to her arms, touching her shaking body. I want to pull her into my arms, but I don't know if I have that right now, if that's something she wants from me.

"I called you," I say, my voice cracking. She shakes her head, but I continue speaking, rushing to explain, to get past this part and to the new, painful realization.

"I was out the morning we were supposed to meet for lunch. I was out... god, I was out to get you flowers." I shake my head and laugh, remembering the bouquet of sunflowers, the wilted bouquet on my chest a perfect match for what lay on my passenger seat for days. "Your mom bumped into me and told me all about your new relationship with her friend's son. That you were happier without me, that she'd never seen you so happy. Showed me a photo of you and some guy laughing at a wedding." I look at her, her face going white as I try and read her to understand what she's feeling.

"Lenore's wedding. My mother made me go, her son was there. Another one of her rich friends she wanted me to hook up with but... we laughed all night about our parents trying to set us up when he was secretly in a relationship. Seems he had his own issues, he apologized for that night in the woods." She shakes her head, panic in her eyes. "I wasn't dating him, Riggins. I haven't dated since...."

She doesn't have to fill in the rest.

She hasn't dated since me.

"I left, and I lost it. There was a liquor store right next door. Grabbed a beer and drank it. I remember.... I remember feeling guilty as if I knew it was the wrong decision, but I couldn't stop. I wanted the darkness to stop; I wanted the grief to stop. Somehow, I was suddenly grieving us all over again, and my dad and it was... it was too much." I shake my head and look up at her again. "I got wasted and then realized how big of a mistake I made. I got in a car to go see you."

"Riggins, no," she whispers, eyes wide.

"I got pulled over. I got a call, Stell, so I called you."

"I wasn't there," she whispers. "I'd moved into an apartment. I haven't lived at home since..." Since before we lived together.

"You weren't there," I whisper, suddenly seeing it all so clearly. "You weren't home, but I thought you were. I only had two numbers memorized."

"My house and yours." We were raised in a time of home numbers and landlines, and neither of our parents ever got rid of them.

"I called that night. You were my... Fuck, Stella." I run a hand through my hair, stalling. "I called. I thought it was you. I was so fucked up. I wanted to go find you, to see you. I wanted to tell you I was going to be better. I remember that clearly, regretting drinking, which had never happened to me. I needed to tell you I was going to get better, to get better, so I could be the person you deserved. Someone picked up...."

I watch her fill in the blanks, but I keep speaking. We spent too long, assuming the other knew what we were saying. That's what got us in this place, after all. Leaving out details to save her some guilt won't help us.

"I called, and someone picked up. It must have..." I shake my head and look at my shoes. A tear I didn't realize had fallen dripping from my shoes. Her soft hand reaches up to my cheek, wiping the trail away. "It must have been her, you know? She always hated us together and wanted better for you. But I was so fucked up, I didn't know. You were my one call, Stell. I called, and... she said you were done. You were moving on. I went to rehab the next day."

I don't tell her that despite the grief I'm feeling, knowing we lost all those years, I'm grateful for it. It ensured I got clean, that I made it long enough to stand on her porch and talk to her like this, to confess this all to her.

"Why didn't you call again? Once you were clean?" she asks, tears of her own now streaming.

"The steps I was taking in rehab... one of them is to recognize harm you've done and how not to continue that harm. To me, you set a boundary by telling me you were done. It was my job to respect that. I did, until I found out we were legally tied. That felt like.... Like a sign." I shrug. "But I wrote you, of course."

"What does that mean?" she asks, confused still.

"Just like when we were kids. At every stop, I wrote you a post-card. The first year after you left, they all got sent back to me. I still have them." Her brows furrow, clearly confused, trying to keep track of all of this new information as we piece our halves together to get a full picture.

"You have those?"

I nod. "I have them all Stella. In a box. I couldn't get rid of any of them. It was therapeutic, writing to you, but I couldn't send them, because I was so sure you didn't want that."

"I *did* want that. I would have killed for that, Riggins."

"I'm getting that now. I'm assuming your mother sent them back, tried to send a message, and I was too young and dumb and drunk to realize. But even when they were sent back, it was like a piece of us I couldn't throw away. So I kept them."

"You kept them." For the first time since I pulled up, she smiles a small, weak smile, like she likes that idea. She likes that I have those letters. I nod. A long beat passes, both of us in silence, my hands still on her arms. I refuse to let go. It feels like if I do, she'll run and be gone for good.

"What now?" she asks finally, what could be minutes or hours later.

"What now?" I mirrored.

She sighs and steps back, my stomach falling to my feet.

"Does this change anything? Everything? Where do we go with all of this? You were angry with me for years, and now I see it wasn't fully out of the blue. I was mad at you, and I think we both can see it through a blurred lens. What are we now? Who are we? How do we move forward? *Can* we move forward?"

I reach up, moving to wipe a tear from her cheek, my heart pounding.

She's scared.

She's terrified, even. Not just because our history is so messy, our shared experiences so skewed, but because she feels vulnerable. She tries to show everyone she's strong and that everything bounces right off of her, but I know Stella. She's soft, delicate. A beautiful flower I don't want to see wilt again. I need to show her how much she means to me, to remind her of who we are and why we're worth fighting for.

I only have one more thing to show her.

"Go away with me," I whisper. Beg, really.

"What?"

"A weekend. Just for a few days. We'll drive. I... I have somewhere I want to show you." Her face goes soft, but her words hold argument.

"Riggs, we have so much to figure out, it isn't the best–"

"A weekend. If we don't figure out how to move on together after, I'll let you go. I'll let you be free, live your life." She stares at me for long, long moments, and I panic. I wonder if this is it, if we're done, and if she's going to end things once and for all.

"Okay," she finally whispers, and her star lights up my sky once more.

NOW

45

ALL MY LOVE.

STELLA

The silence in the car is deafening, but my mind never quiets. In my lap is a box, heavy and laden with postcards. Some battered and bruised, clearly having gone through the mail, all dated and signed. The most recent was just a month ago. As he drives, I flip through hundreds—*hundreds*—of postcards Riggins wrote but never sent, one for every stop of every tour Atlas Oaks went on over the last seven years.

Stell—
We're in Texas today, and it's hot as fuck. I guess it's better than being in Jersey. Says it snowed there. I hope you didn't have to shovel your walk and that you have someone to do it for you.
All my love,
Riggs

Stella—

Remember when you told me you thought Paris would be boring? You were so wrong. You'd love it here. Lots to do and see. And, of course, lots of bakeries. I hope you make it here one day.

All my love,

Riggs.

Little Star—

I wrote for the first time today, and I wasn't angry. I guess that feels like a win, even though it'll never see the light of day. All my songs fucking suck without you.

All my love,

Riggins.

Stell—

It's raining today.

I miss you.

I'm sorry.

All my love,

Riggs.

Stella—

We're in London today and after the show, everyone went to a party because I told them I'd start drinking in the bus if they didn't. I wasn't, of course, but it worked. Once they left I laid outside in the grass outside the bus under the stars.

I miss you.

All my love,

Riggs

He wasn't lying. There was a letter for every stop on every tour. Some of them are filled with silly anecdotes, things that happened, news about one of the guys, deals they made, or new songs being released.

A few mention his mom and how he was missing her. More mention his dad, filled with mixed emotions he'd been wrestling through over the years. Anger and grief and understanding. They all feel like a glimpse into his mind and into his recovery.

If I ever worried for a moment that a future would be hounded by the fear of Riggins drinking again, of falling into old patterns and behaviors, these letters tell me the entire story I needed to hear.

There are even a few dozen cards and letters he wrote when he wasn't even on the road, a bunch from when he went to rehab, and some while he was trying to write albums.

Each one, I fall more and more in love with him again, in a different way than before.

Each one eases the ache, pain, and panic I was feeling over falling for him again. It doesn't ease the nerves of what's next or the grief and anger I feel for what my mother did, but those are all things that I can grapple with later.

Right now, it's all about Riggins and I.

And I'm finally ready to figure out what that will look like, once and for all.

NOW

46

MAINE

RIGGINS

It's a long drive—maybe six, or eight hours, I don't know—but it feels like an eternity before Riggs' truck bumps along dirt roads and finally, we stop. I blink, trying to clear my vision and understand where we are.

"We're here," he says, but doesn't move to leave the truck. We're parked facing a small cabin surrounded by woods.

"Where is here?" I ask. I fell in and out of sleep between reading postcards as we drove, the exhaustion of the emotional turmoil taking its toll.

"Maine," he says simply.

Maine. My head tips up to look at the sky through the windshield, light blue and bright, the sun high in the sky as Riggs drove through the night.

He knows what I'm thinking without even saying it.

"Tonight, we'll come outside. You'll see the stars."

"What is this place?" I ask, not wanting to think about watching the stars with Riggins in Maine, a daydream we had long before everything blew apart.

"My house. Our house. I, uh," he puts a hand to the back of his neck, suddenly somehow shy and nervous. "I built it for you."

"You built it?" I ask, shocked. He shrugs like it's no big deal.

"I didn't know it was for you at the time. I just needed something to do with my hands, with my mind. Clear it out."

I keep staring at him, but he refuses to meet my eyes, staring at the building in front of us. It could be a few seconds or an hour before he speaks again, but I wait patiently, no longer willing to push past things to keep one of us comfortable.

Where has evading these hard topics gotten us besides confused, lost, and angry? Seven years—more, if we're being honest—of avoiding hard conversations to keep the peace or avoid picking at wounds. All it's done has made things worse. All it's done was put seven years of distance between us and fueled miscommunication and misunderstanding.

Finally, he sighs, realizing I'm not going to let this go, and starts to explain, still refusing to meet my eyes.

"After I got sober, there was a gap in our touring schedule. Management wanted us to make a new album and wanted me to fix my image. I'd gotten the DUI, and even though they were about to keep it low-key, the news I was a fuck up and wrapped too tight in the lifestyle was still spreading and not in a fun, all-press-is-good-press way. So they put us on a mandatory break, told me to get my shit together before I showed my face again."

He sighs, his eyes far off like he's lost in another world, another time before he continues.

"I went to rehab, did the whole thing, but I didn't trust myself to be anything but alone. Locked myself in a hotel room and tried to write an album." A self-pitying laugh escapes his chest as he shakes his head. "I couldn't write. Nothing worked. I missed you and needed you. Knew that since you left, but I covered it in liquor. When I got sober, there was nothing left but a gaping hole."

My eyes watch his face, carefully decoding each stretch of skin on muscle, each twitch of his face, each shift of his eyes, but he keeps staring ahead at the cabin before us, eyes glazed, in another life. Another time.

"So I bought land out here to see the stars. I'd say I don't know why I picked here, picked Maine, but we both know that's bullshit, and you were always smarter than I was. You know I bought it because of you." He sighs and I reach out on instinct for his hand, hesitating a split second before I grab it. He twines his fingers with mine but still doesn't look at me, still lost in that world.

"It worked for a bit, but nothing... nothing great came of it. I couldn't write anything worth the ink in my pen. Before that, I was angry. I wrote about that, about you leaving when I thought I did nothing wrong, about my parents, about Dad. I could write about being on the road, the wild ride that was, but now that the rose-colored glasses were gone, I could see what a train wreck it all was. I wasn't brave enough then, to write about what I'd done, how I'd fucked up everything."

He shakes his head, finally dropping his eyes from the cabin but still not looking at me. Instead, his eyes are locked on our hands, to where I'm holding his. He shifts our hands so he can see my tattoo, then brushes his thumb over the tiny R before he takes a deep breath, continuing.

"I needed to distract myself when I was up here, so I started building. I didn't know what I was doing, not at all, but one thing my dad gave me, though, was knowledge on how to build." I remember that, how his father was a contractor, how he could fix and build anything, and how he helped remodel my parents' living room before Jeanie died. "Something in my brain knew I needed blueprints, permits, or else I'd be fucked, so I did all of that and had everything delivered, but this?" His free hand waves at the cabin, indicating the area in front of us.

"This is all me. I did it all except some of the wiring and plumbing." Finally, finally, his head turns and he looks at me, a small self-deprecating smile on his lips. "Hired that out, so at least we know it won't burn to the ground if we turn the lights on."

I return the small smile, and he turns to the cabin again.

"It worked, you know. Cleared my head enough to write. I'd build during the day, lay under the stars with my guitar at night, writing songs about forgiveness and redemption. Addiction and loss. That was *Barren*. It hit number one."

"I know," I whisper. "I saw it. I was proud of you guys, even though I was still livid and lost and sad still. It hurt seeing you succeed when I felt so lost, like I was drowning. But knowing you guys did that all on your own. I was proud."

Silence takes over the car again as we both get lost in our own thoughts.

I look at the cabin, understanding he did this—built this and chose here—because it was the only place he could feel close to me while giving me my space. I get it. It's why I never left Ashford when LA or New York could have made more sense for a songwriter. It's why I kept working at the diner, why I bought the house and never left the town, and why I fell in love with him.

It was my one last connection to him, a connection that I could deny all I wanted, but it was obvious if you looked.

And in that moment, I know my mind is made up.

I think I made my mind up when I read that first postcard with *Return to Sender* stamped on it, to be honest.

We'll make it work. I'll get a thicker skin to deal with the tabloid shit if I have to, and we'll work together to get over our bumpy past because I've learned over the years that I can survive without Riggins, but I can't *live* without him.

I've been surviving for seven years, and I'm tired of it.

I want my best friend back for good.

"Come on. Show me our house," I whisper, squeezing his hand. His head turns to me and I see a glimmer of hope there, his face looking so boyish, harkening back to when we were kids so much that I almost cry.

"Really?" he asks.

"Yeah, Riggs. Take me home."

NOW

47

CLOSE BEHIND

STELLA

"That one," he whispers hours later as we lay on a blanket under the stars.

He was right all those years ago, the stars are wildly bright out here and the peace that's taken over me soothes every part of me.

Here, I know without a doubt we can make it no matter what. Riggins is more important to me than my fears and I know he'll always be by my side.

We were always supposed to be Riggs and Stella. I'll be damned if I let my mother or anything else change that.

"What?"

"That one," he points to a spot in the sky, the brightest star that isn't the North Star blinking at us.

"I bought it for you. It's named Stella. Went to one of those star-buying places, and it took forever for them to find the one I was looking for, and then I had to contact the owners and convince them to sell it to me. I think the company thought I was insane, but I figured if I had this place, this place I made for you when you were never even going to be mine again, I could have you in this small way. The brightest star in my sky has always been you, little star."

I turn to look at him, his head turned toward me and I think the only thing that could make this moment better would be if Gracie was here instead of with Reed.

"You told me you were going to name a bright star after me," I say, remembering that night when we were kids under the same stars, before we had all of this baggage before there was so much hurt between us.

"I told you, I'm making it my life's mission never to fall down on my promises to you ever again." A lump forms in my throat as he turns to me, his hand moving to my jaw to hold me. I lean forward, pressing my lips to his. They slide easily and carefree, with no rush or urgency, like we have all the time in the world.

It feels like the air is finally clear between us, and we both agree we're going to fight for *us*.

My hand moves, slipping under his shirt, resting on his abs that tighten under my touch, and he shifts, barely breaking our kiss and taking off his shirt.

We kiss for more long minutes under the stars, easy and lazy, before he shifts to take off the rest of his clothes.

"I love you so much, Riggins," I whisper as he slides my thin shorts down my legs, leaving me in just an oversized Atlas Oaks tee shirt.

"I know, little star. And you know I love you."

I do.

To the depths of my soul, I do.

He rolls us, so I'm hovering over him. One hand has a thumb gently rubbing my clit, while his other guides himself into me. We both groan in satisfaction and pleasure when he fills me.

It's been amazing with Riggins, before I left and after, but it's never felt like this. Like there's nothing between us, no lies or misunderstandings or fear. Our slates are clean, we're free to be us.

We don't speak as he lifts his knees, giving me a rest for my back as I use my legs as leverage, sliding up and down on his cock. We pant and moan, and his eyes never leave mine as I move above him, the stars as my backdrop. Hours could have passed as we lazily make love like that before my orgasm starts to peak before the pleasure builds so much in my belly I can barely keep my eyes open.

"I love you," he says, hands tightening on my hips. "I love you, Stella. God, I love you. You're my entire universe."

And I come like that, taking him with me over the edge, nothing more needed to tip me into the most all-consuming orgasm of my life than the slide of his cock and the sweet murmurings of his love for me.

And there, with the stars as our witness, I become Riggins Greene's once and for all.

Riggins

We're lying across the large blanket, another tangled around our bodies. I have no shirt, just my boxer briefs on while Stella is wearing my tee and a pair of panties, her head on my shoulder as we both watch the sun rise. We spent the entire night out here, sometimes talking, sometimes in silence, both of us drifting in and out of sleep.

"How did you find out?" she whispers.

"What?"

"How did you find out that we were married?" A small smile creeps across my lips, and her finger brushes against the dimple I'm sure revealed itself.

"My mom." Her head snaps back.

"What?"

"My mom." She looks at me longer, staring and trying to read my face like she thinks I may have completely lost it, but then I let her off the hook. "You called my mom. A lot, I think. Left messages. You know, no one ever called that phone number. It wasn't listed or anything, so the only way people would find it was if they knew the number. The machine was blinking when I went to clean up, and I hit play."

"My messages," she whispers. My hand tunnels into her hair, and I press a kiss to her forehead.

"Your messages, my sweet Stella."

THEN

48

CALL YOUR MOM

RIGGINS

Ashford will forever be a double-sided coin to me. I love this place; it's where I found myself, my best friends, and my band. It's where I grew up, where I met Stella, and where I wrote music that changed lives—my life, the band's life, and fans' lives if what they tell me is true.

But it will also always be the place where my mother died and where my father essentially killed himself. When I drive from the airport to here, through the Pine Barrens this time of the year, it's nothing but sticks, depressing and empty.

Every time, I'm reminded of the times Stella and I lay beneath those trees, staring at the sky, promising we'd be forever. I can look at the stars from anywhere in the world, but when I do it with my feet planted in Ashford, it's like I'm still here with Stella, and that hurts more than anything ever could.

Even more so in the house I grew up with. It was left to me when Dad passed, with no siblings or other family to take it on, and since then, it's been my sole remaining tether to Ashford. A tether I've avoided like the plague to the best of my ability. It's not that I haven't been in this house since my dad died. I have, just not for any stretch of real-time.

I haven't *lived* in this house.

I surely haven't explored it.

This house is so still, so quiet, a time capsule of my childhood and my father's pain and the life my mother lived that ended too quickly. When I walk through the door, boots hitting on the same carpet my mother hated but my father never replaced, it's like I'm seventeen again.

I feel a strange mix of anxiety that creeps up my chest and makes me want to turn around like I've done every other time I tried to clear this place out but fight it back. I didn't learn how to control or conquer until it was too late, and I have an unending hope that I still have a huge, full life in front of me, a life where I can make dreams and hopes come true.

Hopes that would have undeniably included Stella.

I think I've put off cleaning and selling this place for so long because it felt like the one remaining strand of hope for her, the last of the invisible strings tying me to Stella that I haven't severed.

But it's time. Time to leave this behind, to finally sever this part of my life.

To finally try and move on.

Maybe if I cut this tie to Ashford, I'll cut the part of my soul that always aches for Stella.

Wishful thinking, maybe, but I'm a desperate man.

Rubbing my hand over my forehead, I stare around the time capsule that is my childhood home and grab a hair tie to pull up my hair, only the top half making it into the small bun Reed would absolutely make fun of me for.

I start with the bathroom, seemingly the easiest spot that would hold the least memories, but when I see the cabinet above the sink holding every product my mother used, half full like the day she left it when she passed, the knife turns.

I hated my dad for the longest time.

My mother passed, and I was just a kid, a kid without a mother. Then, he took my father away from me, drowning his emotions and sorrows until he died.

But I get it. I might have been deep in the rockstar life when Stella was with me, but as soon as she left, I fell off that cliff, drowning my sadness, filling that hole she left with whatever would numb the pain.

The shoes she left when she ran are still on the top shelf of my closet, and I built an entire fucking shrine for her in Maine. I get how he couldn't bear the idea of clearing out Mom's things, even if it would have made his life easier, his grief less suffocating.

I get it now.

It's an uncomfortable realization that despite my best intentions, I became the man who angered me so much as a kid. And that now, I feel a bit of guilt knowing I got so mad at him for being human and not having the tools or ability to cope.

I push it back and begin the heartbreaking and harrowing work of packing up my past.

Hours and hours later, uncovering more frozen memories of my mother and even more uncomfortable realizations about my father, I head into the living room to run out and grab lunch for myself. Before I leave, my eyes catch the black box on the side table next to the couch. The family phone we never used, but never got rid of because the answering machine had my mother's voice.

I get it, not wanting to hear that, the way it would tear open wounds that have barely healed. God, do I get it.

Every fucking day I'm on stage where I sing and play the songs we wrote together; it's her voice that I hear.

It's why I fell so far off the cliff when she left. Even when I wanted to get over it and her, to run away from it and forget her altogether, every fucking day, I was reminded of what I lost.

I'm old enough, wise enough, to know now that's what it was: me losing her. She'd talked to me so many times about the spiral I was on, and not only did I ignore her, but I started to hide things, and worse.

She left without a word and ignored the call when I needed her most, but I ignored her for months and months before that. My bitterness about it all is gone now, washed away with time, age, and clarity.

I wonder what my father saw with time and clarity and how that gutted him.

I don't blame him anymore. I had Stella as *mine* for barely over a year, and it destroyed me. My dad was married to my mother for fifteen years.

But now I'm looking at the old phone, the cord spiraling down the table, and see the red blinking light of a message. It could be years old, for all I know. It's probably just telemarketers, but before I head out to get food, I sit and tap in the password—my mother's birthday—and listen to the message.

"Hi! You've reached the Greene's. We're unable to make it to the phone right now, but please leave a message with your name and number, and we'll call you right back."

God, it still hits me, hearing the voice I forgot all these years later.

Somewhere buried in this house are home videos my mom made, her voice saved forever, but I don't even think I would have the ability to play the old VHS tapes. And even if I did, would I want to risk finding footage of Stella and I, of watching our once sure history being written?

But the world shifts on its axis a moment later, breaking me out of my thoughts about home videos and how to play them when the first message plays.

"Hey, Jeanette," the voice says, and instantly, I know it's her.

Stella.

I haven't heard her voice in five years, but I could hear it whispered on the wind and know it was her. It instantly takes me back to late nights under the stars, writing songs, watching her gorgeous face pull out similes and analogies that still can bring me to my knees, and doing it with ease like she was born to do it.

Sometimes I wish I had recorded those sessions, that I had her voice saved somewhere so when the memories start to fade, I can replay them, resharpen the memories, since they're all I have of her anymore.

It's actually cruel that our mind saves memories, the more painful, the more crystal clear ones, but doesn't save sounds the same way, doesn't capture the way the end of a sentence dips lower, the way one single word can contain three emotions at once.

"It's me. I know no one listens to these, and I feel so fucking lost right now, so I thought... I don't know. You were always so smart. I can't talk to my mom about it, and Evie's at school... He's been drinking a lot. Riggs, I mean. And it's probably because I'm young and overreacting, but... Well, you know. I don't know. I just wish you were here. You always knew what to say. Miss you."

The machine beeps, and I hit back, wanting to listen once more and commit it to memory, and this time I catch the date.

She left this in November after our first tour, those days when we were happy to be together when I started to drink and party. But she was doing it too, I remember. I remember her smiling at me, watching me with those eyes that never left me.

But I also remember the panic in her face when I would grab yet another beer, the way she'd pick at her nails or bite her lips with nerves.

I think I knew then.

The machine beeps and goes to the next message, and I hear her voice again.

"Hey, Jeanette. It's me. I finally got the nerve to talk to Riggs about his drinking. It's getting out of hand, and it makes me nervous because some days, he drinks more beer than water. I think it helped. I hope it did, at least. And we just found out the guys have been nominated for Song of the Year! I'm so proud of him. He's... he's doing everything he said he would. You'd be so proud, too. I know it."

The hope in her voice kills something in me, knowing how this story ends. The next message is months later, a few months into our first headlining tour and a week or two before we got Gracie.

"Hey Jeanette," she says and this time, there's tears, painting her voice. She's been crying, the words strained. "I'm so lost, and I don't know who to talk to. But you always knew how to handle Riggs and... I wish you were here. He's falling apart, and I don't know how to help him. He's drinking so much, and I'm so scared I'm going to lose him. I just... I wish you were here. You'd know what to say."

I don't hit back to relisten to this one, hating it more than anything else. The next beep comes, and her voice comes again, this time filled with joy and excitement.

"Hey Jeanette, it's me. I think... I think I got through to him. We talked and it went so much better than I feared. And we got a dog!" Her voice sounds so happy, so ecstatic and I remember that day.

I remember feeling heavy, soul-breaking guilt at the look of disappointment and hurt in her eyes when she asked me to stop drinking.

That was the day I started hiding the full extent of my drinking.

In the years following her leaving, I thought it was her fault she didn't see it, that she didn't notice the signs that I was drinking much more than she thought.

And then I'm reminded how fucking young we were and how fucking in love with me she was.

"Her name's Gracie. After you, of course. Jeanette Grace. Wish you were here. Thanks for keeping an eye on us still. Gracie, no!" The sound rumbles, like her phone falling and there's a giggle before the message ends.

I collapse to the floor as the tears start, the memories jagged as they rip through me, causing me true, physical pain at everything I've lost.

At *whom* I lost.

Another beep and another message, this time staring with laughter.

"No! I'm calling your mom!" Stella's voice says, and in the background, there's my voice laughing, "What!?" Before she laughs again. "I do this! Leave me be, Riggins Greene. Sorry, hey Jeanette! It's me! Guess what!? I'm officially your daughter! Well, in law. We got married! It was very last minute, and no one knows yet, but... god. I'm so damn happy. Wish you were here."

It cuts off abruptly, but I don't even care.

Because all I can hear is, *We got married!*

We got married...

We got married?

We. Got. Married.

I hit back, listening again and, this time, paying attention to the date.

I look back, try and think of where the band was that date, to figure out what happened and why I don't remember, but I know.

It's Vegas, the day before she left me.

I let the machine play the next and final message.

"Hey, Jeanette." It slices through me, the sadness, the hoarseness of her voice. She's destroyed. The contrast between this and the previous message is actually painful. "Uhm, I, uh... god. I don't know. I won't be calling you again. He lied. He lied, and I don't even know what to do anymore. I'm so sorry. I thought I... I don't know. I thought we'd be okay. But I can't do this to myself anymore. I can't let him do it to me either. I love you, Jeanette. And I love him. But I can't do this."

The message cuts off on a sob.

Suddenly, without warning, the morning I had torn apart a million times before comes back to me in a new light.

Waking up in the fancy hotel room with Stella, wondering why the fuck we paid so much for the lover's suite. The headache I had, the urge to find a drink as soon as I woke. The wide smile on her face.

"Good morning, husband," she had said, her eyes soft as she brushed my hair back from my face, looking at me like I was her entire fucking world.

And I threw her away.

NOW

49

GODLIGHT

STELLA

We spend five days in Maine. Five perfect, peaceful, healing days. We hike, and we lay under the stars, and we talk, and we laugh, and we fuck. But most importantly, we write.

God, we write. We write and it's natural and beautiful and it heals a part of me I thought was destined to be shattered for life.

But like all good things, it too, comes to an end. Reality comes knocking at our door when we have to make our way back to Ashford because Riggins has a meeting in New York in three days he can't put off any longer. Turns out, he's been putting it off for weeks, doing his best not to leave Ashford in order to be as close to me as possible.

Just in case, he said.

Just in case I needed him.

Just in case I changed my mind.

"I don't want to leave," I whisper, standing outside the cabin as he locks up behind him. It's deceptively large inside, with a primary bathroom, two bathrooms, a small but cozy kitchen-living room combo, and two extra, small bedrooms.

"We'll be back. A lot," he says, pulling me into his arms, pressing his lips to my hair before walking me to his truck, tucking me in, and closing the door before getting in and driving us home.

"When do you have to go to the city?" I ask, staring out the window as we pass from New York State into New Jersey, a bright green Welcome to New Jersey, the Garden State! sign greeting us.

"Day after tomorrow," he says. I nod. "Gracie will stay with you. Want my girls together." It warms me, those words. His hand reaches out, his fingers tangling with mine before he speaks his next words. "We'll have to talk to her, eventually, you know." I swallow, knowing exactly what he's talking about.

My mother.

My mother sent Riggins' letters back to him and never told me about them.

She cornered him at the grocery store and told him I was dating someone I was very much not dating, and she knew it and tipped him toward self-destructive behaviors.

And she answered when he called at his darkest moments and told him I was done with him.

I remember sitting at the coffee shop the day after his father's funeral, waiting for him to come, for us to finally talk. I remember feeling guilty that I stole that opportunity from him, the opportunity for him to explain, to get closure, or maybe to mend things. I remember the excitement I kept trying to douse every time I let my mind drift too far, letting myself think about us being together again.

I remember waiting for thirty minutes and checking my phone, checking the time. I remember the eyes on me as I sat there, alone, and how they felt pity even though there was no chance they knew who I was waiting for or if I was waiting at all.

Most of all, though, I remember going to my parents' house where Evie was living to talk to her and finding my mother instead.

She consoled me when I broke down and told her about Riggs not showing up for coffee that day, where she acted like it was his loss. I remember thinking it was a moment for us, a small white flag she was waving. It was the final catalyst to trying to be whatever she wanted me to be. The small moment of motherly love I never had, something I kept chasing until recently.

Except it was all a manipulation. It was all pretend, another layer on the bullshit my mother contrives to keep people under her thumb, performing and acting the way she sees suitable.

I deserve closure. I might be done with her, but I need to know why. Why did she work so hard to keep us apart? Why has she seemingly hated me since the day I was brought into his earth? What great reason did she have to make me miserable?

"Hmm hmm," I say instead of sharing all of those thoughts, thoughts that we've already rehashed under the stars. Silence fills the car once again.

"I'm happy she did it," he says long after.

"What?" I look at him, and he has his eyes on the road

"I'm happy she did it, fucked with us,"

"I don't—"

"I'm glad she did it. I was trying to get clean, but I kept failing. Losing you is what pushed me to get sober. I'm not sure I would have gotten clean without it. And look at you: look what you became. You're beautiful. You're successful. You've done it all on your own. You told me you felt like you lost yourself when you were on tour. I know you. You're beautiful, and you're kind, and all you wanted to ever do was make everyone else happy. Would you have been this version of yourself if we stayed together? I would have continued to dull your light until you went out. So I'm happy, Stell. I'm happy it happened."

I sit there in shock, confused and unsure, as his words start to process.

But he's right. It makes sense. I wouldn't have found my own footing in the music world without him, and I would have always felt like I was in his shadow. My mother stepping in was fucked up, but it did me some good, I suppose.

"I guess," I say, my voice low. He squeezes my hand.

"Can't see stars without darkness, Stella. I don't regret anything that happened, not when I got my star back in the end."

NOW

50

HURT SOMEBODY

STELLA

It feels strange to knock at the door of my parents' house, the house in which I lived in the final years of my childhood, knowing I probably won't be coming here ever again.

I just need closure.

"You are not welcome here," my mother says when she opens the door in lieu of a greeting, looking at Riggins.

"That's fine, we won't be here long," I say, stepping in without her permission. Her face pinches in irritation, and I don't know how I didn't realize how ugly she was until just now. She used to be pretty, gorgeous, even, but that all left long ago, the more bitter and cold she got.

"What is this about, Stella? I have things to do." I turn to her, standing in the living room of my childhood house. Looking around, there are photos of Evie—graduation photos, dance, and cheer photos —all of her accomplishments are celebrated.

There is one photo of me, half hidden behind another of her and my dad.

There's no point in trying to be civil, or salvage this relationship. I don't think there was ever a relationship to be had, to be honest.

"Did you tell Riggins I was dating Tripp five years ago?" I ask.

Her arms cross on her chest. "Yes."

"You're not even bothering denying it?"

"Why would I deny it, Stella? I did it. I always told you if you were going to take action, make sure you'd stand behind it. I'd do it again, Stella, though it didn't really work in the end, did it?" She sighs like I'm a nuisance. "I tried so hard, *so hard* to set you up with good men, make you fucking useful for once in your life, but no. He," her head tips to Riggins without looking at him. "Always was in the way. I knew when we moved in that he was going to be a problem, the way you always looked at him with wide, doe eyes."

"Did you answer the phone and tell him I was done when he called?"

"When he called drunk, gave a whole sob story about how much he *loved you* and how *sorry* he was? Of course, I did." The knife in my chest twists.

"And the letters?" I ask through a tight throat.

"Oh, I sent those back. I threw out a few, but I figured if I sent them back, he'd be more likely to get the hint. And he did. He stopped sending them, you know." She says it like it's a challenge, a reason not to love him.

"So when I was so depressed I couldn't leave my bed when I thought he didn't give a shit about me when I was in the depths of my sadness, you were getting letters and sending them back?"

"You weren't depressed, Stella. Jesus. You're just lazy. I've told you this a million times."

"Did you put the articles in my mailbox?" I ask, Riggins' hand tightening against mine because I haven't mentioned this theory to him.

"I thought that would work," she says, disappointed. "You needed to see that the night he married you, he was out getting drunk like a loser. Don't you see that he doesn't care about you? He's only using you for your songs, Stella."

A beat passes and I weigh my answers. I could tell her how much

Riggins loves me or how much she hurt me, but does it even matter, does it? Is it going to change her mind? No. So instead, I ask the only one question I need an answer for.

"Why do you hate me so much?" I ask, my voice small.

"I don't hate you, Stella, god. You're always so dramatic."

"Fine, why don't you love me enough to care about me?"

"I don't—"

"I'm done, Mom. I'm done with these games. Not a single thing I ever did made you happy. Not a single thing was good enough for you. Everything was a manipulation, something to pit Evie and me against each other, something to use to control us. Just tell me why, and I'll be gone. You won't have to look at what a disappointment I am ever again." I shake my head. "I just want to know why. Why were you so adamant that I wasn't good enough when all I wanted for so long was for you to accept me. To fucking love me."

She sighs like I'm an inconvenience then steps forward, anger and irritation written all across her face.

"Fine, Stella. Do you want to know? Do you want to know why I resent you so much?"

A chill runs through the room, and I don't have to ask her to continue.

"I was almost out of this fucking town," my mother says finally, venom in her words. "I was almost done. I had a man—a good man, with fucking prestige and money. We were engaged." My eyes go wide because this is all new to me. "Old money, house in the Hamptons. The whole nine. I was getting out of this shit town."

"And?"

"And you two happened." My head snaps back in confusion, but I don't have to ask to get answers. "I went and got drunk at a party of losers and low-class schmucks in this stupid fucking town that ruined my life, and I got pregnant."

Silence fills the house, my ears ringing.

"Your father got me pregnant. My fiance dumped me and said I was used goods. My mother had always loved this god-forsaken town, so she was pleased as a punch. Hank thought the only right thing to do was get married for the kids. Then I had daughters."

She sighs again. "Two girls, two chances. I raised you to be what we needed to get out. To get to the next level, to be someone who *mattered*. God, how much money I spent on dance and etiquette classes, matching you with the right people, and setting you up on dates. And are you even thankful? No. Never."

She waves her hands like it's *my* fault. "No, all I got was you accusing me of being a shit mother and your sister always falling short. You, leaving to be with a fucking rockstar, spitting in my face every chance you could get as a kid. What choice did I have, Stella? How could I love you when you were my biggest disappointment?"

The door creaks open, but I barely notice as I stare at my mother, trying to understand. But I know I never will.

It's impossible.

"Hey, Stell," my dad says with a bright smile, walking into the house. His smile melts off before anyone can say anything, reading the vibe of the room. "What's going on—"

"I'm done with you," I whisper.

"Excuse me?" My mother asks.

"I'm done trying to please you. I'm done being what you want me to be. I'm done caring. I'm done giving you power." I shake my head. "A mother is supposed to love her children and put them first. I don't know what happened to you to make you this bitter, this vile, this self-ish, but I'm sorry. I am. I'm sorry that someone turned you into *this*, sorry you let it happen, but I won't be letting that happen to me. I was almost a shell of a person because of you, and I won't be risking that again." I turn away from her to look at my father, whose face is confused and conflicted.

"I'm sorry, Dad. I love you so much, but I can't be around her anymore. She's dead to me. You're not innocent in this, in letting her be this way, letting her treat us like this, but you're not the villain.

You don't have to choose me; I'm okay with that. But I'm begging you to keep Evie safe from her. She will do anything to make her love her, and you and I? We both know there's no way she can love anyone but herself. I don't know why you stayed so long, but that's your business. I'm done."

He opens his mouth, and my mother says my name, but I don't listen.

Instead, I squeeze Riggins' hand and walk out the door forever.

I don't cry when we drive back to my house, *our* house.

No, instead, for the first time in my life, I am completely free.

Riggins

"I love you," Stella whispers hours later in the dark. She didn't cry when we left her mother's. She didn't even want to rehash it; she just looked at me and said *I'm done with her.*

I was proud. So fucking proud because this is what I always thought she had to do. But seeing her do it, seeing her do it with confidence and without fear, was fucking beautiful.

"Love you more," I tell her. She giggles, the noise filling the room.

"That's my line." I shake my head, something she feels more than sees, and her head picks up.

"No, you don't get it. I love you more. I love you more than my career. I love you more than songs. I used to say the bass of a good song was my heartbeat, but that's not true. My heartbeat is your heartbeat; you were gone for seven years, and I didn't feel it once. Not once, Stella."

Silence fills the room and she shifts over me, putting a hand on each side of my face and staring into my eyes. Long moments pass before finally, she whispers. "No one."

"What?" I ask, confused and a bit concerned.

"No one," she repeats.

I wrap an arm around her waist, holding her close and the other moving to brush her hair back.

I don't understand.

"No one has ever loved me more."

"Stella—" I try to say, but she cuts me off.

"No one has ever loved me more, Riggins. There's always been something, someone above me."

"Never again," he whispers in my hair. "I'll always love you more. You've got all my love and more forever."

"I love you," Stella whispers hours later in the dark. She didn't cry when we left her mother's. She didn't even want to rehash it; she just looked at me and said *I'm done with her.*

I was proud. So fucking proud because this is what I always thought she had to do. But seeing her do it, seeing her do it with confidence and without fear, was fucking beautiful.

"Love you more," I tell her. She giggles, the noise filling the room.

"That's my line." I shake my head, something she feels more than sees, and her head picks up.

"No, you don't get it. I love you more. I love you more than my career. I love you more than songs. I used to say the bass of a good song was my heartbeat, but that's not true. My heartbeat is your heartbeat; you were gone for seven years, and I didn't feel it once. Not once, Stella."

Silence fills the room and she shifts over me, putting a hand on each side of my face and staring into my eyes. Long moments pass before finally, she whispers. "No one."

"What?" I ask, confused and a bit concerned.

"No one," she repeats.

I wrap an arm around her waist, holding her close and the other moving to brush her hair back.

I don't understand.

"No one has ever loved me more."

"Stella—" I try to say, but she cuts me off.

"No one has ever loved me more, Riggins. There's always been something, someone above me."

"Never again," he whispers in my hair. "I'll always love you more. You've got all my love and more forever."

NOW

EPILOGUE
FOREVER

I wake up in a cold bed.

I'm unhappy about it, which is new, considering I haven't been unhappy since Maine, not really.

It's been an interesting few months since Riggins and I went to Maine since we uncovered our history and put it back together. We've written under the stars, finishing the songs for the next Atlas Oaks album, and I've sent a few to my agent. It seems songs written by the duo of Riggins Greene and Stella Hart are a hot commodity, and more than one bidding war has occurred.

We finished the upstairs of our house and two weeks ago, we threw a much delayed house warming party. The whole band and friends the band and Riggs have made over the years came over. Some of which I knew, and it was great to see them again, others I'd never seen before.

Evie came too, though she's in a strange position between our mother and me. I've stuck to my promise to cut her out completely, but my twin's entire personality is so intertwined with getting reassurance and positive reinforcement from her.

In my gut I know one day, she'll hurt Evie, but when that happens I'll be here waiting.

I haven't spoken to either of my parents, though somehow (I blame Reed, who has the biggest mouth on this planet), word of what she did to Riggins and me has gotten around, making her even more of a pariah than she was before.

All that to say, life has been good. Really fucking good. We still have our struggles, and we absolutely argue—that's a given. But every night, I go to sleep with Riggs next to me, and every morning, I wake up with him in our bed, which is why I'm irritated with this morning's proceedings.

I shuffle out of the bedroom, squinting and grumpy. When I get to the kitchen, I blink a few times and see the clock reads 10 am.

How did I sleep so late?

Opening the cabinet above the coffee maker, I reach for the bread. Yawning as I untwist the bag, I place a piece into the toaster before reaching for my pills. On one of the bottles is a bright yellow post.

Had an early meeting.
Text your sister.
All my love, R

I roll my eyes at the note, grabbing the bottles and tapping out my pills before downing them with water before starting my coffee. When it's brewing, I reach for my phone to text my husband.

> Where are you?

He texts back quickly.

> Had a meeting. You text Eve yet?

> I just woke up.

> Where's Gracie?

> With me. Text your sister, little star. See you later.

> You took our dog to a meeting?

> When are you going to be home?

> Where are you now?

> Also, why didn't you tell me you had a meeting?

I send the texts in an irritated, rushed sequence.

> Explain later, I can't be on my phone. Text Evie. Love you.

> You're annoying.

> You're the worst.

I leave it like that for a moment, grabbing milk for my coffee and a plate for my toast before I decide to send one more.

> Love you too.

He doesn't respond, but I don't expect him to. Instead, I sit at the kitchen island with my coffee and toast before texting Evie.

> Why is my husband telling me to text you?

> Because I'm awesome.

> What's going on?

Something is going on, and both Riggins and Evie are in on it.

I'm coming over for lunch

That doesn't answer my question.

She doesn't respond.

Everest.

There's still no reply five minutes later when I finish my toast. I could text Reed or Wes or, maybe, worst case scenario, Beckett, except he hates texting, but I have a feeling it wouldn't be of any use.

Instead, I get dressed and grab my notebook to sit on the porch swing while I wait for whatever my sister and husband have planned to fall into place.

I've learned to go with the flow.

I'm just getting out of the shower, my hair dripping onto the Aspen Oaks tee that goes almost to my knees when the front door opens. Gone are the days of forgetting to set my alarm or lock my door, considering Riggins outed my pen name and a literal rock star is living here, which means it's someone who has a key.

"Oh, perfect," my twin says when she closes and locks the door behind her. "Let's play dress up." She lifts what looks like a dress bag in the air.

"What?" I look at my watch. "Didn't you say you'd be here at noon?"

"Yeah, well, I had a meeting that went too long trying to secure my next tour," she says. Her first spread following a band on tour skyrocketed her career, and the magazine wants her to keep doing them.

"Say the word, and I'll talk to Lee about getting you on the Oaks tour," I say, half joking, half hopeful. I've been saying it for nearly two months now, and each time, she shuts me down.

"I don't want to deal with the nepotism shit, Stell. I told you."

"Yeah, but we're going on tour next summer, and I'm going to miss you," I say with a pout, sitting on my couch.

"No, no. No sitting. We're playing dress up." I glare at her change of subject. "Up, now. Go to your room, the vanity."

"What's going on?"

"We're having sister time, obviously," she says, tugging my hand until I'm still. "I want to play dress up just like when we were kids. I want to do your hair and makeup."

"Evie, we never played dress up."

"That's because you were too busy running after Riggins, but you're all married and shit now, so you have no excuse."

"Evie—" I start, but then her face gets serious.

"Stell, please. Trust me, okay?" I sigh.

I have no choice, so I walk toward my room, my dog walking behind me.

"Evie, it's almost dark," I say as we sit in her car, driving... I'm not sure where. She spent a full hour doing my hair, blowing it out, and adding gentle waves before moving to my makeup, which took another hour.

It felt like I was getting ready for the prom I never went to. Evie was always the more high-maintenance twin, mostly because it was what our mother wanted.

Now I'm sitting in a cream-colored dress tight around my nonexistent boobs and loose around my hips, ending just past my knees with puffy short sleeves, a pair of my own short booties, my face fully made up and heavily... confused.

"That's the point," she says, pulling down a familiar street.

Beck's street.

"Evie..." We stopped in front of Beck's house, and I noticed the cars there. Reed's, Beckett's, Wes', and Riggins' are all parked out front. "Evie," I repeat, this time starting to get nervous.

It melts when my door opens, Riggins standing in front of me, smiling. His hair is down but brushed and less unkempt than normal, a short sleeve white button down and a pair of tan pants on, boots on his feet.

"Hey, little star."

"Where have you been all day?" I ask.

His smile goes wide, his dimple coming out. "Somewhere."

"Why are you all being so weird and vague?" He grabs my hand, ignoring my question and tugging me out of the car.

"Come on," he says with a tip of his head toward the woods.

"Come on?"

"Yeah. Come on, Stell."

"What do you mean, *come on?*" He shakes his head at me.

"I mean come with me. Follow me. God, you're the one who writes songs. You're supposed to know what words mean." I sigh but begrudgingly start walking with him. Evie, in a loose light green dress, walks quickly toward the woods ahead of us.

My pulse starts to beat.

"Where are we going?"

He doesn't answer as he pulls me into the woods, but he doesn't really have to, does he?

As we near the clearing, I hear it.

The jingle of tags.

A bark.

I don't have to catalog it this time since I hear it regularly, but my hand still tightens in Riggs'. I open my mouth to say something but close it again when we finally step into our clearing.

"What is this?" I whisper, looking around.

There are sunflowers everywhere.

Sunflowers and wildflowers with a small arch at one end. A man I don't know is wearing a small smile, and I barely notice the photographer snapping shots as my eyes meet the guys, all dressed in shirts and light green ties. I almost laugh when I see how uncomfortable they look, but I can't when Riggins answers.

"Our wedding," he whispers. "The way it should have always been. In our place, under the stars." I tip my head up to see a few stars out, the sky not all the way dark but getting there, now that summer is coming to its end.

Then, my husband gets down on one knee, holding up a ring to me.

A real ring, not the thin promise ring I've taken to wearing on my right hand after I dug it out of my jewelry box. A large round diamond in the center with smaller triangular ones surrounding it.

"A star for my star," he whispers. My voice catches as the world crashes into me, as understanding hits.

"Are you proposing?" He just smiles.

"I can't do it without you, Stell."

"Do what?" I whisper.

"Anything. Life." Giving him a small, soft smile, I shake my head. Not saying no to his unasked question but refuting his words.

"You *can* do anything you want, Riggings. You're you. You're amazing." It's familiar, words we once exchanged in this clearing what feels like forever ago.

I wonder how those kids would feel seeing us standing here now.

"Fine," he says, proving he remembers it the same as I do. "I don't want to do it without you. Marry me, Stella. For real. Be mine forever."

Words don't work for the first time in my life, a cry hitching in my throat, and he keeps speaking.

"I won't ever let you go. I'll loosen my grip so you can breathe, so you can chase your dreams, but Stella, I'm never letting you go again. I'm honored I get forever to see how bright you burn."

And there, under the stars, in the meadow, I first fell in love with Riggins Greene; I married my best friend.

Again.

ACKNOWLEDGMENTS

It's time for what has become my favorite part of these books, the part where I scream from the rooftops about how much I Leo every single person who helped make this book happen.

As always, thank you to my person, the one who babies me so I can get everything I can dream of done, the one who brings me lunch and makes sure I stay hydrated and don't stress myself too much, Alex. Thank you for making sure I get outside time and for holding me together when I feel like I might break. Thank you for letting me chase my dreams and holding down the fort so I have somewhere soft to land when I get home. I love you so much.

Thank you to Ryan, Owen, and Ella. You three are the reason I continue to chase my dreams, so one day you'll see if you want something, it can be yours. I'm so honored I get the privilege of being your mom. Also, close this, you know you're not allowed to read my books.

Thank you to Madi. I genuinely don't understand some days how we stumbled into each others lives, but I'm grateful every day. In barely a year, you've become one of my best friends, the Jack to my Taylor. You're the best cover designer a girl could ask for and It's been an honor watching you make a name for yourself. Thanks for never balking (much) at my crazy ideas and sorry I never have page counts on time.

Thank you to Regan. When I say I couldn't do this without you, I think you know I mean that incredibly literally. From helping me when I'm have rough mental health days to making sure everything gets done to just hanging out and forcing me to do what I need to.

Thanks for letting me text you at random hours and no firing me. I'm so grateful you were on my approved list of social media managers last year.

Thank you to Salma, who helped make sure this wasn't a heaping pile of shit (hopefully) and for being so kind and insightful. I can't thank you enough!

Thank you to Emily for being the literal best little influencer girl and always popping' that puss. I'm so proud of everything you've accomplished since SEPTEMBER!

Thank you to Ashleigh, the prettiest princess that ever has princesses. You're the sweetest, kindest human and you deserve the entire world. Thank you for always sitting on calls with us while you do your big girl job.

Thank you to Coop-dog, the best dog who ever lived. This is the first book I (successfully) wrote a dog into and the fact that you left just a few weeks before it was out in the world means you're watching over it. We miss you like crazy.

Thank you to Kayla for helping to edit this beast - you are a lifesaver!

Thank you to Noah Kahan, whose music inspired the vast majority of this book and whose music has helped me in some really dark times.

Thank you to my ARC team who always does the absolute most, screaming about my babies from the top of the rooftops. You all are the reason this book will find any success, the reason my career even exists, and I'm forever grateful for all of you.

Finally, thank you to the readers. I started this as a crapshoot, a silly goofy thing I started to get spending money as a stay at home mom and because of you I've made an entire career out of it. I've been able to support my family, to let my husband have time with our kids he's never had before, and fulfill life long dreams. I love you all so much and I can't tell you how much it means to me. Thank you for trusting me, for reading the crazy stories that come into my head, and for loving me.

ALSO BY MORGAN ELIZABETH

The Springbrook Hills Series

The Distraction

The Protector

The Substitution

The Connection

The Playlist

Season of Revenge Series:

Tis the Season for Revenge

Cruel Summer

The Fall of Bradley Reed

Ick Factor

Big Nick Energy

The Ocean View Series

The Ex Files

Walking Red Flag

Bittersweet

The Mastermind Duet

Ivory Tower

Diamond Fortress

Atlas Oaks Series

All My Love

ABOUT THE AUTHOR

Morgan is a born and raised Jersey girl, living there with her two sons and daughter, and mechanic husband. She's addicted to iced espresso, barbeque chips, and Starburst jellybeans. She usually has headphones on, listening to some spicy audiobook or Taylor Swift. There is rarely an in between.

Writing has been her calling for as long as she can remember. There's a framed 'page one' of a book she wrote at seven hanging in her childhood home to prove the point. Her entire life she's crafted stories in her mind, begging to be released but it wasn't until recently she finally gave them the reigns.

I'm so grateful you've agreed to take this journey with me.

Stay up to date via TikTok and Instagram

Stay up to date with future stories, get sneak peeks and bonus chapters by joining the Reader Group on Facebook!

WANT THE CHANCE TO WIN KINDLE STICKERS AND SIGNED COPIES?

Leave an honest review on Amazon or Goodreads and send the link to reviewteam@authormorganelizabeth.com and you'll be entered to win a signed copy of one of Morgan Elizabeth's books and a pack of bookish stickers!

Each email is an entry (you can send one email with your Goodreads review and another with your Kindle review for two entries per book) and two winners will be chosen at the beginning of each month!